REMEMBER WHEN

REMEMBER WHEN

A RAVENSWOOD NOVEL

MARY BALOGH

Berkley

New York

BERKLEY
An imprint of Penguin Random House LLC
penguinrandomhouse.com

Copyright © 2025 by Mary Balogh
Penguin Random House supports copyright. Copyright fuels creativity, encourages diverse voices,
promotes free speech, and creates a vibrant culture. Thank you for buying an authorized edition of
this book and for complying with copyright laws by not reproducing, scanning, or distributing
any part of it in any form without permission. You are supporting writers and allowing
Penguin Random House to continue to publish books for every reader.

BERKLEY and the BERKLEY & B colophon are registered trademarks of
Penguin Random House LLC.

Library of Congress Cataloging-in-Publication Data

Names: Balogh, Mary, author.
Title: Remember when / Mary Balogh.
Description: New York : Berkley, 2025. | Series: A Ravenswood novel
Identifiers: LCCN 2024020478 (print) | LCCN 2024020479 (ebook) |
ISBN 9780593638415 (hardcover) | ISBN 9780593638422 (ebook)
Subjects: LCGFT: Romance fiction. | Historical fiction. | Novels.
Classification: LCC PR6052.A465 R468 2025 (print) | LCC PR6052.A465 (ebook) |
DDC 823/.914--dc23/eng/20240506
LC record available at https://lccn.loc.gov/2024020478
LC ebook record available at https://lccn.loc.gov/2024020479

Printed in the United States of America
1st Printing

Book design by George Towne

REMEMBER WHEN

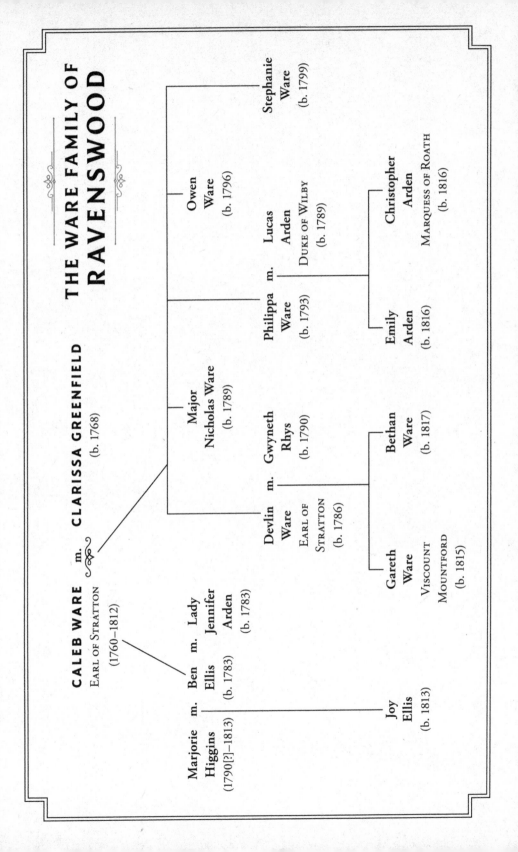

THE WARE FAMILY OF
RAVENSWOOD

CALEB WARE m. **CLARISSA GREENFIELD**
EARL OF STRATTON
(1760–1812) (b. 1768)

Marjorie m. **Ben** m. Lady
Higgins **Ellis** Jennifer
(1790[?]–1813) (b. 1783) Arden
(b. 1783)

**Major
Nicholas Ware**
(b. 1789)

**Owen
Ware**
(b. 1796)

Stephanie
Ware
(b. 1799)

**Philippa
Ware**
(b. 1793) m. Lucas
Arden
DUKE OF WILBY
(b. 1789)

Joy
Ellis
(b. 1813)

**Devlin
Ware**
EARL OF
STRATTON
(b. 1786) m. Gwyneth
Rhys
(b. 1790)

**Gareth
Ware**
VISCOUNT
MOUNTFORD
(b. 1815)

**Bethan
Ware**
(b. 1817)

**Emily
Arden**
(b. 1816)

**Christopher
Arden**
MARQUESS OF ROATH
(b. 1816)

PROLOGUE

1785

It was a moment Matthew Taylor knew he would never forget. A fanciful thought, perhaps, when he was eighteen years old and all of life and life's experiences stretched ahead of him. Or so it was said, most notably by his parents, as though his childhood and boyhood were of no consequence.

He knew, though, that he would always remember. He stood watching Clarissa Greenfield, drinking in the sight of her, willing the present moment not to end, hoping she would not move or speak again for a while.

She was leaning back against a tall tree, her arms slightly behind her on either side, her palms pressed to the trunk. A breeze he could scarcely feel fluttered the sides of her long, full skirt and her dark hair, which she had shaken loose when she'd dropped her straw hat to the ground. She was achingly pretty, with all the freshness of youth and the innate warmth and charm that were an essential part of her.

She was seventeen years old.

Their families were neighbors. She had been his closest friend for most of their lives, though they could not be more different in nature and temperament if they tried. She was even-tempered, devoted to her parents, and obedient to them and her governess. She wanted to be the sort of young lady they wished her to be. They loved her, after all. She had a deep affection too for her brother, a good-natured lad who was five years younger than she. It seemed to Matthew that there was never discord within the Greenfield family.

He, on the other hand, was a misfit within his family. He had tried to love his parents and Reginald, his brother, who was ten years his senior. In his more generous moments he admitted they had probably tried to love him too. It just had not worked. His mother and father had very rigid ideas about the sort of person a second son ought to be if he was to expect a prosperous and respectable future. His father, though a gentleman of property, did not have a large fortune. Everything he did possess would pass to Reginald upon his death, just as his father's property had passed to him while his younger two brothers had forged successful careers, the elder as a diplomat, the younger as a solicitor. Matthew had not met either uncle or their wives and children, his cousins. His uncles wrote to his father but never came home for a visit. His father used them as examples of what Matthew must aspire to be. He must be educated to enter one of the professions suited to his birth.

The whole of his boyhood was designed to prepare him for that future. Any idle activity, any behavior that ran counter to the plan, was firmly discouraged. It seemed to Matthew, looking back from the age of eighteen, that he had never been allowed to be simply a boy, exploring his world and perhaps finding enjoyment in it.

He had decided early in his life that he could not always, or even often, conform to the sober, joyless expectations of his parents.

He gave up even trying after repeatedly being scolded and punished for behavior that came naturally to him—falling into streams, for example, while trying to cross them on mossy stones he had been warned were unsafe; whittling away at pieces of wood with a knife he was not supposed to have and being careless about clearing away every last scrap of shavings that gathered about him on furniture and floor; being late home when visitors were expected for afternoon tea—late and grubby with dust and mud and sweat from head to foot. The list went on and on. He spent more time in his room with only dry bread, stale water, and a Bible for company and sustenance than he did anywhere else, he sometimes thought.

Even his grandmother—his mother's mother, who lived on the estate adjoining theirs and next door but one to the Greenfields— upon whom he called quite frequently as a young child, told him one day that unless his behavior at his own home improved, he would no longer be welcome in hers. He had never again gone there voluntarily.

Matthew gave up trying. He developed into a moody, rebellious boy, until the worst thing of all happened. His brother, the beloved Reggie of his early years, began to punish him for bad behavior by refusing to do things with him such as fishing in the stream or flying a kite in the meadow or going to the village shop for the rare treat of buying sweetmeats. When Matthew had rebelled even more in protest, Reggie had washed his hands of him and become Reginald ever after. Their mother sometimes wept and complained that she did not know what she had done to deserve such a disobedient, ungrateful child. And the more his father tried to insist that Matthew toe the line for his own good, the more Matthew deliberately did just the opposite.

Life at home became intolerable—for all of them, perhaps. It had seemed to Matthew as he grew up that his only real friend was Clarissa Greenfield. She was the one person in the world who accepted him as he was, though she had never tried to excuse his least admirable exploits, such as the time he had been told to take his ball farther from the house lest he break a window and had instead hurled it quite deliberately through the one at which his father was standing while issuing the order. Clarissa had merely asked him why.

It was a question she asked frequently as they grew up, but it was never rhetorical, an accusation in disguise, as it was whenever his parents asked the same thing. It was, rather, a question in genuine search of an answer. She always waited for his explanation. More important, she always listened and never told him afterward that he had been wrong or bad, that he ought to do this or that to make amends. She allowed him to rant when he needed to and pour out all his bad temper and self-pity. She listened until he ran out of complaints and instead talked about his dreams and listened to hers.

She could always bring out the best side of his nature, though he was never sure quite how she did it. Just by being a good listener, perhaps? By never judging him? She was also a good talker, given the chance, a cheerful and amusing companion. They had often laughed together over the merest silliness, sometimes quite helplessly. She was one of the few people with whom he ever did laugh, in fact. She was the only person who seemed to give him leave to be happy, to frolic with no purpose but pure enjoyment.

And frolic they did through long summer days, always remaining within the boundaries of her father's property because that was where she was expected to be. They walked and ran and waded in the stream and lay in the grass and picked daisies to fashion into chains and talked endlessly about anything and everything that came to mind. They often just sat cross-legged in the grass, their knees almost touching, while he whittled a piece of wood and she tried to guess what he was making.

"A beaver," she would say. "How darling it is, Matthew."

"A squirrel," he would say, and they would both laugh.

She never told him to be careful with the knife. She always admired what he carved and called him marvelously clever, even when she mistook a squirrel for a beaver.

Even in winter they had spent time together, sometimes tramping about the park side by side, dressed warmly with little more than their eyes exposed to the elements, but more often in a small, little-used salon inside, where cakes and biscuits and warm chocolate or tea were brought to them in a steady stream and Mrs. Greenfield would ask him if his mother knew where he was.

"She will guess," he would say.

She would smile and tell him she'd send a note so his mother would not worry, and she would include in the note the time at which she would turn him out of the house and direct his footsteps homeward. But those words to him were always spoken with a good-humored smile. And the funny thing was that he always left at the appointed time and hurried home so his mother would have nothing for which to blame Mrs. Greenfield.

Now Matthew watched Clarissa leaning back against the tree, all but grown up, just as he was. But after all these years, she had just broken his heart. Oh, it was an extravagant way to describe his feelings. But he was about to lose her and was trying to postpone the realization that he might find the loss unbearable. It was a silly idea—yes, silly was the right word—to describe his heart as broken, whatever that meant. He was eighteen years old, for the love of God.

He watched as she gazed ahead at a seemingly endless expanse of lawn and trees stretching off into the distance across the park. The afternoon sunlight was upon her face, but he could not tell what she was thinking. Was she staring off into the brightness of her future or back with nostalgia to the past she was leaving behind? Or was she fully present and feeling the breeze on her face and in her hair while being consciously aware that everything familiar was about to change? Was she aware of his silent presence close by, almost in her peripheral vision, or had she forgotten he was there? Did she know she had broken his heart?

Surely she was feeling at least some sadness. She loved him, after all—as a friend. But sadness was not her dominant mood today. He knew that. She had told him so.

"He is so . . . gorgeous, Matthew," she had said. "So good-looking and charming and good-natured. And his smile! Everyone admires him. Mama says he is possibly the most eligible bachelor in all England. Yet he has chosen me."

She had been talking about Caleb Ware, Earl of Stratton since his father's death three or four years ago. He lived about ten miles away at Ravenswood Hall, an imposing mansion and park close to the village of Boscombe. Matthew had seen him a time or two and knew him to be well thought of by his neighbors. But he had no personal acquaintance with the man. Stratton must be twenty-four or twenty-five years old and, yes, a very eligible bachelor since, in addition to everything else, he was said to be fabulously wealthy.

Two days ago the earl, with the countess, his widowed mother, had taken afternoon tea with the Greenfields, by appointment. Before they left, Stratton had arranged with Mr. Greenfield to return three days hence—tomorrow—to discuss a matter of some significance to them both. His mother, meanwhile, had had a private word with Mrs. Greenfield, and the two ladies had agreed that a connection between their families, specifically a marital connection, was greatly to be desired.

Stratton was coming tomorrow, then, to have a word with Richard Greenfield, and it was no secret what that word was to be. In all probability it would be followed immediately by a marriage proposal to Clarissa herself.

She intended to accept, even though she was only seventeen years old. If she asked to postpone her decision for a year or two until she was eighteen or nineteen, she had explained earlier, she might very well lose her chance altogether. The Earl of Stratton would marry someone else, and his choices would be limitless. His mother had apparently explained to Mrs. Greenfield that she would far prefer to see him married to the daughter of a respected near neighbor than to someone of possibly higher rank about whom she would know very little. It was time Caleb settled down. He had the succession to ensure, besides which he had been restless lately and clearly needed a bride who would have a settling influence on him. He would almost certainly not wait, then, nor would his mother, if Clarissa asked for more time.

Richard and Ellen Greenfield, though surely somewhat uneasy about the tender age of their daughter, nevertheless must be very conscious of the great honor being bestowed upon her and the dazzling prospects such a marriage would bring her. She would be the Countess of Stratton, with all the prestige and security of position and untold wealth the marriage would bring her. And she would remain relatively close by at Ravenswood. It would have been strange indeed if they had not encouraged the match.

They had not pressed it upon Clarissa, however. Indeed, they had been careful to point out to her that she was very young, that it would be perfectly understandable if she wished to have a few more years to enjoy all the pleasures of a presentation at court and a social Season in London, where she could hope to capture the attention of numerous eligible young gentlemen. If that was her wish, then her father would inform Stratton of her decision before he could embarrass himself by making her a formal offer.

Their caution and consideration for the feelings of their daughter were typical of them. They had raised her to be a lady with high expectations, but they would never force her to do anything about which she had any doubt.

Clarissa was hugely flattered, however. And excited. The prospect of an early marriage and of a title and new home at Ravenswood of all places would not perhaps have been enough in themselves to sway her, but . . . well, there was the Earl of Stratton himself. She had seen him only a few times in the past and mostly from afar until he came for tea with his mother, but . . . Well.

"He is so gorgeous," she had told Matthew. And he had understood that she was quite in love with the man, though she did not know him at all.

She had known him, Matthew Taylor, almost all her life. They had been close friends for years, but only friends, Matthew reminded himself as he stood, feet slightly apart, hands clasped loosely behind his back, watching her gaze off into the distance.

He wished he could capture this moment for all time. But he had never been much good with paint and brushes. Somewhere between the picture he saw in his head and the image that came through his hand onto paper or canvas, there was a gap in communication. It was very frustrating, because the images were always vivid and insistent. His fingers itched at his back at the thought and he flexed them. He would love to carve her out of wood. Not that he had any great skill at whittling either, but it was wood carving he yearned to do almost more than anything else. He saw life and shape in wood. He saw soul there and longed to reveal it with the aid of his knife.

But he had never been encouraged to discover any real talent he might have. Quite the opposite, in fact. So he had never been able to develop his meager skills. One day, perhaps . . . Oh, one day he would carve this scene.

Or would he simply forget?

No. He would never forget.

She had no idea that he loved her not just as a friend but as a lover. He was in love with her and had been for some time. For the last year or so anyway. It was not a love he would ever reveal to anyone, of course, least of all to her. For he was the younger son of a landed gentleman of only modest means, while she was the daughter of Richard Greenfield, who was untitled but nevertheless of the upper gentry, with an impeccable lineage on both his side and his wife's. He had a home and park at least twice the size of the Taylors', a correspondingly profitable farm, and a sizable fortune. The Greenfields had always been kind to Matthew, but there could never be any question of his marrying their only daughter. Everyone understood that. It had never had to be put into words. Matthew had understood it, even as he was falling in love with his childhood friend. He had known that in doing so he was dooming himself to heartache, even heartbreak. For the time would come when she would inevitably marry.

Someone else, that was.

He had just not expected it to happen so soon. He had been

totally unprepared for what she had told him today. He had not had time to fortify his heart. He had expected that he would have at least another year or two before it happened.

She had turned her head, he realized, and was gazing directly at him. She was not smiling.

"Matthew," she said softly. "You are not happy for me?"

He strode closer and stood in front of her, cutting the sunlight from her face. Putting her in shadow.

"I am happy if you are," he said. "Are you?"

Her eyes were searching his, but he could still not interpret her expression. Usually he could read her well.

"I am," she said. "I believe this will be a good marriage for me—and that is surely an understatement. But it means everything will change. Even though I will not be far away, this will no longer be home, will it? I will be Clarissa Ware of Ravenswood Hall, Countess of Stratton. Yes, I am happy, Matthew. I am even excited. I believe I will be happy with him. He is amiable and charming. I was quite bowled over by him when he came with the countess to take tea with us. But what is going to happen to our friendship— yours and mine? If you were female, it would continue regardless, but there is the minor inconvenience of your being male."

She paused to smile at him.

"Yes," he said.

"It would not be the thing, would it," she said, "for us to be forever traveling back and forth to spend time with each other."

"No," he said. "Not the thing at all." He tried to smile back, but he could not seem to command his facial muscles to do his will.

"What will you do with your life, Matthew?" she asked. "Do something that will make you happy."

He shrugged. "I will find something," he said. "Not the church or the army or navy or a courtroom, but something. I will never be able to satisfy my father, unfortunately. He and I will never be able to sit down and discuss my options as two equals even though I am eighteen now. You must not worry about me, however. All will be well."

"Will it?" She almost undid him then. She lifted one hand and cupped her palm about his cheek. "You are a searcher," she said. "And one day you will find what it is you seek, and you will be happy. You must not settle for anything less, though I do not doubt your father is well-meaning in his efforts to secure your future. Seek, Matthew. Do something positive. Do not just rebel."

There were tears in her eyes then, and he was not sure there were not some in his own too. He blinked rapidly to clear his vision.

"Promise me," she said.

"I promise," he told her, though he had no idea how one sought what one could not even name. Or where one went to look for it. And this was surely the first time in their long acquaintance that she had given him actual advice. Urgently, forcefully given it.

They gazed at each other, their faces only a foot or so apart, and he felt a dreadful urge to kiss her. Just once. A goodbye kiss. A good luck kiss. But it would be a terrible mistake—for her, for him, for them. For if he kissed her, she would know, and she would definitely be sad. And he would know—though he already did—that it was hopeless, that any image to which he clung of their being tragic lovers about to be driven apart by circumstances would be dashed forever. He would end up looking foolish and knowing he would feel it every time he saw her in the future—which was bound to happen from time to time.

"Now you promise me," he said, "that you will be happy. That you will live happily ever after."

Her smile turned instantly brighter. "I promise," she said.

She stooped down to pick up her hat and the ribbon she had placed inside it. She tied back her hair and secured the strings of her hat beneath it at the back, brushed her hands over her full skirts, and raised a smiling face to his.

"Time for us both to go home," she said, and turned in the direction of the house. She waited for him to fall into step beside her.

Clarissa walked homeward, Matthew at her side, and thought how bewildering it was to be seventeen, to be bursting with happy anticipation of a dazzling future on the one hand yet heavy with heartache on the other. To love two men, one she had known all her life, one she scarcely knew at all.

She had always loved Matthew Taylor. They were close in age, while his brother was ten years older than he, and George, her brother, was five years younger than she. She and Matthew had enjoyed doing the same things. They could walk for miles while scarcely noticing the distance. They could wade in the stream and sit for hours in the branches of a tree, seeing shapes in the clouds above their heads. And always they talked endlessly about everything and nothing.

They were very different, of course. She was eager to learn all a young lady should know by the time she grew up. She wanted to conform, to fit in, to be liked, even loved, by everyone, young and old, rich and poor. She knew that the life of a lady was often a life of service to her family and friends and neighbors and servants, and she wanted to do it well. Matthew sometimes called her a dullard, though he always said it fondly and it made no difference to their friendship. He was a dreamer and a rebel, both of which attributes got him into constant trouble at home, some of which he deliberately courted, as though he enjoyed incurring the wrath of adults and drawing the punishments they could mete out. She occasionally called him reckless. But it never, ever occurred to her to put an end to their friendship.

She wished now that he was not in love with her. But she feared he was. And she wished she was not a little bit in love with him, though she feared she might be. She was too sensible, too rooted in reality, however, to encourage the budding feelings either in herself or in him.

She was the beloved only daughter of a wealthy, privileged landowner, a member of the *ton*. She had always known she could expect to make a good, even brilliant marriage when she grew up. Matthew was the second son of a landowner of moderate means and must make his own way in the world when he grew up. His brother would inherit everything, including his maternal grandmother's estate after her passing. She had never made a secret of that fact.

Unfortunately, Matthew did not fancy any of the careers his father had tried to thrust upon him—the church, the military, a seat in Parliament. Not even the diplomatic service or the law, though his uncles had apparently declared their willingness to help him get a start. Nor did he fancy trying to snare a wealthy heiress—his mother's suggestion. Perhaps it was just as well, he had told Clarissa, that no wealthy heiress in her right mind would ever fancy him.

His father had lost patience with him long ago. So had his brother, who had married three years ago and produced two sons in rapid succession. Matthew had always been a rebel. Clarissa had frequently shaken her head at him, but she had rarely if ever scolded him. She had always listened to him and sympathized with him, for she knew that all his bad behavior was a cry for help, a plea to be accepted and loved for who he was. She had once held him in her arms while he wept on her shoulder, though he had been only ten at the time. It had not happened again.

It was all stupidity. For Matthew Taylor just did not know who he was or where he belonged in life. And he had been blessed with the worst possible family to help him find answers—in Clarissa's opinion anyway. They were well-meaning. She was sure that deep down they loved him and were genuinely concerned about his future. But they had not an ounce of imagination among them. They simply could not understand that Matthew would never fit into any mold of their devising. The more they tried to insist, the more outrageously he would rebel.

To be fair, though, she did not know how anyone could help someone who would not help himself. She had given Matthew her friendship and her love and sympathy all her life, but she knew they were not enough. At least she had let him know he was not all alone in the world, that someone cared, really cared, for the precious, intelligent, talented person who lay somewhere deep inside the troubled boy.

Yet now she was making matters worse for him, and she feared he would feel she was abandoning him. For she believed he was a fair way to being in love with her, while she was about to make a brilliant marriage with the man of every young girl's dreams.

Ah, life could be very cruel. What would become of Matthew?

Clarissa had always looked forward eagerly to the future, though she had known it would not include him. A young lady of her social stature did not marry a younger son who would have neither property upon which to settle her nor the means with which to support her in the manner to which she was accustomed. More important, he would not be able to provide their children with any sort of secure prospect for their future. It all sounded a bit calculated and unfeeling, perhaps, but it was how society worked.

Besides, she was young. She wanted everything the world had to offer her. Did that make her shallow? Surely not. The future did not just happen. At least, one did not have to let it just happen. One must try to shape it into something that would bring stability and security as well as happiness to one's life.

She desperately wanted to be the Countess of Stratton, especially as merely thinking of the earl made her feel breathless. He was terribly good-looking and amiable and charming. At tea two days ago, he had demonstrated impeccably good manners and made conversation with her parents and even with George, her twelve-year-old brother. But when he had talked to her, or listened to something she was saying, she had felt herself really seen and heard. She had felt his liking, his admiration. And it had seemed natural, not forced in any way. It perhaps seemed conceited to believe he had been enchanted with her, but . . . well, she really believed he had been.

Yet not many minutes ago she had desperately wanted Matthew to kiss her. She had wanted to kiss him. For over the last year or so she had found her feelings for him changing, and she had not been firm enough with herself to quell them before they developed into something troubling. She had always loved him more than she loved anyone else except her parents and George. Matthew was her friend, almost the other half of herself. But now she was a little bit in love with him too. If she was perfectly honest with herself, it was more than a little bit.

He was slender and wiry in build, not particularly tall. He had very dark hair, one heavy lock of which was forever falling down over his forehead. His face was narrow and angular, interesting more than it was handsome. It was often a frowning face, sometimes even sullen, though occasionally a smile would transform it and make him irresistibly appealing. He had lovely white teeth. His eyes were very dark. Clarissa sometimes described them to herself as fathoms deep. She also thought he was a bit like the tip of an iceberg, as her governess had once described it to her. What one saw of Matthew Taylor, what he allowed the world to see, was only the merest fragment of all that was within him.

All muddled up within him.

He was the most exasperating, contradictory, tortured person she had ever known. Sometimes she felt she could shake him. Yet she loved him.

"Matthew." She stopped walking and turned toward him. She was almost home. This was the most convenient place for him to branch off and return to his own home. "You are very quiet."

"You have not exactly been prattling yourself," he said.

"Do you think I am being foolish?" she asked him, suddenly all doubt and uncertainty. "To marry someone I scarcely know? When I am only seventeen? When most girls do not even make their debut into society until they are eighteen? Am I doing the wrong thing?"

"Oh no, Clarissa," he said, raising both hands, palms out toward her. "You are not going to do this to me. This has nothing to do with me. It is something you must decide—with the advice of your parents."

Even now—stupidly—she wished he would grasp her by the shoulders and pull her against him and . . . Well.

She wished he would tell her not to do it.

But she wanted more than anything in the world to do it—to accept the marriage offer the Earl of Stratton was almost certain to make her tomorrow. He was surely the most attractive man she had ever met—not that she had met many in the course of her life except neighbors, it was true.

"You are right." She smiled ruefully at him. "I am sorry. You will come to my wedding?"

"No," he said. Baldly, just like that, with no hesitation at all.

"No?" She raised her eyebrows in surprise. "Why not?"

"Clarissa," he said with soft reproach.

She felt deeply hurt even as she understood and was relieved that he would not be there.

"If you were female," she said, "you would have to come. You would be my bridesmaid and would be needed to hold my gloves and flowers if I was carrying any."

"I am not female," he said.

"No." She laughed shakily. "And you would look silly holding my flowers. Oh dear, this feels very like goodbye. It is not, surely. Is it?"

He drew breath as though to answer her, but then he shook his head slightly and remained silent. His face tried a smile but settled upon a frown instead.

She opened her mouth to speak, found there was nothing to say, and closed it again.

They had never been at a loss for words with each other. Until now.

She turned and made her way with long strides toward the house. It was goodbye, even if they continued to see each other from time to time in the future. She could feel a single teardrop running down her cheek.

It was goodbye.

And tomorrow was a new beginning. For her it would be the beginning of happily ever after. She felt a spring in her step, and a leftover heaviness in her heart.

What would tomorrow bring for him?

CHAPTER ONE

1818

Clarissa Ware, Dowager Countess of Stratton, drew in a deep breath of fresh air as she stood looking out through the open window of her private sitting room. It was sheer bliss. She could smell the freshly scythed lawn below that stretched ahead as far as the ha-ha. She could smell the sweetness of the wildflowers in the meadow beyond it and see the sheep grazing there. Sunlight sparkled on the river below the meadow and shone bright upon the village of Boscombe on the other side. Was there any lovelier place on this earth to be?

Ravenswood.

Home!

It was so different from all the bustle and stale air and limited horizons of London, where she had spent the past few months, rushed off her feet as she presented Stephanie, her youngest daughter, to the queen, and introduced her to the *ton*. That latter duty had meant attending as many balls and routs and garden parties and soirees and other entertainments as could reasonably be fitted into the twenty-four hours each day allowed. The spring Season had an overabundance of pleasures to offer as one mingled with as many of one's peers as one could. There had been scarcely a morning in which to linger in bed, or an afternoon in which to relax with a book or her embroidery. There had been almost no evenings to spend at home in the familiar company of her family. Even the nights had frequently been shortened by a particularly glittering ball.

At last she was home, however, and, for the first time she could remember, she was home alone. Alone except, that was, for the army of servants who kept the vast mansion running smoothly and administered the farms and kept the park surrounding the house in pristine condition. She was alone, however, in the sense that there were no other family members here with her and no guests. And it was going to remain this way for at least the next couple of months.

She felt slightly guilty at the delight she felt at the prospect of being alone for so long, for she dearly loved her family and close friends. Sometimes, however, she yearned for solitude, for time to be alone with her own thoughts and reflections. Now, after the insanely busy months in London, she craved it more than ever.

And there was the added fact that in a few short months she was going to turn fifty. It was all very well to tell herself, as other people had been telling her with annoying frequency lately, that fifty was just a number, that she was only as old as she felt, that she would be the same person the day after her birthday as she had been the day before.

Fifty was a number of undeniable significance. It was a reminder that her youth had been left behind so long ago that sometimes it felt like something from another lifetime or something that had happened to someone else. Her young womanhood was long gone too. Her children were all grown. Stephanie, her baby, was nineteen years old. Clarissa had already been married for two years when she was Steph's present age. Devlin had been born when she was eighteen.

Caleb had died of a sudden heart seizure six years ago.

Oh, fifty seemed so much larger a number than forty. Or even forty-nine. There was something very decisive about it. Half a century.

One of the sheep in the meadow baaed indignantly at a bird that had swooped too low over its head. The bird perched on the edge of the ha-ha close by and serenaded the sheep with cheeky indifference to any danger posed by the much larger animal. Clarissa smiled as she watched.

It was not that she was feeling particularly maudlin about her advancing age. There had been considerable happiness in her life up to this point, and there was every chance that there was more to come. As far as she knew, she was in excellent health. Her children were all doing well. Her grandchildren were an endless delight to her—four of them so far, with two more on the way. Pippa and Lucas were expecting again sometime after Christmas, as were Ben and Jennifer, though it was the first for them as a couple. Five-year-old Joy was Ben's daughter from a previous marriage. Clarissa's parents were both still in good health. George, her brother, was happily married to her longtime friend Kitty, both of them after a lengthy widowhood.

There was much cause for contentment, then, in Clarissa's life. It was true that Stephanie had not enjoyed her debut Season, but at least she was now officially out, and her confidence had surely been boosted by the two perfectly eligible offers for her hand that had been made very properly first to Devlin, Clarissa's eldest son, now Earl of Stratton. Steph had refused both offers, but Clarissa had hopes that one of these days her daughter would surprise herself and actually welcome just the right marriage. It was not a good idea, after all, for a woman to remain a spinster all her life, though Devlin and Gwyneth would always welcome Steph to continued residence here at Ravenswood, as they had assured her after she refused the second offer. And the choice between marriage and the single state was Stephanie's to make.

It had not helped this year, of course, that Owen, Clarissa's second youngest, had also been in town for the Season, enjoying himself with a group of friends, most of them from his Oxford days. One of those friends was Bertrand Lamarr, Viscount Watley, who had spent a few weeks at Ravenswood with Owen a couple of summers ago. He had been a delightful young man then and still was now. He was in town with his twin sister, Lady Estelle Lamarr, this year and had been delighted to introduce her to the Ware family, whom he remembered with great fondness. He was the sort of young man girls dreamed of—tall, dark, handsome, and genuinely charming. Lady Estelle was outstandingly lovely too. Poor Stephanie had lived through agonies during those weeks here two years ago. She had been seventeen and self-conscious and convinced she was the ugliest young woman in existence. She had gone to great lengths to avoid the young god with whom she had clearly been smitten.

Poor Steph.

Two years had not changed her. She had reacted exactly the same way to him this year, though it had been admittedly easier to avoid Viscount Watley among the crowds in London than it had been in the family setting at Ravenswood.

Almost the whole of Clarissa's family had been in London this year, though Ben had remained home at Penallen with Jennifer and

Joy, and Nicholas, now a full colonel with his cavalry regiment, was still somewhere in Europe, though he expected to return soon to England, where he would take up a military post at the Horse Guards in Whitehall.

In many ways it had been a wonderful few months for Clarissa, surrounded by family and friends, always busy, always with interesting new acquaintances to make—and even a beau of her own, who had actually hinted at marriage. She had been tempted. But when Lucas, Duke of Wilby, had announced that he was taking Pippa and the children back home to Greystone for the sake of his wife's health, and Stephanie had jumped at the opportunity to go with them to see her sister through her confinement, Clarissa had declined the invitation to go with them then or to join them later, after the Season was over. Instead, she had announced her intention of returning home to Ravenswood.

There had been a chorus of protests, for no one else had intended to come back here yet. Devlin and Gwyneth were planning to go straight to Wales with their children after the parliamentary session and the Season ended to visit Gwyneth's Welsh relatives. They had wanted Clarissa to go with them. Her relatives would be more than delighted, Gwyneth had assured her. She had pointed out that Sir Ifor and Lady Rhys, her parents and Clarissa's closest neighbors and friends, would be going there too for a month or so. George and Kitty had begged Clarissa to remain a little longer in London and then return home with them for the summer. Owen had offered nobly to escort his mother home to Ravenswood and spend the summer there, though there was nothing in particular to attract him. There was to be no grand summer fete this year, the organizing committee having decided that there was just too much work involved to make it an annual event.

Clarissa had smiled at the reason they had given for the decision. While Caleb was alive, he had always insisted upon the summer fete as an annual event, proclaiming that all the effort involved
was in itself such a delight that it hardly qualified as work. But there
had been no committee in those days. It was Clarissa who had done
the huge amount of planning and organizing, with help from the
servants and from her children as they grew older. Caleb had simply
paid the bills.

She had refused Owen's offer, and he had gamely tried to hide
his relief.

She had come home alone yesterday—apart from an entourage
of servants and outriders, of course. It had felt and still felt like a
very special treat, though it was more than just that. She needed to
adjust to the fact that she was about to turn fifty, that she was moving into a new phase of her life—had already moved, in fact, for she
had been a widow for six years.

It was not easy when one had been a wife for twenty-seven
years. It took far longer to adjust than anyone who had not experienced the death of a spouse could possibly understand, even when
the marriage had not been entirely an easy one. Was there such a
thing as an easy marriage, though? But she was going to be fifty
soon, and it was time she embraced her freedom.

Whatever that was going to look like.

She was not lonely. There was a difference between loneliness
and aloneness. She was about to discover what aloneness felt like.
Not total solitude, however. She was not going to be a hermit for
the next couple of months until Devlin and Gwyneth returned
from Wales. She had friends and acquaintances here to visit and be
visited by. There would be certain obligations she had no intention
of neglecting. But she would keep it all to a minimum and make

sure she spent most of the time alone with herself. It would be something quite new.

There was one other thing she wanted to do, however, and perhaps today would be the very day to do it—before she lost her courage, as she had done a number of times over the past few years. She just had not known what she would say to him. But now she had the perfect excuse—no, reason—to call upon him. Ben and Jennifer were expecting a baby. She would go and talk to him about that, and slip in the other thing—if she could find the right moment and if her nerve held.

How very foolish she was being! She was not usually either timid or indecisive.

She turned from the window at last and cast a rueful eye at the clock on the mantel and then at the nightclothes she still wore. She had spoiled herself this morning and had breakfast brought up to her sitting room rather than sit in lone splendor in the breakfast parlor, waited upon by a silent, attentive butler and footman.

She crossed the room and pulled on the bell rope to summon her maid. It was time to get dressed and begin this precious interlude of aloneness, when she could be entirely her own person and do whatever she pleased—even have breakfast in her rooms every single morning if she chose.

What a luxurious adventure she was embarking upon.

Matthew Taylor had spent the morning at the home of Colonel Wexford just outside Boscombe. The colonel's unmarried sister, who had lived with him for years, had decided that it was high time they replaced their old, battered dining table with a new one.

"Even though it is polished twice a week and covered permanently with a linen cloth and then a lace one, Mr. Taylor," she said, speaking of the old table, "I am still fully aware of all the scratches and nicks and water stains upon it. I am always anxious when we have dinner guests lest for some reason the cloth has to be peeled off and our guests will see the sad state of a table that was probably as old as the hills even when Andrew first allowed it into his home."

It had come with the colonel's bride many long years ago. "It was her pride and joy and her mother's before her," the colonel explained to Matthew rather sheepishly. "No one else in the regiment had anything to compare with it in size and grandeur. Especially a humble lieutenant, which is what I was at the time."

"I know it is of sentimental value to you, Andrew," his sister said more gently. "But it is time for a new one, you must admit."

"If I must, I must," he said with a mournful sigh and a wink for Matthew. "Measure away, then, Taylor. Prue will tell you exactly what she wants, and you can draw up plans for her approval. What am I, after all, but the man who will pay your bill and eat at the new table?"

"Oh, take no notice of him, Mr. Taylor," Miss Wexford said. "If Andrew had lived on Noah's ark, he would probably still be there now, comfortable with its familiarity."

Matthew had measured and taken notes of exactly what Miss Wexford envisioned, and promised to return the following day with drawings for her approval.

Matthew Taylor was the village carpenter. He had both his living quarters and his workshop in rented rooms above the smithy in Boscombe. Cameron Holland, the blacksmith, was his friend, as was Oscar Holland, who had announced his retirement several years ago and since then had made an appearance almost every day back at the smithy, interfering with its smooth running, if one listened to Cam—making sure that everything was kept in good working order, as it had always been in his day, if one listened to Oscar. Matthew chose not to listen too attentively to either one. Father and son bickered and outright argued at least once a day, but they were clearly fond of each other and both were excellent smiths and well-liked members of the community.

Matthew was not nearly as outgoing as they were, but he was not a hermit. He was friendly with almost everyone in the village and the countryside surrounding it. Most people did not seem to know—or they had forgotten—that he had been born and raised a gentleman, that his brother was a prosperous landowner a mere ten miles or so away, that he himself owned the property next to his brother's, which his grandmother had left to him on her passing.

He had not settled there, however. He had chosen instead to lease it out and hire a good steward for the farm. He was known here simply as the village carpenter. The rooms in which he lived and plied his trade were modest, to say the least, not to mention the fact that they were above the smithy, with all the noise and smells that fact entailed.

He was content with his life. Perhaps even happy, though he thought of happiness as an active, sometimes volatile thing, and his feelings about his life were more muted. That suited him. There were too many ups and downs associated with happiness or active emotion. Contentment offered a more attractive alternative, though he was realistic enough to realize that events could not always be controlled and might at any moment upset the habit of years.

Miss Wexford had ideas for a very ornate dining table indeed. They were not to Matthew's taste, but they were the customer's choice and he would give what was asked of him, perhaps with an attempt to tone down some of the more extravagant excesses. He would do all in his power, though, to give her what could be her pride and joy, as the old table had been her sister-in-law's.

He arrived home with his head full of the design he would commit to paper to show Miss Wexford tomorrow and noticed that one of the more modest carriages from Ravenswood was drawn up outside the village inn. Ah, the Wares were home from London, then, were they? He would have to be more careful about his jaunts to the poplar alley inside the park, though the whole of the park was open for the use and enjoyment of the public at large for three days out of every week. Indeed, Stratton—Devlin Ware, that was—had often been heard to say that he and his wife would be happy to see their neighbors strolling there or enjoying a picnic by the lake any day of the week. It seemed selfish, he had explained, to keep such spacious beauty all to themselves.

They were decent folk, the Wares, Matthew thought as he made his way up the outside stairs that led to his rooms above the smithy and heard the familiar ringing of a hammer on the anvil. They were not at all high in the instep. Years ago he had wished they were, so he would have some reason to hate them, but he had never been able to find any such excuse. Even if he had, it was a spiteful wish that was unworthy of him.

"Mr. Taylor," a female voice called from the street below as he turned the knob on his door and was about to step inside. He had not locked it when he left. He never did. As far as he knew, no one did. Boscombe was a decent, safe place to live.

He would have known that voice anywhere, anytime. He turned to look down at the Dowager Countess of Stratton, his hand still on the doorknob.

"I was wondering," she said, looking up at him, "if I might have a word with you."

She was alone, he saw, though there was presumably a coachman inside the inn, keeping an eye on the carriage while he enjoyed his pint of ale and awaited the return of his mistress. There was no sign of a maid. It was not a shocking breach of decorum, of course, since Boscombe was in many ways just an extension of Ravenswood. But . . . Did she mean a private word? In his rooms?

"May I come up?" she asked, almost as though she had heard his thoughts.

"Please do," he said, and stepped inside in order to hold the door open for her as she ascended the stairs, holding up the skirts of her dark blue carriage dress, which had surely been newly and expertly—and expensively—fashioned in London.

"Good morning, Lady Stratton," he said briskly as she reached the top stair and raised her head to look at him again.

She smiled. "Good afternoon, Matthew," she said.

"I suppose it is past noon," he said, closing the door after she had stepped inside.

And suddenly the place felt not quite like his home. It seemed filled with her presence, and he felt half suffocated. It was a strange fact, when he had seen her with fair frequency for years past and had occasionally exchanged a few words with her. He had even danced with her once in the ballroom at Ravenswood. But she had never been here inside his home before. She was looking around with unabashed curiosity.

"What a cozy home you have," she said, and it did not sound as if she was mocking him.

The room was not large, but it suited him. It was uncluttered—as was his life. There was a couch that would seat three at a push. It had seen better days, but it was marvelously comfortable. There was a rocking chair and a small table with two upright chairs, all of which he had made himself. There was a knotted cotton mat on the floor and, on the walls, a few pictures he had acquired on his travels. A bookcase he had also made stood beneath one of them, stuffed with his favorite books. There were wooden candlesticks, again his own handiwork, on a shelf above the stove, plus a couple of his wood carvings, though not his favorite one. That was in his bed-chamber, a smaller room next door.

The smithy was large. The rooms above it, the original home of the Hollands, were of an equal size. Most of the space now, though, was given over to Matthew's workroom. His living quarters were small, but he liked them that way. They served his needs.

"It is a little smaller than Ravenswood," he said, and she smiled at him again.

"A trifle smaller," she agreed. "It has a low ceiling. It must be warm in winter."

"And stifling in the summer," he said, "especially with Cam working below me. Ah, he has stopped hammering. That is better. Now we can hear ourselves think."

He actually liked the sounds of the smithy and even the smells, though they had taken some getting used to at first. There was, of course, the additional smell of wood coming from his workroom.

"You have a pleasant view through the window," she said, approaching it to look out over the village green to the river on the far side of it and the park of Ravenswood beyond that, though the house was out of sight from this particular window.

"Yes," he said, and recalled his manners. "Will you have a seat?" He indicated the couch, but she pulled out a chair and sat at the table. "May I make you a cup of tea?"

"I will not trouble you, but thank you," she said. "I came to find out if you are very busy at the moment."

He was always busy, though he was careful never to allow work to dominate his waking hours or overwhelm him. He had learned to say no when he felt he had to. People came from near and far with commissions for him, both minor and major. He had wondered when he first set up here if he could possibly make a living from the proceeds of what he could make—or mend—with his own hands. He would not have been destitute if it had been impossible, of course, as there were the lease payments he received annually for the manor house that had been his grandmother's and a considerable income from the farm. But he had vowed he would never use that money to live upon. He had decided long ago that he would make his own way in life, and stubbornness was one of his besetting sins, or one of his virtues, depending upon one's point of view.

"Not too busy," he said. He stood looking down at her, his hands clasped behind his back, and marveled at how well she had aged. She had been a very slender, vividly pretty dark-haired girl with a warm charm that seemed to be the very essence of her being. She no longer had the extreme slenderness of youth, but she was still slim and shapely in a more womanly way. She was no longer pretty. She was beautiful instead—and there was a difference, the first characterized by the sparkle of youth, the second by the calm dignity of maturity. Her hair was still dark, though if she removed her bonnet perhaps he would see some silver threaded through it. She was, after all, fifty years old or close to it. Her birthday was in the autumn.

She had been married to Stratton for well over twenty years before he collapsed and died in the taproom of the inn just down the road from here. They had had five children, all now grown up, two of them already married with children. She was a grandmother. And there was also Ben Ellis, the sixth child, who was not hers but a by-blow of the late Stratton's with a mistress he had kept in London. Matthew had always marveled that she had agreed to take in the young child when his mother died and Stratton brought him to Ravenswood, a mere few weeks after Devlin was born. That had all happened before Matthew left England and stayed away for more than ten years.

She was a remarkable woman, Clarissa Ware, Dowager Countess of Stratton.

"Ben and Jennifer are expecting their first child just after Christmas," she said, again as if reading his thoughts.

Ben had done well for himself despite his illegitimacy. Stratton must have left him money. He had apparently purchased his home down by the sea from Devlin. Last year he married Lady Jennifer Arden, sister of the Duke of Wilby, who was married to the former Lady Philippa Ware. Matthew had had dealings with Lady Jennifer while she was staying at Ravenswood two years ago.

"Ah," he said. "I made her a wheeled chair and a stout cane the year before last, both with help from Cam Holland. I hope she is doing well. John Rogers made her shoes at the same time to help her walk."

"She uses them all with skill and determination," Clarissa said. "The chair has given her great freedom of movement, and she actually walks, twisted leg notwithstanding, far more than anyone could have predicted just a couple of years ago, thanks to the special boot and the cane."

"I am delighted to hear it," he said.

She bit her lip and proceeded to one of the main purposes of her visit. "Do you have time to make a crib for their new baby? A bed that is practical and cozy and safe but with your distinctive touch of artistry? I cannot even give you ideas on the latter. I do not have an artistic imagination, alas, though I can appreciate it when I see it. I would love to give them the crib as my gift."

"It would be my pleasure," he said. He would have to give priority to Miss Wexford's dining table, of course, and that would be time-consuming, to say the least. But most of his other, smaller jobs were nearing completion, and the crib would not be needed much before Christmas, he supposed. Making it would be a personal indulgence, since it sounded as though he would be given free rein with its design. He already had images running through his head of plump, smiling elephants and pop-eyed giraffes, of grinning, curly-tailed monkeys and perky terriers.

"Thank you." She was beaming up at him. "I thought of it when I was in London, and I could hardly wait to come home and ask you."

"I will make some sketches for your approval," he said. "Will sometime within the next week suit you?"

"Perfectly," she said. "Shall I return a week from today?"

She had got to her feet, and he felt stifled again. Her face was eager, almost with the bright radiance of her youth.

"It would be better if I came to you," he said. "This is rather a public part of the village."

He worried that people might believe he was compromising her, though that was absurd. He was, after all, merely the village carpenter, while she was the Dowager Countess of Stratton of Ravenswood Hall.

"Very well, then," she said. "If it is not too much of an inconvenience to you."

He expected her to cross the room back to the door then to take her leave. But instead she went to stand in front of the stove to look at the candlesticks and the wood carvings on the shelf above it. She did not touch any of them.

"You did not enter anything for the wood-carving contest at the fete last year," she said.

"No," he said. "I won the year before and twice in a row before that." There had been a gap of eight years when there had been no summer fete at all. "I thought it ought to be someone else's turn."

"That was thoughtful of you," she said. She was still staring upward, though he had the feeling she was not really seeing the shelf. There was a tenseness about her stance. "What do you do with all your carvings?"

"Most of them are on shelves in my workroom," he said. "A few have sold or been given as gifts."

"And the one from two years ago?" she asked.

He winced inwardly. He should never have let anyone see that particular carving. He certainly ought not to have entered it in the contest at the village fete. That had been a rash indulgence, for it had aroused a great deal of attention and had won first prize. He had been sorry immediately after entering it, but by then it had been too late to enter something else instead.

"I believe it is in my bedchamber," he said. It was the only one of his carvings that was there.

She turned to look at him, her cheeks slightly flushed, and they gazed at each other until he turned abruptly and went to fetch it—the wood carving of a woman standing against a tree gazing off into the distance, the carving that had seemed to create itself independent of his will, almost as if it were something that had come through him rather than from him and had simply made use of his hands and his eyes and his skills. All art was a bit like that, of course, but this, more than anything else he had created, had consumed his whole being until it was finished.

He set it down in the middle of the table, and she came to stand beside him and look at it for a few long, silent moments. And of course, he realized, this was why she had come here today, the baby's crib merely an excuse. She might have summoned him to Ravenswood for that.

She sat on the chair she had recently vacated in order to view the carving at eye level.

"Is she me?" Her voice was a mere whisper of sound.

He considered his answer. A blurted *No* was not going to sound convincing.

"She is woman," he said carefully at last. "Or, rather, she is humanity. All of us, gazing off into . . . what? The future? The past? The very present moment? All three at once? She is dreams and hope and nostalgia and endurance and yearning and . . ."

His voice trailed off. He felt the inadequacy of language, something that had always frustrated him until he had learned to let go and simply let some things be. It worked except when he was trying to explain his ideas to another person.

She was leaning back against the tree, her hands flat against the trunk on either side of her, as though she were drawing life and energy from it and feeling her unity with all of nature. An unseen breeze was fluttering her long, loose hair and the full skirt of her dress.

"She is me," Clarissa whispered.

He opened his mouth to protest but then shook his head slightly and closed his mouth. What was the point of denying it?

"It was a pivotal moment, a turning point in both our lives," she said. "The day we left our childhood and youth behind and became adults."

"Yes," he said.

"Most people could not possibly point to one specific day when that happened," she said. "For most it must be a gradual process, not one giant shock."

"You were happy," he said.

"And also very, very sad," she said.

He drew breath to ask if she had been happy after that day, if she felt she had done the right thing in marrying Stratton. But it was none of his business, and he did not particularly want to know that she had indeed been happy. He wanted even less to know that she had been unhappy.

"Life's two extremes," she said.

"Yes."

She turned her head to look up at him. "Thank you," she said.

For a moment he thought she was going to say more, but she did not. She smiled at him instead as she got to her feet and turned to the door.

"I will send word when I have sketches for the crib to bring for your approval," he said.

"I shall look forward to seeing them," she said, her hand on the doorknob.

Only after she had stepped outside and closed the door behind her did it occur to him that he ought to have opened the door for her. He listened to her footsteps as she went down the stairs to the pavement. Cam had still not returned to his anvil. He had probably gone home for his luncheon.

CHAPTER TWO

Over the next few days Clarissa kept herself pleasantly occupied. She called upon Sir Ifor and Lady Rhys, who had not yet left for their annual visit to Wales, and was able to take them firsthand news of Gwyneth, their daughter, and the grandchildren in London. She called too upon her friends Prudence Wexford and Lady Hardington, and met more neighbors and friends at church on Sunday. She spent almost the whole of one day visiting her parents. She was able to report to them that her brother George's marriage to Kitty was continuing to bring them both considerable contentment.

But she spent most of her time alone, as she had planned to do. If she had wanted a busy social life, she might have had it. But if that was what she had wanted, she would have stayed in London for what remained of the Season. She might have stayed, for example, to discover if her beau remained attentive and if she wanted their relationship to develop further. She smiled to think of Lord Keilly, with his silver hair and rather austere courtliness, as her beau. She wondered what he would think if he knew she amused herself by describing him thus to herself.

But she really did not miss him. The whirl of the London Season had never held any great allure for her, even when she first participated in it as a young bride. She soon forgot it when she was back home, or remembered it as an alien world for which she did not yearn any more than she did for Lord Keilly. It was very unlikely she would ever marry him if he asked.

She roamed the vast house, absorbing the memories each room brought her—memories of Caleb and their children, more recently of their grandchildren too. She strolled the long gallery on the upper floor of the west wing, looking at all the portraits of Wares, going back generations and culminating in those that included her and her children. Devlin had commissioned a painting of himself and Gwyneth and their two children just last year. There were actually smiles on their faces, unusual for formal family portraiture. Bethan, still a plump, bald baby at the time, was standing with crooked legs on her father's lap while he kept a close hold on her waist, and appeared to be waving one chubby hand at the painter and therefore at the viewer. Gareth was sitting more properly on his mother's lap, but he seemed to be doing more than just smiling. He was surely laughing. Both Devlin and Gwyneth looked delighted with life.

Devlin had chosen the artist well.

She was so very well blessed in her family, Clarissa thought afterward as she sat in the turret room atop the front corner of the west wing. Some people referred to it irreverently as the onion room, or more poetically as the raindrop room, but everyone loved it, especially children, who were attracted by the illusion that it was perched on top of the world and used it mainly for cushion fights.

How so many cushions had accumulated there Clarissa did not know, but they were bright and cozy, and it had never occurred to her—or to Gwyneth since she became countess, it seemed—to pare them down.

She sat now surrounded by them, holding one to her bosom. She had brought a book up with her, but she had known even before she picked it up that this was not the place where one typically read. There were glass windows above and all around the room with magnificent views in all directions. It was drizzling rain outside today, as it had been on and off since she came home, but that somehow made the room even more cozy. She could see the lake way off to her right, the sweeping front of Ravenswood Hall to her left, the river and Boscombe ahead. It was a picturesque village and enhanced rather than spoiled the rural loveliness of the view.

It was also where Matthew lived.

It was where he had lived and worked for more than twenty years. She had long ago grown comfortable with the fact. So had he, apparently. As far as she knew, he had never been tempted to go back to what she still thought of as his grandmother's house, where he had lived during his brief marriage—he had wed a mere month after her own marriage to Caleb. His poor wife had died soon after giving birth to a stillborn child the following year, however. Within days of the funerals, according to Clarissa's mother, he had disappeared and not returned for many years. During that time his grandmother had died and left everything to him. According to Clarissa's father, her recently changed will must have come as a severe shock to Horace Taylor and Reginald, Matthew's father and elder brother.

No one had seemed to know where Matthew had gone, though someone must have known, for the house and park had been leased out in his absence, something that must surely have been done at his direction. Captain Jakes, a retired naval officer, had lived there with his wife and, more recently, her unmarried sister too, ever since. Matthew had reappeared after ten or twelve years and settled in Boscombe of all places, as a carpenter. He was skilled at his work, and his services had soon been in high demand. But he had always enjoyed working with wood, Clarissa remembered. He had been talented but unskilled through his boyhood. His father had never encouraged Matthew to develop his one passion.

Clarissa had smelled the smithy a few days ago as she climbed the stairs to Matthew's rooms, where she had never been before. But when she had been inside, it was the wood she had smelled, and she had thought it a lovely, comforting scent. She had thought his small living room a cozy and inviting place. She had thought a person could be happy there, though the room was surely not much larger than this onion turret.

She had spoken to him for longer than she ever had before— since she was seventeen anyway. She had seen to it that she had a good reason for going, of course. But finally, before it was too late, she had mustered the courage to ask about the wood carving that had haunted her memory ever since he had entered it for the contest at the fete two years ago.

It was the most exquisite wood carving she had ever seen, though it could be no more than two feet high. Visually it was perfect. But it was far more than just something upon which to gaze with admiration. From the time she first set eyes upon it she had felt all its emotional force, its profundity, its essential ambiguity. Yet it had taken her a moment to recognize the figure standing against the tree as herself. He had been right, though, when she questioned him about it a few days ago. The woman he had carved was both young and old and everything in between. She yearned toward something, as we all yearn. She was hopeful for the future, nostalgic for the past, rooted in the present. She was Everywoman. And more even than that. She was Everyperson. She was the human experience.

How on earth had he managed to convey all that in one relatively small, exquisitely fashioned carving? It was, after all, just a piece of wood. But at the heart of it all, catching at Clarissa's breath every time she had thought of it since, was her conviction that the woman against the tree was her.

If she could go back, she thought now as she hugged the cushion more tightly to her bosom, knowing all she knew now, would she decide differently? Probably not. Undoubtedly not, in fact. And on the whole she did not believe she had made a disastrous choice. Her adult life had brought her security and contentment and many moments of outright happiness. It had not been perfect, of course—good heavens, it had not been perfect!—but she had this home and a deep sense of belonging. She had neighbors and friends she valued. And she had her children and grandchildren, all of whom—and this included Ben and Joy—were an enormous blessing.

A maid had toiled up all the stairs to the turret room in order to bring her a tray laden with a pot of tea and freshly baked scones with clotted cream and strawberry jam. Clarissa often wondered how the staff seemed to know instinctively where she was at all times and even when she was ready for her afternoon tea—before she knew it herself, in fact.

"I am being spoiled," she said as the maid set down the tray and curtsied before withdrawing. "Thank you."

Matthew's child—Clarissa had never discovered whether it was a girl or a boy—would have been Devlin's age now or a month or two older. She wondered how much pain Matthew had lived through at the time and later, even perhaps to the present day. She wondered where he had been all those years he was gone, and what he had been doing, apart from perfecting his carpentry and carving skills, that was.

Somewhere along the way he had also learned the art of archery. He was famously good at it. Any arrow of his that did not pierce the bull's-eye of the target was considered a shocking failure by all who ever watched him, and his arrows flew fast and true as he pulled them at seemingly lightning speed from the quiver he carried on his back. Owen, Clarissa's youngest son, declared that he himself could hit the broad side of a barn on a good day, while Matthew Taylor could miss the center of the target by a fraction of an inch on a particularly bad day. Yet it never occurred to Owen to resent the village carpenter. He came closer to revering him.

Clarissa poured herself a cup of tea and cut a scone in half before spreading jam on both halves and heaping a sinful amount of cream on top. She bit into one half, careful to hold her mouth over the plate as she did so. Ah. Her eyes fluttered closed as she savored the taste. Was there any culinary delight to compare with scones, jam, and cream?

She sat back against the comfortable cushions of the sofa when she had finished both halves and let her eyes roam over the slightly misty countryside outside. She was home, and there was nowhere on earth she would rather be—though she had loved that sparsely furnished, low-ceilinged room above the smithy, with its view over the village green and its pervading aroma of wood coming from what she guessed must be his workroom beyond.

She waited eagerly for him to send word that he had a design for the new baby's crib to present for her approval.

Ravenswood had been intended by its architect to strike something like awe into all who beheld it. The man had succeeded, Matthew thought, not for the first time, as he climbed the steep flight of steps to the great double front doors and rapped the brass knocker against its pad. It was amazing that one family could use all this space, though there was also, of course, the army of servants who catered to their needs and made any exertion on their part more or less superfluous.

Though that was an unkind thought. They were a busy family, all of them, and went to great pains to serve the community in every way they could. They were well liked and respected. It would be difficult to dislike or despise any of them. Well, the late Stratton perhaps, though even that was questionable. There had been some good in him, a fact Matthew admitted only very grudgingly. There had also been the one great evil, for which he would never forgive the man.

The doors opened—both of them—and Matthew explained to the butler that he had an appointment with her ladyship. It occurred to him that perhaps he ought to have presented himself at the kitchen door, but though he had chosen to live and work as a humble craftsman, he never abased himself. The butler, inclining his head in acknowledgment of his claim, led the way and announced him formally at the drawing room doors.

Clarissa rose from her chair and came toward him, smiling, one hand extended. She was alone. Matthew had learned since her visit to his rooms that she was the only one who had returned from London, that the other members of her family were not expected for at least another couple of months. He took her hand and held it for a few moments before releasing it. Her eyes sparkled. She looked happy.

"Prudence Wexford described to me the sketches for the dining table you are going to make for her," she said. "It all sounds very grand. However have you found time to design a crib too?"

"The table is going to be something of a monstrosity," he said with a blunt lack of tact he rarely expressed aloud no matter who the customer or who the listener. "But she seems inordinately pleased with the drawings."

"She is," she said. "She even went so far as to say she can scarcely wait to unveil the table to all her neighbors and friends. I would not be at all surprised if she holds a special dinner party to celebrate when the table has been made and installed. I assume it was precisely her instructions you followed when you drew up the plans? For I do agree with your opinion. It sounds rather . . . busy. You are making her very happy, though, Matthew."

"I aim to please," he said, and smiled back at her.

He still felt embarrassed about what had happened when she called on him last week. Entering that carving for the contest at the fete two years ago had been done on a whim. He had been hesitant about exposing it to public scrutiny because it was so precious to him. More important, though, he had wondered if she would recognize herself in it. He had been unable to resist finding out. He had convinced himself that she probably did not even remember that brief moment in her youth, the day before all the excitement of receiving and accepting a marriage proposal from the Earl of Stratton. Even if she did remember, he had assured himself, she would hardly see herself in what he had carved in a burst of creative energy.

But it seemed she had remembered, and she had recognized herself. He wondered if she understood the significance of the fact that he kept it in his bedchamber rather than more prominently displayed in the living room or with most of the others in his workroom.

The whole thing had been a self-indulgence he rarely allowed himself. For that incident had happened more than thirty years ago, when he had lived upon raw emotion, something he would not go back to for any consideration in the world. Anyone who thought youth was the best time of one's life was clearly an ass.

"Shall I show you the preliminary design for the crib?" he asked, raising his left hand, in which he held a large scroll of parchment paper. "It is only preliminary. You may change anything or everything about it."

"Why do you not spread it on the table over here?" she said, leading the way and removing the bowl of flowers and the lace cloth upon which it stood so he would have plenty of space. She set the bowl on a sideboard and folded the cloth neatly beside it. She brought back with her two small, heavy-looking crystal candlesticks to hold down the outer edges of the drawing so it would not immediately snap back into its roll.

"Oh, just look at it," she said in obvious delight as she leaned over the table.

The crib itself would be a solid, but not too heavy, structure of simple design, though he would contrive to have one of the longer sides movable so it could be lowered almost to the level of the mattress for easy lifting in and out of the baby. He had made a rough indication on the main drawing of what he intended for the headboard and footboard, on both the outside and the inside. The smiling elephant with curled trunk and ears like huge fans would dominate the inside of the footboard, while a laughing monkey would climb the post on one side and a giraffe would be featured on the whole of the leg and post at the other side, munching upon the leaves of a tree whose branches spread out over the top of the board. A puppy, a kitten, and a baby rabbit would cuddle together and smile down at the baby from the headboard. Two of the legs and the bars would be twined with climbing plants and flowers and small birds and butterflies and ladybirds. He wanted to make it all shamelessly unrealistic. Even the flowers and the ladybirds smiled.

"Oh," Clarissa said again after gazing in silence for several minutes. "How absolutely adorable, Matthew."

"Everything will have smooth curves and no sharp edges," he told her. "Nothing that could hurt a baby."

She straightened up and looked at him with flushed cheeks and eyes that still sparkled. "It will be a masterpiece," she said. "Ben and Jennifer are going to absolutely love it. Joy too."

Joy, he recalled, was Ben Ellis's daughter from a previous marriage.

"Is she happy about the new baby?" he asked.

She laughed. "Apparently she has not stopped bouncing since she was told," she said. "Though I hope for all their sakes that is something of an exaggeration. She has longed for a brother or sister. She is five years old and will be a splendid older sister."

He marveled anew at how Clarissa had accepted Ben into the family. It must have been incredibly difficult for her. Had Stratton claimed that the mother, recently deceased, was a former mistress, dismissed before he married Clarissa? Or had she known then, and had she always known, what sort of man she had wed?

It was really none of his business, though. She had seemed happy enough when he had returned from his long travels and settled in Boscombe. She had been as beautiful as ever, and as warmly charming. They had made a handsome couple, she and Stratton, and had seemed devoted to each other—until the end, or what Matthew thought of as the end, though Stratton had lived four or five years longer before his sudden death.

"You trust me to proceed, then, Clarissa?" he asked, indicating the plans.

He heard the echo of her name. Was it offensive for a village carpenter to call a dowager countess by her given name? Had he done it at all when she called in his rooms last week? He could not remember, though he was pretty sure he had not done so in all the years since her marriage. Yet she called him Matthew more often than she did Mr. Taylor.

"Absolutely," she said. "I would have no idea how to arrange all these flowers and creatures into one harmonious whole. I know you will do it to perfection."

He removed the candlesticks from the edges of his drawing and rolled it up neatly again while she replaced everything as it had been when he arrived.

"There is no hurry, of course," she said. "Though I would love to see the finished product tomorrow. Prudence's need is greater than mine. She would love nothing better than to have her table yesterday. And doubtless you have other work too."

"I never take on more than I can comfortably handle," he said.

"May I come and see the crib after you start on it?" she asked. "I would love to see it develop from pieces of blank wood into a child's paradise. However, I do know that many artists of all kinds—painters, writers, musicians—do not like any outside interference in their creations until they are complete."

He was one of those artists—if *artist* was not too pretentious a word to apply to himself. But it was not for that reason he hesitated. She really ought not to come to his rooms again. Not that it would seem indiscreet to her. For all her amiability with him and her use of his first name, she must see him merely as a tradesman. But for him . . . ? And for other villagers, who would hardly be able to avoid seeing her coming and going? Well. Perhaps when the time came, he would suggest that she bring a maid with her.

"Perhaps," he said vaguely.

"It is time for morning coffee," she said. "Will you join me, Matthew? Oh, but not in here. It is such a lovely day after all the clouds and drizzle we have been enduring. I will have it taken onto the terrace outside the ballroom. There will be a sunny corner there by now. Will you come?"

What the devil would her servants think and talk of among themselves? Would they assume it was merely business they were discussing over their coffee? And would they be right? Did it matter?

He had decided many years ago that the rigid British class system no longer meant anything to him, that all people mattered equally, that he could not care less whether people knew or remembered that by accident of birth he was a gentleman. That designation had never served him well anyway. It was not that he resented the facts of his birth. He truly did not care. He mingled socially with everyone alike. And he spent a great deal of his time—most of it, in fact—alone with his own company. He liked it that way. A solitary man who was nevertheless sociable.

"I will welcome both the coffee and the fresh air and sunshine," he said, and she smiled happily and turned to pull on the bell rope.

The butler must have been hovering close to the drawing room doors. He appeared within moments, and Clarissa requested that a tray of coffee for two be taken outside.

"Come," she said, crossing the room to the door and allowing him to open it for her. "I decided to return home early from

London, though my children and friends tried to persuade me to stay until the end of the Season and then join them in their various plans for the summer. Jennifer and Ben also invited me to spend the summer at Penallen. I wanted to be alone, however. Solitude is such a rare and precious luxury. But I will welcome some company. Is that very muddleheaded of me?"

"Life is made up of opposite extremes," he said. "A contented life comes from finding a balance of those extremes, though it is not always easily achieved."

"What a wise understanding of life," she said, turning toward the west wing and the ballroom. "And have you found balance in your own life, Matthew?"

"I believe so," he said. "With the understanding that I cannot always control events, of course."

He fell into step beside her.

CHAPTER THREE

Clarissa led the way along a lengthy corridor toward the west wing and then through the ballroom and out onto the terrace, where two comfortable chairs had already been brought out, a small table between them. They had been set up in the corner of the terrace where the shade cast by the building had already receded to admit the warm sunshine.

Clarissa had decided to invite Matthew Taylor to stay for coffee on impulse. After looking over the design for the crib he was bringing for her approval, she had planned to go outside herself to enjoy the warmer weather, perhaps to go up the hill beyond the west wing and sit inside the temple folly, from which there was a fine view over the park and surrounding countryside. She would not even bother with a book this morning, she had thought. She knew she would not read it. Just when she might have expected to enjoy long hours of reading to her heart's content, she seemed to be right off books. All she wanted to do was gaze about her and think and dream. It was unusual for her. She had never imagined that doing nothing would appeal to her. There had always been so much to do and so much she wished to do if only she had the time.

Being alone and idle once she had dealt with the business of the crib, then, had been her plan. Yet here she was, seated on the terrace outside the ballroom, Matthew beside her, waiting for a coffee tray to be brought out. So much for solitude.

But why should even her hours of idleness be mapped out ahead of time? Why should she not sit here with an old friend if she wished, talking about nothing in particular? She was not bound by any schedule, especially a self-imposed one.

It was a concept to which she found it strangely difficult to accustom herself. She had no one to please but herself for the next couple of months. She had come home to Ravenswood for this very purpose, to discover herself anew, to learn how to enjoy her life free of her usual compulsion always to be doing something useful, always trying to please everyone and behave as they expected her to behave. She had done that all her married life and even in the six years since Caleb's passing. It was hard to learn how to be selfish.

She smiled at the thought. Was that what she could be for the rest of her life if she chose? Could she really choose anything? Be anybody? Was that what freedom was?

Matthew had once been her closest friend. Closer in many ways than her own brother, whom she adored. Certainly closer than any of her female friends who sometimes came to spend an afternoon or even a full day with her or invited her to spend a day with them. She remembered very little of all those visits, except a lot of giggling.

But Matthew had of necessity become a near stranger after she married Caleb. Then he had disappeared for more than ten years. When he returned, he had been different. Among other things, he

had come to Boscombe as the village carpenter and did not social-
ize exclusively with the gentry of the neighborhood, although he was
a gentleman himself. She and Caleb had still been married then.
She had been the Countess of Stratton. She had had children to
raise and duties to perform. Any real friendship with him had been
out of the question. It had become a habit to treat him as a mere
acquaintance, to acknowledge him whenever they met, but never to
speak with him at any length.

Yet for the past six years she had been essentially free of the
obligations imposed by her marriage.

She turned her head to look curiously at him now as he squinted
off toward the lake. She tried to see in him the boy of whom she
had been so dearly fond all those years ago. He had been very slender then, to the point of thinness, in fact. He was still slim and wiry
in build. He still had all his hair, though the darkness of it was
sprinkled with gray. There was even still that lock that had insisted
upon falling down over his forehead. His face was as angular as it
had always been, with some lines fanning out from the corners of
his eyes. Those eyes were still very dark, though they were less intense than they used to be. His jaw was hard and firm but not as
stubborn as it had been then. He was not a handsome man, just as
he had not been a handsome boy. But he had always been striking
in appearance. He still was.

Attractive was perhaps the word for which her mind searched.
He was still attractive. And it occurred to her that she had not allowed herself to admit that in all the years he had been living in
Boscombe. She had never allowed herself to be fully free—a startling thought when she had lived such a privileged life of luxury.

She wondered what story lay behind his settling here as a carpenter, specifically in rooms above Oscar Holland's smithy, when his

grandmother had left him her stately manor house and pretty park and accompanying farmland when she died not very long after the death of his wife, the former Poppy Lang. It could not have been more than a year or so after his disappearance. And what was the story behind that unexpected marriage of his, so soon after her own?

There was so much of the more than thirty years since their friendship ended about which she knew nothing—because she had been living her own busy life. She had thought of him occasionally, of course, and wondered about him and worried a bit about him when he disappeared and no one knew where he had gone. After his return and the surprise of his settling so close, she had grown accustomed to seeing him from time to time and not thinking of him too much. Many childhood friendships waned and even disappeared when one grew up and grew apart, after all.

She had put her husband and family and her social duties as Countess of Stratton before all else. It was what she had been raised to do, what all ladies were expected to do. But why was she still doing it when she no longer had a husband, when her children were all grown, and when the bulk of her social obligations had been taken over by Gwyneth?

It was these very questions she had come home to consider, of course, though she had not been thinking specifically of Matthew when she made the decision—except she had known that above all else she must see that carving again and find out if the woman against the tree really was her. She had not asked herself why it was important that she know.

Now she sat and gazed at Matthew and wondered . . . They were thirty-three years older than they had been then, when she had stood against that tree and he had gazed silently at her. But they were still alive. They were both free.

He was a carpenter living and working above an old smithy, while she was a dowager countess with an earl for a son, a duchess for a daughter, a cavalry colonel for another son. She lived at Ravenswood Hall. It might be foolish to dismiss those facts as though they did not matter. But he was a gentleman just as she was a gentleman's daughter. Why should they not resume some sort of friendship if they wished? It could never be quite as it had been, of course. She could not picture them frolicking about the park here almost all day, every day, through the summer. But could it not be something that would offer them both some companionship and simple enjoyment?

She did not know how he would react to such a suggestion. She really did not know him at all. He did not know her. They were virtual strangers. They had been children when they were friends. They were middle-aged adults now. They had lived quite separate lives in the interim, moving along ever-divergent paths.

But . . .

But he kept that wood carving in his bedchamber, and it really was a carving of her, as he remembered her from that last day of their friendship. It pulsed with emotion, if it was possible for wood to do any such thing. It was, of course, the carver rather than the wood who had put the emotion there.

She wondered how he was feeling now. They had been sitting in silence since they sat down. Perhaps for him it was an excruciatingly uncomfortable silence.

"It is lovely out here," he said, as though he had read her thoughts. But his words sounded heartfelt, not just a stilted conversational opener.

"We are very fortunate to live in England," she said. "In Britain."

There was the suggestion of a smile in his eyes when he turned his head to look at her. "Now, how many other countries do you know, so you can make a fair comparison?" he asked.

"None." She laughed. "But I stick by my opinion. I cannot imagine anywhere on earth I would rather be."

"Actually," he said, "nor can I."

"And what other countries do you know?" she asked.

He shrugged. "Most of the countries of Europe," he said. "Countries of the East. India. Nepal."

She stared at him. "They are where you went during the missing years?" she asked.

"The missing years," he said, still looking slightly amused. "They were not missing for me. I was there the whole time, keeping an eye on them. They were crucial years in making me the person I am today."

And who is that? she wanted to ask him. For he was very different from the rebellious, troubled, often sullen boy of her memory.

"You ran away," she said. "Had your life become so unendurable that you could not stay? Though I do not really need to ask. I am more sorry than I can express in words for the grief you were made to endure."

"I did not run away from anything," he said. "I always knew, after all, even as a boy, that I could never escape from myself. It was the one thing I must always carry with me wherever I went, like a persistent shadow. When I left, Clarissa, I ran *to*."

But they were interrupted at that point by the arrival of their coffee, and Clarissa was not sure if he had finished his sentence or not. The footman who brought the tray poured them each a cup before withdrawing, and Clarissa waited for Matthew to add cream to his before she offered him the plate of freshly baked shortbread biscuits.

"Thank you," he said, setting one in his saucer. He stirred his coffee. "You cannot know what guilt a man feels when his wife dies as a consequence of childbirth. And the child . . . She was perfect in every way except that she never drew breath. My grandmother and my parents and brother heaped words of comfort upon me, assuring me that it was all for the best since Poppy was beneath me socially and had a bit of a temper and a sharp tongue to go with it and an unsavory reputation as a woman of questionable morals. It was even possible, they hinted, that the child—she was Helena, but they never called her by name—was not mine. Poppy, they implied, had lured me, a gullible, mixed-up boy of eighteen, four years her junior, into giving her respectability."

"Oh." Clarissa grimaced as she absently stirred cream into her own coffee. And the thing was that his relatives, his parents at least, would truly have intended their words to be comforting to the bereaved husband and father. They were respectable, well-meaning people, Mr. and Mrs. Taylor, both now deceased. They had done their best to sort out their troubled younger son and form him into the sort of man they believed he must learn to be. The fact that what they were trying to do was impossible had only ever frustrated them and made them try harder. They had been totally without imagination or sensitivity. They had lacked the ability to discover who their son was and how they might best guide and help him to a future that would bring him both security and personal fulfillment. "I am so sorry, Matthew. But the thing is that they must truly have believed they were saying what would soothe your grief."

"Strangely enough," he said, "I can see that now. I can understand them as I doubt they ever understood me. I can forgive them and hope that before their deaths they forgave me for making their lives a true hell for many years."

"Did you find what you were searching for after you left here?" she asked. "Or is my question too intrusive?"

He took a bite of his biscuit and chewed and swallowed before answering. He was gazing off toward the lake again.

"I am not sure I was consciously searching for anything," he said. "I just wanted to be away from everything and everyone familiar. I wanted to be alone with myself in places I had never been and with people who did not know me. I wanted to let go of my self-centeredness, my bitter hatreds and disappointments. I felt them poisoning my whole being and needed to be rid of them. I did find one thing after I arrived in Switzerland, however. I even stayed there for a few years. I found wood carvings everywhere. They were on every building—beautiful and exuberant. They were in churches and in village squares and on mountaintops. They were in shops and workshops. I was in awe of the vision and skill of all those workers. I stayed and apprenticed myself to one I admired particularly, who was willing to take me on and teach me what he knew. And suddenly my hands felt like an essential part of me again and I knew I was doing what I wanted to do, what I needed to do and would always do no matter what else the future held for me."

Clarissa set down her empty cup and saucer on the table beside her. She did so quietly in the hope that she would not break his train of thought. But he turned his head to look at her cup and the coffeepot, and she poured them each a second cup and offered the plate of biscuits again. He stirred cream into his cup but did not take another biscuit.

"It was not until I finally left Switzerland, though, and went to Italy," he said, "that I understood what I really wanted to do, what I must do with wood. I went inside St. Peter's church in Vatican City, as all visitors to Rome do, I suspect, and I saw the *Pietà*, sculpted by Michelangelo. It is a depiction of the crucified Christ, newly taken down from the cross and splayed across his mother's lap while she looks down at him. I stood there for hours without moving, for almost the whole of one afternoon, in fact. I could not tear my eyes away from it. Someone approached me eventually and took my arm and spoke gently, asking if I needed to sit down, if I needed a glass of water or wine. It was only then that I realized my cheeks were wet with tears."

The coffee had cooled in Clarissa's cup, but she did not even notice.

"The skill and design of the sculpture were beyond perfect," he said. "It would be a masterpiece based on those alone. But it was not those things that held me in a sort of trance for so long. It was the sheer raw passion coming through it that enthralled me. And the word *through* is the right one. There was no emotion in the material of which it was made. It was cold white marble. The passion was in the sculpting of it. Michelangelo is long dead, but he left an essential part of himself in that work, and probably in others too. He had left himself, his whole being, in it, in fact. You will think my words impossibly extravagant, Clarissa, and I have never spoken thus to anyone else. But that sculpture changed my life. I would never work with either stone or marble. Wood was my medium. But I knew that skill was not enough. A true artist puts everything that is himself and beyond himself into every serious work he creates. And I believed I was a true artist."

Clarissa was taken with the magic of speaking to an old friend again, and how quickly they had both fallen back into their openness and familiarity. She scarcely breathed lest he stop talking before he had finished his story. But a few words struck her with more force than all the rest—*I have never spoken thus to anyone else.*

It was as it had been between them all those years ago.

It was almost as though he had the same thought. "You were always too good a listener, Clarissa," he said, turning his head to look at her again. "And I was always too much of a talker. You must be thinking me very self-absorbed indeed. What of you? You have a lovely family. Have they brought you happiness? Has this brought you happiness?" He indicated the park and the house behind them with one sweeping gesture of his arm.

"Happiness, unhappiness, and every feeling between the two extremes," she said. "In fifty years of living it would be strange indeed if I had not experienced them all numerous times. One thing age has taught me, however, is that one ought not to be deceived when one is at an extreme into believing that it is permanent. The worst unhappiness fades, as does the brightest happiness. One learns to flow with life's ups and downs if one is to know a pervading contentment. On the whole I have done my best, especially in my dealings with other people. I have made most of the right choices, with one or two exceptions, a few of them huge. But I would not go back to change them even if the chance were offered me." She did not speak unkindly, but she did look directly at him.

"You would not go back, then, to the age of seventeen and make a different choice?" he asked.

"No, of course not," she said.

"Well, there is a slap in the face to me," he said.

She looked sharply at him, but that suggestion of a smile was back in his eyes.

"What nonsense," she said. "There is no way on earth I could have chosen you or you me."

"You might have lived in abject poverty if you had," he said. "No one knew at the time that my grandmother would take pity on me and leave me everything."

"That was the very least of the reasons, Matthew," she said, frowning. "As you know very well. We were friends. Any closer connection would not have worked even if you had known about your grandmother's will. We would have been wretchedly unhappy within a year. Less."

"Would we? Because I was so addled in the head that sometimes I did not know up from down?" He grinned unexpectedly. "Do you remember when we always used to talk like this, Clarissa? About our feelings and frustrations and triumphs? No subject was barred, was it? Except perhaps the weather and the state of our health in order to keep the silence at bay."

"It is rare, that sort of friendship," she said. "I have known it with only one other person, though most of our ramblings down the years have been shared in long letters to each other more than in person. We met when we were both new brides. Coincidentally, we were married on the same day at the same hour, though in different parts of the country. Kitty was widowed before I was. She married George last year."

"Your brother?" He raised his eyebrows. "The former Lady Catherine Emmett, then?"

"Yes," she said. "I'm surprised you remember. But let me ask you something else. Do you feel like climbing the hill to the temple folly, Matthew? The view from up there is worth the climb."

He hesitated a moment before getting to his feet. "I am a workingman," he said. "I scheduled one hour for my appointment here and have already exceeded that. However . . ." He gestured with one hand toward the hill.

"Thank you. Now, you asked about my family," she said as they stepped off the terrace onto the grass. "But we went off on a conversational tangent, as we always used to do. Let me answer your question. They have been and still are a constant source of delight to me. I have been very fortunate. Perhaps it was sheer luck on my part that I learned early that children of the same parents and home and upbringing are nevertheless all completely different from one another. To expect or to try to demand that they all behave in a similar manner is pointless and can only cause a fractious relationship and a frustrated parent and child."

Too late she realized that she might have been describing Matthew himself and his brother. He did not say anything in the short silence that followed as they began to climb the steep slope to the temple. He offered his hand to help her climb.

It was a strong hand, she discovered when she took it. A workman's hand. There was a roughness to it, perhaps even some calluses on his palm.

"Devlin was always fated to be the next Earl of Stratton, of course," she said. "Tentative plans were made for Nicholas, as the second son, to have a military career and Owen, as the third son, to have a career in the church. We never pressed the point, but Nicholas embraced the idea. He never wanted anything else for his future but to be a cavalry officer. Owen, on the other hand . . . Well, we soon gave up on the idea of his being a clergyman. He was full of mischief from his infancy on. He lived for the pleasure of playing practical jokes on all of us, especially poor Stephanie, as the one sibling younger than he. Though I must not describe her as 'poor Stephanie.' She always gave as good as she got. She used to merely roll her eyes when she discovered long-legged spiders in her bed or frogs in her rain boots and would transfer the creatures to his bed and his boots. I do not believe I have ever heard Steph scream. Owen still does not know what he wants to do when he grows up, though he already is grown up."

"How old is he now?" he asked.

"Twenty-two," she said. "He told me a few weeks ago when we were both in London that he sometimes thinks he would be quite happy devoting his life to the church if it were not for the religious part of it."

"He is mildly muddleheaded?" he said, releasing her hand as they reached the top of the hill and turned together to look at the wide view over parkland and farmland and river and village.

"He told me that if being a clergyman required only love and service, which after all are at the very heart of our religion," she said, "he would be at the front of the queue to sign up."

They both laughed.

"He would have a congregation of at least one," he said. "I believe I might attend his church."

He did not attend the church in Boscombe.

They went to sit on the sofa inside the temple. The view was somehow enhanced from in there by the fact that it was framed by tall stone pillars, which held up the pedimented roof.

"Your daughter—Helena—would have been Devlin's age now," she said quietly, wondering if all her talk about her children had struck a nerve with him.

"Yes," he said. "Almost exactly."

Almost exactly. Yet he had married Poppy after she married Caleb. Which must mean . . . But it was none of her business.

"Did you ever consider remarrying?" she asked.

"No," he said.

He obviously did not want to talk about what must have been

the most painful period of his life. They sat in silence for a few minutes—a not uncomfortable silence.

"I was at the ball here during the summer fete ten years ago," he said. "I did not usually go, you know. I always enjoyed the activities of the day, but I never had energy left to come back here in the evening to trip the light fantastic with all my neighbors. On that occasion, however, Oscar Holland and his wife would not take no for an answer, so I came."

The culminating event of every fete had always taken place in the ballroom here. The dancing usually spilled out onto the terrace, where she and Matthew had drunk their coffee a short while ago. They had almost always been fortunate enough to have lovely weather. Indeed, she could not remember a year when they had not.

"I was sorry for what happened that evening," he said.

Caleb had come up here to this very place after supper with one of the guests at the ball—a newcomer to the village, a pretty young woman who had described herself as a widow in search of some peace. In fact, she had been Caleb's mistress, whom he had brought from London with him after the parliamentary session came to an end. He had crossed an invisible line that year. He had spent a few months of every spring in London, leaving his family here, and of course Clarissa had known he did not remain celibate during those months. But never before had he tried to bring his two worlds together.

Devlin, who had come up to the temple folly with Gwyneth on some sort of romantic tryst of their own, had found the two lovers inside the temple under compromising circumstances. And Devlin had chosen to make a fuss, a very loud and public fuss, which had ended down on the terrace outside the ballroom and put an abrupt end to the ball. There had been no way of glossing over what had happened.

"It was one of those catastrophes from which it seems recovery is impossible," she said. "I believed the world as I knew it had come to an end. I sent Devlin away. He saw it as open rejection on my part, and in some way perhaps he was right—to my shame. But mostly, I believe, I wanted to shield him from the crashing inward of his world. For he had not known. I do not believe any of our children had."

"But you had?" he said.

"Of course," she said. "I had been married longer than twenty years at the time, Matthew. It would have been impossible not to know. But no word was ever spoken between us. And, if it is possible to believe, ours was in many ways a good marriage. We were fond of each other, and we both adored our children. He would weep when it was time to return to London and again when he returned for the summer. It was not hypocrisy. He genuinely loved his home and family."

She knew from his initial silence that he was not convinced.

"I am not sure if you know how you were spoken of in the village and neighborhood after it happened," he said. "It was never ever with derision or condemnation, Clarissa, though I know women are often blamed when their men go astray, as though there was some deficiency in them that excused the men for seeking comfort elsewhere. You were always spoken of with respect and sympathy and admiration. You were seen as the perfect lady before it happened, and that did not change afterward, though for a long while you became almost a hermit."

She sighed. "And what did you think of me, Matthew?" she asked before she could stop herself.

He turned to look directly at her, and suddenly she could see the boy he had been in the burning light of his eyes.

"I wanted to kill the bast—. I wanted to kill him with my bare hands," he said.

"Ah." She could not think what else to say. She despised herself for the thrill of pleasure his words gave her.

"At this rate," he said, getting abruptly to his feet, "the Ellis baby is going to be born before I even make a start on his crib. Or hers. And Miss Wexford is going to don full mourning over the absence of her new table. Not to mention all the other jobs that need my attention. I must take my leave, Clarissa."

She rose too, and they stepped outside the temple into the sunshine. She paused there, and he came to a stop beside her.

"Matthew," she said, not looking at him. "Has it occurred to you that for the past six years there has been no reason at all why we cannot be friends again?"

"I believe we always have been friends," he said.

"You know what I mean," she said. "We have been friendly. It is a different thing. The past hour or two has taken me back to the way it used to be between us. We could always talk of things we did not confide to anyone else."

"Yes," he said. "It was usually me, spewing anger and frustration."

"Not always," she said. "You shared dreams too, just as I did. We used to find a great deal to laugh over. I want you to know I am going to be here alone at Ravenswood for at least the next couple of months. It was a deliberate choice on my part. I do not feel lonely. But I do feel that with the approach of my fiftieth birthday I need to rethink my life, look to the future more than I do the past. Will you be a part of that future? May we be friends again? May we spend some time together? When you have some to spare from your work, that is. And if it is something you want too. It is altogether possible you do not. Thirty-three years is a long time, after all. There may be nothing left to bring us together again except nostalgia."

She was embarrassed by her own words and wished with all her heart she had kept her mouth shut.

"You want me to come here and spend time with you?" he asked, frowning. "People would inevitably see us. And people talk."

"Does it matter?" she asked.

"The dowager countess and the carpenter?" he said. "It sounds like the title of a rather lurid tale, does it not?"

She shook her head and laughed. "But will you come?" she asked. "Just sometimes?"

He continued to frown. "I come into the park occasionally on open days," he said. "I practice archery in the poplar alley."

"Thursday is an open day," she said. "Three days from now. May I have the pleasure of watching a private demonstration of your skill with a bow and arrow?"

"At three o'clock," he said. "After I have finished work. Weather permitting."

"I shall put in an order for fine weather and look forward to seeing you," she said.

He began the descent of the hill without another word, though he stopped close to the top in order to offer the support of his hand again.

"Thursday, then," he said abruptly when they reached the terrace.

And he strode away without further ado, along the outside of the west wing and around to the south wing and out of sight.

Clarissa stood on the terrace and watched him go.

She was still half wishing she had kept her mouth shut. He had not been vastly pleased by her suggestion. She was not sure she was. It might be quite impossible to recapture anything of the friendship that had been so precious to them both all those years ago, when they had been different people. Yet they had talked together easily today, as though they had been doing it all their lives. And he had told her things he had never told anyone else—about the years he had spent in Switzerland, learning the intricacies of carving wood, about his discovery of the *Pietà* in Rome and its effect upon him.

How she wished she could see that sculpture for herself.

No, she was not going to regret her impulsive decision to delay his departure this morning or her suggestion that they be friends again. People would talk, he had said. Let them. Friendship was too precious to be abandoned just because of wagging tongues. Besides, she had never found the people of this neighborhood to be particularly malicious. Even after the great scandal of that ball ten years ago, they had somehow been able to pick up the pieces of their lives, she and Caleb, and limp on together, largely because the people of Boscombe had chosen to behave as though nothing momentous had happened that night.

Matthew had gone in search of himself all those years ago, though he did not see it that way. And it seemed to Clarissa that he had found himself. She had never undertaken a similar search—until now. She had not realized that perhaps she ought. She had busied herself instead, made herself useful, tried to make herself warm and lovable to those who depended upon her. But it seemed there was less and less to busy herself about. Her usefulness had diminished, especially after Devlin's marriage.

Perhaps almost more than anything else she needed a friend.

CHAPTER FOUR

What Clarissa must be in need of, Matthew guessed, was a friend for the summer, someone who was not family. Some sort of crisis, if that was not too strong a term, must have brought her home to Ravenswood early and alone, when she might surely have remained in London until the end of the Season and then gone with one of her children or her brother to wherever they intended to spend the summer months. He could not remember her being alone here any other time.

It would be impossible, of course, for the two of them to be anything like the close friends they had once been. Her family would not approve. Nor would their friends and neighbors. Besides, their lives, hers and his, were almost as different now as it was possible for them to be. Apart from the memories they shared, they had nothing upon which to build an enduring friendship.

Twenty years or so ago, after returning to England from his long travels, he had given up all interest in and adherence to the very rigid British hierarchical system. The fact that he was a gentleman by birth and upbringing meant nothing to him. Nor did any interest he might once have had in rebelling and deliberately not being a gentleman. He still spoke like one, he supposed, because that was the way he had always talked. But to himself he was simply a person doing what he chose to do with his life, earning enough money to satisfy his modest needs, as he had done during his years abroad, mingling with people who pleased him, whether they were aristocrats or farm laborers.

There had been need of a carpenter in the village of Boscombe, and he had decided to settle here, not because Clarissa lived close by but despite that fact. He would not go to the house his grandmother had left him. She had given him a home there after his father turned him out following his abrupt marriage to the already pregnant Poppy Lang, and she had shown a stiff sort of kindness to his wife. But she had let him know at every opportunity that he was a disgrace to her and his whole family. Why on earth she had decided to surprise everyone—it must have been a hideous shock to his father and brother—by changing her will in his favor, he had no idea. Perhaps she had done it while Poppy was still alive and pregnant and had simply forgotten afterward to change the will back to the way it had been.

In choosing Boscombe as his home and place of business, Matthew had also moved close to Clarissa, of course, but that fact had meant nothing to him. He had a lingering fondness for her, perhaps, but nothing more than that. Except . . . Well, he had carved that image of her as he remembered her from the last day of their friendship, one of the most deeply emotional experiences of his life.

Now she wanted them to be friends again. Not just friendly, but friends. Her invitation to him to stay for coffee after their business meeting and his acceptance had seemed innocent enough, but it had not taken long out on the terrace for the years to fall away and send them back to when they had talked to each other as though they were talking to their own souls. She had asked about his travels, as other people still did occasionally, but he had not been content to give the usual vague description to satisfy her curiosity. Rather, he had delved right in and given her a lengthy account of his enchantment with the wood-carvers of Switzerland and of his fateful encounter with the *Pietà* in Rome. He had even told her about shedding tears in a public place.

What was it about Clarissa that had always induced him to bare his soul to her? Had she done the same with him? Certainly it had never been on the same scale. Yet the friendship had been genuine.

He was uneasy about encouraging any permanent sort of renewal of that friendship, however. But he could, he supposed, spend a little time with her at Ravenswood until her family returned home. He had his work as an excuse—actually, as a reason—not to go too often or stay too long. Besides, she claimed to have come home in order to spend time alone while she came to terms with her advancing age. She would not expect any new friendship that sprang up between them to be like the old, when they had often spent long hours and even whole days together. So he had suggested she come to the poplar alley, where he went to practice archery a couple of times a week if he could get away and the weather was decent.

Thursday was overcast and a bit cheerless, though there was no sign that rain was imminent. He went there after working all morning and through the luncheon hour on Miss Wexford's table. Perhaps Clarissa had changed her mind, he thought, not sure if he would be disappointed or relieved if she had. But he could see her strolling at the far end of the alley, close to the summerhouse, as soon as he turned off the path that ran along the southern edge of the park above the meadow. He propped his bow and quiver against one of the tall trees and went to set up the target the correct distance away. She had seen him and was coming toward him.

Sheer grace and beauty, as she always had been.

He stood and waited for her and felt again the long-forgotten lifting of his spirits at the sight of her approaching.

"I hope I will not be a distraction to you," she said as she drew close. "But I am looking forward to a private demonstration. I have never been able to watch you compete in any of the contests at the summer fetes. I have always been too busy with the craft and baking displays at the hall."

"Perhaps," he said, "you have not missed much."

"Oh, but I believe I have," she said. "My children are in awe of your skill. Owen in particular once told me that if you were ever to miss the bull's-eye during a contest, the whole nation would go into mourning."

He laughed. "He has a little trouble with accurate shooting," he said. "Though I believe it is the matter of concentration that is his main problem. He is a game one, however. He competes regardless."

"Concentration," she said. "Is that your secret to success?"

"That and a great deal of practice," he said. "Hours and days and weeks and months of it."

She tipped her head to one side. "Where did you find the time for it?" she asked him. "And what made you try it in the first place? I do not remember your ever picking up a bow when you were a boy."

"It is a long story," he said, bending to take up his bow and checking to see that it was tautly strung. "I will tell you sometime."

He had never told anyone else. He would be looked upon as some sort of freak if he did. Not that he would be particularly bothered by that, but why describe something he knew no one else would understand?

"I had no idea a bow could be so large," she said. "It is huge compared with others I have seen at home. Did you make it yourself? But of course you would have. How did you bend it into such a perfect arc? It must have taken a great deal of strength as well as skill and patience. And how did you manage to string it?"

He laughed. She was reminding him very much of the eager girl she had been.

"Rule number one of asking questions," she said, looking from the bow to his face, amusement in her own. "Wait for the answer to each one before moving on to the next."

"I will show you how it is done one day," he said. "Have you ever shot an arrow?"

"No," she said. "And no woman has ever entered the contests here, if I remember accurately. It is a shame. I know there are some quite renowned women archers, though I would defy any of them to handle that particular bow. Matthew, will you pretend for the next while that I am not even here? I know you covet your practice time, and I will leave you to concentrate. I will prop myself against this tree to watch and not open my mouth until you are finished."

She suited action to words, though he could sense that she had the same sudden thought he did—Clarissa leaning back against a tree. Not to end his world on this occasion, however, but merely to watch him shoot arrows at a distant target.

He had wondered if he would be able to do it today, if it had been wise to suggest she join him here of all places. He still wondered. He was not sure it would be possible to get to that space inside himself—though it was not actually a space, was it, or inside him?—that enabled him to ignore all else except sending his arrows unerringly into one small ring a seemingly impossible distance away. He hoisted his quiver onto one shoulder, took up his position, and raised his bow. He drew and released a few breaths, listening to the quiet rhythm of them, feeling the freshness of the air as it came in, the warmth as it left, and he was there. It was not a conscious thought. That would have been intrusive. Rather, it was an awareness. All else had receded. The world had faded away.

He shot one experimental arrow, drawing it from his quiver, fitting it to the bow, and letting it loose, all as one fluid motion. It caught the outer edge of the bull's-eye and stuck.

She neither applauded nor said anything. He was unaware of any sign of her in his peripheral vision. But she had flickered into his consciousness, and he had to bring himself back to full concentration before releasing a barrage of arrows, one after the other. He went to fetch them, returned without looking at her, shot them again, and fetched them once more. Usually he continued for an hour or more, not because he needed the practice, as most people interpreted that word, but because he craved, even needed, the feeling he got from doing it. Though *feeling* was a poor choice of word. Words were terribly inadequate to explain the deeper meanings of life. *Feeling* would imply that he was inside his body and his mind. He was in neither place while he practiced, though he had never tried to explain that apparent absurdity to anyone who did not know and understand it for themselves. He had once lived among people who did.

He shot and collected one more round of arrows and reluctantly gave up the idea of continuing today, though it had been a very brief practice. It would be unfair to Clarissa, who had stayed still and silent against the tree. He went to stand in front of her as he had done on another, far different occasion.

"I am sorry, Clarissa," he said. "I am not good company when I shoot."

"I have been trying to work out in my mind what it is about watching you that has so caught at my breath," she said. "It is not just the incredible speed and accuracy with which you shoot your arrows. It is something about . . . you. About the way you and your bow and arrows seem all . . . one. I do not know quite what I am trying to say. But I can understand now why everyone stands in awe of you as an archer, when one might expect some of them at least to be annoyed with you, even jealous. I believe everyone else competes for the pure prestige of being able to tell others that they came second to you."

"I suppose," he said, "I ought to sit out some of the contests."

"Never do that," she said. "Everyone would be terribly disappointed, Matthew."

He shrugged, a little embarrassed, and propped his quiver and bow beside the tree next to the one against which she leaned.

"I have had some freshly squeezed lemonade and newly baked currant cakes taken to the summerhouse," she said. "Will you join me there?"

"Are the cakes as tasty as the biscuits were a few mornings ago?" he asked her.

She smiled. "We have an excellent cook," she said. "I have to exercise an extraordinary amount of self-discipline in order not to overindulge."

They made their way along the alley, and it struck Matthew as it never had before how the straight line of trees on either side of the long, grassy walkway gave a marvelous sense of seclusion in contrast to the wide-open spaces of the rest of the park. He had never been inside the summerhouse, but he had often thought how perfectly it had been positioned for maximum beauty and privacy despite its walls having been constructed almost entirely of glass.

He opened the door—it was unlocked—and held it for her to precede him inside. The glass windows had trapped warm air in there and made it a pleasant place to sit. It was furnished with comfortable-looking sofas dotted with a number of cushions and a few woolly blankets. Two side tables held books, whose creased spines suggested they were not there just for show. On a longer table before one of the sofas a pitcher of lemonade stood on a tray with two glasses and a plate of currant cakes arranged in a pyramid. There were tea plates upon which to serve them.

"Do have a seat," she told him as she poured them each a glass and placed three of the cakes on a plate before handing it to him. She put one cake on her own plate and sat beside him on the sofa he had chosen, though there was one empty place between them.

"I hope," he said, "you are still enjoying your time alone at Ravenswood."

"I am," she said, "though I keep receiving invitations to tea or dinner—and to one young lady's birthday party. They have been sent in the belief, I suppose, that I must be very lonely here on my own. So far I have been able to refuse every invitation without, I hope, giving offense. I have called upon each sender for the obligatory half hour. People really are very kind. Mrs. Danver made a brief call here the day before yesterday. She apologized that the Reverend Danver had not come with her. It was his afternoon for visiting the sick. Lady Rhys called on me yesterday afternoon. She had received a letter from Gwyneth and was kind enough to share it with me. She and Sir Ifor are leaving for Wales next Tuesday. He will play the organ for Sunday service one more time, and then there will be a long dearth until he returns. So I have not been alone for long stretches of time since my return, Matthew. But I never did intend to make a hermit of myself for the whole summer. I just hope to keep a balance between solitude and company."

Just as he always did.

"I have certainly looked forward to this afternoon," she said. "And I have been amazed and awed."

"You successfully launched Lady Stephanie Ware upon society?" he asked her, changing the subject.

"I did." She sighed. "She is nineteen and the daughter and sister of wealthy earls. She is enormously eligible, in other words. But she would not go last year and went this year only because Pippa was going to be in London with Lucas and the twins, and Gwyneth persuaded her that she would be sadly missed by all of them if she did not go too. What a gem of a daughter-in-law I have there. But what is it with my own daughters? Pippa would not go to London until she was twenty-two, an alarmingly advanced age even for a young woman of such beauty and eligibility. Fortunately she met Lucas—now the Duke of Wilby, no less—at her first social event, even before she made her official come-out. Something comparable did not happen to Steph this year, alas."

"She is very young," he said. He had never quite understood the compulsion young girls felt to marry almost before they left the schoolroom—before, in Clarissa's own case. Most of them would surely benefit from a few years of experiencing life for themselves before settling down. However, that was the way their society worked, and very few people seemed to rebel against it.

"She also has such a poor opinion of herself that sometimes I could weep," Clarissa said. "But there is no point in telling her over and over again that she is beautiful and sweet-natured and accomplished, that she will have no trouble at all attracting the sort of husband who will value her and make her happy. She is made for love. People are drawn to her, especially children. But until she can see these things for herself, she will never be happy, I fear."

Lady Stephanie Ware was indeed a pretty young lady, though Matthew could understand why she could not see it herself. Physical appearance was of such importance to young girls. She was large in build and always had been. She had a round, youthful face that always seemed to glisten with good health. She had good skin. She wore her blond hair in a double row of heavy plaits wound about her head. The hair must be very long. He wondered if she had ever had it cut.

"She had two perfectly eligible marriage offers within a month of her presentation at court," Clarissa said. "She rejected both. I was not entirely displeased. I might have been a little concerned, in fact, if she had jumped at the first offer. It might have suggested a certain desperation. But then she grasped the opportunity to go to Greystone with Pippa and Lucas when they decided to return home early so Pippa may be more comfortable during the months of her confinement."

"So parties and balls held no attraction for Lady Stephanie?" he asked.

"No," she said. "Though I believe there was a specific reason as well as a general one. Do you remember Viscount Watley? Did you meet him when he spent a few weeks here a couple of years ago with Owen? They were at university together."

"The handsome lad who had all the village girls sighing over him?" he asked.

"Tall, dark, and handsome," she said, nodding. "Not to

mention kind and charming—a natural charm, not an assumed one. He quite inadvertently made that summer insupportable for poor Steph."

"Inadvertently?" he said. "He was not unkind to her, then?"

"Quite the contrary," she said. "Owen tends to treat her with some carelessness at times. She is, after all, just his younger sister. But Viscount Watley went out of his way to draw her into activities when she held back and to talk to her and smile at her and praise her for her singing, among other things. He could not have treated her worse, as it turned out."

Ah. Matthew was beginning to understand.

"She sees herself as fat and ugly, to put it bluntly," Clarissa said. "And she fell painfully in love with a man she saw as a god. She was miserable. Oh, it would be funny if it were not also so tragic. And I am her mother."

"He was in London this year?" he asked.

"Indeed. Two years older and even more handsome," she said. "And delighted to meet Steph again. He made a point of introducing her to his twin sister, who is his female counterpart. Lady Estelle Lamarr is slim, elegant, dark-haired, beautiful, and charming, and she tried her best to make a friend of Stephanie. But . . . well, Steph fled to Greystone, when Pippa and Lucas had expected her to wait until the Season ended before joining them there with me."

"It is not easy being a mother, then?" Matthew said.

"No, it most certainly is not," she said. "But only because love hurts. Not all the time, of course. But sometimes."

Yes, it did. He held himself aloof from the extremes of love now, but he still believed, even at the age of almost fifty-one, that what many adults dismissed as puppy love in the very young could be very real indeed. Very exalting. And very, very painful. The pain he had felt over Clarissa was long gone, but he could remember what it had been like. He would not wish to be young again.

"Do you sometimes wish we were young again?" she asked, again as if reading his mind.

"Young and carefree?" he said.

She turned her head sharply to look at him. "That was not very tactful of me, was it?" she said. "My own family life was rather idyllic. I had parents who adored both George and me. They instilled firm principles in us, but they also allowed us a great deal of freedom to become the persons we wanted to be. There was almost never any discord in our home. All my needs were met. I would not have had a care in the world throughout those years if I had not known you, if we had not been friends."

"My apologies," he said.

"Oh, no, no, no." She set a hand briefly on his arm. "I did not mean that the way it sounded. I valued our friendship more than I can say. My heart bled for you when you were frustrated and troubled and rebellious and in trouble, as you so often were. I learned empathy from our friendship. But it was not all gloom and doom. We had good times, did we not, Matthew? We had fun."

He smiled as he thought back. "They were not always fun times for you," he said. "Do you remember all the trees I made you climb?"

"Even though I was afraid of heights?" she said. "You used to call me a girl. There is no worse insult than to call a girl a girl. And then you would dare me, and up I would go, shaking in every limb."

"So that we could be closer to heaven," he said. "So we could have at least the illusion of being away from the world. So we could give wings to our dreams. And we did enjoy all the hours we spent in the boughs of trees. Admit it."

"We often told outrageous stories too," she said. "We used to feed each other lines until we ended up helpless with laughter. But I always dreaded the coming down again. Why is it always so much harder to go down than to go up? I might have broken every limb and bone in my body."

"I always went down ahead of you," he said. "I would not have allowed you to fall. I would have caught you."

"Ha," she said derisively. But she was smiling. So was he.

"Do you remember when we used to cross the river between our properties by swinging from a rope I had tied to a tree branch that overhung the water?" he asked.

"Oh," she said. "Matthew, you were cruel. I cannot believe I allowed you to goad me into something so dangerous."

"But every time after you did it, you were exhilarated and bubbling over with triumph and laughter," he said. "You never once fell into the water, did you?"

"But you did," she said. "You were showing off and trying to do it one-handed. You lost your grip."

"Not to mention my dignity," he said. "I tried to persuade you that it was deliberate, but you set your hands on your hips while I dripped like a drowned rat on the bank before you and clamped my chattering teeth together. And you said, 'Ha!' just as you did a few moments ago."

"Oh, Matthew," she said, tapping his arm. "We did have good times. You put some adventure into my life."

"And you put laughter into mine," he said.

"Will you have more lemonade?" she asked him. "More cakes?"

"Neither," he said, getting to his feet. "It is time I was getting home."

"You will come again?" she asked him, getting to her feet to stand beside him. "Perhaps on a day when you do not practice archery? The day after tomorrow?"

It was a Saturday. He usually took both Saturday and Sunday off from work, having decided long ago that he would never make himself a slave to his working life. Occasionally there was an exception, but not often.

"It will be a Saturday," she said, echoing his thoughts. "Perhaps you could come earlier in the afternoon."

He looked through the glass windows at the park surrounding them.

"Have you ever been up into those hills?" he asked, nodding east toward the line of them in the distance. They apparently formed the boundary between Ravenswood property and that of Cartref, home of Sir Ifor Rhys.

"Many times," she said. "They do not look particularly high from here, but the view in all directions from the crest of the highest hill is quite magnificent. There is a roadway along the top, just wide enough for two riders to go abreast or for a gig or curricle. Have you never been up there?"

"No," he said.

"Then we must go on Saturday," she said. "I will have the gig made ready."

"What, Clarissa?" he said, grinning down at her. "Have you grown into a staid old age? Is there anything wrong with your feet?"

"It would be a long walk," she said. "With a stiff climb at the end of it. Do not look at me like that. We will walk if you insist. And then we will trudge up to the top. Weather permitting, that is."

"You have two days in which to pray for rain," he said.

"Or, better yet, for snow," she said.

They walked back along the alley so he could retrieve his equipment.

"Do you make your own arrows?" she asked.

"Of course," he said. He drew one out of the quiver and handed it to her. He watched as she slid her thumb and forefinger along the smooth, straight length of it and noted the perfection of her hand and manicured fingernails. He thought of his own callused fingers and short nails and rough palms in contrast.

"Amazing," she said. "You must tell me the full story sometime. Perhaps when we are at the crest of the hill on Saturday, admiring the view and catching our breath."

"Perhaps," he said.

He hoisted his quiver over one shoulder and took the target and his bow in his hand, and they fell into step along the path. When they reached the driveway, he turned toward the village and his rooms above the smithy while she made her way back to Ravenswood Hall.

Two totally different worlds, which they would apparently bridge for the summer with some sort of resumption of a long-ago friendship.

So be it. It was not, perhaps, the wisest idea either of them had ever conceived, but when had he ever considered wisdom as a motive for any of his actions? And was she not entitled to a short break from devotion to her family and other duties? Did she not deserve some time just for herself, to do with as she pleased?

It seemed to please her to spend some of her time with him.

CHAPTER FIVE

Clarissa spent the following morning in the library, writing letters. She had been amused and rather touched at how many she had received since her return. Her family and friends must have started writing almost as soon as her carriage drove out of sight of the group of them gathered outside Stratton House to wave her on her way.

They had probably felt guilty at allowing her to return home alone. They would fear that she was going to be lonely. Obviously she had failed to convince them that it was something she really wanted to do.

Kitty and George reported that they were still enjoying the Season in London, though they would return home soon—home being the dower house on the estate now owned by Sir Gerald Emmett, Kitty's son. Clarissa must never forget that she was welcome to join them there at any time. Lord Keilly had asked particularly about her at the soiree they had attended the evening before and had appeared a little taken aback and *hugely* disappointed to learn that she had returned to the country.

Kitty had underlined the one word.

Gwyneth was missing both Clarissa and Stephanie, as well as the frequent visits from Pippa. Devlin would probably be pleased, however, to receive fewer bills from her shopping trips now that her mother-in-law and sisters-in-law were no longer available to accompany her. There was very little pleasure to be had from shopping alone, alas. She was looking forward to leaving for Wales as soon as the parliamentary session ended. It was still not too late for Clarissa to go with them. Everyone—she had underlined the word—would be delighted.

Owen—yes, he had actually written his mother a letter, a rare feat for him—was missing her and "even that pest of a sister of mine." He had started to help out at a home in London for delinquent boys, and his hair might well be a uniform gray by the time his mother saw him next. He would still be happy to join her at Ravenswood for the summer if she felt herself in need of company. All she had to do was let him know.

Stephanie reported that she was very happy indeed to be at Greystone, which was far better for Pippa's health than London. The twins, now two years old, were exhausting, and Lucas kept assuring her that she need not feel she must amuse them during their every waking hour since they had a perfectly competent nurse, not to mention a doting mother and father. But playing with them was fun. She hoped her mother did not need her at Ravenswood just yet. She did wish, though, that Mama would come to them. Both Pippa and Lucas would be delighted, as would the children. And she would be over the moon.

Pippa had written with very similar news and sentiments. She was feeling considerably less tired than she had much of the time in London. In fact her energy had surged back now that she was home. Even so, she was so glad of Stephanie's company. Only Mama's company too could make her happier.

Ben had written from Penallen as soon as he learned Clarissa had returned home alone from London. Jennifer was blooming with good health and exuberant spirits despite—or maybe because of—her condition. His aunt Edith, who now lived permanently with them, was enjoying fussing over her, and Joy kept bringing both women gifts of wildflowers and shells and pebbles from the beach. Joy was enormously excited at the prospect of a new brother or sister, though she had almost seven months to wait. Both Aunt Edith and Jennifer were in the process of writing letters of their own to Clarissa, and Joy was drawing her a picture of Carrie, her collie, now two years old and as frisky as ever. But Mother did not have to wait for letters. She would be more than welcome to come and stay whenever she wished and for as long as she wished. Ben would even come and fetch her if she would but say the word.

Clarissa wrote to them all, a time-consuming process since she could never be satisfied with writing just a brief note. And she felt a welling of love and gratitude for all of them. She felt slightly guilty too, since she knew she had worried them and made them wonder if they had done something to drive her away, despite her firm reassurances to the contrary. It seemed absurd that after fifty years of active living she sometimes felt as though she knew and appreciated everyone and everything around her except herself. Her family seemed to be in an unconscious and entirely well-meaning conspiracy to keep things that way.

Who exactly was Clarissa Ware, née Greenfield, Dowager Countess of Stratton? Sometimes it seemed that she had dreamed her way through life, that it was all something that had happened to her rather than something she had lived with conscious intent. Yet she had never had much time to dream. There had always been so much to do, and she had wanted to do it all well, to be perfect, not to neglect even the smallest duty.

How fortunate it was that at least she knew beyond any shadow of doubt that she loved her family. All of them. She had even loved Caleb in a way it would be hard to explain. It was a bit surprising she had loved him at all, since in many ways he had been a weak man. He had left the running of the estate entirely to a steward and later to his eldest sons, Ben and Devlin. He had left the raising of the children and the running of the home and social events like the grand annual summer fete to her. He had left them all behind for a few months every spring while he went to London, supposedly to fulfill his duties as a member of the House of Lords, though Clarissa had suspected he had little interest in politics. He had spent those months partying with the *ton* during the Season, flirting, committing adultery, betraying both her and their children over and over again.

Yet he had undoubtedly had a great fondness for them all. His pride in his children and his admiration for her had been genuine. He was a man with an enormous amount of natural charm. He loved people, and people loved him. Until the great upset at the summer fete ten years ago, they had been seen as a happy family at the heart of a happy neighborhood. And it had not been all illusion, though it would be hard to explain that to any skeptic.

Matthew Taylor leapt to mind.

But had she been equally weak? Had she convinced herself that it was better to have half a life than none at all? Had Devlin's moral outrage when he found his father up in the temple with that woman in the middle of a ball exposed her own weakness of character as much as it had Caleb's? Was that why she had sent Devlin away? Had it been not so much to protect him as to save herself from having to look inward and admit the truth about herself? She and Caleb had never talked out all the sorry mess that had been made of their lives. Rather, they had moved onward as though nothing monumental had happened. She had genuinely grieved when he died suddenly of a heart seizure four years later.

Human relationships were never as simple as it seemed they ought to be. Nor was understanding oneself.

But she had fallen into a daydream. She picked up her bundle of letters and took them out to the hall, where she set them in the silver bowl that held outgoing mail.

She loved her family. They were the anchor of her existence. So was Ravenswood. And Boscombe and the neighborhood surrounding it. She had dear friends and many friendly acquaintances here. She belonged here. But was it all something to which she clung because there was nothing else? Just a void at the center of herself? It was a thought that disturbed her. She had come home to find and confront the answers.

She went upstairs to her room, found a warm woolen shawl, and left the house after informing the butler that she would probably not be back for luncheon but would have something cold if she was hungry when she did return.

Then she walked, taking the lower path west of the house, veering off among the trees between the path and the river after she had passed the end of the meadow, and reducing her pace as she wound her way among the trunks and looked up through the branches to the sky and the clouds floating lazily by. It was closer to heaven up there, she thought, her eyes upon the upper branches. And she smiled. She had always liked that idea, concocted one day by Matthew to persuade her to climb. And he had been strangely right. They had seemed to leave cares behind them whenever they did climb, and they would relax on a sturdy branch and dream away the hours together, or laugh them away as they composed one of their ridiculous stories.

She set a hand flat against the rough bark of one of the trees and imagined, as she had all those years ago, that she could feel the energy push its way through the roots and the soil, up through the trunk and into the boughs, all the way to the topmost branches and on up into the heavens. Trees lived for a long time, sometimes even centuries, stalwart and rooted in one place. Did they know of their own existence? Someone—was it Matthew?—had once told her that when a tree fell, whether brought down by a storm or by an axe or even old age, the whole forest wept.

She stepped back out onto the path and across it instead of following it to the lake. She struck off north, across rolling grassland with its upward slopes and dips into unexpected little flower arbors.

They were very different from each other, she and Matthew. She was securely established at Ravenswood. She enjoyed the love of an ever-growing family. She had roots here that ran as deep as those of the trees she had just touched. This would be her home for the rest of her life, though she would never be fully dependent upon Devlin. She had her own modest fortune upon which to live in comfort. She had, in fact, everything for which her upbringing had prepared her. Hers was a success story. It had not been without its upsets, it was true, but that same upbringing had enabled her to smooth them out and live through them and beyond them.

Matthew, on the other hand . . . He had made a life for himself that must have seemed a shocking failure to his father before he died. Matthew did not live as a gentleman lived. He seemed uninterested in doing so, though it would surely have been possible, since as far as Clarissa knew he still owned the home and estate his grandmother had left him. He had cut himself off from what remained of his family. She had not heard of there being any communication between him and his brother. He worked as a carpenter, a job that financed his basic needs, she supposed, but would not allow for many luxuries. Yet he was not reputed to spend long hours and days on more and more work so he could earn more. He seemed to be a man without ambition.

Some people might say he had crawled home after years of travel, exhausted, defeated, unfulfilled, having never made his fortune or even found the place in life the younger son of a gentleman of property might have expected. But it was impossible to know Matthew Taylor, even in the limited way Clarissa now knew him, without seeing that he was a man . . . Oh, how did one describe it to oneself? At peace with his world? At one with it? Living just exactly the sort of life he had been born to live?

His prevailing mood was so different from what it had always been when he was a boy that it was impossible to explain to herself what had caused the change. But she wanted to know, to understand. She suspected that most if not all the answers lay in those lost years, about which she still knew very little. They had not been lost, though, according to him. He had lived through them and come out the other side a changed and, he said, happier person.

He had gone away to find himself all those years ago, and it appeared he had done just that. In contrast, she had stayed at home all her life, at her parents' home until she married, at Caleb's after that. And she had never been on any search for herself. Why should she? She had always known perfectly well who she was and where she belonged. Until now.

It occurred to her suddenly that in many ways she and Matthew had reversed roles during the thirty-plus years since their friendship ended. It was a startling thought.

She found one of the quiet flower arbors over a rise of land and went to sit on the seat at the center of it. There was always a seat, though she knew these little arbors were intended primarily for the viewing pleasure of anyone who rode in the park or traveled about the perimeter in a light carriage. She was surrounded by quiet, fragrant peace. She breathed slowly in and out with conscious contentment. How privileged she was to have her home at the heart of all this beauty and tranquility.

How could she possibly be feeling restless?

She looked forward to tomorrow with the eagerness of a child awaiting a treat. Perhaps it was a mistake to try to recapture the friendship she and Matthew had enjoyed during their youth. Perhaps some things were best left to memory and not tampered with. But she had so enjoyed watching him shoot his arrows in the alley yesterday and then talking with him in the summerhouse, reminiscing.

Tomorrow she was going to get him to talk more about the missing years. She wanted to know when and why he had taken up archery and become such a master at it.

So often when one looked forward to an outdoor activity too eagerly one ended up horribly disappointed when the weather did not cooperate. Clarissa knew a moment's dread the following morning when her maid woke her as usual with a cup of chocolate and crossed to the window of her bedchamber to pull back the heavy curtains. But she need not have worried. She could see clear blue sky out there even before she sat up to hug her knees and confirm her first impression that there was not a cloud in sight. She could hear birds singing their hearts out from the trees down by the river. She breathed in fresh air and the smell of recently scythed grass from the open window.

It was going to be a lovely day, perfect for a long walk.

"I will have breakfast up here in my sitting room, Millicent," she told her maid. "Afterward I will need my green walking dress and bonnet. A parasol too. The floral one, I believe. And my stout walking shoes."

"Yes, my lady."

Her maid cast a look of mild surprise her way, though she did not question her mistress's choices. She knew that Clarissa thought those shoes the most unattractive footwear ever invented and kept them to wear only in heavy rain or when she knew there would be mud she could not avoid. That clearly was not the case today. And the parasol! It was garish, to say the least. It had been a Christmas gift from Joy, who had chosen it herself, according to Jennifer as she smiled sympathetically at her always quietly elegant mother-in-law.

The shoes had one virtue, however. They were marvelously comfortable, and Clarissa guessed she was going to need that comfort today. As for the parasol, well, she was feeling in a giddy mood and she knew she would enjoy telling Matthew where it had come from and how Joy had bounced up and down with excitement as her grandmother unwrapped the parcel on Christmas morning.

How ever had she agreed to trudge all the way out to the hills and back—and up over the hills, which would be no mean feat in itself? But he had always had a gift for persuading her to do things she had no wish to do, like climbing trees. Or at least he could as long as they were not strictly forbidden activities. She had never gone swimming with him in the river, for example, because it was specifically not allowed. She guessed no one had thought it necessary to forbid tree climbing, since her fear of heights was well known.

Did Matthew believe she was still that girl of long ago? They had walked endlessly when they were very young, it was true. But neither of them was young any longer.

Yet she felt young a while later as she turned off the main driveway into the village, onto the narrower path that led east, and could see that he was waiting for her at the southern end of the poplar alley, where they had agreed to meet. Like her, he was early. He stood with his back against one of the trees, his arms crossed over his chest, one booted foot flat against the trunk. There was what looked like a canvas bag on the ground beside him. He watched her come, a smile on his face.

"Ever the elegant lady," he said as she drew close, his eyes sweeping over her small-brimmed bonnet and her dark green walking dress and black shoes—which were anything but elegant.

"You have not seen my parasol unfurled yet," she said. "When it is raised it looks like an overabundant flower garden in full, blinding, unlikely sunshine. It was surely intended for a very young woman to twirl about her head to draw admiring glances in a crowded park. It was not meant for an aging matron out on a sedate walk. But my granddaughter chose it specifically for me and told me so at great length on Christmas morning."

"Is that how you see yourself, Clarissa?" he asked. "As an aging matron? There must surely be a full-length looking glass somewhere inside Ravenswood. But you probably see in it what you expect to see or what you believe you ought to see since you are a dowager countess and have five adult children—six if you count Ben Ellis, as I daresay you do. I myself, however, see a woman of vibrant beauty, who has every right to twirl a garishly bright parasol above her head. Clearly your granddaughter sees you the same way."

She laughed as he hoisted the canvas bag over one shoulder, and hoped she was not blushing. But yes, her title, amended to dowager countess after Devlin married Gwyneth, and the existence of grown children and growing grandchildren did make her feel—oh, not old exactly, but . . . unyouthful, if there was such a word.

He did not appear youthful either, but he did look like a man who took care of himself and was in the prime of life. He was lithe but looked strong despite the lines on his face and the gray in his hair. He was certainly not dressed for elegance—or to impress. His coat was not so form-fitting that he would need a valet to squeeze him into it. It fit him comfortably. It had seen better days—quite a while ago, surely. His shirt was plain and unadorned and clean. His boots, though freshly polished, were creased with age. His tall hat was not in the first stare of fashion—or the second or third. Clarissa guessed his ever-so-slightly shabby clothing had nothing to do with any inability to afford better, but rather had everything to do with a certain carelessness over material things.

He looked strangely appealing.

"What is in the bag?" she asked. "It looks heavy."

"I thought," he said, "that by the time we get to the crest of the highest hill we will be thirsty at the very least. Probably hungry too."

"How thoughtless of me," she said. "I did not remember to have a picnic luncheon sent out there in one of the wagons. Now I feel bad that you have to carry everything."

"It is part of the fun of going on a walk with a friend," he said. "Do you not remember, Clarissa, when we used to do it all the time? Usually with food and drink from your kitchen. Your parents were very kind and your cook extremely indulgent."

They made their way at a fairly brisk pace toward the hills and the eastern boundary of the park. And they talked. At first about daily matters. She told him how exuberant with delight Stephanie was at being at Greystone with her sister and brother-in-law and twin niece and nephew and how it made her, Clarissa, wonder why she had gone to all the trouble of presenting her younger daughter in London this year. She told him of the letter from Gwyneth that had been delivered just this morning, informing her that Bethan, Gwyneth and Devlin's daughter, had taken her first steps—five of them in a row, in fact, before she looked suddenly alarmed and plopped down on her padded bottom before laughing and clapping her hands but refusing any repeat performance.

He told her about moving his tools and equipment and piles of wood with Cam Holland's help to Colonel Wexford's last evening and setting up a temporary workshop in a barn there. He could do a lot of work on Miss Wexford's table at home, particularly the numerous and intricately carved legs and feet. But his workshop would scarcely hold the table itself once he put it together, and what would he do with it when it was finished? How would he move it, vast and weighing a ton, out of his workshop and down the steep stairs to the pavement and out to the colonel's? So he was going to work on it there, and it would be up to the colonel himself to mobilize an army of burly servants to get it from the barn to his dining room.

"Miss Wexford buzzed around us like a particularly persistent bee when we arrived," he said. "She had a thousand suggestions and a million questions. She did promise before we left, however, that she would not disturb me once I start work there but will leave me alone to get on with it."

"By which words you understood that she will be forever in your way, I suppose," Clarissa said.

"I am afraid so," he said with a laugh. "One cannot help liking the woman."

"Can you not shut and lock the doors to the barn?" she asked.

He laughed again. "I would not even if I could," he said. "She is so terribly excited about this table, Clarissa. I will humor her. I do not believe there has been a great deal of excitement in her life. More than that, I do not believe she has ever done much purely for herself. She has been an excellent sister and housekeeper to the colonel and a good aunt to his daughter. She has never had her own family or home. I suspect her only personal possessions are what she has in her own room. She has been well loved and appreciated and cared for in return, but I am not sure those things have been enough to satisfy her . . . soul."

"And a new dining table will do that?" she asked.

"One she has commissioned and will pay for herself in defiance of her brother's assumption that the expense will be his," he said. "One she has more or less designed for herself. Yes, curiously, I believe her soul is being nourished."

"Matthew," she said, pausing to look at him while she opened her parasol, having felt the slightly uncomfortable warmth of the sun against the back of her neck. "You are a very perceptive and very kind man."

Even she would not have described him as kind when he was a boy. He had been too needy, too disturbed by frustration and rage.

He looked at the parasol as she raised it over her head. "I like your granddaughter's taste," he said. "And I am glad her parents allowed her to indulge it."

"So am I," she said. "Do you by chance remember the very garish and cheap jewelry with which both Joy and Jennifer bedecked themselves at the fete two years ago?"

They were on a not particularly steep section of the narrow roadway that went up over the crest of the hills from the low land near the river before descending at the far end and winding its way back west on the northern side of the park. It was easy enough to ride up or to go in a light carriage. Clarissa had done it numerous times, though not recently. She had never done it on foot. It felt very steep indeed today after the already long walk from the house. The roadway ahead looked like an endless, undulating ribbon of pure torture.

"Give me your hand," Matthew said.

She did, and the climb seemed much easier with the steady support of his strong workman's hand as it closed tightly about hers. She felt ashamed at having to accept his assistance when he was carrying that heavy bag over his other shoulder.

"We will sit and rest at the top, and we will doubtless agree that the long walk and the climb were well worth the effort. Not too far now," he said with a smile.

"Hmm," Clarissa said. It was hard to catch her breath and impossible to say more. But her eyes already told her he was right. She had seen the view before, of course, but never as a result of her own exertions. Somehow it made a difference. And the sun was shining down from a sky that was still as clear of clouds as it had been when she woke up. It was a perfect late spring day, the air not quite as hot as it would be in a few weeks' time. There was a welcome coolness to the breeze.

When they finally stood at the very crest of the highest hill, they turned slowly in all directions. Sir Ifor Rhys's neatly cultivated farmland stretched away to the east of the hills, the large manor house that was Cartref in the distance. The pretty cottage in which Idris Rhys, Sir Ifor's son and Gwyneth's brother, lived with his wife and family was a short distance beyond the main house. There was a pretty, though not large, park surrounding the buildings.

And on the other side of the hills there was Ravenswood, with its vast park, closely packed trees to the south and north of it and others dotted pleasingly across it, and the river winding past with the main road on the other side, along which a heavily laden stage-coach was swaying. And, slightly back from the road, the village of Boscombe, with its picturesque houses and village green and church with a tall spire and the stone bridge that connected the village to Ravenswood. The mansion itself looked vast and imposing from here, its four wings surrounding cloisters and gardens at its center.

"You were right," Matthew said, setting down his bag. "These are not particularly high hills, but the view from the top is spectacular. Shall we sit for a while?"

He did not wait for her answer but opened the bag and drew out a light blanket, which he spread on the scrubby grass before gesturing for her to sit on it. He followed her down and gazed over the park, one leg stretched straight ahead of him, the other bent at the knee with one arm draped over.

It was a relaxed, informal pose. The very size of the blanket dictated that they sit rather close to each other. They were not touching, but she could both feel and smell the heat coming from him. She was very aware of him, of his masculinity, and wondered how he could be so relaxed. She felt taut with something that was not quite discomfort.

He glanced over his shoulder at her, a lazy smile on his face. His hat was tipped slightly forward to shade his eyes from the sun.

"Are you as parched as I am?" he asked her. "I am too lazy to take the drinks from my bag. There is a flask of water and one of tea. I could not remember if you take milk and sugar. I packed a little of both separately."

She delved into his bag and pulled out both flasks. It was water she wanted more than anything. She could not find any cups.

"I decided to travel as lightly as possible," he told her. "No cups and no plates, I am afraid. We will have to drink directly out of the flasks."

Oh my! How very ungenteel. She smiled with inward amusement.

She drank from the water flask first before wiping off the top with a clean handkerchief—there were no napkins either in the bag—and handing it to him. The water tasted faintly of whatever had been in the flask before it—tea? Coffee? It did not matter. It tasted as good as the finest wine to Clarissa.

There were two packages of food, both wrapped securely in clean cloths. One held two sandwiches made of thick slices of bread with an almost equally thick layer of very yellow cheese in between. The sandwiches were quite inelegant and the bread a little stale, as were the large slices of seed cake he told her Mrs. Holland had brought for him a few days ago. But to Clarissa it seemed like the most delicious feast she had eaten in a long while. Perhaps ever.

The problem with bringing milk and sugar for the tea but no cups and no spoon, of course, was that they were virtually impossible to use. And Clarissa did remember that as a boy he had drunk his tea black. That was how she drank hers from the flask today—lukewarm, very black, and so strong that a spoon, if there had been one, would surely have stood upright in it without touching the sides. But it was like the perfect ending to a perfect picnic.

"Thank you," she said as she shook out the crumbs and folded the cloths before putting them back into the bag with the empty flasks. "That was delicious."

"Liar." His eyes laughed lazily into hers.

"Oh, not so, Matthew," she said in protest. "It was the best picnic ever. The best meal ever."

But she laughed with him at the extravagance of her words, true though she was convinced they were.

"Are you ready to leave?" he asked her.

She shook her head. "You were going to tell me about the archery," she said.

"Was I?" He turned his face away to look out over the park again. "Are you sure? It is a long, boring story."

She did not answer him. She sat still and waited until at last he pushed himself to an upright sitting position on the blanket, crossed his legs at the ankles, and draped his hands over his knees.

"Well," he said. "It all began when I was in India and decided to go on a hike with a couple of holy men."

CHAPTER SIX

Matthew waited hopefully for her to laugh, to tell him that if he could only talk nonsense, then she did not want to hear it and it was time to make their way back home anyway.

It did not happen.

But he might have known better than to expect she had changed. She had always waited for him to speak when she knew he had something to say. She had always listened to him too—really listened. In those long-ago days of their childhood, it had seemed to him that she was the only one who ever did.

He turned his head to glance at her. She was slightly behind him but very close. The blanket had determined that. She was hugging her knees and looking steadily back at him. And, Lord, she was more beautiful than any woman her age had a right to be. And full of vitality. She had walked here stride for stride with him, talking and laughing with him and twirling that garish parasol behind her head, making him forget that she was no longer that girl he had loved once upon a time. Just as he was no longer that boy.

"I will try to make a long, boring story as short as I can," he said as he turned his head back to look out over the park. "After a few more years in Europe, first learning carpentry, then working at whatever job I could find to support myself, I thought I would probably end up coming home, though I never felt I was quite ready. I just did not know what ready would look like. Then I made the acquaintance of Joe Hopkins, who was a bit like myself—a wanderer, a man with itchy feet, as he liked to describe himself. We were soon firm friends, and off we set for the East. He had an uncle in northern India who had a senior position with the East India Company. Joe was confident he would offer us employment and enable us to make our fortunes. Not that either of us was particularly interested in being rich. It took us a long time to get there, but we did eventually arrive and miraculously were offered work with the company—as the lowliest of lowly clerks."

Matthew had hated it. The supposed superiority of the white man. The contempt for all things Indian—its people, its customs, its religions. Especially its religions. To company men, even God was white and superior and contemptuous of all that was not white or superior or a worshiper of the English God. Matthew had soon grown almost ashamed of being white and English. He saw himself as an interloper in the country of these people, and he found himself wanting to get to know them—but from their point of view, not from that of his fellow countrymen.

Fortunately for him, Joe felt much the same way, and together they plunged into the life of India as it was lived by the Indian people. They acquired some friends and friendly acquaintances and a gradual knowledge and understanding of a culture very different from their own but just as richly steeped in history. Perhaps more so. It was a civilization far older than theirs. They acquired a smattering of the language so they would not have to rely wholly upon the services of an interpreter.

"I was particularly intrigued," Matthew said, "by the holy men who roamed the streets and the countryside, begging for their food with bowls they held out whenever they were hungry, but with never a word of pleading and always a murmur of thanks when food was given. They were seen as dirty, lazy beggars by my own people, of course, but they were treated with deep respect, even reverence, by their own people. There was something about them that fascinated me. I never could quite put my finger upon what it was. They seemed always to be content and at peace, though they apparently had nothing beyond their robes and sandals and begging bowls. They never seemed to feel the urge to do anything or go anywhere. They just were wherever they happened to be. They spoke to people who spoke to them, but never in the form of lengthy sermons or speeches. They gave blessings when asked for them. They sometimes sat unmoving for long hours, seeming to stare into space, though they never looked bored or as though they were simply daydreaming. They never seemed to fall asleep. I had the impression they were very present at every moment. When Joe told me one day that two of them were about to return to their monastery in the mountains north of India and that he had decided to go with them, I chose to go too, abandoning the job I so hated. I expected it to be an interesting adventure for a week or two." He paused, turning to look at her. "I must be boring you horribly, Clarissa."

He had been droning on for what seemed a long time. He turned back to gaze out over the park spread below him, and marveled as he often did at the green serenity of England, which he had taken so much for granted as a boy.

"You are not," she said, and he turned his head to glance at her again.

"The monastery was a long way into the mountains," he told her. "It took more than two weeks of rough walking and rugged scrambling to get there. It was cold and stark. There was little to eat, and even water was not always easy to find. The pace was very un-British. We took longer breaks than I expected, sometimes not moving onward after a night's rest until almost noon by my watch, stopping again when there was still an hour or more of daylight left. Sometimes we went a whole day, once two days, without moving onward at all, though there was never any apparent reason for the delay. I had to learn the rhythms of their lives. Life was not always about getting somewhere. One was not at the mercy of time. What was time anyway? I grew less and less impatient as the days went by, so much of them apparently wasted. But we arrived eventually, and Joe and I were accepted without question. We were each given a tiny room in which to set our things and sleep. We were fed twice a day with everyone else. We were given mats upon which to sit cross-legged alongside all the monks for hours on end, meditating while staring at a blank wall a couple of feet or so in front of us."

He had been a bit taken aback at first. They were neither questioned nor treated as temporary visitors or curiosity seekers. It was assumed they had come to seek something specific. *Enlightenment* was the word Joe had used. And so Matthew had sat and tried to meditate and achieve enlightenment.

"We were supposed to still the body and the mind," he said. "We were to listen to the ebb and flow of our own breath and, if necessary, chant a mantra silently to ourselves until we moved into a state of understanding. We were not told what that was exactly or how we would recognize it when we got there. It was nothing to do with what we would call God, since they did not seem to see God as an entity separate from all else. To them it was not helpful to use that word to describe the divine, since it immediately made of it a separate being, someone to be worshiped. No one could tell me what the divine was, however. In fact they did not even use that word. The whole experience of enlightenment could apparently not be described in words. And it could never be achieved if one thought in terms of success and failure. It could not be willed. The more one strove to achieve it, the more one moved back into one's mind, and that never worked."

He must be sounding like a madman.

"Why did I persist?" he said. "Why did I want to achieve something no one could even explain to me? It was not as though I was being forced. I was not stranded in that monastery. After the first couple of weeks or so, a small group was going down to the plains to bring back supplies, and Joe went with them, his curiosity satisfied. I do not know which of us was the more surprised, him or me, when I chose to stay. By then I was deeply frustrated and more and more determined to succeed at all costs. Why? It seemed to me that I was searching for the missing link that would make me whole after all my years of rebellion and restless wandering. And it seemed to me that the answer lay there. I would not leave until I had found it."

He fell silent again, wondering ruefully why he seemed unable to cut the story short, as he had promised to do. He had never told this story to anyone else and very much doubted he ever would again. But he had always told her everything. Well, almost everything.

There was one monk at the monastery who was deeply revered by all the others. He rarely emerged from his small room. Matthew had never seen him. He apparently spent his days and most nights deep in meditation. One day Matthew was summoned into his presence. Until then he had thought of the man as a sort of mythical being.

"I knew at that moment," he said to Clarissa, "that I was a failure, a nuisance, that I was about to be dismissed, asked to leave. I sat cross-legged, facing him, on a mat identical to his own and no fancier than those in the meditation room. I was on the verge of tears. I did not understand why. I was not interested in their religion or any other. I did not want to join them permanently. But when he spoke, it was not to reprimand me. He told me that for some people, particularly Europeans, stilling the mind in meditation was a near impossibility. Our culture frowned upon stillness, he said, which it equated with laziness and a waste of precious time."

Do not send me back, Matthew had begged him. He had been quite abject, to the point of self-pity. *I have been in pain all my life. I need to find peace.*

I do not have the power, nor do I want it, to send you anywhere, he was told. *Those who come here to seek may stay until they find or until they choose to leave of their own free will. There are other ways of stilling the mind, however, ways that involve a disciplined exercise of the body. You may wish to try one of these ways. Have you ever shot an arrow?*

Matthew had raised his eyes to look in surprised puzzlement at the monk. *With a bow, you mean?* he had asked foolishly. *No.*

We have a master of the art living with us at present, he was told. *He has helped a few men like yourself who desperately seek but cannot find because they cannot let go of their desperation. He is willing to instruct you if it is something you wish to try.*

It is, Matthew had said eagerly, though he had not for the life of him been able to imagine what archery of all things had to do with this monastery or his search for inner peace.

"And what did it have to do with your search?" Clarissa asked, and he realized he had been talking aloud.

"I was embarrassingly awful at it for a long, long time," he said. "I could not hit a target to save my life. More often than not, my arrows died an ignominious death at my feet. Even when I improved, I could still shoot only one arrow before having to stop and set up all over again. I watched my teacher in despair. His arrows flew straight and true and so close together, one after the other, that it was hard to see where one ended and the next began. But I did improve—over a long, long time, though I could not see how what I was learning was helping in my search. My teacher explained it to me—but only after I had become proficient with my bow. When I understood, he explained, that the bow, the arrow, the target, the air through which the arrow flew, my arm that held the bow, the arm that fitted and shot the arrow, my stance, my eyes, my whole person, were, in fact, all one, then I would understand everything. And then suddenly, one day, it happened. I no longer had to think of what I was doing. I no longer had to think of success or failure. I was one with the whole process. Unfortunately, it is an experience impossible to explain adequately in words. Or perhaps it is not unfortunate, for if we could explain it, we could also manipulate it and change it, personalize it, make some sort of monument of it."

He dropped his chin to his chest and closed his eyes. He was very glad she was Clarissa. She did not rush into speech. She had always been the same. She had always listened. She had never said much afterward. She had never lectured or advised or even given an opinion most of the time. Her silence had always brought him infinite comfort. The comfort of acceptance for the person he was— a not very pleasant person when he was a boy, according to most people who knew him.

"Thank you," she said at last, and he turned his face toward her.

"It is a foolish story," he said.

"You know it is anything but foolish," she told him. "And so you came back home."

"And so I came home," he said. And for some strange reason he felt close to tears.

"And you are a happy man," she said.

He laughed softly. "Making a home of rented rooms above a smithy?" he said. "Earning a modest living as a carpenter? How could I possibly be happy?"

She smiled at him. And oh, that smile. He wondered if she had ever realized the power of it. It was not her social smile, charming and genuine as that was. It did not involve sparkling eyes or a flashing of teeth, only a curving of her lips and a softening of her whole facial expression and something from within that beamed from her eyes and wrapped about the recipient like a woolly blanket or a warm hug. It was a smile intended for that person alone.

Ah, he had missed it. For more than half his lifetime.

"If I do not stand soon," she said, "I may never be able to stand again."

He jumped to his feet and held out his hands to help her up. She both laughed and groaned as she stood, clinging tightly to his hands.

"Oh, Matthew," she said. "We are no longer young."

"Thank goodness," he said. He far preferred the age he was now. He preferred her the age she was now too, with all the poise and dignity the years had given her to add to the vibrancy she had always had.

She smiled at his comment. Their hands were still clasped between them. And he could see the sudden awareness arrest her expression. He released his hold on her and bent to pick up and fold the blanket while she shook her skirt and smoothed out the creases.

"Shall we continue on our way?" he said, pointing to the downward and upward undulations of the road ahead, which would eventually take them down to the park and back to the house along the northern path.

"Yes," she said. "It would be as far to go back as it will be to continue."

"A long way, in other words," he said. He felt suddenly guilty. Even with the lengthy tea break they had taken, this was a long walk. He ought not to have ridiculed her idea of bringing a gig. But they had no choice now but to trudge onward. Unless . . .

She raised the bright parasol over her head and gave it a twirl.

If they had brought a gig, of course, they would have no choice but to keep to the roadway. But since they were on foot . . .

From the bottom of the next dip, the drop down to Sir Ifor's land was almost sheer. But on the Ravenswood side it was a far more gradual slope. It also appeared to be all grass with just a few protruding stones. He stopped and moved closer to the edge to peer downward.

"No," she said firmly before he could voice his thoughts.

"It would be relatively easy to go down here," he said. "We would cut off a huge corner and at least half a mile of our journey. Probably more like a whole mile."

"No," she said again.

He turned his head to grin at her. "It would be exhilarating," he said. "It would be like being children again. And it is really quite safe. There are even a few large flat stones in conveniently strategic places upon which to rest. I will help you. You are not a coward, are you?"

"You are doing what you always used to do," she said, narrowing her eyes. "You are goading me into doing what I know is madness and what is entirely against my will and better judgment. It is how you got me to climb trees."

"Did you ever fall?" he asked.

"Utterly irrelevant to the present situation," she said.

He held out one hand toward her. "Come and see," he said.

She shook her head, exhaled with audible exasperation, and came to stand beside him, though she did not take his hand. "I suppose you do not remember," she said, "that I am afraid of heights."

"All the more reason to get down from this one by the quickest, easiest route, then," he said. "Look at it, Clarissa. There are no difficult obstacles, like sheer cliffs, for example, and there is no dangerously steep part of the slope. We seem to be high up only because we are up rather than down. From down there it will look like nothing at all. Shall we find out?"

"You are quite determined to do this, are you not?" she said.

He merely turned his head to grin at her again, and she huffed out another exasperated breath.

"I might have known," she said, "that deep down you have not changed at all."

He laughed. "Ah, Clarissa," he said. "Nor have you."

She lowered her parasol with a snap, and he took it from her. "We will do it," she said. "And if I survive the ordeal, I will call you the monster and the idiot you are."

"Take my hand," he said.

They descended the first part of the slope very slowly as she felt out every foothold and clung to his hand as though her very life depended upon it. They paused when they came to the first rock, which was flat enough on top to give them firm footing. She looked ahead for perhaps the first time.

"Oh," she said. "We have scarcely started. I think we should go back."

"Look behind you," he said.

She did so and let out one of her huffs. "Did we really come down all that way?" she asked.

"It would certainly be foolish to change our minds now," he said.

"And it is not foolish to go on?"

"Well," he said. "We could stay here. Perhaps for the rest of our lives. Or possibly someone will come looking for us after a week or so. I believe there is a little tea and water left in the flasks."

"Oh," she said. "You are enjoying this. Come along, then."

The grass was thin on the next stage of the descent and they did some slipping and sliding on loose stones that had not been visible from above. But there was never any real danger. And the slope became far more gradual and grassy below the next big boulder, which was not as flat as the other one had been but nevertheless gave them a firm base upon which to stand and catch their breath.

"It is easy from here to the bottom," he said. "You can walk it sedately, Clarissa, or you can take it at a bit of a run. I'll show you. I'll go down first and be there to catch you at the bottom."

"You are not going to leave me?" she said, alarmed.

"No," he said. "I'll come back up if you need help. But you will not."

It was a fairly gradual slope, though admittedly longer and steeper than it had looked. It was far easier to take it at a run than at a walking pace. He ran down most of it. Children could have a feast of delight rolling down here, he thought, and wondered if children ever had. The hills were a long way from the house.

He watched her begin a gingerly descent, holding up her skirt with one hand to show her still-trim ankles, her eyes on her feet and the grass immediately ahead of them. But after a short distance the slope became too much for her and she had no choice but to fall or run for it. She ran, holding her skirts up with both hands now, and shrieking as she came. She reached the bottom just as she was about to topple over, but he caught her in his arms and swung her off her feet and around in a complete circle. They were both laughing helplessly.

"Matthew," she said as he set her feet back on the ground. She tipped a flushed face to his. Her arms were wound tightly about his neck. "You reckless, utter idiot."

"Guilty," he said. "And aren't you glad of it?"

He watched the laughter fade from her face even as he felt it drain from his own.

"Yes," she whispered. "You idiot."

And suddenly they were kissing with passionate intent as though they would fold themselves into each other if they could. A whole lifetime of yearning went into that kiss, it seemed to Matthew, and who could ever say which of them had initiated it? Perhaps it had been entirely mutual. It was very definitely a kiss. Their mouths were open, their tongues clashing and twining and exploring, their breath mingling. They were not going to be able to convince themselves afterward that it had been a mere pecking of lips, a mere extension of their exuberance and laughter.

"You idiot," she murmured again when he softened the kiss and moved his lips almost away from hers. And she deepened the kiss for a few moments longer until full awareness returned to her, as it had already begun to do to him.

Awareness of what they were doing, he and Clarissa Ware, Dowager Countess of Stratton. Their first and only kiss at the age of almost fifty in her case, going on fifty-one in his. And as impossible now as it had been when she was seventeen and he eighteen. More so, in fact. At least then he had been a gentleman and she a lady without all the trappings of title and aristocratic status. Now he was a carpenter and wood-carver by his own choice. His closest friends, the people with whom he most often associated, were fellow workmen and shopkeepers. And she was a dowager countess.

He raised his head, and she drew hers back at the same moment, though they did not immediately release each other. Her eyes were large and slightly dreamy as they gazed into his. Her cheeks were rosy from surely more than just the exertion of running downhill. Her lips were soft and moist and deep pink.

"When you stood against that tree," he said. "After you had told me Stratton was coming to offer for you the following day and you were going to marry him. When I came to stand in front of you, I wanted desperately to kiss you then."

"I know," she said softly. "And I wanted desperately for you to do it."

"What would have happened if I had?" he asked her. "Would the whole of the rest of our lives have been different? Would you have changed your mind?"

She thought about it, her eyes lowered, her teeth sinking into her lower lip before shaking her head. "No," she said. "But there would have been more heartache."

She had loved him, then? But she had married Stratton anyway? Because his offer had been too dazzling, too tempting to resist? No, he must not be bitter. There had been other reasons, all of them sensible.

"I loved you," he said.

"Yes, I know," she said, moving her hands to his shoulders and patting them. "And I loved you. But love would not have been enough, not for us. We would have ended up desperately unhappy."

He was about to argue the point, but he was no longer the love-sick eighteen-year-old he had been then. And even at the time, he had known that love would not have been enough for them.

Whoever thought love was all that mattered was living with his head in the clouds. Though romantic love was not the only kind of love, of course. Not nearly.

He bent to retrieve his bag and her parasol.

"Oh, Matthew, you lied!" she cried suddenly. She was gazing up the slope they had just descended, a look of horror on her face. "You told me the hill looked high just because we were up there, looking down. You told me that from down here looking up, it would seem like nothing at all."

"Well," he said. "Almost nothing at all."

"Look at it!" she said, flinging out her arm and pointing with the parasol. "It goes on forever, and it is almost sheer."

It had been a longer, steeper descent than he had estimated from above, it was true. And there had been that tricky bit in the middle.

"Are you not all the more proud of yourself for doing it?" he asked.

She drew breath to make some sharp retort before closing her mouth with a clacking of teeth. After a moment she laughed. "Ah, Matthew," she said. "You have made me feel young again today. And very foolhardy again. We might have killed ourselves."

"Nonsense," he said. "Besides, I was there to catch you, as I always was."

"But who would have caught you?" she asked.

They were on grassland, halfway between the southern and

northern riding paths. They set out straight across rolling lawns dotted with trees and surprising little sheltered nooks of flowers and ponds and rustic seats. Matthew wondered if they were ever used, though a whole army of gardeners must be kept constantly busy tending them all.

"I believe some people from the village bring their picnics to these more isolated parts of the park," she said as though she had read his thoughts. "They come on open days, as they are invited to do, but some of them are too shy to use the more obvious attractions closer to the house. My children would often come back from rides in the park and tell me I simply must go and see the lilies or the sweet peas in such and such a spot or the daffodils or bluebells turning a whole grassy slope yellow or blue in another place. I would go with them to see, though riding has never been one of my favorite activities. They were good days. I suppose Devlin and Gwyneth's children will drag them off to appreciate similar sights when they are older."

He took her hand in his as they walked, and she made no objection. It was something he had never done as a boy, he realized. He did it now only because he had not thought before he did it. It felt natural. It felt . . . comfortable.

Two gardeners were at work in one of the flower nooks. Matthew thought perhaps he and Clarissa would pass unseen, since they were about to descend another dip in the land some distance from where the men were working. But one of the men straightened up to remove his cap and cuff his obviously sweating brow. He caught sight of them and raised the cap as he bobbed his head.

"A fine afternoon, my lady," he called, and the other gardener looked up and snatched off his cap too.

"It is indeed," Clarissa called back.

So much, Matthew thought ruefully, for meeting at the end of the poplar alley earlier instead of at the house. He did not doubt that within a very few hours everyone who worked at Ravenswood, indoors and out, would know that the dowager countess had been strolling in the park with the village carpenter.

Hand in hand.

By tonight there would hardly be a soul in Boscombe or on the neighboring farms who did not know it.

Dash it all! But he did not release her hand, and she did not pull it away. And when she asked him as they took their leave of each other on the driveway if he would join her on Tuesday for a picnic at the lake, he did not say a firm no as common sense told him he ought.

"I can come after work," he said. "About four o'clock?"

"Come to the house," she said. "We can take a picnic basket in the gig."

She had clearly realized too, then, that there was no further point in trying to keep their friendship to themselves.

"Thank you for today," she said. "I have enjoyed it more than any other day this year. Maybe last year too. Thank you for thinking to bring food and drink. It was quite delicious."

He laughed, and she laughed back.

"It was," she said as she turned away from him.

He watched her walk up the drive to the house before he strode past the meadow and crossed the bridge toward home.

He was still smiling.

CHAPTER SEVEN

Clarissa was glad she had made arrangements to visit her parents again after church the following day. It was her mother's seventieth birthday. She needed to put some distance between herself and Ravenswood and her memories of yesterday. She needed to clear out her head.

The journey was a long one, however, and though she had the company of her maid in the carriage, Millicent was not a talker. Even among her fellow servants she apparently had a reputation for taciturnity. Whatever was one expected to do with one's mind under such circumstances? One could not gaze mindlessly upon the scenery beyond the windows for all of ten miles—it was eight, George had once explained to her, if one were a crow, ten if one were a human traveling the carriage road, nine if one knew the occasional narrower, more heavily rutted shortcuts.

George and Kitty had sent with her from London a magnificently painted fan as a gift for Mama for her birthday. Clarissa's gift was a cashmere shawl so soft it felt almost like silk.

Think about those birthday gifts, then, and about family.

Not that kiss!

She had been unable to shake off the memory of it for the rest of yesterday. It had kept her awake after she went to bed. It had figured prominently in her dreams. She still could not forget it today. She had tried in vain to dismiss it as a mere part of their exuberant reaction to their safe—though madly perilous—descent of the hill.

She could not convince herself.

It had been a kiss.

Goodness, they were both in their fifties—well, she was as close to being there as made no difference. And he had never kissed her before. Though he had confessed to having wanted to do so when he was eighteen. As she had confessed to wanting it too. But that was over thirty years ago. Over half her life ago.

She had not been kissed for a long time, not in that way anyway. Caleb had been dead for six years, and for the difficult four years before that their physical encounters had become fewer and less passionate. She would almost be willing to swear they had not kissed at all during those years.

Yesterday's kiss, no matter how she tried to rationalize it, had shaken her to the core. And it had not even been just one kiss, which might the more easily have been dismissed as a mindless conclusion to the swinging about and the laughter. No, there had been two kisses. And she very much feared she had initiated the second if not the first. In fact, she knew she had.

And then, almost all the way home across the park, he had held her hand. It seemed a simple enough thing in itself since they had walked side by side, and it had been a long way. But . . . well, no. It had not been a simple thing. She could not recall ever walking hand in hand with Caleb. She could not remember holding hands with any other man either. She would take an offered arm, it was true. But never a hand, unless it was offered briefly to help her in and out of a carriage or something similar.

It had been a glorious, wonderful afternoon. The long walk had exhilarated her and made her feel young again. And they had fallen into easy conversation, just as they always had. She had thought they could be friends again. And she had been right. It had been lovely to walk and sit with a friend her own age, someone she had known a long time, one with whom she could relax and talk and laugh without conscious effort. The memory of his picnic tea set her to smiling again even now, and she glanced surreptitiously at Millicent on the seat across from her own. Her maid was staring woodenly out of the window, however. Those sandwiches! She had had to open her mouth very wide to bite into hers. And that tea-flavored or coffee-flavored not-quite-cold water! The tea itself so strong it might almost make one's hair curl! No plates or cups or spoons or napkins. She had never enjoyed a picnic more.

And his story—that incredible account of how he had come to be an archer. She felt marvelously privileged that he had told her, when she knew he had not told anyone else. That story had explained one thing about him that had puzzled her for more than twenty years. How could the troubled, restless boy she remembered have become the man who was even-tempered and quietly content with his very simple way of life, who seemed at peace with himself and his world? It had always seemed to her too great a change to have come naturally with advancing age and maturity. She knew now that he had had a profound spiritual experience up in those mountains—the Himalayas, were they? It had not been the sort of experience that had set him on fire with religious zeal or a crusading spirit, but rather one that had brought him an inner tranquility that had continued to the present.

Clarissa wished that kiss had not happened, or the hand-holding. She had wanted, and still did, an uncomplicated summer friendship with Matthew Taylor, not a romance. The very idea of a romance between the two of them was absurd after all this time. They were middle-aged.

She wished the kiss had not happened, but it had. And she wanted more—more of his friendship, that was. She had invited him to drive to the lake with her on Tuesday. They were bound to be seen, he had warned her. But they had already been seen, strolling hand in hand, and those gardeners were not likely to keep such a story to themselves. But she and Matthew were neighbors. What was so reprehensible about their enjoying each other's company once in a while?

She knew the answer—why such a friendship was remarkable, anyway, even if not reprehensible. The village carpenter and the dowager countess. Not merely walking together but walking hand in hand.

She would not give in to any sense of wrongdoing. That carpenter was also a gentleman. Besides, it was no one's business whom she befriended. And it was not as though the friendship was going to consume her every waking hour. He was a man who worked for a living. And she had certain social obligations she would keep up, though she would also continue to cut them to the minimum in order to spend time alone—she still intended to give priority to that.

It was just a shame that the mind could so often have a mind of its own—she smiled at the absurdity—and take one's thoughts in a direction they did not wish to go. Her mind was more undisciplined than ever these days, thoughts tumbling all over one another in their eagerness to grab her attention and take her off on unwanted mental journeys.

Perhaps she needed to take up archery.

The journey to her parents' home seemed more interminable even than usual. She was very glad when the carriage turned onto her father's land and the house came into sight. Perhaps the visit would take her mind off yesterday. Indeed, it almost certainly would, she thought as she saw two carriages, a curricle, and a gig drawn up to one side of the house, minus their horses. There were other visitors, then. Someone must have organized a birthday party of sorts for her mother. How lovely!

Although the ten-mile journey was a long and tedious one, Clarissa had made the effort to visit regularly since her marriage. In all that time, however, she had only rarely encountered any of the neighbors she remembered, or the few who had come to live in the neighborhood more recently. It would be a pleasure to see some of them again.

The vicar was new here since her day, though Clarissa had met him a time or two. Captain Jakes and his wife and Miss Jennings, her sister, had lived as tenants on Matthew Taylor's property for many years. Clarissa had met them before but had only a very slight acquaintance with them. And then there was Matthew's brother and his wife, Reginald and Adelaide Taylor, and Philip, their elder son, with Emily, his wife.

Clarissa had not very much liked Reginald, more than ten years her senior, when she was growing up, though admittedly she had taken most of her information and opinions about him from Matthew, who had hardly been an impartial reporter. Reginald had been the good son, perfect and dutiful, an old sobersides—Matthew's word for him—who frowned upon imperfection and indiscipline and frivolity. He had seen his younger brother as guilty of all three.

After kissing her father on the cheek and hugging her mother and wishing her a happy birthday, Clarissa shook hands with all their other visitors. She would have been happier if the Taylors were not of their number, though that was selfish of her, she admitted. They were, after all, the closest of her parents' neighbors, and it was good of them to have come to pay their respects to her mother. Even so, she would just as soon have had no reminders of Matthew today. She smiled and set herself to being her usual sociable self, mindful to include everyone in the general conversation and careful to speak individually, however briefly, with each one.

The vicar and his wife were a genial couple who agreed with everyone on every topic, a fact that made meaningful conversation with them virtually impossible. But Clarissa did not doubt that their kindliness was a great comfort to their parishioners. Her parents adored them. Captain Jakes told Clarissa that he had been very happy living in the neighborhood for so long, but that he and his wife were experiencing a growing longing in their old age to be closer to the sea again. When their lease expired next year, they intended to move to Plymouth if they could find a suitable house there. Miss Jennings was also eager to make the move, he added, and his sister-in-law nodded and explained that she and her sister had both been born and raised in Plymouth.

"When I retired," the captain said, "I thought I would never want to see either a ship or the sea ever again, and Mrs. Jakes felt the same way."

"I most certainly did," his wife said. "But one changes one's mind as one grows old, Lady Stratton. One starts to long for home."

"For the smell of the sea," the captain said.

"And even of fish," Mrs. Jakes said, and they both laughed.

"And for the company of old friends," the sister added.

"I must ask you, Lady Stratton," Philip Taylor said when Clarissa spoke with him and his wife. "Do you know my uncle?"

"Matthew Taylor?" she said. "Yes. He is a carpenter and lives in Boscombe, just a stone's throw from Ravenswood. He and I are virtually the same age. We grew up as friends and neighbors here."

"Yes," Philip said. "That is what Papa says. I wish we knew him, especially as he lives relatively close. I believe he must be . . . interesting."

"But you know that Papa-in-Law says you should stay away from him, Phil," his wife said gently. "He says Mr. Matthew Taylor would not welcome your acquaintance."

"How would Papa know that?" Philip asked. "He has not seen my uncle—his brother—for what must be thirty years or more. I was little more than a baby when he left. I do not even remember him. Should grudges be borne forever? And by people of our generation who had nothing to do with whatever happened to cause the estrangement? But I do apologize, Lady Stratton. I really ought not to have raised the issue with you at all, let alone gone on like this. As you may have inferred, it is a bit of a sensitive one in our family."

Clarissa smiled at the couple and looked up at Adelaide Taylor, Philip's mother, who was coming to join them.

"It is always a joy, Lady Stratton," she said, "to see that Mr. and Mrs. Greenfield have retained such good health into their seventies. They have always been excellent neighbors. We are very fortunate."

"I believe the feeling is mutual," Clarissa said.

"Mr. George Greenfield married in London last year?" Adelaide said, making a question of it as though she did not know for sure. "I hope he is both well and happy."

"Yes, thank you," Clarissa said. "He married one of my closest friends, and it appears to be a perfect match. Your younger son and your daughter are no longer at home with you?"

Anthony, their second son, Mrs. Taylor explained, was a junior solicitor with a prestigious London firm, and was doing very well and expected promotion before the end of the year. Mabel, their daughter, had married a prosperous landowner from no farther than twelve miles away and had presented her husband with two healthy children, one girl and one boy, both of whom were adorable.

"Though I am quite sure you would say exactly the same of your grandchildren, Lady Stratton," she said.

"But of course," Clarissa said. "Grandchildren are a special breed." She included Reginald in her remark as he came up to stand beside his wife.

"They are indeed," he said. "We do not have the disciplining of them, only the loving of them."

His words took Clarissa a bit by surprise.

The conversation became more general after that as they all moved to the dining room for a sumptuous banquet of a tea and the opening of birthday gifts. Clarissa was the first to leave afterward, at her parents' insistence, since she had a long journey home.

It had been a thoroughly pleasant visit, she decided when she and Millicent were a few miles upon their way. However, her thoughts had not, after all, been diverted from Matthew. What would he do if Captain and Mrs. Jakes did indeed leave his home next year in order to return to Plymouth? Lease it to someone else? Go and live there himself? The latter seemed unlikely. He appeared happy with his simple life and his small, slightly shabby rooms above the smithy.

And what were Matthew's thoughts about his brother and his nephews and niece? She had not asked him. She had the impression, though, that he had had nothing to do with them since he left home. Reginald's elder son and his wife had seemed to confirm that impression today. But Philip Taylor wanted to know his uncle.

Would it ever happen? Would Reginald allow it? And would Matthew rebuff any attempt Philip made to meet him anyway, even though the younger man had had nothing to do with the estrangement and could not even consciously remember his uncle?

Had the estrangement been the best thing for the brothers, Reginald and Matthew? Did it remain a good thing? Times and people changed.

But oh dear, this was absolutely none of her business, Clarissa decided, trying to take her thoughts in another direction. She had never interfered in Matthew's troubled family life. She was not about to start now.

But thoughts were stubborn, unruly things, and hers eventually brought her right back to that kiss. To the wild happiness and exuberance of the whole afternoon outing, in fact, when she had felt almost like a girl again. Or at least like an adult without a care in the world, untrammeled by status, in particular the title of dowager. How she hated that word.

She pondered yet again the wisdom of pursuing their friendship. She thought of the final slope of the hill, which she had tried to descend at a sedate walk but had ended up hurtling down, shrieking and laughing—right into Matthew's arms. She thought of what had followed.

Perhaps she ought to send word to him, canceling their plans for Tuesday.

But she knew she would not do it. It was possible that the nature of their friendship was one of the things she needed to explore if she was to learn what she had set out to learn about herself during these months alone.

Was friendship . . . No. Was romance something she could no longer welcome into her life? Because she was about to turn fifty and it would be unseemly? Because she was the Dowager Countess of Stratton and was expected to behave like a dowager? By whom? Her family? Her neighbors? Society at large? Was she going to allow her behavior and her very feelings to be dictated by others? For the rest of her life?

Oh, this introspection, which she had never really done before, was giving her a headache.

Matthew had gone to Colonel Wexford's house on Sunday morning, when he knew the family would be at church. He had brought home with him several of the table legs and broken his usual rule about Sundays by working all day on them. He worked the following morning, afternoon, and evening in the colonel's barn, knowing he would not be interrupted since Miss Wexford had gone shopping with her niece in a town several miles away. He started work very early again on Tuesday. He intended to continue through the luncheon hour so he could justify finishing in time to go to the lake for a picnic with Clarissa.

It was something about which he had been feeling uneasy since Saturday, it was true, for there was to be no attempt this time to keep their outing a secret. The servants' quarters at Ravenswood were bound to be abuzz with the news that yet again their dowager countess and the village carpenter were going to spend time together.

However, he had said he would go, and go he would. And as luck would have it, they were not even to be saved by rain, which could often be relied upon to ruin the best-laid plans for an outing. The weather was not only fine; it was sunny and hot, more like summer than spring. It was hotter than Saturday had been. It was the perfect day, in fact, to sit by the lake and enjoy a picnic tea.

He did not work uninterrupted today, alas. The door of the barn opened at nine o'clock, three hours after he had started work, though it seemed less.

"Oh, Mr. Taylor, there you are," Miss Wexford said, stepping inside. "One of the grooms told the cook, who told my maid, that you have been here for hours already. That must mean you came here without having your breakfast first. That will not do, you know. Breakfast is the most important meal of the day, especially for a workingman. I have brought you a little something to eat with your tea."

He stepped forward to take the cloth-covered tray from her hands and guessed from the weight of it that she must have brought him a banquet. He really did not want to have his work interrupted, but it was a kind gesture on her part. He set down the tray and removed the cloth.

"Thank you, Miss Wexford," he said. "This is very generous of you."

"I will not keep you," she said, "as I am sure you want to eat quickly and get back to work. May I have a little look while you eat?"

Without waiting for an answer, she almost skipped over to the tabletop upon which he was working, and was soon exclaiming with admiration and delight though it was not even half finished.

She had brought him a large china mug of tea. Milk had already been added to it, and probably sugar too. He took neither in his tea. There were two biscuits propped on the saucer. On a separate plate were two thick slices of lavishly buttered toast together with a heap of thinly carved cold beef. There was a pot of what looked like raspberry jam and another of mustard beside the plate. A large jug of steaming custard stood next to a bowl containing a great wedge of apple tart.

I have brought you a little something . . .

He shook his head and nearly laughed out loud.

"It is going to be even more magnificent than it appears in my fondest dreams," Miss Wexford said, her tone rapturous, her hands clasped tightly to her bosom. "You are indeed a genius, Mr. Taylor, and I shall tell everyone so who asks. Not that everyone does not know it already."

Matthew tried to make a dent in the food while she talked and was surprised to find that really it was not difficult. He had not realized he was hungry, and the food was delicious, strange as it seemed to be eating apple tart and thick custard for breakfast.

He took one sip of the tea, grimaced, and set down the cup. He would wait until she left and find somewhere to pour it so she would not see and be hurt.

"I will not disturb you any longer," she said, turning from his worktable and glancing at the tray. "I hope I brought you enough, Mr. Taylor. I know you are a workingman and must therefore have a larger appetite than Andrew and I have or even Ariel. The beef and the tart and custard are from dinner last evening, but they were kept in a cool pantry overnight and are still quite fresh. Heating the custard again has thickened it considerably, but I actually like it that way."

"So do I," he said.

"I see you have left your tea and biscuits until last," she said. "I will not take the tray with me, then."

"I will return it to the kitchen before I leave," he said.

She turned to go, hesitated, and turned back. "Mr. Taylor," she said. "May I offer you a word of friendly advice?"

He raised his eyebrows.

"In a neighborhood like ours," she said, "there are certain . . .

expectations. People can get upset, rightly or wrongly, when they are not strictly observed, and gossiping tongues can begin to wag. It is not always wise to take the risk of that happening."

It looked for a moment as though she was going to say more, but instead she turned away, hurried out of the barn, and closed the door quietly behind her.

It would be easy to pretend not to understand. She had not been at all specific, after all. But Matthew had understood clearly enough and felt a bit of a sinking feeling in his stomach. Quite predictably, then, there was already gossip. Because he had been walking in the Ravenswood park on a Saturday afternoon with the Dowager Countess of Stratton. Not just walking, but also holding hands with her.

The talk could only grow after this afternoon.

He did not care for his own sake. Well, yes, he did. He was a quiet and private man, who hated drawing attention to himself. The closest he ever came to doing so voluntarily was on the day of the summer fete, which had now become a biennial event instead of a yearly one. He could never resist entering the archery contest, and except for last year he had not resisted also putting an entry into the wood-carving contest, even knowing that he would probably win both contests and have to face the excruciating embarrassment of receiving his prize ribbons from Stratton while the other fete-goers applauded and slapped him on the back and shook his hand.

He did not relish the prospect of being the subject of local gossip.

He cared far more deeply, though, about how such gossip would affect Clarissa. She was generally known as a woman of great dignity and decorum, someone who had never set a foot wrong since her marriage to the late earl despite the provocation of his adulterous behavior. She was deeply respected by all and loved by many.

It would be a great scandal if now, alone at Ravenswood without the support of her family around her, her name became coupled with his. There must be some, of course, who would remember that he was a gentleman by birth and the owner of a manor house and sizable park and farm ten miles away. But even those who did remember would say his virtual rejection of his birthright for the past twenty-some years, his chosen profession—if it could be called that—and his choice of abode and friends disqualified him from being accorded the deference a gentleman might expect. Certainly those facts set him universes apart from the Dowager Countess of Stratton.

It simply would not do, Matthew decided, trying to bring his mind into focus on the inlaid mosaic he was creating for the table-top out of wood of various shades. He would go this afternoon since he had said he would. But that must be it. With her permission, he would let it be known that he was working on a project for the dowager, designing and making a gift she wished to give the child whom Ben Ellis and his wife were expecting. Such a story would probably not put an immediate end to the gossip, but if there was nothing further to feed it, then eventually everyone would shrug and assume that their meetings must have been for the principal purpose of planning the project. There would be those, of course, who would not quickly let go of the damning detail of the hand-holding. But if there was no more . . .

Matthew returned to his work.

CHAPTER EIGHT

Clarissa called at Cartref early on Tuesday morning. Sir Ifor and Lady Rhys were to leave for their annual family visit to Wales before nine o'clock, and Clarissa knew they liked to be punctual. Along with a number of other people, she had given them her best wishes after church on Sunday, but they had always been close personal friends, even before their daughter married her eldest son. Now the three of them shared two grandchildren.

She went to see them on their way and found them just getting up from the breakfast table and being fussed over by their son, Idris, and Eluned, his wife, who would not be accompanying them. Idris was exhorting his father to take the journey in more gradual stages than was his custom.

"Just remember, Dad, that Mam is not as young as she used to be," he said.

Lady Rhys turned back to her son after greeting Clarissa. "Well, there is cheeky you are getting, Idris," she said. "I am not in my dotage yet, young man."

He threw up his hands, palms out. "It is just a suggestion, Mam," he said. "But you know how you sometimes complain that as soon as Dad's nose is pointed in the direction of Wales, he cannot get there fast enough and forgets about eating and sleeping. And even changing the poor horses half the time."

"It is a sad day," Sir Ifor said, "when one has to be told how to live one's life by one's own son. But never mind that. Clarissa, did I see you up on the crest of the hills on . . . Saturday, was it? I made a spectacle of myself by cutting a caper and waving my hat at you, but neither you nor your companion saw me. I did not see any carriage or even a horse. Never tell me you went there on foot."

"Well, I did," Clarissa said as everyone looked at her with interest. "We walked all the way from the house and all the way back. I was very proud of myself. And if any of my sons had been at Ravenswood, I would have defied them to imply that I am in my dotage."

She smiled at Idris to show she was not being serious.

She wondered if Sir Ifor had seen whom she was with, since it certainly was not one of her sons. Sometimes it was easier simply to provide information than let people speculate.

"Matthew Taylor is going to make a crib for me to give Jennifer and Ben for the baby they are expecting," she said. "He has already shown me sketches. It is going to be quite gorgeous—all covered with carvings of animals and plants and birds and butterflies. He accompanied me on that long walk on Saturday. We go back a long way, Matthew and I. We were close friends when we were growing up. His father's land adjoined my father's."

"And a very gentlemanly man he is too," Lady Rhys said. "Are you quite, quite sure you will not come with us, Clarissa? You know Devlin and Gwyneth would be more than happy, and the relatives would roll out the red carpet for you. I hate to think of you all alone at Ravenswood for what may be more than a month while we are enjoying ourselves."

"Sometimes it is good to be alone for a while," Clarissa said, not wanting to dwell on the relief she felt in her friends' apparent disinterest in Matthew and the crib. "I am enjoying my quiet time here, though I am quite sure I will be more than eager to welcome my family home when they come. I will feel a renewed appreciation for their company."

"Well, that is one way of looking at it," Lady Rhys said. "Though being alone is not something I would choose for myself, especially when Wales beckons."

As she spoke they had all been making their way out to the traveling carriage that was awaiting her and Sir Ifor. Clarissa stood back now to give the Rhyses a chance to hug and take a fond leave of one another. Idris handed his mother into the carriage, Sir Ifor climbed in after her, the coachman shut the door securely and climbed up to the box to gather the ribbons in his hands and give the four horses the signal to start, and they were on their way. Idris and Eluned waved until the white handkerchief fluttering from the carriage window was withdrawn and the vehicle disappeared from sight.

"Come and have some breakfast, Lady Stratton," Eluned said. "You must have missed having it at Ravenswood. There is plenty of food left."

"Thank you, but I must be getting home," Clarissa said.

"To your nice quiet life," Eluned said, smiling. "Enjoy it while you have the chance, Lady Stratton."

Clarissa spent the rest of the morning partaking of a late and leisurely breakfast in her sitting room and gazing out through her open window, ignoring both books and embroidery. The letters she needed to write could wait too.

Had Sir Ifor known who was with her up on the hills three days ago before she told him? He very probably had. Neither he nor his wife had shown surprise when she told them. Lady Rhys— Bronwyn—had even been ready with her kind description of Matthew.

Were her friends really uninterested in her friendship with Matthew? Or had Sir Ifor raised the matter this morning as a sort of warning to her? That if he had seen them together, someone else might have too? And of course someone else had—two of the Ravenswood gardeners, in fact. They had seen the two of them walking hand in hand.

Did she care that word was probably spreading? Not really, she thought at first. Only the truly malicious gossips would try to make something of it. Many people would know Matthew was a gentleman. He spoke like one, after all. A few would even recall that his father and now his brother were close neighbors of the Greenfields, her parents.

However . . .

Well, perhaps she did care for Matthew's sake. He was such a quiet and private man. He would hate to be the focus of any sort of gossip. It was no doubt pure selfishness on her part to like the idea of pursuing a friendship with him while she was alone here. She had enjoyed their two encounters, and she was looking forward to this afternoon's drive to the lake and the picnic tea with an eagerness she had not felt at all in London, despite the glittering parties she had attended and the congenial company. The weather was perfect again, more like summer than spring.

Perhaps, after all, she needed to put an end to the friendship. This afternoon everyone in the house would know with whom she was going to share the picnic tea for two that was being prepared.

But why end it now? People would grow accustomed to seeing them together from time to time. Or would they? Would they perhaps grow more scandalized the longer she and Matthew were seen pursuing a friendship that might be considered unbecoming for two people whose stations in life were so far apart?

How annoying to discover so early in this time alone she had snatched for herself that her freedom was not limitless after all. For it was not only her own reputation she was risking. She had no right to risk Matthew's too. In many ways he had more to lose than she did.

It would be wrong and selfish to continue, she decided at last, gazing through her window at the sheep in the meadow without really seeing them. A continued friendship might destroy his peace of mind, a peace that had been hard-won during the year or years he had spent at that monastery north of India. It had served him well since then. One could see it in his eyes and in the quiet, modest life he enjoyed, earning his living with the labor and skill of his hands.

She could not in all conscience threaten that peace.

She would explain to him this afternoon. In the meanwhile she was going to enjoy every moment of their picnic. Memories could be very precious, and she knew she would remember these few encounters with him with great fondness in the years ahead.

But . . . would the memories be enough?

When Matthew arrived at Ravenswood, he saw an open barouche standing outside the main doors rather than the gig he had expected. A groom stood at the horses' heads while a coachman used a soft cloth to rub off what must have been a smudge of dust from one gleaming door of the conveyance. Both men nodded politely when Matthew greeted them.

Clarissa must have seen him walking up from the village. She was stepping out onto the flight of steps to the front doors, wearing a summer dress of light figured muslin and a floppy-brimmed straw bonnet. She was carrying the brightly colored parasol her grand-daughter had given her for Christmas. She was smiling brightly and looking for all the world like a woman half her age.

"Could the day be any more perfect?" she asked as he went to meet her at the bottom of the steps.

She was referring, of course, to the weather. He was very aware, however, of the two silent men behind him. He had sat with them a number of times in the taproom of the village inn, where he went occasionally in the evening for a pint of ale and a bit of male com-pany, and where they went for a similar purpose. These very men, as well as other servants from Ravenswood, always treated Matthew as one of their own there and included him in their conversation. He was just the local carpenter to them, as well as the man they admired for his superior skill with a bow and arrow.

"I was pleasantly surprised half an hour or so ago when I stepped out of Colonel Wexford's barn to discover that spring had passed into summer while I was hard at work," he said, handing her into the barouche and following her in. "There are no windows in the barn and only lamps for light. It might have been raining or snowing outside for all I knew."

"You were working on Miss Wexford's dining table?" she asked.

"I was," he said. "She seems pleased with what she has seen so far. She keeps assuring me on the one hand that she will not disturb me so I can get on, and finding frequent excuses on the other hand to come into the barn for a look."

"It must be quite disconcerting for you," she said, laughing as she raised her parasol over her head and the groom moved back from the horses' heads and the carriage wheels crunched over the stones of the terrace on the way to the lake.

A large picnic basket was standing on the seat across from them. Matthew looked from it to her and raised his eyebrows.

"When our cook is asked to prepare a picnic tea for two," she said, "I believe that in her mind she sees two companies of soldiers, all with voracious appetites that must be satisfied so that not even one of them will go away just a little bit hungry."

"I would guess it will be somewhat more elaborate than Saturday's picnic tea," he said ruefully.

"Somewhat more," she agreed, looking amused. "But I do not believe I will ever taste cheese sandwiches or seed cake more delicious than the ones you brought then, or water more refreshing."

He laughed. Though the thing was, she seemed to mean what she said. He tried to relax. It was all very well to tell himself that class distinctions no longer meant anything to him, that he was done with all that nonsense. For years he had successfully mingled with all classes and had been comfortable with all. But a few days ago he had felt anything but comfortable when those two gardeners had seen him walking hand in hand with the Dowager Countess of Stratton. They were men he spent time with at the village pub as well. And today he was very conscious of the broad back of the coachman up on the box before them, a mere few feet away, a functioning ear on either side of his head.

"I decided after all not to bring the gig this afternoon," Clarissa said. "It occurred to me that the poor horse would be stranded down at the lake for at least a couple of hours, waiting for us to return. This way the horses can be taken back to the stables and we can walk back from the lake whenever we are ready to leave."

"A good idea," he said. "And we will carry the hamper of left-overs back between us?"

"No." She laughed. "Someone will fetch it later. But I wanted to tell you I wrote to Ben and Jennifer last evening to tell them about the crib. Not that you will be making it, but that it will be my gift for the new baby. I would hate to give it as a surprise when the time comes only to discover that they already have another set up in the nursery. But all the wonderful carvings with which you are going to cover this one will remain a surprise. It is going to be a unique piece of furniture. I can hardly wait to see it finished."

"I thought," he said, "I might include a chest of drawers to match it."

"That would be wonderful." Her face lit up with pleasure as she twirled her parasol.

He understood what she was doing. She was keeping the conversation focused upon the work project that had brought them together. It probably came as second nature to her to say in the hearing of servants only what she wanted them to hear. She might even be doing it now quite unconsciously.

It was not far to the lake. Matthew felt a bit helpless as the coachman lifted out the hamper and carried it into the shade cast by the boathouse a short distance away. The man then hauled a large blanket out of the boathouse and spread it on the bank a little farther along where they would have sunshine and an unobstructed view of the water and the landscape around it. Then he climbed back to his box and drove off without a word.

"Awkward," Matthew said.

"Was it?" She looked after the retreating carriage and then at him. "I am sorry. Have I made life more complicated and less comfortable for you? I have not thought much about our friendship for years past. It was something that needed to end at the time, and it was ended. But recently I have looked back with a great deal of nostalgia and have come to the realization that there is no further need for us to keep an almost total distance from each other. We live close—even closer than we did during our childhood. You have no wife or other attachment as far as I know, and I have been a widow for six years. It seemed such a good idea for us to renew our friendship this year while I am here alone, without the distraction of family and house guests. And I have indeed enjoyed your company and conversation. I have felt honored by your confidences, which I know you have not shared with anyone else but me. But it seems I have been selfish."

Here was his opportunity to end it. He could even walk away right now and leave her to solitude and the lake for however long she wished to stay before she walked back to the house.

Alone.

It would be most ungentlemanly of him.

"I have enjoyed your company too, Clarissa," he said. "Since we are here now, shall we enjoy this afternoon too? Shall we feast our appetites on the contents of that hamper and our senses on the beauty all around us?"

For this one afternoon. This last afternoon. That was what he was really saying, and he could see that she understood and very probably agreed.

She was looking youthfully pretty this afternoon, he thought again, standing in sunshine in her light muslin dress and floppy-brimmed straw, the incongruously bright parasol over her head. She was smiling.

"I do not want to sit sedately on a picnic blanket admiring the view until it is time to eat and then walk home when we are finished," she said. "I want to do something. Can you row a boat, Matthew? Not that I am helpless. I used to bring the children here all the time when they were small, and I would take the oars when the boys tired of trying and would row them a couple at a time around the lake. Sometimes I would pile them all in and row them across to the island to explore or to swim from what we called the beach at the far end of it. Those were lovely days."

He wondered where Stratton had been when all this had happened. Still in London performing his parliamentary duties? Busy about estate business? Matthew had never had much use for the man. He could understand his popularity, for he had been endlessly and apparently genuinely charming and genial to everyone. He had been a perfect host at the many social events that had happened through the summers and winters. But Matthew had always suspected that he was essentially a lazy man and shallow of character. It was his countess who had appeared to do most of the work of organizing the elaborate entertainments and seeing that they ran with seamless perfection. Matthew had never had proof until that disastrous summer fete ten years ago that Stratton did not remain faithful to his wife during the months he spent in London, but it would have been surprising to hear that he did.

"I believe I can row without taking us in endless circles," he said. "And without tipping us into the water and capsizing the boat."

"Then take me rowing," she said. "I will sit in the boat looking decorative." She laughed.

Ah, Clarissa, he thought as he dragged out one of the boats and made sure there were no leaks and no sign of splits or wood rot in the oars while she carried out a small pile of towels and put them in. How happy could her life have been? She would have made the best of it, of course. She had lived a life of luxury here, she had fulfilled all her duties with meticulous care and grace, she clearly adored her children, even the one who was Stratton's by-blow, and she had friends and friendly neighbors all around her. No doubt she now had financial security for life, and she had sons and daughters who would always love her and care for her. She had had a good life following her decision to marry a virtual stranger when she was very young.

But happy? How happy had she been all this time? How happy was she now? Her decision to come home early and alone from London had been a pretty drastic one. Her children must have offered her alternatives so she would have company through the summer. Her brother and his new wife, her friend, must have tried too. But she had come home, she had told him, for the express purpose of being alone with time to think and assess. And one of her early decisions had been to renew her friendship with him.

"Allow me," he said, holding the boat steady against the bank with one hand while he offered her the other.

She stepped carefully in and sat down and watched him release the boat from its moorings before taking his place across from her. He used one oar to push them off from the bank.

"Let the adventure begin," she said, and laughed again. "All the children used to chant that whenever I pushed off, and they would cheer as I rowed away."

Matthew felt an ache of something in his chest. He had missed so much of her life. And how different his own life would have been if his daughter had survived her birth. She had been so perfect. He rarely thought of her—or of poor Poppy. They were from a former life.

"I do not hear a cheer," he said.

She cheered and pumped her parasol in the air a few times while she laughed yet again.

He rowed around the south side of the island, mostly under the shade of the trees on the bank. Then he rowed into the more open water west of the island and saw the sloping bank that must be the beach from which she had swum with her children. There were very few trees close to the western and northern banks of the lake. A footpath had been constructed all around. It had been made for the viewing pleasure of those who walked there as well as those who rowed on the water. It was bordered on the landward side with flower beds just now coming into their own and ornamental bushes that must have bloomed earlier in the spring. And there was a rustic-looking shelter on the bend between the western and northern paths, looking very picturesque with its thatched roof and open, pillared front and hanging baskets of flowers that would bloom from now until the autumn.

It was an idyllic place, the lake at Ravenswood. Somewhere to relax. Somewhere to make one forget the world beyond.

"I loved the evening picnics we used to have here for the whole neighborhood," she said. "I would always find an orchestra to play from the pavilion on the island, and everyone would feast on the east bank and converse and listen and be happy. Did you ever come to any of those?"

"To one," he said. "I came with the Hollands. It was magical with all the colored lanterns strung from the trees, their light reflected in the water. And the music."

"I used to think of it as our own private little Vauxhall," she said. "Have you ever been to Vauxhall Gardens?"

"In London?" he said. "No."

"Our entertainments were better," she said. "Not that I am boasting or anything obnoxious like that. Of course, we never had fireworks, as they do at Vauxhall." She sighed. "I am not ready to return to the real world yet, Matthew. Shall we go to the island and explore?"

"Will we need a ball of string to find our way out?" he asked.

"Make fun if you wish," she said. "I know it is a very tiny island, but it is ours. Come and explore it with me."

Instead of pulling the boat back in to the bank after rowing all about the lake, Matthew turned it in the direction of the island, where he could see the mooring place. Reaching it, he jumped out, secured the boat, and offered a hand to help her out.

"So," he said, "let us explore."

And he felt a strange welling of happiness.

CHAPTER NINE

She was going to squeeze every ounce of pleasure out of this afternoon, Clarissa had decided anew as soon as the barouche disappeared back along the narrow road toward the house. If it was to be the last of their friendship, then so be it, but let it at least be an afternoon to remember.

The weather was perfect, a sumptuous banquet awaited them in the picnic hamper, and they were all alone in what must surely be one of the outstanding beauty spots of all England. Memories abounded of those lovely years when her children were young and she had been a lot younger than she was now. But today she wanted to create a new memory.

Those days of their youthful friendship, hers and Matthew's, had been so very long ago. And at the end of them, when they had both married and thus taken their lives along vastly divergent paths, they had only just begun to be aware of each other as a man and a woman. Neither had admitted it to the other at the time because any relationship but friendship had been impossible for them.

Well, now they were friends again, and they had those feelings again. There was no point in denying it to herself. There was no ignoring the sexual nature of that kiss on Saturday and the way they had held hands all the way back to the house afterward. It was probably why they both seemed to have decided they must put an end to whatever was between them. But the end had not come yet. They had given themselves today to enjoy first.

And there was an island to explore.

"Stay close so you do not get lost," she said when he had tethered the boat securely so they would not be stranded. Actually, the idea of being castaways had its appeal, but it was a bit of an unconvincing one. They could swim back to the boathouse without any great effort, after all. Besides, the food hamper was over there.

"Very well," he said, grinning at her and taking her hand in his. "I will trust you to bring me back safely to civilization."

"The pavilion here is an almost exact replica in miniature of the temple up on the hill by the house," she said. "As you have probably noticed before. It is a lovely place to come and sit and dream, though I always loved it best by lantern light at night when there was an orchestra playing inside and crowds of neighbors and friends on the bank. That has not happened for a long time."

For a moment she felt a pang of nostalgia for those days.

"And then there is the forest," she said. "Come and see. The children called it the Dark Forest and tried to frighten one another or catch bandits or hunt down lions and bears."

"A strange mixture," he said.

"Not to children," she said. "And not to adults who think like children. Are there not to be elephants and giraffes and dogs and monkeys and bears all coexisting with numerous other forms of life on a certain crib that awaits the carpenter and wood-carver's skills?"

"Touché." He laughed.

They moved among the trees, running their fingers over rough barks as they had always used to do, as though to feel the very life force of the tree within, and gazing up through boughs and branches and leaves to the sky above. They listened to the songs of unseen birds and the chirping and whirring of equally unseen insects in the undergrowth. They stepped carefully as they drew close to the water lest there be unexpected marshland to clog their shoes with mud and perhaps unbalance them. They clutched each other's hands in mutual warning and stood very still as a duck led her line of ducklings out of an inlet into open water before they all bobbed away into the sunshine.

Soon—it really was not a large island—they came out onto open ground and the gently sloping grassy bank that had always been called the beach, perhaps because it sloped right into the water and retained its gradual incline for some distance out. One had to be careful not to ground a boat when one rowed close to here, but it was a young swimmer's delight—and that of the adult who had charge of even younger ones who could do little more than splash and shriek in the wide shallows. There was no sudden drop into deep water and no great danger provided the adult watcher remained vigilant.

The beach was partially shaded by trees on three sides. The afternoon sun sparkled on the water of the lake on the fourth side. Flowers and bushes were blooming along the edge of the footpath on the western bank beyond, as they had seen from the boat a short while ago.

"This is a little piece of paradise," Matthew said.

"It is," she agreed. He was still holding her hand. He looked relaxed and contented. And—yes—virile and masculine. Why pretend she did not notice? She might be close to fifty, but she was not dead yet. And perhaps that was what was wrong with Lord Keilly, her beau. Not that he was dead either. He was a seemingly healthy, good-looking man with everything that might recommend him to her as a beau. He was a gentleman of good birth and property and solid fortune, a man of good character, according to all reports, and a man of impeccable breeding and what seemed like an amiable disposition. But there was no . . . Oh, what would be an appropriate word to describe what it was about him that failed to attract her? There was no sizzle. It sounded like a very frivolous word to use in such a context. But that was it exactly. There was no sizzle in her relationship with Lord Keilly and no chance of there ever being any.

One ought not to expect sizzle from a romantic relationship when one was firmly established in middle age.

Oh, what utter nonsense!

Was it sizzle she felt with Matthew, then? It was certainly more than just friendship and even more than mild attraction. Goodness, they had wanted each other during that kiss. She had no doubt it had been mutual.

"A penny for them," he said.

For her thoughts? She smiled, imagining how he would react if she answered truthfully. "I was thinking," she said, "that perhaps we ought to have brought the picnic hamper over here with us."

"I can go back for it if you wish," he said. "But I think I would prefer to wait for my tea. Shall we sit down?"

"I did put a few towels in the boat," she said. "Old habit. There was almost always a need of them with the children. They do not serve well as blankets, however."

"And what is the matter with bare grass?" he asked, releasing her hand in order to bend down to rub a hand over the ground. "Bone dry. And looking and feeling like a thick carpet. Would you like my coat to sit on?"

"No," she said, and sat, arranging her skirts carefully around her before removing her bonnet and fluffing up her flattened hair as best she could. The air felt deliciously cool against her bare head. The grass was lush and springy all about her. He sat and turned his head to smile at her.

"Definitely paradise," he said.

"Yes."

"Our last outing was almost all about me," he said. "It is your turn today, Clarissa. Tell me more about this crisis with which you are dealing."

"Crisis?" She frowned at him, startled. "That is rather a strong word."

"I believe you have reached a definite juncture in your life," he said. "It is probably something you consider impossible to discuss with your family, or even your women friends. It is, rather, something you feel you must work through alone. Tell me."

It was something she had never done, strangely enough. Even in the days when they had spoken freely to each other and he had poured out his heart and frustrations to her, she had never had anything remotely similar to share with him. Her life had been almost unbelievably trouble free. Even when she had learned years after her friendship with Matthew was over that her marriage was not going to be all she had hoped it would be, she had had her training as a lady to fall back upon and had been able to ignore what might otherwise have been unbearable. One thing her education had not trained her for, however, was coping with widowhood and the sense that somehow she was superfluous to the life at whose very center she had lived and functioned for so many years.

How could she possibly talk about it?

Where would she even begin?

"Nobody can fully understand widowhood who has not actually experienced it," she said. "You were married for a short while, Matthew. I do not know how much of this applies to you, though everything did end in horror for you, and I do not imagine you recovered quickly or even at all. Losing a spouse is not like other bereavements. Most people assume, and one assumes oneself, that after a certain time—a year, perhaps two—one will have recovered from the worst of the grief and adjusted to the changes in one's life and will be forging onward with renewed purpose. One assumes it especially, perhaps, if the marriage itself was less than perfect, as mine was, particularly during the last years. There was a certain . . . distance between Caleb and me, though we never really talked things through with each other—or perhaps because we did not. And of course I had sent Devlin away and Ben had gone with him. I feared I had lost both of them forever, and I knew their absence weighed heavily upon Caleb. It was a dark time, and then he died in the middle of it."

He did not break the silence when she paused.

"There is an emptiness in my life where he was," she said. "Other people might think his sudden death was a fortunate release for me, a blessing in disguise. Indeed, especially in the early days, I expected that it would be. But then the emptiness set in, sometimes a sort of absence of all feeling, but often a little more painful. An ache of something missing at the core of myself. For of course it was not just my husband I had lost. I lost my position too, after a few more years, when Devlin came home and married Gwyneth and she became Countess of Stratton in my stead. It is rather a jolt to the system to become a dowager when one is still only in one's forties."

"The mother-in-law / daughter-in-law relationship is not an ideal one?" he asked.

"Oh," she said. "I do not wish to give that impression. Quite the opposite is true, Matthew. Gwyneth is wonderful and I adore her. She makes Devlin happier than I have ever seen him, and she is the perfect mother and countess. She is much beloved in the neighborhood, as you must have seen for yourself. She is the perfect daughter-in-law. She took over her duties immediately after her marriage instead of dancing delicately about me, as so many new brides tend to do, pretending she still considered me to be the real countess and looking for a tactful way to take command. But she involves me in many of her decisions. She asks for my thoughts and suggestions and even help. But she is never obsequious about it. If she disagrees, she will say so and give a reason. She never rides roughshod over my feelings, though. I believe she genuinely loves me, just as I love her."

"But—?" he said. "I can hear a *but* in your voice, Clarissa."

She was quiet for a while, watching what was surely the same duck leading her ducklings back to the inlet on the southern shore.

"Much of my sense of purpose has been stripped away," she said. "There is still Owen to settle, of course, though I do not suppose a mother's influence or interference will be of any great service there. He will find his own way. He has too much intelligence and too much . . . conscience to fritter away his life as an idle gentleman about town. And if he does need a guiding hand, then it will surely be Devlin's he will seek. I have Stephanie to settle also, though I have done all I can do already. I presented her at court this year and introduced her to the *ton* by taking her to dozens of parties and balls. Devlin and Gwyneth gave her a glittering come-out ball. I do not believe she will allow me to do much more by way of presenting her with eligible young suitors for her hand. She can be very stubborn. No, that is an unfair word to use. She is of very firm character, and I respect that. I just wish she had a more positive image of herself. But that is something she must discover within herself, if she ever does. It is not something I can teach her or persuade her of. A mother's power is far more limited than she expects it to be when she gives birth to her children."

She fell silent and hoped he would change the subject—perhaps suggest again going to fetch the picnic hamper or returning to the bank to eat there. But he remained silent too, and she had the feeling his attention was fully focused upon her. Oh, this was difficult. She was so unused to talking about herself to other people—really talking, that was. She had come closest to it down the years with Kitty, but for most of those years they had lived far away from each other and communicated only in long, long letters. It was not the same. It was easier by letter. There was time then to think before one wrote, to choose one's words carefully, to filter out what one could not fully understand oneself.

"Hence the crisis, if you still wish to call it that," she said. "I know that in innumerable ways I am one of the world's most blessed and fortunate of women. I have all this for my home." She made a sweeping gesture with one arm. "I am dearly loved by all the members of my family—including, I believe, both of my daughters-in-law and my son-in-law. But I am not sure I am needed. And the very fear that I may be right about that annoys me, for I do not wish to descend into self-pity as I approach my fiftieth birthday. I am quite determined, in fact, that it will not happen. But I need to . . . find my place."

Still he said nothing.

"Do you notice how life is lived in quite distinct phases, Matthew?" she asked. "There was my childhood, my first seventeen years before I married Caleb. Then there were the years of my marriage. Each phase was very different and very clearly defined. I knew my role in each and embraced it. Now I have entered the phase of my widowhood. I am already six years into it, in fact, but I still do not understand what my role is to be, if any. Or how I will fill the dwindling years. And what a horrid word that is—*dwindling*. Where on earth did it come from? It is not a word I remember using ever before. It has occurred to me only recently how strange it is that despite the vast size of the park here, no one has ever thought to build a dower house. I think I might be happy living in one— close to my family and all I have loved since I was seventeen, but separate from them. In a place where I could close the door and be alone with myself if I chose. Is that how you feel in the rooms above the smithy?"

"Yes," he said.

"Yet my very wish for a dower house is selfish," she said. "Many people live in hovels, if they are fortunate enough to have a home at all, while I have all the vastness of Ravenswood to call my home."

She drew her knees closer to her body and wrapped her arms about them while she felt Matthew's gaze still upon her.

"This is how I see the three phases of your life," he said. "The first two were all about obligation—what your family and society expected of you as a lady. You spent your childhood and girlhood learning what would be expected of you and preparing yourself for it. You were very single-minded about that, Clarissa. I remember. You were always very happy, but there was no breath of rebellion in you. The future you were expected to prepare for was the future you wanted. Your marriage was about obligation to husband and family and your role as Countess of Stratton. And again you did your duty superlatively well. You have raised a lovely family. You have carried out your obligations to the neighborhood around Ravenswood with dedication and grace and . . . humility. You have the respect of all and the affection of many. You have left the present countess with the difficult challenge of being your equal. Now, in this third phase, you no longer have pressing obligations. This phase is for you. It is a phase without the weight of duty or obligation upon your shoulders. And while you drew pleasure and a sense of fulfillment from the performance of those duties, you never did know much about freedom, did you? About the freedom to be the person you really are, living the life you really want to live."

"But that is the whole point," she said, turning her head to frown at him. "Who exactly am I, Matthew? What is the life I really want to live?"

"Alas," he said, "I cannot answer those questions. Only you can. But I have seen you happy a few times recently. Not happy in the way I witnessed down the years when you fulfilled the role of countess and were known for your warm cheerfulness, which always seemed genuine. And not happy in the way you must have been as a young mother, when you brought your children swimming and exploring here and no doubt did numerous other things with them to keep them entertained. More recently I have seen you happy in yourself. Just in brief, snatched moments, perhaps, but very real. When you walked all the way from the house to the hills and then toiled up them to the crest of the highest peak, you were weary and desperate for the rest we took. But you should have seen the look on your face as we stood there at the top and gazed at the countryside all around. You were panting and flushed and vividly happy. I am not even sure you were aware of it, but it was . . . breathtaking to see."

"Well, it was an accomplishment," she said, laughing. She rested one cheek on her knee and continued to look at him. "My children are very solicitous of my comfort, you know. They insist that I ride everywhere in a well-sprung carriage. They pamper and care for me. They make me very aware that I am the matriarch of a grown family and a grandmother of four, with more on the way. They would be horrified if they knew how you dragged me on that long walk."

He grinned at her. "Is that what I did?"

"Absolutely," she said.

"And are you sorry you gave in to tyranny?" he asked.

"Absolutely not," she said. "When else have you seen me happy in myself?"

"When you ran down the hill," he said, "instead of taking the safe long way down by the road."

"Happy?" she said, raising her head. "Matthew, I was terrified."

"And laughing helplessly when I caught you and twirled you about," he said. "And kissing me with reckless, scandalous abandon."

They locked eyes. Neither spoke for several moments.

"Was I happy then?" she asked. "It was a mistake."

"It was a spontaneous outpouring of joy," he said. "It did not come from any of the disciplined rules of behavior you have followed so meticulously all your life."

"It most certainly did not," she said. "I was not taught to kiss random men."

He regarded her through slightly squinted eyes, his head tipped a little to one side. "Is that what I am?" he asked her. "A random man?"

She sighed. "How did this get started?" she asked him, though she did not wait for an answer. "I have loved two men in my life, Matthew. I have kissed two men. One of them was my husband."

"And the other was me?" He phrased it as a question, though the implication was perfectly obvious. She had definitely kissed him at the foot of that hill a few days ago.

"When we set off on this outing earlier," she said, "I did it with the firm conviction that it must be the last. I had the feeling that you had made a similar decision. For any friendship between us, no matter how casual or innocent, cannot be kept secret. Already word is spreading, and that is hardly surprising. We have been seen by various gardeners and other servants here. I have already received a very gentle warning from Sir Ifor Rhys, who saw us on top of the hill a few days ago and tried and failed to attract our attention."

"Yes," he said. "I had a warning this morning too. From Miss Wexford."

"Ah," she said. "So we must put a firm and abrupt end to our renewed friendship because gossip might be bad for your business and it might tarnish my reputation and that of my family, who will be seen as neglectful and unable to control me. So how am I to express this freedom of which you speak, Matthew? It is an illusion. I am bound hand and foot for the rest of my life by the expectations of society. And you cannot throw away the productive life of contentment you have spent more than twenty years building here, and years before that cultivating."

"You are right, you know," he said after a few moments of silence. "I did intend to make this the last time I would accept any of your invitations here. I could not see any comfortable way forward for our friendship. I had decided that maybe it was a mistake to have believed it could be renewed. For myself I did not fear notoriety. I have never deliberately courted the approval of my neighbors here. People may bring their business to me or go elsewhere with it. It has never mattered much to me. My financial needs are few. It does not take much to cover them, and I have never craved more. But I have been concerned about your reputation, especially now, when you are here at Ravenswood alone. I have not wanted to do it damage, even with an innocent friendship. But—"

"But?" She looked at him and smiled ruefully.

"But as time has passed this afternoon and I have seen you happy again," he said, "that part of me that lived in perpetual rebellion when I was a boy asks why we should end it. Must we live only for the approval of others, who really do not know us or care deeply about us at all? Must everything be about unfailing respectability? Even at the expense of personal happiness?"

"One lesson was given great emphasis when I was a girl," she said. "I was taught that reputation was a lady's single most valuable possession. Give up reputation, and everything was gone. Probably forever, for people have long memories."

"A dowager countess throws away her reputation, then, does she," he said, "when she befriends a carpenter?"

"That or her happiness," she said. "She cannot have both. And so, if she bows to the expectations of society, she really has no freedom to choose. She loses her power to shape her own future, to engage with friends and activities of her own choosing. She loses her ability simply to be happy, running down hills, shrieking and laughing, kissing random men, exploring an island scarcely larger than a pocket handkerchief with a carpenter just because she enjoys his company more than that of all others at the moment."

She blinked several times so she could see his face more clearly and realized it was tears that were blurring her vision. But before she could lift a hand to swipe them away, he did it for her, cupping her face with two large, slightly callused hands and wiping away her tears with the pads of two roughened thumbs.

And he kissed her, softly, warmly, his lips light and slightly parted over her own. She felt instant comfort, a sense of rightness, and sighed as she moved into his embrace, parting her own lips so she could feel his heat and taste him. And she lowered her knees, turned toward him, and wrapped her arms around him so he would not end the kiss almost before it had begun. She unbalanced herself in the process, and he lowered her backward onto the grass, holding the kiss as he did so, and following her down so she felt half his weight heavy across her.

He raised his head and gazed heavy-lidded down into her eyes.

"So beautiful," he murmured.

"Matthew," she whispered. And it seemed miraculous to her that this man with the lines of age beginning to form on his face and the silvering dark hair, one lock down over his brow, was the boy she had adored as a girl, the boy with whom she had been falling in love when her upbringing and the excitement of being singled out for elevation to the dizzying heights of the aristocracy had persuaded her to marry Caleb. Yet here he was now, that boy, all these years later, just as dear as he had been then. Matthew Taylor. Calling her beautiful and meaning it.

He was kissing her again then, more fiercely and with greater heat, and she was kissing him back with all the longing of the years that had passed since they had gone on to lives that did not include each other. His hands were moving over her on top of her clothing, cupping her breasts, outlining her waist and her hips, pausing over the slight mound above the junction of her legs. Worshiping her. Making her feel young again and desirable again and full of an answering desire. Her hands found their way beneath his coat and waistcoat to the smooth warmth of his shirt, and she felt the wiry strength of his back, the straightness of his spine, the powerful muscles of his shoulders. She could feel, after he had removed his hand, the hardness of his arousal pressed to her through the layers of their clothing and wanted him with a fierce desire she had not felt since the early years of her marriage. Oh, so long ago.

"Matthew." She was whispering his name again into his mouth, and he raised his head to look down at her. She watched regretfully as the slightly glazed look in his eyes turned to a frown.

He sat up abruptly and pushed the fingers of both hands through his hair. "Oh, God," he said. "I am sorry. I am so sorry."

She reached out a hand to reassure him, but he had leapt to his feet and moved a short distance away. His eyes were on the water of the lake as he began to peel off his clothes. Her eyes widened as she watched him, but he seemed almost unaware of her. When he had stripped down to his drawers, he ran into the water and kept going until it reached his waist. Then he waded a little farther and dived under, to reappear a few moments later farther out in the lake. He shook his head and glanced back but then swam away with powerful strokes.

Ah, Clarissa thought, trying to bring order back to her hair before clasping her knees and gazing after him. This was why any sort of friendship between them was unwise. For it was definitely more than just friendship, and more too than just romance. She had already admitted it to herself. She had felt it, surely, from the beginning, when she had gone boldly to his rooms to ask if he would make a crib for Ben and Jennifer's baby, hoping she would also find the courage to ask him about the wood carving he had entered in

the contest at the fete two years ago. She had known she was playing with fire. She had known it with greater clarity at each subse-
quent meeting.

Must it be ended, then?

Common sense said yes.

Something inside herself she had never explored before argued
back.

Why not have the boldness, the backbone, to reach for what she
wanted and to . . . to . . . to what? To disregard, to assign to perdition, what anyone else might think of them? Or say of them?

It was not a decision that involved her alone, of course.

For a few moments she was tempted to strip down to her shift
and follow him into the water. It was an age since she had last
swum in the lake or anywhere else. The desire to do it now, when
she was still feeling a bit flustered after their kiss, was almost over-
powering. But it would be the wrong thing to do. He had taken to
the water himself because he had needed to get away from her, to
compose himself.

There was something she could do, however. She got to her feet
and made her away across the island to retrieve the pile of towels
she had brought with them in the boat. She carried them back and
sat again to wait for him.

CHAPTER TEN

At first Matthew thought Clarissa had left without him and half hoped she had. He wondered if she had taken his clothes with her. But when he looked again, he could see that she was back sitting on the beach, something white on the grass beside her. The towels she had brought in the boat, he guessed. The maternal instinct still burned bright in her. She had gone to fetch them.

His blood had cooled and the unaccustomed exercise of swimming had restored his equilibrium. But he still felt shaken. He had known he was attracted to her, a fact that complicated any chance there might have been of a casual friendship with her over the summer. He had not expected it to prove beyond his control, however. Saturday's kiss had not bothered him unduly. It had been a spontaneous and understandable reaction to that breathless run down the hill. It had been an extension of their laughter.

Today's kiss had not been at all like that.

She had been baring her soul to him, something he could not remember her ever doing as a girl. She had never seemed to have

troubles in those days, unlike him. Now she was caught in the dilemma of wanting both freedom and reputation. Yet she did not
believe it was going to be possible to have both.

Clarissa had always chosen respectability over freedom. Though
she had not called it freedom a while ago, had she? She had called
it happiness. And he wondered again if she had ever been truly
happy. For happiness came from freedom, it seemed to him. When
had Clarissa ever been truly free, except perhaps in brief bursts very
recently? Or had she always been free but used her freedom to
choose duty and loyalty and respectability? There were never any
clear answers to the deeper questions of life, were there?

All of which speculation was beside the point. The point was
that he had kissed her when she had been at her most vulnerable.
Oh, he might have started out with the idea of comforting her, but
soon he had been kissing her with a panting need. One she had
returned, it was true, but he had started it. When more than ever
before she had needed a friend, he had responded as a lover. And so
he had compounded her unhappiness, especially as they had more
or less agreed that this would be the last afternoon they would
spend together.

He did not know how long he had been swimming, but it was
long enough. It was time to return and apologize. Not that a simple
apology was going to be anywhere near enough. Unfortunately, he
did not know what would be.

He waded out through the shallow water and saw that she was
watching his approach, her expression quite unreadable—deliberately
so, perhaps? The air felt downright chilly on his dripping body. He
took up two of the towels in one hand, gathered his clothes with
the other, and walked back a little way into the trees to dry off and
dress—minus his drawers, which he squeezed out and wrapped in

the towel he had used to rub his hair dry. He made his way back to stand beside her and dropped his two towels to the grass. She did not look up at him.

"After all the times I spilled out my troubles to you when we were growing up," he said, "you never once said or did anything to upset me further. You never scolded or sermonized or suggested that I was the author of my own woes. You never told me I was tiresome or too much of a troublemaker to be associated with you any longer. Instead you smiled and sometimes reached out a hand and somehow made me feel that I was special to you and worth knowing. You made me feel valued. You made me feel good about myself. I always went home happier and calmer than I was when I came. Today you opened your troubled heart to me, and what did I do? I dived at you and mauled you. I made your unhappiness all about me. I reached for my own gratification. And . . . What?"

He stopped talking, for she was gazing up at him now and she was smiling—a full-blown smile that lit her eyes and curved her lips. He would have called it a mischievous smile if mischief weren't contrary to Clarissa's personality.

"Oh, Matthew," she said. "You did not dive. Or maul. What an absurd visual picture those words conjure. We ended up in each other's arms. You responded to my need and kissed me. And I kissed you back because I wanted to do something entirely free. Because . . . why should I not? Whom was I harming? Not you, I judged. You wanted to kiss me as much as I wanted to kiss you. I was glad you had the good sense to end it when you did because it would have been unseemly to continue in what is a secluded place but not entirely private. But, Matthew, you must not take all the blame upon yourself for what did happen, or any blame at all, in fact. What blame?"

"You want to end our friendship," he said, "because all the servants here must already be buzzing with talk of it and Sir Ifor Rhys has given you a gentle warning. And because Miss Wexford has warned me, albeit gently too, and she is your friend. I take the blame for making things even more complicated."

"Things," she said as she got to her feet and brushed creases and grass from her skirt while he realized too late that he ought to have offered her a helping hand. She took up her bonnet and tied the ribbons beneath her chin. "You want to end it too, Matthew. I can believe Miss Wexford's warning was tactful. She is of no more a malicious nature than Sir Ifor is. Nevertheless it was a sure sign that word is spreading and that those who feel kindly toward one or both of us are concerned."

He bent to pick up the towels. He held the dry ones under his arm and the wet ones in his hand.

"I do not know about you," she said, "but I am awfully hungry. I could devour one of your cheese sandwiches with no effort at all."

"Instead," he said, "you are going to have to settle for some of the exquisite dainties with which that food hamper by the boathouse is probably stuffed."

"And champagne, alas," she said, "instead of water from your flask."

"I do not suppose I will ever live down that picnic fare," he said. "You will have to excuse me—or not—on the grounds that I am just an old bachelor."

"Widower," she said softly. "And there is nothing to excuse, Matthew. I am not teasing you when I tell you it was the loveliest picnic of my life. Shall we go and have tea?"

He followed her back to the boat. He wondered how many people in the village and neighborhood realized that he was indeed a widower, not a bachelor. It was something he normally preferred to keep to himself. He celebrated his daughter's birth and mourned her death and his wife's on the same day each year. He did it quietly and alone with lit candles and meditation. One thing he had never done since his return to England, though, was visit their grave.

He hurried on ahead as they passed the little pavilion in order to be at the bank ahead of her to hand her into the boat.

S he told him some amusing stories of things that had happened in London earlier in the spring. She told him of the picture of Carrie, the dog, that Joy had enclosed with a letter from Jennifer. She told him of the most recent letter from Pippa at Greystone. She frequently felt exhausted, she had written, just from watching Stephanie play with Emily and Christopher while they took shameless advantage of her energy and good nature.

"I am a typical mother and grandmother, you see," Clarissa said. "Boring everyone who is polite enough to listen with doting stories of my children and grandchildren. I am sorry, Matthew. I do not mean to be tedious." She smiled ruefully at him.

"You know," he said, "despite the wide brim of that bonnet and perhaps because your parasol is lying idle beside the blanket, you will be fortunate indeed if your face is not sun bronzed tomorrow."

"With freckles too?" she said. "Horror of horrors. Nobody will be able to look at me without swooning." But she did not reach for her parasol.

"I would always want to look at you," he said, grinning—the first time he had smiled since he went dashing into the lake earlier. "And I could not find you tedious if I tried."

"How very gallant of you," she said.

At her request, he told her about some of the wood carvings he had done in his spare time during the past couple of years. His favorite was a short-eared owl perched on the stump of a tree and poised for flight but delayed by the long staring match in which it was engaged with the man who would soon capture it in wood.

"I love to convey the idea of movement or imminent movement in what I carve," he said. "It is a huge challenge but makes all the difference to the completed carving, I believe. That bird was ready to go, but it was absolutely not going to concede the staring victory to me. I was the first to step back and look away and so release the owl into flight. We might still be staring at each other if I had not."

"The sense of movement is one of the things that most astonishes me in your work," she said. "It would seem to be impossible to achieve when the carving itself does not move. But you make it possible."

"I aim to satisfy." He grinned at her again, though she knew what he had said was not quite true. In his wood carvings, he was the true artist. He carved for himself and his vision and, in doing so, pleased all who were privileged to behold his creations. But how could she convey that thought in words? She did not try.

"I would love to see it sometime," she said.

He merely smiled. Perhaps he would enter it in the contest at the next fete, though that would not be until next year. Perhaps he would show it to her . . . But no. Today was supposed to be their last day.

They were busy tucking into the contents of the picnic hamper, which were quite as sumptuous as he had predicted. There were cucumber sandwiches—the bread was fresh and sliced wafer-thin, as were the cucumbers—and sausage rolls with pastry that flaked to the touch and lobster patties that melted in the mouth and slices of cheese and fried chicken legs.

And then there were the sweets, usually to be resisted as much as possible but today to be indulged in because . . . well, simply because. There were biscuits made with lots of butter, small apple tarts, thin slices of fruitcake, and equally thin slices of a white four-layered cake, a creamy icing and strawberry preserves spread lavishly between each layer—but not oozing out. How did the cook accomplish that?

But before they started on the sweets, Clarissa suggested they carry them, along with the as-yet-unopened champagne, along the footpath north of the lake to the thatched arbor at the junction with the western path.

"It is such a lovely spot," she said, "though I rarely go there. I only ever see it from afar." She was about to add that it looked utterly romantic, standing just where it did in all its miniature rural beauty. But she really must not bring up the idea of romance.

She wrapped some of the sweets in two neatly folded linen napkins within a white cloth that had been laid over the top of the hamper before it was closed, and made a bundle she could carry in one hand. Matthew meanwhile took up the bottle of champagne in one hand and two glasses in the other.

And so they walked along the path, just for the pleasure of finishing their tea inside a small grotto, which held a single table of bare wood and a backless bench on either side of it, if memory served her correctly. But the walk was lovely, the lake water glimmering and lapping on one side, the undulating green landscape dotted with trees on the other, a few low bushes and flower beds bordering the outer edge of the path. They walked in a silence that felt comfortable, and it seemed to Clarissa that there must have been silences when they were growing up. They had often spent hours at a stretch together. They surely could not always have talked nonstop, though that was how she remembered it.

"I often avoid being in company with others," he said. "Silence is seen as the great enemy of people gathered together, and they will do all in their power to fill it with the sound of conversation, no matter how meaningless. You are one of the few people I have known with whom I have always felt perfectly at ease, even happy, when we are silent with each other. Do you remember when we could sit for hours, often in the branches of a tree, without speaking a word but nevertheless comforted by each other's presence?"

Ah. There had been such times, then, and he remembered them.

"And now see what I am doing," he said. "I am breaking the silence in order to extol its virtues."

They both laughed.

"In fact," he said, "I believe it was our silences I valued most about our friendship. They were so soothing. I have not fully understood that until now. How strange."

"It says a great deal for the quality of my conversation," she said.

But he laughed again. "Clarissa," he said, "you were quite perfect."

She blinked a few times, unwilling to show any sign of tears. He had always treated her as though she were perfect—that troubled, sullen, rebellious boy, who was such a trial to almost everyone else who knew him. Caleb, for all his affection and admiration, had never really considered her perfect, had he? He would not have needed other women if he had. Though she was not going to think of that now. Or ever.

The gardeners must have been along here recently, she thought as they approached the grotto. In beds and pots and hanging baskets, pink, white, and lilac hyacinths bloomed in profusion along with pink peonies; yellow pansies; blue, purple, and white irises; and great balls of white and pale green allium. The combined perfume of them wrapped about her senses like a tangible thing. Someone had cleaned off the table and benches and swept the floor. They stepped inside and set the remains of the picnic on the table, using the cloth that had wrapped the sweets as a tablecloth. The grotto was open at the front, two pillars holding up the roof at the corners. The wide opening was framed by thatch above and flowers and greenery on both sides. The whole vista of the lake and the island was spread before them. The lake water was very blue.

He opened the bottle of champagne.

And this was the end, she thought.

But was it? Must it be?

Why?

"The glasses add a definite something to this picnic feast," he said, filling them both.

"Though there was much to be said for drinking straight from the flask at your picnic," she said, seating herself on one of the benches while he took the other, facing her. "Both of us from the same flask."

"This is more genteel, Clarissa," he said, grinning as he placed one of the glasses before her and raised the other in his right hand. "One must make a toast when drinking champagne, must one not? I believe there is a law." His smile faded as he gazed thoughtfully across the table at her. "To friendship," he said.

"To a lifelong friendship," she said. "Even when it lies dormant for years at a time."

They drank, their eyes lingering upon each other. The champagne was bubbly. She could feel it tickling her nostrils and dampening her cheeks.

"Is that what ours is?" he asked.

"Yes," she said.

"And it lies dormant for years at a time. Why?" he asked.

They both set down their glasses.

"Sometimes one of the friends is way up high in the mountains north of India learning to shoot arrows," she said.

"And sometimes one of them is married to someone else for twenty years and more," he said.

"Sometimes one has all the grandeur and burden of being a dowager countess," she said, "while the other chooses to live as a humble workingman."

"And all too often each of them worries about what will happen to the other's reputation if there is gossip or even scandal," he said.

"Even when they do not worry about their own reputation," she said.

"And sometimes," he said, "the friendship threatens to turn into something else."

"And they both end up terrified and running a mile in opposite directions," she said.

They had gone far enough. They stopped talking in order to take another sip of their champagne and look over the sampling of sweets they had brought with them.

"It would be a sin not to try everything that has been so lovingly prepared for us," he said.

"But would it be more of a sin actually to eat it?" she asked.

They looked at each other.

"No," they said simultaneously.

And so she ate a biscuit and a tart and a slice of both cakes, and thoroughly enjoyed every mouthful. She had brought three of everything, and he ate what she did not. Which meant that he ate twice as much as she did.

"Did I bring enough for you?" she asked.

"Far more than enough," he said. "But how could I burden you with having to carry any of it back?"

"Ah," she said. "And I thought you were eating the food because you really wanted it."

They finished their champagne and he poured them another glass each. They drank that too. She took the cloth to the doorway and shook out the crumbs before folding it and sitting back down at the table.

"Is this not the loveliest place on earth?" she asked.

He looked about him and inhaled the scents of all the flowers. Then he looked at her with laughing eyes. He set his hands palms up halfway across the table on either side of their glasses, and she set hers palms down upon them and felt his strong, callused fingers close around hers.

"At least the loveliest place," he said, "until you are somewhere else. Then that will be the loveliest."

"You have become adept with flattering words," she said.

"Ah, but the word *flattery* implies insincerity," he said. "I never speak insincerely. Not to you or about you, at least."

He was rubbing his work-roughened thumbs lightly over the backs of her hands, and she was thinking she had been quite right about this grotto. It was surely the most romantic place on earth, as well as the loveliest.

"Why did you not go home to the house you inherited from your grandmother after you returned from your travels?" she asked him. "Why here instead?"

She had not meant to ask.

"I was never interested in the life of a gentleman for the sake of social status," he said. "And at the time I had little interest in farming. The same man had run the farm for years and years, and he was very efficient at his job and very protective of his authority. I wanted to live a simple life, but not shut up in a manor house, where I would not feel any real sense of belonging either with the class into which I had been born or with any other. I wanted to be a wood-carver with a side occupation of carpentry to pay the bills. I discovered there was need of a carpenter in Boscombe, and when I went there, the first thing I did was call at the smithy to make inquiries. That same night, my meager belongings were upstairs in the rooms where the Hollands used to live. I have been there ever since."

"Your brother and his wife and their elder son and his wife were at my parents' home last Sunday when I went there for Mama's seventieth birthday," she said. He raised his eyebrows in surprise. "I found that someone had arranged a small party for her. Captain Jakes was there too with his wife and her sister. They are considering going to live in Plymouth after their lease expires next year. They want to be close to the sea again."

"Yes," he said. "I have been informed of that."

She felt she had encroached upon forbidden territory and must go no further. "I am glad you came to Boscombe," she said. "But it must have taken some courage."

"I stayed away from England for longer than ten years," he said. "In that time I freed myself of all lingering traces of obligation to be the man I was apparently born to be. A gentleman, in other words. I became simply a person. A person with an unfocused dream for a long while. But it became more focused with time. I wanted, I needed, to work with wood and a knife, just as some people need to work with canvas and paints or with paper and pen or with a violin and a bow. Who knows why certain people are born with these cravings? But nothing brings contentment or peace of mind to such people except the decision to answer the calling and become the person one was meant to be. By the time I returned to my own country, Clarissa, it needed no courage at all simply to do what I had to do. I came here specifically because it was a familiar part of England and there was need of a carpenter. I have stayed here because I have never felt the urge to move on to something different. I was done with both restlessness and traveling."

"And so," she said, "it turns out that you are far stronger than I, Matthew. Yet it seemed the other way around when we were children."

"Ah," he said, "but it was you who always believed in me, who always encouraged me, often without the medium of words, to be the person I needed to be. Almost your last words to me on that final afternoon were to seek the fulfillment of all my yearnings and thus be happy."

"Did I say that? Aloud?" she said. "So I encouraged your rebellion?"

"No, nothing as negative as that," he said. "Quite the opposite. You . . . How do I express it? You permitted me to be the person I was deep within. You liked me just as I was and as I was becoming. It felt almost like love."

"It was love," she said. "Long before I knew anything about other kinds of love, I loved you."

They smiled at each other and he squeezed her hands. Before he could let them go, she lifted her right hand and his left, drew them across her body, and set the back of his hand to her cheek.

"What do we do now, Matthew?" she asked. "Make this the last, glorious afternoon we spend together? Because of what people will say? Or will we continue? I am finding it difficult to be the person I want to be. Being the person I think I ought to be and the person other people expect me to be is very deeply ingrained in me."

He drew a breath and released it slowly.

"I will be in the poplar alley on Thursday, as usual, practicing archery," he said. "Weather permitting."

And so they would delay their decision for another day.

He drew their clasped hands toward him across the table and kissed the back of hers before releasing it and getting to his feet.

She stood too and picked up the folded cloth. He gathered up their two empty glasses and the almost empty bottle of champagne, and they made their way back along the northern path to restore everything to the picnic basket, which he set inside the boathouse to be picked up later.

He carried his towels as they walked back to the house in near silence—and hand in hand.

CHAPTER ELEVEN

Clarissa had spoken of the various phases of life one could distinguish as one grew older. For her, there had been her childhood and girlhood as one phase and her marriage and motherhood as a second. Now she was into the third, which had started with the death of her husband.

It seemed to Matthew that his own life had been lived in three distinct parts too so far, and that the third was the longest and the most satisfying. He wished it could go on forever. But nothing did. Change was inevitable even when one scarcely noticed it happening. And actually one had very little power to prevent it.

For more than twenty years he had lived in much the same way—in the same rooms in the same village with the same friends and acquaintances, doing the same work. He earned his living with carpentry, and he spent his spare time carving and practicing archery and reading and socializing. He was known as an even-tempered man. The closest he had come to losing his temper had happened ten years ago during that disastrous ball at Ravenswood on the night of the summer fete. He had been a witness to the ghastly scene Devlin Ware had created on the terrace outside the ballroom, when he had accused his father of having brought his mistress from London and of having behaved in a most unseemly fashion with her up in the temple folly while his wife and children and their friends and neighbors were dancing, oblivious, in the ballroom a mere few yards away.

All of Matthew's suspicions had been confirmed, and Matthew had wanted to throttle the man right at that ball. He had wanted to throttle him when he heard that it was Devlin who had been forced to leave Ravenswood as a result of the fracas, not Stratton. He had wanted to throttle him when he heard stories of how Clarissa had withdrawn from society as much as she could and hidden away in that vast house, which had so often flung wide its doors to the community at large. He had wanted to throttle Stratton when he heard that most people had stopped going to the park on open days because they wanted to give the countess the privacy she seemed to crave—and they feared the terrible embarrassment of a chance meeting with her. He had wanted to throttle Stratton because all his sons and daughters had been negatively affected by his behavior, even the youngest two, who were still children at the time. They were Clarissa's children too.

He had wanted to hurt Stratton because the man had been in possession of one of the most precious gifts the world had to offer—Clarissa herself—and had spurned her and sullied her and hurt her beyond imagining and possibly ruined all that remained of her life.

Matthew had not throttled the man. Doing so would have solved nothing, and if there was one thing he had learned in all the years after he left home, it was that acting violently was almost never justified and almost never brought lasting satisfaction. He had not hurt Stratton, but he had steadfastly avoided being in his company. If he went to the village inn for a pint of ale and discovered Stratton there before him, he simply closed the door of the taproom without stepping inside. If Stratton arrived after him—as had happened on the night of his sudden death—then Matthew simply left and went home.

He had hated the man with a passion. He had not mourned his death. Indeed, if he was strictly honest about it, he would have to say he had rejoiced.

In the main, however, the twenty or so years he had spent in Boscombe had been years of tranquil contentment. Yet now he could sense definite change coming, and he seemed helpless to do anything about it. Or perhaps he was unwilling to do anything about it. He went about his daily routine as usual and waited for his life to settle back to normal, though he suspected it was not going to happen.

For one thing, there was his renewed friendship with Clarissa. Though *friendship* was not an adequate word, for it had become increasingly obvious to him that it was a romance that was developing between them, and a romance was far less convenient than mere friendship. Yet even *romance* was not quite a strong enough word. They wanted each other—he was in no doubt that she shared his hunger. And that would certainly not do. There was no way on God's earth he was going to begin an affair with Clarissa Greenfield.

Yet the desire was very real and must somehow be dealt with. The most obvious way would be to put an end to the whole relationship, but that seemed not to be working. On either side.

Then there was the gossip, which bothered him more than he cared to admit and probably bothered her too.

He went into the village shop after work the day after the picnic at the lake and found there were two women ahead of him at the counter, enjoying a cozy gossip with the Misses Miller, to whom the shop belonged. It was not an unusual occurrence. Normally Matthew would cheerfully have awaited his turn and even joined in the conversation. He was well known to everyone and accepted as one of their own. But on this occasion a strange hush fell over the shop as soon as he entered it, and the hush was succeeded by a self-conscious rush to comment upon the weather. The customers soon took their baskets of goods and left, favoring him with self-conscious nods as they edged past him, and he was left to the tender mercies of the Miller sisters.

"You had a lovely day for your picnic with Lady Stratton yesterday, Mr. Taylor," Miss Jane, the younger of the two, said.

"The dowager Lady Stratton, Jane," Miss Miller reminded her.

"Yes, of course." Miss Jane smiled as Matthew handed her his shopping list. "You had a lovely day anyway. It is lovely, the lake at Ravenswood. Did you take out one of the boats?"

"We did," Matthew said.

"Lovely," she said, setting the items from his list one by one onto the counter. She seemed to have become stuck on the one word as a descriptor.

"The late Mr. and Mrs. Taylor lived right next to the Greenfields," Miss Miller said. "The dowager countess's mama and papa, that is," she added, lest Matthew be unaware of the fact.

"Yes," Matthew said. "We were neighbors. And friends. The dowager countess and I are less than a year apart in age."

"Ah," Miss Jane said. "That would explain it, then. We sometimes forget that Mr. and Mrs. Taylor—such a lovely couple—were your mama and papa, Mr. Taylor."

Everything that was on his list stood before him on the counter.

"I think that is all for this week," he said. "How much do I owe you?"

And Miss Jane had no choice but to add the prices to his list and work out the total with the stub of a pencil that had never seemed longer than it was now and never seemed to get shorter either. Perhaps the sisters kept an array of identical stubs under the counter.

He paid the bill, bid them a good afternoon—a wish they returned with bright cheerfulness—and made his way home, half smiling and half resigned to the fact that if all the staff at Ravenswood knew, and the Misses Miller at the shop, the very center of village life, knew, then there could be no one for at least a five-mile radius around the village and Ravenswood itself who did not know that he had gone picnicking yesterday at the lake and had walked hand in hand with the dowager countess through the park a few days before that and had taken coffee with her one morning on the terrace outside the ballroom.

Change was coming, unless both he and Clarissa put a firm end to whatever was developing between them right now and provided the gossips with no further fuel to feed their curiosity and mild sense of outrage. At least, at the moment it seemed to be mild.

His relationship with Clarissa and the reaction to it was not the only change that was pending in his life, however. There was also the letter that had been awaiting him in his rooms—Cam must have brought it up and pushed it under the door—when he returned from the picnic.

It was a brief note from his nephew, Reginald's elder son, asking if he might call upon his uncle one day. He had informed his father that he was making the request, he had explained in the letter, but though his father had warned him that his uncle might refuse to have anything to do with him, he had nevertheless not tried to forbid his son from making the attempt. The nephew had signed the letter Philip Taylor, Matthew's obedient servant.

He had been just a toddler when Matthew left home. His brother had been little more than a baby. Their sister had not yet been born.

So here was some definite change coming, Matthew thought. Not inevitably, of course, for he could refuse the request or even simply ignore it.

But he sensed change was happening.

First Clarissa had mentioned that his brother and nephew and their wives had attended Mrs. Greenfield's birthday party. It had been the first mention of his family anyone had made since he could not remember when. After his return from his travels, he had made no attempt to see any of them, and none of them had made any attempt to see him.

There had been a total estrangement ever since. No one had begun it—unless he had, years before, when he left home without a word to anyone except his grandmother's solicitor, who had agreed for a reasonable fee to keep him informed of any essential information he needed to know, provided Matthew always made the solicitor aware of how and where he might be reached, of course.

No one had formalized the estrangement after his return. By what had seemed mutual consent, he had ignored their existence and they had ignored his. He had never gone even as close as his grandmother's house, now his, since his return. He had found out about the deaths of his grandmother and his parents from the solicitor. He had not reacted to any of those events. Not outwardly anyway. He had wanted things to remain as they were. Life was more peaceful that way.

But he had always known that it was the one area of his past life—a rather large area, actually—with which he had never dealt. Ignoring its very existence would perhaps not serve him until the end of his life. He pondered his response to his nephew's letter, but there was really no doubt in his mind how he would respond. He had no quarrel with the boy—no, not a boy. Philip was a man in his thirties now. Matthew had no open quarrel with his brother either. Just an estrangement that neither of them had confronted in the more than twenty years since Matthew had come to live in Boscombe.

He invited his nephew to call upon him the following Tuesday at four o'clock in the afternoon, if that was convenient to him.

And then there was tomorrow, his regular day for practicing archery in the poplar alley at Ravenswood. Weather permitting, of course. He had told Clarissa he would be there. He had not suggested that she come too, and she had not said she would—or would not. They had come to no explicit decision on what to do about their friendship despite the fact that they had both begun the picnic intending that it should be the last of such meetings. They had walked back to the house from the lake hand in hand and in near silence.

He did not know if she would come tomorrow. He did not know what it would mean if she did not, though he would assume it was the end of an experiment that had just not worked. Except that it had worked all too well.

He expected to come very close to finishing Miss Wexford's dining table tomorrow. He would go to the poplar alley after that. If Clarissa did not come, he would need to practice longer even than usual. Life was changing, but he must not disintegrate with the changes.

Clarissa was late arriving at the poplar alley the following afternoon. Deliberately so, which was unusual for her. But she did not want to delay or interrupt his archery practice if she could possibly avoid doing so. Besides, it was a cloudy, chilly day and she wondered if he would be there at all. It would not hurt to have a look, however. One ought to take some outdoor exercise each day, after all, though it was easy to make excuses when the weather was not to one's liking.

She dreaded seeing him again and dreaded not seeing him.

She did not know where it was headed, this friendship that was quickly renewing itself after so long and at the same time turning into something else. Romance? Sexual desire? Love?

At the age of almost fifty she had no experience with the first. She was surprised when she considered the matter and realized it was true. Yes, there had been a great deal of external romance surrounding her marriage to Caleb. They had been the golden couple, the fairy-tale couple, the happily-ever-after couple. She had been completely dazzled by her bridegroom and head over heels in love with him. There had even been seeming romance within the marriage itself, for he had remained charming and attentive, and she had made no effort to hide her infatuation with him. Why would she? In addition to everything else, she had had something resembling a palace in which to live and luxury wherever she turned. The physical side of their marriage had been, and had remained almost to the end, sensual and satisfying and frequent. He had been proud of her and almost worshipful of her until the end of his life. He had not once spoken a harsh or indifferent word to her.

She had equated it all with love and romance. For a long while, even after she had begun to suspect and then knew that all was not paradise with her marriage, she had thought of herself as the most fortunate and the happiest of women.

But there really had been no romance.

They had never stolen off to the summerhouse alone together, she and Caleb, to watch the sunset—or sunrise. They had never picnicked alone together at the lake or sat in the thatched grotto to drink champagne and gaze into each other's eyes. They had never walked hand in hand in the park or anywhere else. They had danced together, but only in the presence of their neighbors and really for their benefit so all could see them as the eternal golden couple. Though maybe she was being overly cynical. Caleb had loved to open a ball with his countess. He had loved to set the tone for an evening of happy revelry with his friends and neighbors.

But he had never taken her in the middle of a ball up the hill to the temple folly to marvel at the night sky—and to steal a few kisses and perhaps a bit more while their family and friends danced in the ballroom and on the terrace below them.

No. Romance was new to Clarissa, as she had admitted during a day spent alone yesterday, most of it either in her private sitting room or up in the turret room. It was so new and so intoxicating that she really did not want to put a stop to it.

She still did not want to end it today, even after the morning visit three of her friends paid her together—Lady Hardington; Mrs. Danver, the vicar's wife; and Miss Wexford. They were amiability itself, their faces wreathed in smiles as they invaded the drawing room, where she had hurried after witnessing their arrival in Lord Hardington's carriage through the window of her sitting room. They hugged her and kissed her cheek and apologized for descending upon her with no prior warning.

"But it is such a gloomy morning," Mrs. Danver explained. "We needed to find a way to cheer ourselves up. And we could only imagine how lonely you must feel here sometimes, all alone, especially on a raw day like today, Lady Stratton. So here we are."

"We are sorry if we have interrupted some congenial activity, Clarissa," Lady Hardington added. "But here we are indeed, and we do not intend to go away until you have warmed us up with some coffee or, better yet, chocolate."

They all laughed and sat down, and Miss Wexford informed Clarissa that Mr. Taylor was hard at work on her dining table in her brother's barn.

"It is very close to completion," she said. "He may even finish it today, but will almost certainly do so no later than tomorrow. I cannot wait to see it set up in the dining room and to invite a party to dine with us—provided each guest promises solemnly to admire it profusely, that is."

They all laughed again.

And they continued to speak of Matthew, all three of them, with the greatest good humor and tact. They spoke of his marvelous skill as a carpenter—and they had heard he had taken on a commission from Clarissa herself. They spoke of the wonderful wood carvings he had entered in contests at the summer fetes and wondered if he had made many others and what he had done with them. They regretted that the long estrangement with his family had apparently never been resolved. They wished at least that he would find a more genteel home in which to live. It would surely be more comfortable for him than those rooms above the smithy and more indicative of the social status he could claim by right of birth. As it was, no one who did not know his history would even suspect that he was a gentleman.

"Except for the way he speaks," Mrs. Danver said.

"And as far as anyone knows," Miss Wexford said, "he does still own the manor house and property his maternal grandmother left him."

"As things stand," Lady Hardington said, "there is an unfortunate air of near poverty about the dear man. When did he last purchase a new coat? Or new boots? One does wonder, since there must be income from the lease of the home that was left him, why he needs to pretend to be nothing more than a humble carpenter living on the edge of poverty. Perhaps it is because he does not have a wife. You have been gracious enough to extend some hospitality to him lately, Clarissa. Perhaps you have asked him some of these questions?"

"I have not," Clarissa said, and smiled.

It was more or less the answer she gave to all their musings over the half hour of their visit.

"It might almost be said, Lady Stratton," Mrs. Danver said eventually, "that Mr. Taylor is not being fair to you. If you are kind enough to invite him to walk with you in the park and enjoy a picnic with you at the lake, the very least he can do in return is try to look and behave more like the gentleman he is. Not that it is any of my business."

"But I do not issue invitations on the understanding that the person concerned rise to any preconceived conditions I may set," Clarissa said. "How presumptuous of me that would be. Besides,

Mr. Taylor has always been the perfect gentleman when in my company."

"Well, that is good to hear," Miss Wexford said, beaming at her. "And it is not at all surprising, given the fact that he was raised a gentleman. He has always treated me with the utmost respect whenever I have gone to the barn to ask about his progress with the table. I have never felt the necessity of taking a maid with me. Nor has Andrew ever suggested that I ought. I daresay you have never felt the need either."

"I would not dream of any need for a chaperon when I am with him," Clarissa said. "We grew up as close neighbors and friends, there being less than a year between our ages. I never needed a chaperon then. My parents trusted us while we spent hours together roaming the park and climbing trees and making daisy chains."

"Climbing trees," Miss Wexford said. "Oh my. I am envious, Lady Stratton. My mama and papa would never allow me to climb any, though Andrew was forever pretending they were the high tower of a fortress or the mast of his imaginary ship and climbing to the very top to survey the land or sea around him. I do wish girls were allowed to do at least some of the adventurous things boys do all the time."

"Well, do be aware, Clarissa, that there are comments being made about your apparent friendship with Mr. Taylor," Lady Hardington finally said, getting to her feet at last as a signal to the other two ladies that it was time to take their leave. "None of them openly malicious, of course, as far as I have heard."

"There are probably comments too about Mr. Taylor working in our barn and me taking him cups of tea there a couple of times each day," Miss Wexford said. "I know myself innocent and you know yourself innocent, Lady Stratton. But it behooves friends to watch out for one another and pass along gentle warnings."

"Perhaps," Mrs. Danver said, "your family will all be home soon, Lady Stratton, as the Season in London must be drawing to a close. Then there will be no further cause for gossip. It really is sad that women are never quite trusted to behave rationally when they are alone."

"Alone with a houseful of servants," Clarissa said, rising too to see them on their way.

They all laughed again. The three of them hugged her once more and beamed at her—and were genuinely concerned for her.

But Clarissa was not having any of it. She had decided that during her blessed day of solitude yesterday. She was going to live in future as she wished to live. That did not mean that henceforth she was going to throw upbringing and respectability to the winds and live a life of open scandal. But it did mean that her behavior was not going to be determined by what others expected of her, whether those others were her family or her friends or more casual acquaintances—or servants.

There was nothing scandalous in her enjoying a friendship with Matthew—or even in her indulging in a mild romance with him. She was, after all, a free woman. She had no husband or betrothed. She had no children dependent upon her. She was independently wealthy.

And she was going to be fifty years old in a few months. It was time to do some living on her own account.

So she was not going to change her mind about going to the poplar alley this afternoon. The raw weather would not deter her. Nothing else would either. But she would go late so that he would have time to set up and immerse himself in his practice.

If he went at all, that was.

There was always the chance that he had decided differently from her and would never again set foot inside the park at Ravenswood. If that was the case, then she must accept it. She would not force her company upon him if he did not want it.

But oh, how dreary that would be.

She did not realize the full extent of her anxiety until she came to the end of the poplar alley and saw that he was there. He had his back to her, and she could tell that all of his concentration was upon his shooting. She went quietly to sit on the grass before the first of the poplars on the eastern side and propped her back against the tree while gathering her woolen shawl more warmly about her shoulders and across her bosom.

He had removed his coat and hat and stood there in his shirt and waistcoat over breeches and top boots. His large quiver was over one shoulder. One arm was holding his bow in position while the other hand plucked arrows from the quiver, set them to the bow, and shot them into the center of the target a long distance away.

Clarissa gazed with frank admiration at his long legs and narrow hips, at his powerful shoulders and arms. Only the silver threads in his dark hair betrayed his age from this back view. She loved those silver threads and the laugh lines on his face. She was so glad he was no longer the deeply unhappy boy of her memory and that she was no longer the girl who had the whole of her future life happily mapped out for perfection.

She expected that after he had stridden along the alley to retrieve his arrows and turned to make his way back, he would see her. But she could tell from the look on his face and the language of his body that he was in another world. No, not exactly that, for he had to be fully present to shoot the way he was shooting. But she knew his concentration did not include what was peripheral to the task at hand.

She watched him shoot all his arrows again and go to fetch them—and again and again until at last when he returned from his walk to the target he looked up and looked around, frowning, first back to the summerhouse, then to this end of the alley, then to the tree where she had stood last time. And finally his head turned her way and he saw her on the other side of the alley. He set down his bow and quiver on the grass at his feet and came striding toward her. She smiled up at him.

"You came," he said, stooping down on his haunches and reaching out his hands, palm up, for hers.

"Did you think I would not?" she asked, setting her hands in his and feeling their familiar roughness and hardness as his fingers closed about them.

"I did not know," he said, and smiled back at her.

And she knew something had changed between them in the days since the picnic. An awareness and acknowledgment, perhaps, that this was far more than just a friendship, and that it was not about to end.

"And I did not know if you would come," she said.

"I am glad I did," he said. "I am glad you did."

He squeezed her hands as he stood up again, bringing her with him and wrapping her tightly in his arms.

Ah, it felt good. So very, very good.

"So am I," she said. "Glad that you did and I did, that is."

They both laughed before he kissed her.

CHAPTER TWELVE

Are you not cold, Matthew?" she asked when he raised his head a minute or two later. She was rubbing her hands briskly up and down the outsides of his arms. Up and down his shirtsleeves, that was.

"Strangely," he said, laughing, "I am feeling quite the opposite of cold at the moment. But I am shockingly underdressed. Excuse me a moment, Clarissa."

He went to pick up his coat and pull it on before fetching the target and stacking all his equipment against the tree where he had left them last time. He glanced up at the grayish, lowering clouds. It was hard to know if they were rain clouds, but the sky had looked exactly the same all day, and it had not rained yet.

"I have it on the reliable authority of our head gardener," she said from just behind him, "that it will not rain today. I trust him utterly."

"He has never been wrong?" he asked.

"Not to my knowledge," she said. "And he has been at Ravenswood longer than I have. Of course, there are the times when he squints up at the sky and then off to the western horizon before he nods sagely and says that she may rain and she may not. The weather to him is feminine, it seems. But even on such occasions—especially on those occasions, in fact—he has never yet been wrong."

"You are in a cheerful mood today," he said, taking in the sparkle of laughter in her eyes and the upward curve of her lips, as well as the rosy glow in her cheeks and at the end of her nose. A bit of cold and wind had always done that to her.

"I am," she said. "I came, having convinced myself that in all probability you would not be here. But you were, and I was glad. Did you finish Miss Wexford's table? She called here this morning with Lady Hardington and Mrs. Danver. She was quite exuberant because you were very close to finishing."

"It is all done except for a few final touches," he said. "Mostly a bit of sanding and varnishing. And I will need to see it in place in the dining room to make sure it sits solidly on the floor and will not rock as soon as someone rests his elbows on it."

"I am glad you said '*his* elbows,' " she said. "A lady would never do anything so shockingly ungenteel."

"Never," he said. "Ladies are invariably perfect. Shall we stroll?" He indicated the long alley.

They walked very slowly despite the chill of the day. He set an arm loosely about her shoulders, and she wrapped an arm about his waist. She smiled up at him now and then, and a couple of times he kissed her. Something, he realized, had changed in their relationship since the day of the picnic.

"We are going to be friends, then, are we, Clarissa?" he asked.

"Yes," she said. "We are."

But of course they were already more than just friends. There was some sort of romantic or sexual attraction between them, and they were just going to have to see what came of it. They would have to make decisions as they went along. But ending the whole thing abruptly now, before anything had properly started, had not seemed to suit either of them.

"I am going to ask Devlin if he would very much mind my having a dower house built somewhere in the park," she said. "I can afford it. I was thinking down by the river, perhaps to the east of the drive and the bridge, between the river and the meadow, with a pretty garden all my own and perhaps a rustic fence."

He smiled at her. He had learned long ago—from her, in fact—that when someone had a story to tell, it was better to allow that person to tell it without interruption. She had mentioned a dower house when they were at the lake. Obviously she had done more thinking since then.

"Of course Ravenswood is large enough for an army," she said. "And of course all four massive wings are available for my use except for a very few private apartments. I have one of those myself. It is spacious and comfortable and overlooks the front of the house. But . . ." Her voice trailed off and she shrugged. "But that is not the point."

"My rooms above the smithy have a front door," he said. "I believe maybe that is the point, is it?"

"Yes, exactly. You do understand," she said, stopping to beam up at him. He kissed her. "Those rooms are your very own, Matthew, even though I suppose they still belong to the Hollands. But you have your own front door and can retreat behind it whenever you choose. You have your own things and your own dreams there. You can keep out the world when you choose or step out into it whenever you wish. You can decide whom to invite in and whom to keep out. I was honored that you invited me in that morning."

He did not point out that she had really given him no choice. And she could presumably do the same things with her private apartment at Ravenswood. But he understood what she meant. Total independence and privacy were very precious. Probably she had never had either, despite all the spacious luxury of Ravenswood. She had a loving family, which would always draw her in to share their lives and their company and their love. But her private rooms were only a part of the larger house, which now belonged to her son.

Matthew was beginning to understand more clearly why she had come home alone a few weeks ago and why she had some serious thinking to do about her future.

"I want a whole house to myself," she said. "Nothing very large. A cottage. I do not want to run away. I love it here and I love my family. But I want a place that is all my own."

He kissed her briefly and they strolled onward.

"Does this all sound very selfish to you when I already have so much?" she asked.

He looked at the poplar trees in their straight, regimented lines on either side of them, keeping them in, keeping the world out, and understood the lure of the alley—and of a home that was all one's own, even if it was just in the form of rented rooms.

"It must be difficult," he said, "to adjust to major change when one is a parent. For years and years you raise your children and love them. For years they depend entirely upon you, a dependence that dwindles as they grow up until the time comes when your roles appear to reverse. Yes, I understand, Clarissa."

"Ah, Matthew," she said, stopping yet again. "And our roles have been reversed too. Those words—*Yes, I understand*—were always mine."

"And infinitely comforting to me," he said.

"They are now to me when it is you speaking them," she said. "I have not spoken explicitly to my children about these things, perhaps because the ideas have been all muddled up in my head and are only now becoming clearer to me. But I have hinted at them, and I can tell they do not understand at all. They are merely concerned about me and determined to redouble their efforts to love me and include me in their lives."

"Perhaps you will marry again," he said, "and begin a wholly new life somewhere else." Perhaps her interest in their friendship was simply a symptom of a broader need, one he could not fulfill any more than he could thirty years or so ago.

"Well, there was someone," she said. "Or rather there is someone, as I have not heard that he has expired since I left London. He is everything I could possibly want in a husband, Matthew. He is titled and wealthy and a fine figure of a man. Like me, he has been widowed for six years, though he is childless. He is courtly and well respected and . . . interested. He has the approval of my children and my brother."

Matthew hated him, sight unseen. He did not want to know the man's name.

"Has he made you an offer?" he asked.

"I escaped before he could do so," she said.

"Escaped?" he said.

"Well, yes," she said. "I was tempted, you see. Tempted to be sensible, to slip back into the role for which I was raised and educated, the comfortable role of lady and wife and hostess. I would be mistress of my own home again if I married him. I would not merely be the Earl of Stratton's mother. I would be a person in my own right again. He was—is—amiable, as far as I can tell without a more intimate acquaintance. He liked me. He was a good conversationalist."

"Yet you seem to be more inclined to talk of him in the past tense than the present," he said.

"Yes." She sighed. "For other people's commonsense opinions cannot guarantee my happiness. I need to think with my heart as well as my head. But why are we standing out here getting colder when we are very close to the summerhouse? It traps warm air, as you know, and is probably several degrees warmer than it is out here. There will be no lemonade awaiting us today, though."

"And no cakes either?" He frowned at her.

She laughed. "And no cakes."

He tightened his arm about her shoulders and led her toward the summerhouse. They settled side by side this time on the long sofa after he had closed the door behind them. So it seemed she was not going to marry her London beau even though she had been tempted? It was probably one of the decisions she had come home to think through. And then she had renewed her friendship with a man who was unsuitable for her in almost every imaginable way, thus further complicating her life.

"Your heart and good sense have not agreed with each other upon the right course for you to take?" he asked her.

"About marrying Lord Keilly?" she said. "Assuming he intended to ask me, that is? Alas, no. But I really was tempted. I have been horribly envious of George and Kitty, you see. They are very happy with each other. They both look ten years younger than they did a year ago, I swear. I have never been jealous of them, I hasten to add. Only envious. They have something I realize I would like for myself.

Not necessarily marriage, though. I have understood that since I came home. Just . . . Oh, how do I express it? Just . . . renewed life. Something to make the world seem new again and fresh again and full of possibilities once more. In fact, I believe I definitely do not want to marry again. Not yet anyway, and never unless I am convinced it is the only thing that can fulfill all my yearnings."

He settled her head against his shoulder and held it there with one hand while he kissed her forehead.

"Hence our friendship," he said. "And ignoring the warnings and advice of all your friends—I assume that was the reason for the call the three ladies paid you this morning."

"They are very dear," she said. "And really quite tolerant. But they are concerned. Because they care about me. I appreciate that. But I must live my own life. Every day I become more firmly decided upon that. Have you had any such visits?"

"Not quite," he said, and chuckled. He told her about his experience at the village shop. "But like you, Clarissa, I live my own life my way."

"It is not entirely easy to do, is it?" she said.

"When you attended your mother's birthday party," he said, changing the subject, "did you talk about me at all?"

"No." She turned her head to look at him in some surprise. "Well, actually yes, very briefly. Your nephew asked if I knew you and I told him that yes, I do. I told him you are the carpenter at Boscombe and that we were close friends as children. I daresay he knew that first fact already, and apparently Reginald had told him about our childhood friendship. Mr. Philip Taylor told me he would like to meet you. But his wife reminded him that her father-in-law would probably disapprove."

"He is coming to call on me next week," Matthew said. "My

nephew, that is. He wrote to ask if he might, and I gave him the definite date of next Tuesday."

She gazed into his face. "How do you feel about that?" she asked.

He shrugged. "I could hardly say no," he said. "I have never had any quarrel with the boy. Man. He is over thirty. It is hard to believe."

"Yes," she said. "You have never reached out to your brother? Or he to you?"

"No," he said.

"Was there a definite quarrel between you?" she asked him. "Something neither of you could forgive, that is?"

"No," he said. "I left without a word to anyone after we buried Poppy and Helena. When I returned, I came straight here."

"I beg your pardon." She sighed. "This is none of my business. I told myself I would never ask."

"You did not ask," he said. "I told you that my nephew is coming to call."

"Yes, you did," she said, and sighed again.

"Change is happening," he said, resting his cheek against the top of her head. "I hoped it never would. I have been happy here just as I am for more than twenty years. Well, contented anyway, which is often more desirable than active happiness. I would have been grateful for twenty more such years. But there are those phases of life you spoke of, those changes that press themselves upon us whether we want them or not, and there is no point in fighting against them. We must simply discover where they will lead and which ones will become permanent features of our lives and which will pass on through."

"And I have forced some of these changes upon you," she said.

"I invited you to drink coffee with me one morning, and I suggested that we be friends again, at least for the summer. Possibly I am responsible for another change too. If I had gone to see my mother the day before her birthday or the day after, I would not have seen your nephew and perhaps put the thought of calling on you into his head."

"Even if we were total hermits, Clarissa, we would not be immune to change," he said. "It happens. It is what life is about. But we are not hermits."

"I feel responsible anyway," she said. "I am sorry for upsetting your life."

"In truth," he said, "I am glad you invited me to stay for coffee that morning, and I am glad I said yes. Those biscuits were delicious."

She laughed. "You ate only one."

"The power of self-control," he said. "And I believe I am glad my nephew is coming."

They lapsed into silence, and he gazed along the poplar alley and off across the park to the west. From where he sat he could just see the back edge of the stable block, which formed the northern wing of the house, and a little farther along to the trees that climbed the back side of the hill upon which the temple folly stood.

How strange a thing life was. He could never have predicted this particular twist in his own. Clarissa had cut herself off from him more than thirty years ago in order to marry into a stratum of society far above his own even if he had chosen to live the life of a gentleman. And he had cut himself off from her, first by marrying Poppy, and then by choosing a different life entirely from the one with which he had struggled all through his boyhood. Now he and Clarissa were oceans and continents and planets apart as far as social position and way of life were concerned. They both had established lives with which they had long been comfortable and contented—until recently, on her part anyway.

And until recently on his part too.

He turned his head and kissed her, and she kissed him back, warmly and willingly—but without the urgent passion that had almost overcome them out at the lake. It was better thus, at least for now. Perhaps if they were able to indulge all the deep affection that had lain dormant within them for so long, it would prove to be enough. Perhaps people would grow accustomed to seeing them together from time to time and life would settle back to a new normal that was not so very different from the old.

Perhaps . . .

Perhaps pigs would fly.

She drew back her head then, and her eyes were shining again.

"Oh, Matthew," she said. "Let me show you where I want the dower house to be. We have to walk back along the alley for you to fetch your things anyway, and the place is very close by. I want you to tell me what you think."

They walked briskly back, hand in hand, and he realized that things were changing rapidly indeed for Clarissa. Her new life was taking shape in her mind, and she was making definite plans. An open friendship with him, regardless of the opinion of her friends and neighbors; no marriage unless or until her heart was able to tell her that the whole of her present and future happiness depended upon it; a greater independence, financial and otherwise, of the family who loved her—and whom she loved; and a home of her own, paid for from her own purse, with a front door she could shut against the whole world if she felt so inclined.

She had commented that her brother and her friend had looked ten years younger since their marriage. He wished he could show Clarissa her image now in a full-length glass, red nose and all. She looked almost like the girl he remembered from all those years ago.

He picked up his things from the end of the alley, and they walked to the main driveway and down it, past the meadows on either side with their wildflowers and grazing sheep. But before they reached the bridge, she turned to her left and led the way along the bank of the river after he had set down his things again. The bank widened after a short distance, and she turned to him, her arms spread wide before twirling once about.

"Here," she said. "Just here. In the park, below the meadow, not far from the house and in sight of the village, by the river. What do you think, Matthew? Is it not perfect?"

He looked critically, mostly at the river. The banks were high on both sides. Although the level of the water fluctuated through the year, he had never known it to overflow its banks. There was no more danger of flooding here than anywhere else in the village on the other side. There was ample room in this particular spot for a cottage and a garden separate from the meadow and the parkland above it. It would even be possible to widen the path between here and the driveway itself to accommodate a carriage. It would be a peaceful spot, somewhat withdrawn from any other building but not totally isolated either.

He wondered how she would cope with a greater solitude than she had now or had ever had. But he thought she would probably enjoy it. She would, after all, still be close to her family and friends and all that was familiar to her.

Closer to him.

She was waiting for his opinion.

"I agree," he said. "I think it is the perfect spot."

She beamed at him. "It will be so good for Gwyneth," she said. "She will be the undisputed mistress of Ravenswood. Not that the matter is disputed now, of course. But there is a tendency when someone says *Lady Stratton* for us to turn our heads simultaneously and say *Yes?* We will both be happier when I am living here. Everyone will be happier. I will."

"When you are living here," he said, repeating her words. "Your mind is quite made up, then, Clarissa?"

"It is," she said. "And suddenly I understand Miss Wexford's excitement over her table."

They both laughed.

They made their way back to the driveway and he stooped to pick up his things before they took their leave of each other. But they both became aware of the sound of horses' hooves and light carriage wheels on the bridge and turned to see who was coming.

It was Owen Ware, driving a smart curricle.

"Owen!" Clarissa exclaimed at the same moment as the young man was hauling back on the ribbons and drawing his horses to a halt. "What on earth are you doing here?"

Despite her words, she sounded delighted to see him. He jumped down from his perch before tossing the ribbons to the groom riding up behind him, glanced at Matthew, and gathered his mother in his arms.

"Coming to beg you to put up with my company for the summer," he said. "How are you, Mama?"

"Surprised," she said. "Delighted. Let me have a good look at you." And she cupped his face in her hands and gazed fondly at her youngest son.

"Come," he said. "I'll give you a ride up to the house. Just leaving, are you, Taylor? I see you must have been working on your archery. Trying to stay one step ahead of the rest of us mere mortals for next year's fete, I suppose. Though you would still be a few miles ahead of us if you did not practice at all, I daresay."

His words were genial, but there was a look in his eyes—a bit steely, a bit haughty—that told Matthew that he knew, and that the knowing was what had brought him home.

"I can but try," Matthew said. "And yes, I am on my way home."

"Goodbye, Matthew," Clarissa said, smiling at him.

He had only a moment in which to decide how he would address her. "Goodbye, Clarissa," he said.

He wondered, as he crossed the bridge and made his way around the village green toward the smithy, if it really was goodbye.

CHAPTER THIRTEEN

For once in her life Clarissa was not entirely pleased to see one of her children. And this was exactly what she had just been talking about. How lovely it would be to have a cottage of her own, or even rooms above a smithy, with a front door she could shut and lock against all comers if she wanted. But how dreadful of her even to think of locking her own children out of her home.

Owen chatted cheerfully about his journey during the short drive. He hugged her again after they had stepped inside the house.

"I would kill for a cup of tea, Mama," he said. "But I will run up to my room first and freshen up a bit before joining you in the drawing room. My valet should be here with all my baggage fairly soon, though it may be too late for me to change for dinner. I hope you will not mind dining informally tonight."

"Of course I will not," she told him. "I will refrain from wearing a tiara and diamonds."

He laughed. "I decided that, after all, Ravenswood held more lure for me than London," he said.

"Even before the end of the Season?" She raised her eyebrows.

"All those parties and such become remarkably tedious after a time," he said, setting an arm about her shoulders. "I'll kick about here for the summer if you can bear my company."

He smiled at her, using all his considerable charm—her tall, lean, handsome young son with his finely chiseled features and slightly overlong near-blond hair.

"What happened to your work at the home for delinquent boys?" she asked him.

"Oh, God, that!" he said, raking the fingers of one hand through his hair. "Whoever had the asinine idea that giving such boys a clean bed and new clothes, nutritious food, and a decent education would render them grateful in return and remorseful for past sins and devoted to virtue and goodness forever after was an idiot. They are, of course, little horrors. But the only remedy anyone can dream up is to concoct a long list of rules and double and triple them until the boys' old lives begin to look vastly more appealing than the new. There has to be another way."

"Go and freshen up, Owen," she told him. "I will have a pot of tea waiting for you in the drawing room."

"Make it an extra-large pot," he said before bounding off, taking the stairs two at a time just as though he were still fifteen instead of twenty-two.

Clarissa was waiting for him when he joined her ten minutes later, rubbing his hands together and still smiling cheerfully.

"I am glad to see you have had the fire lit," he said. "What a chilly day it is out there. I do not know what happened to the sun. You are looking well, Mama. I enjoyed seeing a few familiar faces close to home. Mrs. Danver and Eluned Rhys were coming out of the shop and waved to me as I drove by on the other side of the green. Cam Holland waved from the doorway of the smithy. And then there was Mr. Taylor down by the bridge, on his way home from some archery practice. Walking back from the village, were you?"

He took his cup of tea from her hand and added a biscuit to his saucer before sitting down and smiling at her even more cheerfully. "It is good to be home," he said. "I ought to have come with you and given you my company from the start. I am sorry I did not."

She gazed steadily at him after seating herself beside the fireplace. She took a sip from her cup. "I suppose there was an emergency family conference," she said. "A somewhat depleted one since Pippa and Lucas and Stephanie had already left town. I suppose you were the one chosen, as it was easier for you than for any of the others simply to hop in your curricle and give the horses their head once you had turned them in this direction."

He made a valiant attempt to look blank.

"Who wrote from here?" she asked. "Was it one person or multiple persons?"

"Wrote?" He frowned, his cup suspended halfway to his lips.

"Let me see," she said. "The writer would have been concerned. There were the beginnings of some talk, though nothing vicious, of course. And there was no suggestion of anything improper. The very idea! But perhaps Lord Stratton would wish to consider how it appeared for his mother to be at Ravenswood alone. And how it must feel to her. She must surely be missing her family and the company with which she is usually surrounded. Some possibly unsuitable people were taking advantage of her good nature and pressing their company upon her when perhaps there ought to be someone here to keep such persons mindful of the fact that she has relatives to protect both her and her reputation from such presumption. She was actually persuaded, for example, to walk in the park with Mr. Matthew Taylor and share a picnic with him at the lake. The village carpenter. Am I reasonably close, Owen?"

He had the grace to look a bit flustered. When he bit into his biscuit, a shower of crumbs landed on his coat and pantaloons. He tried to brush them off with the back of the hand that held the remains of the biscuit, but another shower followed the first.

"Idris happened to mention it in a letter to Gwyneth," he said. "He is her brother, Mama, and Devlin used to be his best friend when they were boys. Lord Hardington wrote to Uncle George too, but only to advise him to ignore any foolish gossip he heard about you. In his opinion there is no one more respectable than you."

"Hence the family conference," Clarissa said.

"It was hardly a conference, Mama," Owen said. He set aside his cup and saucer and laboriously brushed crumbs into his hand. "We all dined with Gwyneth and Dev, and the letters were mentioned. That was all. I wanted to come here. Are you not happy to see me?"

She sighed. "I am always happy to see you, Owen," she said. "Even so, I wish you had not come. You will be bored to tears. Besides, I do not need a guardian or a chaperon. I tried to tell you all before I left that I wished to be alone for a while, that I looked forward to enjoying my own company and deciding what sort of future I want for myself."

"Like marrying Lord Keilly?" he said. "You could do worse, but you could probably do better too. He is a bit of a dry old stick, is he not? Though I ought not to have said that aloud. Maybe you really do plan to marry him."

"Future plans for a woman need not always involve marriage," she said. "It was all I thought of once upon a time, admittedly. I married your father when I was seventeen. I did it freely and gladly and did not regret it. But I am going to be fifty soon, Owen. I may want—in fact, I probably will want—something different now. Like friendships with people of my own choosing. Throughout my girlhood, until I married, I had a very close friendship with Matthew Taylor. I am not sure you are aware of that. The Taylors lived right next to Grandmama and Grandpapa Greenfield. They still do."

"But things have changed since then, surely, Mama," he said. "He is a carpenter now. He lives above the smithy, for the love of God. I have the greatest respect for him. He is the best wood-carver and the best archer I have ever encountered, yet he is very modest about both. It would be hard not to like him, in fact. But . . . well, you are a Ware. Of Ravenswood. The Countess of Stratton."

"The dowager countess," she said.

"Even so," he said. "It really is presumptuous of him to take advantage of your being alone here by trying to revive an old—a very old—friendship."

"It was I who suggested that we renew it," she said.

He gazed at her, a troubled frown on his face.

His tea, she could see, was cold in the cup, and his saucer was an untidy mess of crumbs he had dumped there. She emptied the cup into the slop basin and shook the crumbs into it too before removing the cozy from the teapot and pouring him another cup. She placed a fresh biscuit on the saucer.

"In the two and a half weeks since I came home," she said, "I have spent a great deal of time alone, both indoors and out, just as I planned. I have called upon friends and neighbors and received their calls. I have attended church. I have been twice to visit your grandparents—it was Grandmama's seventieth birthday last weekend, as you perhaps recall. I have written letters. I have behaved in exemplary fashion, in fact. But of course I have added a friend to my repertoire. An old friend, now new again. We have sat up in the temple folly and strolled in the park. We have walked to the eastern boundary and climbed the hills for a better view. We have picnicked at the lake and rowed on the water. I have watched him practice shooting his arrows and marveled at his skill. We have sat in the summerhouse and drunk lemonade. And today, just before you arrived home, I took him to see the clearing on the bank of the river where I am going to persuade Devlin to allow me to build a dower house—a cottage that will be all my own while I live."

"A dower house?" He gaped at her. "When you have all of Ravenswood Hall as a home? Mama. Whatever has come over you? It seems to me I have come home just in time."

"To bring me back under control?" she said, smiling fondly and with considerable amusement at him.

"I hardly recognize you," he said.

"Good." She laughed outright. "The time I have spent alone here has borne some fruit, then."

He opened his mouth to speak again, but she held up a hand. "Drink your tea before that too turns cold," she said. "Inevitably, Owen, people have noticed that Matthew and I have spent some time together, though it has not been a great deal. He is, after all, a workingman, and I have come here deliberately to enjoy some solitude—which I have been doing. A few people have given each of us gentle warnings of possible gossip. At first I was a little alarmed, as was he. And he may yet decide that it would be unwise to consort further with me. For my part, I refuse to give up what makes me happy just because the general consensus may be that being friends with a gentleman-turned-carpenter is not quite what might be expected of a dowager countess."

"He makes you happy, Mama?" Owen asked, frowning again.

"Being with him makes me happy," she said. "I am reminded

of my girlhood, a very happy time in my life. And he played a large part in my happiness then. We played and laughed together. We talked endlessly of anything and everything that came to our minds. After thirty-three years we are discovering that all that has not changed. Everyone should be fortunate enough to enjoy such a friendship."

"You play?" he asked, sounding aghast.

She laughed again. "I did tell you we took a boat out on the lake," she said. "We also landed on the island and went exploring. Do you remember the days when we did that, Owen, and you children peopled the Dark Forest with all sorts of monsters and villains and wild beasts and went to vanquish them?"

"You explored the island?" he said.

"We did, though all we found was a mother duck and her ducklings, bobbing out toward open water," she said. She could not resist continuing. "And when we climbed the hills on the eastern edge of the park, we did not walk the whole length of the roadway over them. We found the least steep descent directly to the park and climbed and scrambled and ran down it."

"You were on foot?" he said. "And you ran down one of those slopes? I almost broke my neck the only time I tried it, and Ben threatened to tan my hide if I ever did it again. Not that he ever carried out any of those threats, but I was never willing to take the chance."

She smiled at him. If she had heard about that descent of his at the time, she would probably have had a fit of the vapors.

He heaved a great sigh and set down his almost-empty cup.

"Whatever am I going to do with you, Mama?" he said. "If this connection with Mr. Taylor blows up into a full scandal, you know, all the blame will be heaped upon me."

"I will tell you what you are going to do," she said. "Tomorrow you are going to take me in your curricle all about the perimeter of the park and even up over the hills. And you are going to name to me every flower we see. There are so many of them blooming right now, with many more to come, that I find it impossible to identify more than half of them. You used to be very good at knowing them all. If there was one even the gardeners could not name, we always consulted you."

"I daresay I made things up from time to time," he said.

"Tomorrow," she said. "Right after breakfast."

He grimaced.

Miss Wexford was euphoric. Her new dining table was in place in the dining room, larger and more imposing than the old one, weighing considerably more, steady on its many broad feet, ornately carved, and surpassing in splendor even the most extravagant of her dreams. She would not cover it with a cloth, she told Matthew and her brother. Not, at least, until all her friends and neighbors had been given the chance to admire it.

"I hope you understand, Prue," Colonel Wexford said, "that we are going to be stuck living at this house until we die, and probably Ariel after us. Every one of the male indoor servants and every one of the gardeners and grooms, not to mention my valet, has threatened to quit my service en masse if they are ever again called upon to lift that table."

"Oh, Andrew!" Miss Wexford exclaimed with glee. "My brother does like his little joke, Mr. Taylor. Take no notice of him."

She was going to plan a party to show off her new possession, she announced, and she made her own prediction that within a week of the party Matthew would have so many new commissions he would have to give up sleeping at night. The idea caused her a great deal more merriment, while Matthew wondered if he was doomed to having the Wexford table become his artistic legacy to the world.

But he was touched to have given so much pleasure and was smiling as he climbed the outside stairs to his rooms a little later. Someone hailed him from the street before he reached the top. He was unsurprised to see that it was Owen Ware, who was coming from the direction of the inn. The boy must have been watching for him—though he must get out of this habit of thinking of men in their twenties and thirties as boys. It was a symptom of his own advancing age, he supposed.

"I would like a word with you, Mr. Taylor," Owen said. "Perhaps I could buy you a pint of ale?"

"You had better come on up," Matthew said, imagining how the landlord and any patrons who happened to be taking midafternoon refreshments at the inn would strain their ears to overhear the conversation if they went there. "I'll make us both a cup of tea."

He went inside his rooms and left the door open while he started a fire in the stove and filled the kettle from a large pitcher of water in the corner. He heard the door close quietly.

"Ah, that lovely smell of wood," Owen said. "I suppose you are so used to it that you scarcely notice it any longer."

"I try not to take anything in my life for granted," Matthew said. "Have a seat at the table."

Owen sat and ran his hand over the smooth surface. "I suppose you made this yourself," he said. "It must be marvelous to have a skill like that. One thing about growing up in a wealthy, privileged home is that one ends up pretty useless by the time one reaches adulthood. Everything practical is done by someone else who is paid for doing it."

It was not exactly how Matthew had imagined this conversation beginning. He took the chair across from Owen's, since the stove and the kettle would take a while to perform their tasks.

"One can always learn what one wants or needs to learn but did not learn during boyhood," he said.

"Is that what you did?" Owen asked. "You are Reginald Taylor's brother, are you not? My grandparents' neighbor. I suppose you were a younger son."

"As are you," Matthew said. "Youngest son in your case."

"Except that in my case there is plenty of wealth to go around," Owen said. "I do not have to do a day's work in my life if I choose not to."

"Would a life of idleness satisfy your soul?" Matthew asked.

"That is an odd way of putting it," Owen said. "Satisfy my soul? I suppose you expect that as the third son I am going to be a clergyman."

"I would guess it is something you do not wish to do," Matthew said. "What do you want to do?"

"Well, there you have me," Owen said. "I am twenty-two years old and do not know what I want to do when I grow up. It is as frustrating as hell. I want to use my privilege and relative wealth to help those who have nothing, but as soon as I put the thought into words I feel the distinct urge to stick a finger down my throat and vomit. I expect to look in a mirror to see a halo hovering above my head. I do not like self-righteous piety. I do not know what I want."

"Give it time," Matthew said. "Do not try to press the issue, especially as there is no compulsion upon you to do something in order to avoid starvation. Life has a way of leading a person in the right direction if that person does not try to get in the way."

"Is that what happened to you?" Owen asked. "How did you end up here? It could not have been what you expected when you were growing up. Was it?"

The kettle was boiling and Matthew got up to make the tea. He covered the teapot with the patchwork cozy he had bought at the last fete and set it on the table to steep. He set sugar and milk beside it with a slop basin and strainer, and put the only two matched cups and saucers he owned before them.

"I always felt a compulsion to whittle wood," he said. "I thought of it as a hobby, one at which I was not very good. I never made the association with carpentry and the chance of making a living with it. That understanding came gradually while I was wandering about Europe, not thinking of anything in particular except picking up the odd job here and there and seeing what was to be seen. By the time I came back to England—oh, about the time you were being born, I suppose—I knew without any doubt what I wanted to do and how I wanted to live. I had learned the necessary skills at the hands of masters."

"So you settled here," Owen said, looking about the room while Matthew poured the tea, having ascertained that his guest took both milk and a little sugar in his tea. "You have been here for most if not all of my life. Did you never have the ambition to expand the business with employees working under you and a fortune building in some bank for your future needs?"

"No," Matthew said.

"Are you sorry now you were not a bit more ambitious when you were younger?" Owen asked as he stirred his tea.

"No," Matthew said.

Owen tapped his wet spoon against the rim of his cup and set it down in the saucer. He looked up and met Matthew's gaze directly across the table. He was looking a bit white about the mouth, Matthew thought. He was about to get to the point, it seemed.

"What is your interest in my mother?" he asked.

It was what Matthew had expected him to ask as soon as he walked through the door, but more belligerently expressed, perhaps.

"Lady Stratton was a close friend of mine years and years ago, before she married your father," he said. "Before I married. After that she moved way up on the social scale and I moved way down—deliberately so on both our parts. It is a number of years since your father passed on. It is many years since my wife died. In fact, she passed a year after we married of complications following childbirth. Our daughter died too. We have discovered in the last few weeks, your mother and I, that our friendship never fully expired but lay dormant all these years. We have enjoyed a few outings together—all on Ravenswood land—and lengthy conversations. I am not ambitious, not in my professional life and not in my personal life. And I believe your mother can be trusted always to do what is right and best for her and all who love her."

"She is talking about building a cottage on the edge of the park," Owen said. "A sort of dower house, for the love of God. She showed me the place this morning. As though Ravenswood were not large enough to house the five thousand in some comfort. And as though Dev and Gwyn and the rest of us did not love her. As though she wanted to get away from us and shut the door in our faces. It is dashed upsetting, that is what it is. What have we done to her to make her change like this? What have you done?"

"Perhaps," Matthew said, wading into waters he would probably be better advised to avoid, "you ought to try looking at the situation from your mother's point of view."

"I suppose she has told you we neglect her," Owen said. "And to our shame, we did allow her to come home alone a few weeks ago instead of insisting that she stay awhile longer and then go with Dev or Pippa or Uncle George to spend the summer. Or instead of me insisting that I come home with her. I feel hellishly guilty, I do not mind admitting, about being so selfish and staying in London only because I thought I would be bored silly here. I put my own pleasure before my mother. Whom I adore, I would have you know."

His voice was wobbling a bit. He was not far from tears, Matthew guessed as he poured him another cup of tea.

"Your mother has told me just the opposite of what you assume," Matthew said. "She has told me all her children and her brother and her friend, his wife, shower love upon her and include her in all their activities and make sure she is never alone or lonely. Has it occurred to you—though apparently she has tried to explain to you herself—that she craves some time alone in which to assess her life now that you are all grown up? Has it occurred to you that she is a person as well as your mother? Who loves you all very dearly, I might add."

He wondered if he had gone too far. He had not planned to say anything at all. He guessed that most of what Owen had said so far was unplanned too.

"I beg your pardon," Matthew said. "All this is none of my business."

"I was sent," Owen said, "or rather, I came to warn you off from taking advantage of Mama's being alone here, without any of us to protect her. I suppose . . . it is hard to think of one's own mother as a person. As someone who had a life long before one was born. And who still has a life after one has grown up."

Matthew held his peace and Owen got to his feet.

"Now I feel like an idiot," he said. "I ought to have planted you a facer as soon as I came inside. I ought to have let Dev come. Or Uncle George. Sometimes I wish Nick was already back in England. It seems as though he has been gone forever with his regiment. It has been ten years. Only ten years, you may think. But ten years to me is almost half my life. I have no backbone. That is my problem. And I like you, Mr. Taylor. You have always been my idol as an archer. Where did you learn that, by the way?"

"You have backbone." Matthew set a hand on his shoulder and squeezed. "More important, you also have a heart. I cannot promise that my renewed friendship with your mother will end, Owen. That will be up to her, and up to me too. But I will never do anything to dishonor her. That is a promise I can safely make."

He dared not think how close he had come to doing just that out at the lake a few days ago. It would not happen again.

"That will have to be good enough for everyone," Owen said rather bitterly as he made his way to the door. "Or, if they do not like it, they will have to come and confront you themselves. Thank you for the tea. Mama would consider it far too strong, but I like it this way."

And he opened the door, let himself out, and closed it behind him.

Matthew found himself thinking, of all things, about the tea he had taken for them to drink up on the hilltop. After sitting for several hours in the flask, it had been twice as strong as what he had just drunk with Owen. Yet she had said it was the best picnic she had ever had. How smoothly she lied.

He found himself chuckling when surely he ought to be feeling anything but amusement.

CHAPTER FOURTEEN

M onday morning brought a servant from Colonel Wexford's with a written invitation for Matthew. Miss Prudence Wexford requested the pleasure of his attendance at a reception and soiree to be held at the home of her brother two evenings hence.

A reception. And a soiree.

They were grand names to give a social gathering in the country. But Matthew could almost picture Miss Wexford's dilemma as she planned it. If she had decided upon a dinner, her guest list would have to be relatively small despite the impressive size of her new table. And the table itself would have to be covered, and the guests would have to practically crawl under the cloth in order to admire the artwork beneath. They would not even see the carved frieze around the edge of the tabletop or the mosaic on the surface of it. If, on the other hand, the occasion was a reception, then the table could be left bare of an enveloping tablecloth, with just small mats under the various food dishes from which the guests would be invited to help themselves.

The table would be on view in all its splendor, except perhaps the full effect of the mosaic, while the guests satisfied their appetites and remained on their feet and Miss Wexford gave a guided tour of the table's architectural features.

The word *soiree* would have been added to suggest that the gathering would continue into the evening as a more general party.

And Matthew Taylor was to be one of the guests. Perhaps, in a sense, the guest of honor. He smiled in some amusement at the thought. He almost always accepted specific invitations, no matter who the sender. He was comfortable with the company of all social classes despite his preference for solitude. He would have accepted this particular one without a qualm despite a certain embarrassment at being the maker of the table that had occasioned it. He would have looked forward with a mild sort of pleasure to seeing and conversing with his neighbors. He liked the people among whom he lived, after all.

But he would have given a great deal, he thought as he propped the invitation on top of the bookcase in his living room, to find himself with a plausible excuse for not accepting it.

Clarissa would almost certainly be there.

He, she, they were going to be the focus of attention, more even than the table. There was no doubt in his mind about that. Word had spread. It had even, quite predictably, reached her family in London. Young Owen Ware had been sent home as their ambassador to discover what was going on and to confront the village carpenter, who had dared hold his mother's hand during a walk in the park and ride off to the lake with her in a barouche to enjoy a picnic with her.

Owen's arrival would not have gone unnoticed. Nor would his visit to the rooms above the smithy the following day. And now the three of them would, almost without a doubt, be on public display at Miss Wexford's reception and soiree. It was the stuff of grand drama.

Or farce.

Matthew did not like any of it. He did not like it for himself, and he certainly did not like it for Clarissa. Not a whisper of poor taste or impropriety had ever been associated with her name.

It was all very well for them to have decided last Thursday when they were together, just before Owen drove up in his curricle, that they would defy the gossip and exercise their freedom to choose the sort of life they would live and the friends they would have. It was another thing to feel themselves getting more and more embroiled in what he did not doubt was the conversational topic of the moment in the neighborhood.

The quiet, comfortable life he had enjoyed for more than twenty years was definitely slipping away, perhaps never to be retrieved.

For there was the other thing too. Tomorrow was the day his nephew was coming to call on him, and Matthew, despite what he had said at the time, did not look forward to it one little bit. He really, really did not want to reopen that chapter of his life. Chapter? It was more like a volume. He had put it all behind him long ago, shut his mind to it, and moved on. He did not want any reminder. He had never gone back and had no intention of ever doing so. Why would he? He was perfectly happy with his life as it was.

Or as it had been until it had started to fray at the edges.

Anyway, he had agreed to this visit. It was foolish of him to be making a mountain out of what would in all probability be no more than a molehill. His nephew would surely stay for the obligatory half hour while they chatted politely over a cup of tea. Then they would shake hands and take their leave of each other. And that would be that.

Or would it?

He sighed as he went into his workroom to look over the design for the crib and make a few adjustments before he settled to work on it. Perhaps his mind could be absorbed by his work.

He was starting to have the slightly panicked feeling, though, that he might feel compelled to move away from here and start over somewhere else.

Run away.

Disappear.

Again.

Clarissa showed her invitation to Owen when he came down to breakfast at what was a respectable hour for him. But he intended visiting his grandparents, her parents, today and wanted to make an early start so he could be there in time for luncheon. She was going to go with him even though it would be the third time she had made that long journey in just a few short weeks. She doubted he would have gone without her anyway. He had been sent home to Ravenswood to guard her, after all.

The invitation was addressed to both of them.

"Oh, I say," he said after reading it. "A reception. In Boscombe? And a soiree too? All in one? I wonder what the grand occasion is."

"I believe," Clarissa said, "it is the unveiling of Prudence Wexford's new dining table. She is immensely proud of it, though Matthew Taylor once incautiously described it to me as a monstrosity—fortunately not in her hearing. He gave the making of the table his full attention, notwithstanding."

"Hmm," he said. "So . . . a reception and soiree in honor of a table? I would not miss it for worlds, Mama. Is Ariel Wexford at home? She was gone most of last winter, visiting some great-aunt or other. Actually, I remember now. It was a pair of great-aunts. She has not married in the meanwhile, has she?"

"No," Clarissa said. "She is at home and unattached, as far as I know."

"And I know Cousin Clarence is at home," he said. "I daresay Uncle Charles and Aunt Marian have been invited to this thing too. It could be a jolly affair. We will go, Mama?" Charles Ware was Caleb's younger brother. Clarence was his son, near to Owen in age and a close friend.

"Of course," she said. "Prudence Wexford is my friend. Besides, I must confess to an eagerness to see this table."

She wondered if Matthew had been invited, though he almost certainly had. She did not doubt they would draw considerable attention merely by being in the same room together. She did not know how to proceed now that Owen was home and the curiosity seekers and gossiping tongues must be waiting avidly for further developments.

She sighed as she went upstairs to get ready for the outing.

They really must talk tomorrow evening, she and Matthew. She did not want to give up their friendship. She had already decided she would not, in fact, just before Owen came home. They had both decided. She had not changed her mind. She was not going to have her behavior or choice of friends dictated to her by concerned neighbors and alarmed relatives. She was not.

But Matthew might have come to a different conclusion. This must all be very upsetting for him. She suspected that Owen had called upon him yesterday after driving her all about the park. She had not asked him where he was going and he had not volunteered the information. But she suspected it, and she wondered what had been said. Had harsh words been exchanged? Ultimatums given? Threats made?

It did not bear thinking of, so of course she had thought of little else through a night of disturbed sleep.

They must talk.

Meanwhile, she went with Owen to visit her parents, and allowed him to persuade her to go in the curricle. Actually, it did not take much persuasion, as she liked the vehicle. It was speedier than the carriage and open to the fresh air. It handled ruts and potholes in the road more smoothly. It made her feel more youthful.

Owen hugged his grandmother and wished her a belated happy birthday. He watched her unwrap his parcel containing a pair of black kid gloves, which she told him were almost too luxurious actually to wear. They all had luncheon, and Owen went off with his grandfather to see the new variety of rose that had just been added to the arbor. Clarissa remained indoors with her mother.

"Owen came home?" Mrs. Greenfield said, her eyebrows raised. "Even before the end of the Season?"

Clarissa sighed. "He was sent by the family, who are worried about me being alone at Ravenswood," she said. "I am a bit vexed with them. Poor Owen will be bored speechless within a fortnight."

"Does this have anything to do with Matthew Taylor?" her mother asked.

Clarissa huffed out a breath. "Oh," she said. "You too, Mama?"

"Marian mentioned in a recent letter that you have been spending a little time with him," Mrs. Greenfield said.

"Marian Ware?" Clarissa said, unable to keep the indignation out of her voice. "I suppose she and Charles are concerned. Caleb has been dead for six years, Mama. My brother-in-law ought to mind his own business. And my sister-in-law."

"Perhaps they consider that his brother's widow is their business," her mother said. "Or at least someone for whom they feel a sort of protective affection."

"I do not need protection," Clarissa said.

"Of course you do not." Her mother reached a hand across the space between them and patted her arm. "You are a strong woman, Clarissa, and always have been. You have always done what is right. Your father and I trusted you as a girl. We trusted you during your marriage, though it was difficult at times not to step in to try to protect the interests of the daughter we loved. We trust you now. I was always fond of Matthew when he was a lad, though he was also a scamp—except when he was with you. Or with us. I always thought he would have thrived if everyone who had the care of him had relaxed and treated him as a person with unique needs. But then, who am I to criticize? I never had a problem child."

"We have become friends again," Clarissa said. "We have spent a few afternoons together, walking and picnicking, always within the park, just as we always stayed in the park here. The gossips are wagging their tongues over the story, of course. When we were growing up, we were essentially equals, both of us the children of gentlemen. Now I am the Dowager Countess of Stratton while he is the village carpenter. It ought not to make a difference and does not to me. I intend to continue our friendship, Mama, no matter what my children say, or my neighbors. Provided he does not put an end to it, that is. I think perhaps the gossip is more distressing for him than it is for me."

"Then you must both decide what you want and what you choose to do about it," Mrs. Greenfield said. "The time was not right for either of you when you were on the brink of adulthood. Your father and I were actually relieved—as well as flattered and honored, of course—when Caleb, or rather his mother, came court-ing. We saw what was beginning to happen between you and Mat-thew. And it was not just—or even mainly—the slight difference in your stations that alarmed us, Clarissa. It was the very real pos-sibility that both of you would end up wretchedly unhappy. Forgive us for urging upon you what turned out to be less than ideal."

"You did not urge me, Mama," Clarissa said. "You allowed me to decide for myself."

"At the age of seventeen?" her mother said. "I have suffered many pangs of guilt over that. We ought to have sent Caleb on his way without a word to you."

"It was not an entirely unhappy marriage," Clarissa said. "There was much happiness too. He was never unkind to me except per-haps on that one memorable occasion. And I had my children. And Ravenswood. And you not too far away. And now I have my old friend back and intend to keep him if it is what he wants too."

"You must do what will make you happy," her mother said. "It is time, Clarissa, just as it was time for George last year, to look to your future and what will bring you the greatest sense of fulfill-ment. You owe nothing to anyone. I know your love is already freely given to your children and grandchildren—and to us. Now you must love yourself."

Clarissa blinked several times in an effort to prevent tears from forming in her eyes. Just a few minutes ago she had been bracing for a lecture from her mother. She might have known better. *Now you must love yourself.* Why was no one ever taught to do that? Why was it looked upon almost as a vice? Was the absence of self-love the cause of that void she felt at the core of herself?

"It is why I came home early and alone from London," she said. "I wanted to sort out my life now that Caleb is gone and Gwyneth has married Devlin and taken over my duties so competently and the children are all grown and Stephanie has been launched upon society. You are right, Mama. I no longer owe anything to anybody, except my continued love. It is a freeing thought, but also a potentially lonely one. I need to move consciously into a new phase of my life. Perhaps it will include Matthew, though I do not know in what capacity. But of course everyone has become alarmed. Everyone wants me to remain as I am, or as I was."

"I am not alarmed," Mrs. Greenfield said. "Nor is your papa. Quite the contrary, in fact. We want you to live your life to the fullest, Clarissa. It is all we have ever wanted for you."

Clarissa could no longer control her tears. Two of them spilled over and trickled down her cheeks while she fumbled for a handkerchief, and her mother first patted and then squeezed her arm before drawing her daughter into her arms and murmuring soothing words to her while she continued to weep.

"Come up to my room," Mrs. Greenfield said at last. "You must dash some cold water on your face and comb your hair. It will be time for you to return home soon. And in a curricle, no less. It must have been enormous fun to travel so far in such a flimsy vehicle."

"It was," Clarissa said before hiccuping and then laughing as she followed her mother upstairs.

"If only I were twenty years younger," her mother said.

An hour later Clarissa and Owen were on their way back home. Tomorrow, she remembered, was the day Matthew was expecting a visit from his nephew.

Poor Matthew. She knew he would be dreading it. The quiet life

that seemed to suit him so well had been badly disturbed lately—
and she was largely to blame.

If she did speak to him at that reception, she must keep her
remarks brief. But it seemed such an age since they had been alone
together—last Thursday afternoon. And that might very well be
the last time.

No matter. She would forge ahead anyway with the plans for
her future that were beginning to unfold in her mind. They did not
depend upon the decision of one man. She must never allow that to
happen. She was a free and strong woman.

Matthew had thought about his family as little as he possibly
could during the more than thirty years since he had left
home. Yet when his mind did drift toward his brother and his
nephews, as it inevitably did from time to time, he thought of the
latter as young children. As for his niece, she had not even been
born when he left England.

Philip Taylor, the elder of his nephews, was, of course, thirty-
five or thirty-six years old now, and Anthony, his brother, one year
younger. Matthew had worked it all out before Philip arrived, but
it was still a bit of a shock to actually see him, a neatly dressed
gentleman who bore a distinct resemblance to Reginald—but older
than Reginald had been when Matthew last saw him.

Philip had brought Emily, his wife, with him. She was a pretty,
plumpish woman, probably a few years younger than he. They apparently had two young children of their own. That made him a
great-uncle, Matthew thought.

He heard them, right on time, coming up the stairs beside the smithy but waited until they knocked before opening the door. He shook hands with them—two strangers—and invited them in.

"I am your nephew," Philip said. "Thank you for agreeing to see me, sir. I have taken the liberty of bringing my wife with me. Emily."

"What a cozy place you have here, Uncle Matthew," she said. "May I call you that? I can smell wood. It is a lovely smell. Do you work here too?"

"I do," Matthew said while his nephew stood beside her, looking both awkward and tongue-tied. "I can show you my workroom, if you wish, while the kettle is boiling."

"I would love to see it," she said.

He showed them his workbench and his tools and a half-finished rocking chair he was making for the elderly mother-in-law of a farmer who would need it by the end of next month, when she would be coming to live permanently with him and his wife. He showed them the shelves with his wood carvings, and they spent some time admiring them.

"My father says you were forever whittling pieces of wood when you were a boy and making a mess to arouse Grandmama and Grandpapa's wrath," Philip said. "He says you did not show much talent in those days."

"I did not," Matthew admitted.

"Oh, Phil," Emily cried as her attention focused upon one particular carving. "Look at this. Have you ever seen anything more exquisite?"

It was a carving of two spindly-legged lambs pressed to the side of their woolly mother. Matthew had carved it after watching the lambs being born at David and Doris Cox's farm not far from the village in the springtime two years ago. It was one of his favorite pieces, though everything he carved and kept was his favorite piece when he made it. He would not allow himself to keep anything he did not believe at the time to be at least equal to the best thing he had ever done.

"Oh, and I know just how she feels, that sheep," Emily said. "Look at the smile on her face, Phil."

"She looks just like a sheep to me, Em," Philip said. "She would look a bit silly if she were smiling."

"But the smile is all inside her," she said. "It fills her up. And look at her wool. I feel as though I could sink my fingers in it and feel her warmth. How did you do that, Uncle Matthew? Oh, I do wish our children did not have to grow up. I want to keep them close to me, just like those lambs, for all the rest of my life. And do not say, Phil, that they and I would look a bit silly when they are fifty and I am over seventy."

Philip laughed, but with obvious affection for his wife. "At least I will be able to tell my father that you show a bit more talent now than you did as a boy, sir," he said.

"A bit more?" Emily said.

"Perhaps you would like him to decide for himself, Emily," Matthew said, reaching up to the shelf to lift the carving down and set it on the bench. "Perhaps you will accept this as a gift."

She gasped and clasped her hands to her bosom. "Oh," she said. "Really?" And she took Matthew completely by surprise by flinging her arms about his neck and hugging him. "Thank you, Uncle Matthew. I do not know what to say."

Matthew met his nephew's eyes over the top of her head. Philip was looking embarrassed. He was not smiling. Even so, it was an extraordinary moment. It brought what felt like a knot to

Matthew's stomach. Of something . . . lost. Something missing. He imagined for a moment that she was Helena, his daughter, hugging him like this, overwhelmed with gratitude for some small favor he had done her.

"That is incredibly generous of you," Philip said. "We will treasure it. Thank you, sir."

We, he had said. Not just *she*.

"The kettle will be boiling dry if I do not make the tea soon," Matthew said, leading the way back to his living quarters.

Emily set her carving carefully down on the table and stood gazing at it while Matthew made the tea and covered the pot with a cozy before slicing the fruitcake he had baked himself. Not all the fruit had sunk to the bottom, as it often did, he noted with satisfaction. And there was not that telltale layer of darker-colored cake at the bottom to signify that he had underbaked the cake and left raw dough there. In fact, it looked near perfect, and he could only hope it tasted as good. It had even risen.

Philip explained during tea that he had long wanted to call upon his uncle, the only surviving relative on his side of the family apart from his mother and father, and his children, of course. He had especially wished it after marrying Emily, who had seven brothers and sisters and so many aunts, uncles, cousins, nieces, and nephews that he was not sure anyone had ever made an accurate count.

"And if anyone ever has," he said, "someone new is sure to come along the very next day to be added to the number."

"Oh, Phil," Emily said, laughing. "We have always been a close family. And we can certainly count. This is a very nice cake, Uncle Matthew. You have even learned to cook, something I have never had to do, to my shame."

"It was either learn or starve," Matthew said. "Really, it was an easy choice to make."

"I never knew quite what caused the rift between you and the rest of our family," Philip said. "Your wife, my aunt, died after giving birth to a stillborn baby, I learned when I was growing up. Everyone tried to comfort you—my grandparents, my mother and father, my great-grandmother—but you went away without a word to anyone and did not come back until many years later. Then you came to live here and work here when you might have lived comfortably in the house Great-Grandmama left you. The farm there is prosperous enough. You might have lived right beside us. But you did not even come to see us, and nobody came here to see you. I have never understood it."

Emily reached across the table to pat the back of his hand. "Papa-in-Law has always said that if you wanted to come home at any time, Uncle Matthew, you would do it," she said. "He says that your not coming means you want nothing to do with any of us and is a decision we must respect. He says he never fully understood you and does not now—because you do not choose to be understood. He did not want us to come bothering you when Phil asked him a couple of weeks or so ago if we might. But he did not forbid it. Not that he could, of course, since Phil is a grown man. But he said if we wanted to try, then we must do so, though we must be ready to find that you would not welcome us very warmly."

Matthew sat very still, taking in all her words. Then he sighed. "I was never happy as a boy," Matthew said. "I did not fit in. I do not put all the blame on my parents or upon your father, Philip. They tried their best, I believe. It was just that their best was not what I wanted or needed. Eventually, after my wife and daughter died and the comfort my family offered me was to tell me that it was better that way and God's will had been done, I had to leave. I stayed away for longer than ten years, learning wood carving and carpentry as well as some things about myself and what I wanted of the rest of my life. When I returned, I decided it was best not to renew any ties with my family. And when they did not reach out to me, it seemed they felt the same way, and I was relieved. I never did understand why my grandmother changed her will to leave her property to me instead of to your father as she had always intended. It must have come as a severe shock to him and to my parents, your grandparents."

"Well, no." Philip laughed as he stirred sugar into his second cup of tea. "It could be no shock, could it, since Papa was the one who had suggested it."

Matthew stared blankly at him. "Suggested what?" he asked.

"I was just an infant at the time," Philip said. "I have no memory of any of those events. But apparently Papa suffered terribly after you left. He felt he ought to have done more, made more of an effort to understand you and be your brother. According to Mama, he once said that you had always had three parents while you were growing up, and that was one too many. What you had lacked, he said, was a brother. That was what he ought always to have insisted upon being. I think it very possible that he has felt guilty ever since. I think maybe he has always waited for you to come home."

"But *what* did he suggest?" Matthew asked, staring intently at his nephew. "Why was it no shock to him to discover that our grandmother had changed her will?"

It was Philip's turn to stare blankly at him. "Well, because it was Papa who asked her to do it," he said. "Begged her, actually, since I believe she was a bit annoyed at your going away without a word when she had given you and your wife a home after you married. Papa had always felt a bit bad that he would inherit Great-Grandmama's property as well as everything of ours while you would have nothing. After you left, he did something about it. He talked Great-Grandmama into changing her will and leaving everything to you."

"Did you not know, Uncle Matthew?" Emily asked as Matthew scraped his chair over the bare floor with the backs of his knees and got to his feet.

"I did not," he said. "No, I did not."

He closed his eyes briefly and let this new, all-consuming knowledge seep into his being.

"I did not know," he said again as Emily came around the table and hugged him again.

CHAPTER FIFTEEN

When Clarissa and Owen arrived at Colonel Wexford's the following evening, the house was already humming with the sounds of conversation and laughter. They were welcomed by the colonel and Ariel, his daughter, and by a flushed and clearly excited Prudence.

"Are we last to arrive?" Clarissa asked after smiling at Ariel, kissing her friend on the cheek, and shaking hands with the colonel. "I hope we have not kept you waiting."

"You have not, Lady Stratton," Colonel Wexford assured her. "Everyone else was early. Owen, my boy. Good to see you. Ariel was pleased to hear you had come home to keep your mama company."

"I was pleased to know there would be someone close to my age here tonight," Ariel said. "But there is no reason to look archly at me in that way, Aunt Prudence. Owen and I are old friends, and that is all we are or will ever be—by mutual consent. Come into the dining room, Owen. That is where everyone else is, including your cousin Clarence."

She linked an arm through his and bore him off.

"Ariel says the most startling things—in the presence of a young gentleman," Miss Wexford said. "Young ladies are not what they were in my day, Lady Stratton. I do not know what our world is coming to. But there—she is a dear girl despite everything. Come into the dining room."

The colonel offered his arm.

It was the first evening entertainment Clarissa had attended since coming home from London. There, all was glamour and glitter and the largest crowd that could be squeezed into the space, as every hostess tried to outdo every other. Here, all the guests had gathered in the dining room, and there was room for all of them even though the new table more than half filled the space. They were all neighbors and friends, and Clarissa felt instantly comfortable despite the slight apprehension she had felt all day about almost surely meeting Matthew here and knowing that everyone would be watching curiously to see how they would behave toward each other.

He was here already, she saw instantly, in a group with the Coxes and the Reverend Danver, a glass in his hand, a look of polite amiability on his face. He had not seen her arrive, or, if he had, he had looked away before she looked at him. She hoped they would not be doing that throughout the evening. Self-consciousness was not something from which she suffered often or willingly.

And self-conscious with Matthew? It seemed like a contradiction in terms.

Almost everyone was buzzing with enthusiasm and exclaiming over the table, which was by way of being the guest of honor. The thought amused Clarissa as she slipped her hand free of the colonel's arm.

"It is quite . . . imposing," she said to Miss Wexford. "I hope you are as pleased with it as you hoped to be."

"Oh, more so," Miss Wexford said. "How fortunate we are, Lady Stratton, to have Mr. Taylor living in our midst. Such talent! He could work in London and still be noticed and acclaimed. Do come and have a closer look."

Prudence had wanted a table that was very special. But the trouble with tables, Clarissa thought as she looked closely at this one, was that they had to be flat on top with four legs, one at each corner, with perhaps another pair in the middle if the table was long. There would appear to be not much a carpenter could do to make the piece unique and memorable. Matthew had done both, though Clarissa could see at a glance why he considered the table a bit of a monstrosity.

There were actually eighteen legs in clusters of three, all of them designed to look like Grecian columns, but each of the three a different style from the other two—Doric, Ionic, and Corinthian, if she remembered her ancient Greek history correctly. They were intended, she realized, to make the table look like a Grecian temple— with a flat roof. Right at the center underneath, as though to hold up the table, was a circle of slender ladies in flowing Grecian robes with laurel wreaths upon their heads, each bearing a delicate urn upon her shoulder. The three graces? No, there were too many of them. The nine muses? There were not enough. The Delphic oracles? But they were not plural, were they? There was one at a time— the Delphic oracle. The oracle with her handmaids, then? But did they have to be any group in particular?

The tabletop was undeniably beautiful, with its overlapping diamond mosaics created out of inlaid wood. Were not such mosaics associated more with ancient Rome than with Greece, though?

Perhaps not. A narrow frieze of columns to match the table legs had been carved in exquisite detail all about the edge of the tabletop.

The whole thing, Clarissa thought, was a bit of a confused mess, the product of Prudence's imagination, based very loosely upon what she had read of ancient history. Yet it had an undeniable sort of charm. Her friend was clearly ecstatic over it, and that was what mattered. Fortunately most, if not all, of their neighbors appeared to agree with her. Clarissa moved back so others could see more clearly. She glanced across the room and locked eyes with Matthew for a few moments. She allowed her amusement to show and raised in a silent toast the glass Colonel Wexford had placed in her hand.

His eyes did not twinkle back at her as she had expected. He did not raise his glass, which looked as full as it had when she entered the room. He had an expression on his face that she could not interpret, though it was vaguely familiar. Memory came flooding in as he turned his head to speak with Marian Ware, who had just touched his arm. He looked as he often had when he came as a boy to seek her out. He seemed troubled, though there was no outer sign that would betray him to anyone else. He was half smiling now at Marian and at Thomas Rutledge, Lord Hardington's eldest son, and Thomas's wife. He looked perfectly composed.

Something told Clarissa he was not.

Was it the strain of being the focus of attention as the crafter of the table? But she might have expected the occasion to amuse him more than it would embarrass him. Was it being in a room with her, then, surrounded by a large number of their neighbors, most of whom would be watching them surreptitiously but closely enough not to miss a thing?

Or was it something else?

The table was set with plates and dishes of sumptuous-looking dainties, both savory and sweet. Hot savories filled the warming dishes on a sideboard. Clarissa filled the plate Ariel Wexford placed in her hand, set her empty glass on a side table with others, and began to circulate in the room, intent upon having a word with everyone. It was something that came as second nature to her. She did not detect any great difference from usual in the way she was treated.

It was tempting to keep her distance from Matthew. But she did not want to be constantly dithering, and she did not want to be forever shaping her behavior to what other people expected of her—as she had done all her life until very recently. She had decided on the last day they had spent time together, just before Owen arrived home, that from now on she was going to live the life she wanted to live and cultivate the friendships she chose, regardless of general expectations. She had come home from her parents' house yesterday encouraged that they supported her wholeheartedly. If Matthew had decided differently—was that why he looked as he did this evening?—then she would accept his decision.

Some of the guests were wandering into the drawing room. Clarissa went there too with Eluned Rhys and Mrs. Holland and looked around. Owen was over by the window in the midst of an animated group that included Clarence, Ariel, and Edwina and James Rutledge, younger son and daughter of the Hardingtons. Marian and Charles Ware were seated to one side of the hearth, in conversation with Lady Hardington.

"Shall we join them?" Eluned said.

But Clarissa could see that Matthew was coming into the room, his hands empty, alone for the moment. He looked about at those gathered there with his usual quiet, amiable expression, and it was probable no one but Clarissa realized that tonight for some reason he was out of sorts. She stayed where she was, not far inside the door, as Eluned and Mrs. Holland made their way over to join Charles's group.

She turned and smiled at Matthew, leaving him room to nod pleasantly and join one of the groups if he wished. He hesitated, but then he came toward her.

"Clarissa," he said, and immediately she felt a change in the atmosphere around them. It was nothing dramatic. Conversations continued, apparently without interruption, and no one turned to look specifically at the two of them as they moved away from the door and went to stand beside the grand pianoforte in the corner beside the window. But Clarissa did not believe she was imagining the sharpening of interest from those around them.

"You were right," she said. "The table is a bit of a monstrosity, though the skill with which it has been carved makes one largely unaware of the fact. It might also be called magnificent without either irony or bias. Besides, you have made Prudence very happy indeed. I have never seen her so . . . ebullient."

"Any self-respecting ancient Greek would have an apoplexy at the mere sight of it," he said, and they both laughed. Heads turned their way with unabashed curiosity.

"I am so glad to see you this evening," she said. "It has been almost a week since I watched your last archery practice and showed you where I hope to have a dower house built. Owen arrived, and we were unable to take a proper leave of each other and arrange another meeting. Assuming you wished for another, that is. Have you practiced archery since?"

"No," he said.

"I am sorry about that," she said. "Tomorrow is Thursday again.

Will you practice and then come to the house to take tea with me? If the weather is warm enough, I will have it brought out to the rose arbor in the courtyard. The roses are beginning to bloom, and the scent of them is heavenly."

He frowned, and it seemed to Clarissa that he was not paying full attention to what she was saying. Was he finding it so difficult to say no?

"I will not come to the poplar alley to distract you," she said. "And I cannot promise that Owen will not join us for tea. But I refuse not to invite you for that reason. Matthew, what is it?"

"Mmm?" he asked. "What is what? I am sorry, Clarissa. It is noisy in here."

There was a hum of conversation. It was no noisier than usual for such social gatherings, however. Besides, they were standing a little apart from any other group. Clarissa waited until he closed his eyes briefly, inhaled audibly, and then looked fully at her for the first time.

"It was all Reginald's doing," he said without any clarifying explanation.

"Ah," she said. "His son was to call upon you yesterday, was he not? You mean it was your brother who sent him to see you? Or . . . stopped him from coming?"

"He came," he said. "Philip, that is. His wife came with him. Emily. No, I was talking about thirty years ago, after I had left home and gone off to Europe. My grandmother's will, leaving everything to me instead of to Reginald as she had always intended and my father and brother had always expected. It was not her idea to change it. She must have been openly hostile to doing so, in fact. Reginald not only had to ask her to change it, he pleaded with her. More than half my life has been built upon a lie I told myself—that none of them cared, that none of them truly loved me. Reggie gave up his most prized and enduring dream for my sake."

"Oh, Matthew." She squeezed his hand, remembered where they were, and released it again.

"How am I ever going to forgive myself?" he asked, gazing at her with intent, troubled eyes and looking very like the boy she remembered.

Unfortunately this was neither the time nor the place to continue this conversation.

"I will expect you for tea tomorrow," she said. "Practice first and then come. We will talk."

She smiled at him before turning away to join Alan Roberts, the schoolteacher, and his wife, Sally, Cameron Holland's sister. When she looked a minute or so later, Matthew was part of a group with Colonel Wexford and the Reverend Danver and was looking, outwardly at least, his usual placid, cheerful self.

M atthew had intended to make a start on the crib for Ben Ellis's baby the following day, but he found he could not concentrate or make up his mind about a few details of the design. Should he carve the elephant in relief on the footboard, large and complete and smiling and jolly? Or should he have it peeping over the top of the footboard? But from the inside the child would see only the ears, the eyes, and the trunk. It might look funny, but it was possible the peering eyes might disturb the child's sleep.

Stupidly, he was paralyzed by indecision. Yet he had to decide that one detail before he could feel ready to start on any part of the project.

He spent most of the morning dithering and allowing his mind

to wander in a dozen different directions. He went early to the poplar alley in the afternoon. He felt in desperate need of the archery
practice to restore focus to his mind and peace to his being. He shot
twenty rounds of arrows. A disturbing number came nowhere close
to the bull's-eye. A frustrating number came close but not close
enough. At least one arrow in each round did not even make the
target.

He ought to have given up, he decided wearily, when, after ten
or fifteen minutes, he had failed to get himself to that place or
nonplace of no-thought he needed to be before he shot his arrows.
His mind steadfastly refused to get out of his way. The smiling elephant of his earlier imagination had turned into a leering gargoyle.

After the twentieth round, he picked up one of his arrows from
the ground where it had landed and snapped it in two. He had even
been counting rounds, he realized, something he never did because
counting was an activity of the conscious mind.

He was in no state to take tea in the courtyard of Ravenswood
Hall, in a rose arbor of all places. He would be better off at home
with his door shut and locked, drinking his overstrong tea and eating a slice of the fruitcake left over from Philip and Emily's visit.
Except that he was not hungry. Or thirsty. More reasons he ought
to go home anyway instead of up to the house.

She was his only hope.

It was a thought, an instinct, that came from deep within, from
a past so long ago that it might have been from another lifetime
altogether. When life had overwhelmed him and there had seemed
to be nowhere to turn and no one to go to, he had always stumbled
off to find Clarissa Greenfield, to pour out everything that was
threatening to blow him apart into a million pieces. It had always
worked. It had never failed.

But that was then. This was now.

He had learned long ago the secret of tranquil living. Of contented living. He had learned that he did not need to rely upon any other person for his peace. Everything he needed was within himself. Friendships could enrich his life, but the substance came from inside. He had learned to like himself, even to love himself in a non-narcissistic way that had nothing to do with vanity. He had certainly learned to love his life.

And in so doing he had spurned the incredibly selfless love of his own brother.

Reggie.

He did not want to go back to using Clarissa as a crutch.

He did not want to be the boy he had been when he did just that. He was a fifty-year-old man now. He had thought his life all sorted out. He had liked his life—of which he was already thinking in the past tense, he realized. He had thought himself capable of dealing with any unwelcome change or crisis that might come his way—poor health, loss of business, anything. Yet along had come change in the form of a pleasant young man and woman, his nephew and niece-in-law, and he had crumbled almost before their very eyes.

He had held himself together in the days since by sheer effort of will. After last evening's reception and soiree, his face had literally ached from the half smile he had kept upon it.

Clarissa had known anyway.

He gathered up his equipment, even the broken arrow, which he stuffed inside the quiver, and made his way toward the drive. Until he reached it he was not sure which way he would turn. He was so very tempted to turn toward the village and home. He turned instead toward Ravenswood. He owed Clarissa an explanation at least. He certainly did not owe her the humiliation she might feel if her expected guest simply did not show up. She might even be the laughingstock among her servants. It did not bear thinking of.

The door into one of the arched tunnels on either side of the front steps that led into the courtyard was open. Matthew could see daylight through it, a sign that the door at the far end of the tunnel was open too. He left his quiver and bow beside the steps and walked through.

The courtyard was bright with midafternoon sunshine. Strange—it was only now he was noticing that it was a sunny day. Warm too. The covered cloisters that ran all about the outer perimeter were in shade, but the grass in the large square open to the sky was almost emerald green, and the rose arbor at the center was bright with color and the steady spray of rainbow-hued water shooting up from the fountain there.

He had only ever seen the courtyard before now during fete days, when display tables for various crafts were set up against the cloisters and the place teemed with people. He stopped for a moment to feel the full beauty and serenity of the place.

The most beautiful part of it was walking toward him from the arbor, her hands outstretched for his.

"Matthew," she said. "I am so glad you came."

"How could I not when you had invited me?" he asked, taking both her hands in his and squeezing them tightly. "This is a beautiful place."

"Yes, it is," she said. "I love walking in the cloisters in the winter when it is not too cold or blustery. And I love to sit here during the summer. The four wings of the house keep the scent of the roses inside. And I never tire of gazing at the fountain. There are so many colors within water. Yet it seems colorless in itself."

She had linked a hand through his arm and was leading him toward the arbor, where she sat beside him on a wrought iron seat.

"I did invite Owen to join us, at least for a while," she said. "But he has gone riding with Ariel Wexford and Edwina Rutledge and his cousin Clarence. I believe I have convinced him that I do not need a jailer every hour of every day, or even a chaperon. Now I need to persuade him that he will lose his sanity if he decides to spend the whole of the summer here with just his mother for company."

She made light conversation while a footman and a maid brought out trays of dainties and tea and lemonade. His arrival had been watched for and noted, then, despite the fact that he had not knocked upon the front door.

"Thank you," she said after everything had been set down upon a table before her, and the servants withdrew silently. "Will you have tea or lemonade?"

"Lemonade, please," he said.

She poured them both a glass and put one of everything upon a plate before handing it to him. He wondered if he could find enough appetite to eat at least something. He sipped his lemonade. It was delicious and almost icy cold. How did they do that in what must be a hot kitchen?

"Did you have a good practice?" she asked him.

"Yes, thank you," he said.

She had a way of looking at him, a way that demanded truth and was fully aware when it had not been spoken.

"No," he said. "No, I did not. The bull's-eye was elusive today and my timing was off. Perhaps I did not place the target in quite the right place. Or perhaps I am just tired."

"Or perhaps you cannot forget your nephew's visit," she said.

He bit into a jam tart, which was as light as air and had obviously been made with fresh preserves. He swallowed the mouthful before he answered.

"I ought not to have burdened you with that revelation," he said. "It was not important."

"I will certainly respect your right not to talk about it," she said. "But I will not allow you to get away with telling me it was unimportant, Matthew. Our friendship was always based upon truth telling."

He looked at the other half of his tart but put it back on his plate rather than into his mouth. He took another sip of his lemonade.

"Since Tuesday I have been feeling like the boy I was when we were friends," he said. "And somehow last evening I found myself reverting to that time and blurting out to you the depths of my guilt and misery. I ought not to have done so. It was grossly unfair to you. And it was not . . . who I am now. I am not that boy any longer. I have managed my own life and affairs and problems quite successfully for more than thirty years. I will continue to do so. I am sorry about last night. Truly sorry."

"Matthew," she said softly. "Tell me about Poppy."

He was certainly not expecting that. She had known Poppy, of course. Everyone had. She had been the daughter of a ne'er-do-well drunkard of a small landowner and his slattern of a wife, who had given up early the struggle to keep a tidy home and raise a decent family. Poppy, pretty and spirited and sharp-tongued, had worked at a tavern and had inevitably acquired a reputation for being unchaste. Whether the reputation was justified or not had been questionable.

"You will have heard all the rumors," he said. "She was increasing with . . . Helena when I married her. I had lain with her and took the consequences. She was not a bad person. She was human. She was my wife."

He thought of picking up his glass and sipping his lemonade again during the silence that followed. But he was not sure his hand would remain steady.

"Did you . . . lie with her while you and I were still friends?" she asked.

"No," he said sharply. "No. I did not."

"Was it because I was going to marry Caleb?" she asked.

He set his elbows on his knees, bowed his head, and pressed his two bent forefingers against his eyes.

"I will not answer that," he said. "I lay with her, I married her, and I cared for her. She died, and I buried her with our daughter. That is all."

Except for a terrible ache about his heart. Poppy might have lived all these years if he had not lain with her. And he had not done so out of love or even any real desire. He had done so in an effort to forget another pain, another woman. He had cared for her and he would have continued to do so. But he knew he would never have loved her, not in the way a woman has a right to be loved by her husband.

And if he had not lain with her, of course, and she had already been with child by another man, she might have lived the last months of her life with a reputation shattered beyond repair.

"She seemed happy enough. She had a good home, where she was safe and well fed and cared for. My grandmother, though appalled with me, treated her with surprising kindness. Poppy, impertinent though she often was with everyone else, behaved toward my grandmother with a sort of awed respect."

He realized he had spoken aloud.

"And you would have continued to care for her if she had lived," Clarissa said. "You would have seen it as your duty. And through her you would have found your way through, Matthew, to the person you could be. Not quite as you found it when you went away after her death. In a different way. But you would have done it. You would not have neglected or abandoned her. Or mistreated her."

"Even given the person I was then?" he asked.

"Yes," she said. "Even given that."

He was amazed by her words. He would have assumed she had despised him for marrying Poppy, that she might have seen it as some sort of revenge against his father or perhaps against her for so abruptly marrying the Earl of Stratton. But no. Somehow, despite the odds, Clarissa had always believed in him. She believed he would have stepped up to take responsibility for what he had done so impulsively out of the depths of his misery. Was she right? He would never know.

"But she died," he said.

"Yes."

He picked up the other half of the jam tart again and looked at it before returning it to his plate. He could not finish it or eat anything else.

"I am sorry," he said, getting to his feet. "I am not hungry. I hope I will not offend your cook."

"Don't go home yet," she said. "You are feeling too miserable. Take a walk with me. In silence if you wish. You have reminded me lately that we were always as good at that as we were at talking. And every relationship should consist of both."

"I will not be good company," he said before smiling despite himself. "But I rarely was, was I?"

"You were company I always liked," she said, setting her glass upon the tray and standing up. "I still do. I will walk with you as far as the bridge at least."

"Very well," he said.

CHAPTER SIXTEEN

Matthew shouldered his quiver and bow and picked up the target. She walked beside him along the terrace and onto the drive to the bridge and the village beyond.

"I hope to make a start on the crib next week," he said.

"That will be lovely," she said.

"I am just stuck upon where the elephant should go," he said. "Nowhere seems right, but it must be included. It is central to my whole vision."

"Oh, indeed," she said. "Peering around the corner of one of the footboards, perhaps?"

He stopped abruptly. The meadows on either side of them were a riot of wildflowers, whose heavy scent hung on the air with a promise of summer. Sheep were grazing placidly among them. One ambled closer to the drive and stood looking at the two humans before baaing softly and turning away.

"That is brilliant," he said. "It is one place I had not thought of."

"Sometimes I really am brilliant," she said, and they both laughed.

Inside, of course, neither of them was laughing at all. She had always known she had hurt him by marrying Caleb and thus putting an abrupt end to their friendship. She had known he was in love with her—as she had been more than halfway in love with him. And let no one tell her it had not been true love just because they were so young. He had reacted in a manner rather typical of him at the time. He had rashly and impulsively taken up with the somewhat notorious Poppy Lang and then married her when he had acknowledged that the child she was carrying might well be his.

And the thing was, as Clarissa had told him back in the rose arbor, he would have stuck by Poppy for a lifetime and cared for her and supported her. He would have adored the child and sheltered her from all harm. They would have been the making of him, taking him by sure degrees from rebellious boyhood to responsible adulthood. But they had died. The child—Helena—had not even drawn breath.

Clarissa had always known that those deaths would have been painful for him. She had just not realized until today how painful.

Did one ever recover from the loss of one's child? She had been enormously fortunate in having given birth to five living and healthy babies without any miscarriages or stillbirths. Her children had all survived the perils of childhood. Nicholas and Devlin, as well as Ben, had survived the Napoleonic wars.

How could she possibly understand what it must have been like . . .

"Will you leave your things beside the driveway again and come into my parlor?" she asked him, keeping her tone light. "We will shut the door and be cozy and private together. I am not ready to let you go home yet. Tell me you are not ready either."

He turned to smile at her. "Your cottage is built already?" he asked.

"Except for the tiles on the roof and the chimney," she said. "Or perhaps thatch. I have not decided yet. And except for the windows and floors. Oh, and the walls. And there is no furniture."

"No front door?" he asked.

"Alas," she said. "No doors at all. Come anyway."

"An abundance of imagination was not something either of us ever lacked, was it?" he said as he set down his things where he had put them last time.

They joined hands and walked along the bank of the river until they came to the clearing where she already lived in her imagination. She came here every day, sometimes merely to assure herself that yes, it was perfect, and sometimes to visualize how it would all look, cottage and garden. Alas, she was no architect. No landscaper either. She would recognize the perfection of it all when she saw it, but at present she had only a vague image in her mind, or perhaps more in her heart. An image of home. Her very own.

"A green door, do you think?" she asked. "Or red?"

"You will be surrounded by greenery," he said. "Red would look cheerful."

"Then red it will be," she said. "Have a seat. Take that comfortable sofa."

"The one with all the cushions?" he said. "Come and sit beside me, then. It is too big for just one person."

They sat together on the rough grass, their arms about their updrawn knees as they gazed across the river to the village beyond it and slightly to their right. They could see the main road too from here. It was never very busy, though. One westbound stagecoach passed each day, and one that was eastward bound. Neither came into Boscombe, though both would stop and let off any passenger who was going there. Mostly, though, the view from here was of serene countryside.

"What will you do," Matthew asked, "if Stratton refuses his permission for you to build here?"

"He will not," she said. "He will bluster and complain and wonder what he has done so very wrong that I would choose to leave Ravenswood in favor of a lonely cottage here. But he will not say no."

"You know your son so well, then?" he asked.

"Yes," she said. "It was a close-run thing for a number of years after I sent him away. He did not write—to any of us. Not even after Caleb died. He stayed away for another two years after that happened before coming home, cold in manner and with a heart he had hardened against all finer sentiments. I fear I must have given the same impression to him. Meeting each other again was the most excruciatingly difficult thing I believe I have ever done. Our relationship was strained, to say the least, for a while after his return. I believe it was Gwyneth who thawed his heart. She refused to give up on him. And then he and I had a heart-to-heart talk and we were finally free to love each other openly again. He will find it hard to understand now that his protective love is not enough for my needs, but he will accept my resolve. The real battle is going to be over who will pay for the new dower house. He will insist and I will resist. I will insist and he will resist."

"Compromise?" he said.

"I will pay for the roof and chimney and floor, and he will pay for everything else?" she said.

"Oh, but you must pay for the red door too, Clarissa," he said.

"And the knocker?"

"It would seem only fair," he said, and they both laughed over their own silliness.

It had always been thus between them. They had never allowed gloom to dominate their mood.

"Will you come to visit me?" she asked him. "Frequently?"

"Perhaps Stratton will set up armed guards at the driveway end of the path," he said.

She smiled. "Will you come?" she asked again. "Will you be my friend, Matthew?"

"Always," he said, and he reached out and took her hand in his.

The scent of the wildflowers and the sheep in the meadow behind them mingled with the fresh smells of the river flowing by below the bank. There was a sound to the water too, hardly heard unless one deliberately listened for it. From the blacksmith's shop in the distance came the ringing of a hammer against the anvil.

He raised their clasped hands and kissed the back of hers and then her fingers one at a time. He turned her hand and placed a lingering kiss on her palm. She dipped her head to rest on his shoulder, and he placed his arm about her shoulders and kissed her on the lips. She kissed him back and smiled at him.

He settled his cheek against the top of her head, and they gazed silently outward, drinking in the beauty and peace of it all. He was more relaxed than he had been earlier. He had been taut and ready to snap in two while they were in the rose arbor and walking down the driveway. Or so it had seemed. She had desperately wanted to dissuade him from going home alone like that, just as he had left home earlier. He had had a bad archery practice, surely a rare thing for him. He had lost his equilibrium and had been unable to recover it during tea—which he had not eaten apart from one bite of a jam tart.

He sighed after several minutes.

"I thought I was at perfect peace," he said, "even knowing that I had blocked out a whole segment of my past. I suppose it was never a good idea to do that. I ought perhaps to have confronted my demons as soon as I came home from abroad, but I did not consider it necessary or desirable. I did not want to look backward but only forward. It seemed to work. Until now."

"What will you do?" she asked him.

"Confront those demons?" he said. It was more question than statement. "Confront my own self-pitying and ill-informed assumptions about my family? About my brother anyway."

She did not say anything. She had learned long ago that often with Matthew it was best not to do so. All through his childhood and boyhood he had been told how to think and behave. With her he had always been able to think for himself, to find some sort of calm spot inside himself. She would not give her opinion or advice now, though it was not easy to keep quiet and apparently relaxed.

"I have written my brother a number of letters in the past couple of days," he said. "All of them I have fed to the stove to heat my kettle. But I cannot face him. What the devil would I say? He probably would not want to see me anyway, not after thirty years or so of my apparent ingratitude. I must persevere with the letter writing until I have expressed myself just so."

"Remember," she said, "that his son and daughter-in-law would have gone home a couple of days ago with the news that you never knew why your grandmother changed her will."

He sighed. "I am going to have to go there, am I not?" he said. "It is the very last thing I want to do."

They sat in silence again.

There was a vehicle coming along the main road from a distance, Clarissa could see. Not the stagecoach, but a private carriage. She watched it idly for a few minutes until it made the turn toward Boscombe. It was not a grand carriage, but it was considerably larger than most that belonged in the neighborhood. Except Ravenswood, that was. And Ravenswood was almost certainly its destination.

Clarissa sat up. "I have the distinct feeling that history is about to repeat itself," she said. "There is a carriage on its way here."

He shaded his eyes with one hand and watched it approach the village. "Do you recognize it?" he asked.

"No," she said. "It is not Devlin's. I must go and meet it after it crosses the bridge."

He got to his feet and offered his hand to help her up.

"You may stay here for a while if you wish," she said. "Though I do not mean that the way it might sound. I am not ashamed of our friendship, Matthew. Good heavens, I am not. But you may wish to avoid any sort of confrontation or unpleasantness."

"I am not concerned," he said. "Besides, my things are piled at the end of the path, a sure sign that I am lurking not far off."

"I am sorry," she said. "Perhaps I am jumping to the wrong conclusion, but really I am starting to get very annoyed with my family."

They arrived at the end of the path just as the carriage came rumbling over the bridge. It felt very like last week all over again, though it was a different sort of conveyance from Owen's curricle.

There was a shriek from inside the carriage as it slowed and came to a stop. A little nose was flattened against the window, and two little hands were splayed against it.

"Grandmama!"

The door opened before the coachman could descend from his perch, and Ben swung his daughter down safely to the ground before jumping out himself to join her.

"We came! Great-Aunt Edith is looking after Mama, and Carrie is looking after both of them. She will bark and frighten anyone who tries to hurt them. We are to take you home with us. You can come to the beach with me and collect shells. You can watch me swim."

Why did young children so often feel that they had to talk at full volume, Clarissa wondered as she bent to hug and kiss her granddaughter.

"Slow down, Joy," Ben said. "Give me time to hug Grandmama myself."

He proceeded to do so. "How are you, Mother?" he asked. "We have not come to bear you off to Penallen in chains, you will be happy to know. How do you do, Taylor?" He held out a hand to shake Matthew's. "I was to tell you from my wife that having the wheeled chair you made her two years ago is the best thing that has happened to her. I hope she makes marrying me an exception to that extravagant claim."

"I hope so too," Matthew said while Joy jumped up and down on the spot and held one of Clarissa's hands with both her own. "I will make my way home, Clarissa."

"I will take the liberty of calling upon you tomorrow if I may," Ben said. "But not, I hasten to add, in order to raise any sort of hell with you."

"Tomorrow afternoon will be fine," Matthew said as he bent to pick up his equipment while Joy gazed with frank interest at it all.

"Goodbye, Matthew," Clarissa said. "I will see you soon, I hope."

She watched him stride toward the bridge while the coachman lowered the steps to make it easier for them all to climb inside for the short ride up to the house. While Joy was scrambling in, Clarissa turned toward the son whose illegitimacy she had always steadfastly ignored.

"Ben," she said, "what on earth are you doing here?"

B en had no chance to answer until an hour or so later, after Owen had arrived home from his long ride, bringing Clarence with him. They had already escorted the ladies to their respective homes. The two of them had come to Ravenswood with the intention of bearing Clarissa off to dine with Marian and Charles, her brother-in-law. Clarence wanted to show Owen the new horse his father had recently acquired.

That plan quickly changed, however. The two young men exchanged hearty handshakes and some back slapping with Ben, but it was impossible for them to ignore an excitedly bouncing Joy, who was bursting with the need to impart to her favorite uncle all the news she had just been pouring out to her grandmama almost without a pause to catch her breath. Owen grasped her by the waist, hoisted her high, and tossed her toward the ceiling while she shrieked with fright and glee.

"Come and play," she demanded. "Cousin Clarence can come too."

Owen and Clarence went obediently from the room with her. They were going out to the hill to play one of Joy's favorite games, rolling down the long slope all the way from the temple to the bottom into the waiting arms of one of the two men. Clarissa understood that Clarence was going to dine here at Ravenswood and sent word to the kitchen.

So much for her quiet alone time.

"You were going to tell me what on earth you are doing here," she said to Ben.

"Was I?" But he held up both hands, palms out, when she would have spoken again.

Suddenly all her annoyance had returned. Who was next? Devlin and Gwyneth, just happening to have made a detour here on their way to Wales? In the hope, of course, that she had changed her mind and would go with them after all. Was a woman quite incapable of knowing her own mind? Even when her fiftieth birthday was galloping up on her?

"May I speak first?" Ben asked. "Then you may go for my throat if you wish. I have not come here to be a watchdog. Owen was the one appointed for that role, and it is quite obvious how effective he has been. No one could be less suited for the job. And I have not come to bear you off to Penallen against your will to keep you amused there through the summer until the family returns here. I will gladly stay for a while, of course, if it is what you wish. And I will very gladly take you back to Penallen with us if that is what you wish. But apparently you made your preference quite clear when you decided to come home early from London. And I assume you have not changed your mind since then. You wanted time to yourself, time to be yourself instead of always being someone's mother or mother-in-law or grandmother or sister or even friend, and instead of being coddled and included and protected and loved to death."

Ah. At last. Someone who understood.

"Nobody believes me," she said. "Worse, no one trusts me."

"I do, Mother," he said. "I believe you and I trust you. So does Jennifer. She knows just what it is like to be loved so fiercely that the recipient feels smothered. We both knew as soon as I was appealed to that I would come. But not to rein you in. We both want you to know that you have our full approval and support."

There was an ache at the back of her throat as she swallowed and fought tears. "It is not just my being alone here that has rung all the alarm bells, though," she said. "It is my friendship with Matthew Taylor."

"Jennifer adores him," he said. "He made her chair and gave her more freedom than she had had since early childhood, before her illness. And he made her a crutch, which, together with the shoe John Rogers, the cobbler, made for her, has enabled her to walk after a fashion. She even walked along the aisle of the church to me on our wedding day. She refers to Matthew Taylor as an artist. I have always felt a deep respect for him. He is hardworking and humble and refined—and marvelously talented. He speaks like a gentleman and is, indeed, the son of a gentleman and his wife—which is more than can be said of me. None of which attributes really have anything to say to your case, Mother. You are free to choose your own friends, whoever they are or whatever they are, as well as your own romantic partners. I do not know if Matthew Taylor is only the one or both, and frankly it is none of my business. Or that of any of your children."

"Well," she said. "We have been seen walking hand in hand in the park."

"Shocking behavior indeed," he said. "Mother. Two years ago the alarm was raised in the family when it was observed that Jennifer and I were becoming friendly and perhaps eventually a little more than just that. The sister of the Duke of Wilby and the bastard son of the late Earl of Stratton. It was unthinkable. We almost succumbed to what others thought. We almost deprived ourselves of the love of a lifetime, however long our lifetimes last. It took some courage to go against the accepted norms. I remember it well. But we did it. We did what was right for us. And the sky did not fall upon our heads as a result. You must do what is right for you."

"I am going to build a cottage on the bank of the river below the meadow," she said. "I have the place picked out. There will be just room for the house and a pretty flower garden. It is going to be heaven on earth—with a bright red front door."

He regarded her in silence for a few moments. "Poor Dev," he said.

"Oh," she said, "I intend to pay for it myself. It can become a modest dower house for future generations. Ravenswood has never had one."

"That was not what I meant," he said. "If Dev agrees to have it built on his land, he will certainly insist upon paying for it himself, Mother. You will have what I would guess will be an unwinnable fight on your hands if you try to have your own way on that. I daresay the absence of a dower house until now has something to do with the size of this house?"

"It is rather large," she agreed. "That is part of the problem, Ben."

He smiled at her. "Joy and I will go back home in a few days," he said. "I must confess to being uneasy at being away from Jennifer, though she has excellent company and care from Aunt Edith. You may, of course, come with us if you wish. We would be delighted, as you very well know. But I am not going to press the point. I may, however, persuade Owen to come with us. He always loves being by the sea. You will be alone here again."

"Thank you," she said. "Ben, it is not that I do not love you all. I do."

"Is it not strange," he said, "that children are expected, even encouraged, to make their own lives away from the nurturing love of their parents when they grow up. But when parents try to do the same thing, they cause something like panic in their children. Why should you not have a life of your own now that we are all adults and living the lives we have chosen? Even Steph is spreading her wings."

"I worry about her," she said.

"It is unnecessary," he said. "Many people with a low regard for themselves will grasp at the first opportunity to settle respectably. Yet I have heard that she refused two quite eligible offers in London?"

"She did," Clarissa said. "One of them came with a title."

"That fact alone tells me she will eventually have a strong sense of self and will find what will make her happy," he said.

"Oh, Ben," she said, "when did you become so wise?"

"Perhaps," he said, "it started when I was at the knee of the woman who loved me instantly and unreservedly when I was foisted upon her, while ninety-nine out of one hundred women in the same position would have spurned me and refused to have anything to do with me."

Clarissa was spared the necessity of answering by the sudden bursting open of the drawing room door and the influx of three disheveled, grubby, grass-stained persons, who were still in a boisterous mood.

"Uncle Owen almost broke his leg and his arm when he tried rolling down the hill," Joy shrieked. "He did not tuck in right. I had to show him how to do it."

"I believe I did break my nose, though," Owen said, rubbing it.

"You are a splendid instructor, Joy," Clarence said, beaming down at her. "I rolled down without mishap."

"Yes," she said.

Oh, she would never be a hermit, Clarissa thought as she got to her feet. She loved people too much. She was enjoying herself enormously.

"I assume you are staying for dinner, Clarence," she said. "You will be very welcome. But the butler will be handing in his notice on the spot if you turn up in the dining room looking like a scarecrow. Go with Owen and get cleaned and brushed up. Joy, go with Papa for a scrubbing."

They all filed meekly from the room. Before hurrying off after them to change for dinner, Clarissa tried to decide if she wanted more to laugh or to weep. Sometimes the emotions involved were very similar.

CHAPTER SEVENTEEN

B en Ellis came, as planned, to Matthew's rooms the following afternoon. The surprise was that he did not come alone. Clarissa was with him. His daughter was not.

"Joy has gone off for a swim in the lake with Owen and Clarence," Clarissa explained. "Clarence Ware, that is. He stayed last night."

So, Matthew thought—Owen, Ben, Clarence Ware, Joy. Poor Clarissa. Her lovely solitary late spring and summer had fast changed into a series of visits by family members. He could only wonder if any more of them would turn up. And it was all his fault. Well, not all, he supposed. But he was certainly the cause of these impromptu visits.

"I have come," Ben said after shaking Matthew's hand, "so I may report to my siblings and my uncle in all honesty that I have had a word with you and done my best to sort out the situation. Here I am sorting it. I have known Mother since my father brought me to Ravenswood when I was three years old. I am now thirty-five. In all that time I have never once seen her behave recklessly or improperly. She has always been the perfect lady and the perfect mother and grandmother. I would not presume now to question her choice of friends or style of living. I want only to see her happy. You are a man I have known since I was a lad. I have always looked upon you with the deepest respect and admiration for your talents and skill. I would not presume to confront you on any choice you make about your own life. There, that is done. Now, I seem to recall from two years ago, when you were making a wheeled chair and a cane for my wife, that you keep a display of your wood carvings in your workroom. I will go and have a good look at them if I may. I do not need company. Sometimes art is best viewed and appreciated when one is alone and behind a closed door."

Matthew exchanged glances with Clarissa. She raised her eyebrows but said nothing. Ben did not wait for an actual invitation but strode off into the workroom and shut the door firmly behind him.

It was a good thing, Matthew thought, that he had taken the sketches for the baby's crib into his bedchamber along with the pieces of the frame he had cut out that morning. Not that he had expected their meeting to take them into his workroom, but one never knew. One never did, indeed.

"Ben is your chaperon?" he said.

"I believe he decided that at my age I do not need one," Clarissa said. "He also understands that we need to talk. I am sorry about all this, Matthew. Perhaps I should have predicted it, but I really did not. I hope this is the end of the matter, but I would not wager upon it. Ben is going back home to Penallen the day after tomorrow. Owen is going with him."

She went to sit at the table, in the place she had sat last time, and Matthew took the chair across from her.

"Perhaps your family's reaction to any change you decide to

make in your life is something you needed to discover," he said. "There is a quotation hovering at the outer edges of my mind. Ah. I have it. *No man is an island*. By John Donne, the poet, though that particular work was not poetry. Perhaps what you wanted to do this summer was never something you were going to be able to decide all alone, Clarissa."

"Every man is part of the main," she said, recalling the words as closely as she could from a little later in that passage by Donne. "Presumably he meant every woman too. I think perhaps it would be altogether better for your peace of mind, Matthew, if you stopped seeing me. I would absolutely understand."

"Is it what you want?" he asked her.

Her hand came partway across the table and then started to withdraw. He took it in both his own before she could do so.

"My family's concern and the concern of my friends and neighbors here is rather touching from my point of view," she said. "It shows me how much they all care. However, from your point of view it is more than a little insulting. There would not be all this bother if you were Lord Taylor of such-and-such, with a grand stately home and property. My family was mildly encouraging of the budding courtship of Lord Keilly earlier in the spring. This must all be humiliating for you. Yet when all else is stripped away, I am merely Clarissa Greenfield and you are Matthew Taylor, children of neighboring gentry."

He drew a couple of breaths but still seemed not to have filled his lungs. "I am going back," he said.

He saw the incomprehension in her eyes change to understanding. She set her free hand over their clasped hands. But she said nothing. Typical of the way she had always been, she waited for him to continue.

"I am going to talk to Reginald," he said. "If he will talk to me, that is."

He felt sick to his stomach, as he had been feeling ever since Philip's visit. He had tried to ignore his new knowledge. There was little point now in raking up all those old troubles. His brother had probably lived a happier life without him. He himself had lived a happier life free of his family. His childhood and boyhood were like a bad dream that had faded almost to nothingness. He had been at peace with himself and his world. His life for more than twenty years here had been exactly as he had wanted it to be.

He felt even worse now that he had put it into words—*I am going to talk to Reginald.* As though he had burned a few bridges behind him. As though he could not now change his mind.

"And I am going to visit their graves," he said. "Poppy's and Helena's."

If he could find them. They were probably completely overgrown. He had not even had a headstone made for them. His stomach gurgled quite audibly.

"How will you get there?" she asked.

"I will hire a horse or a carriage," he said. "It is what I do whenever I have a distance to go."

"Let it be a carriage from Ravenswood," she said. "Let me come with you. I can visit my parents for as long as you need."

Their eyes met across the table.

Strangely, it was what he had dreaded most, the journey there. The anticipation. Ten miles without anything to think of except what it was going to be like to see his brother again after all these years and what he was going to say. Wondering what it would be like to walk into the churchyard to hunt for a grave he had treated with such disregard he had not even made arrangements to have it marked. And then there would be the long journey back to Boscombe, alone with his thoughts again.

"I cannot go tomorrow or the day after, though," she said.

"The day after that?" he said. "It would be a great imposition upon your good nature, though."

"Matthew," she said softly, and tears welled into his eyes.

He felt horribly humiliated. He snatched his hands from hers and scraped back his chair to scramble to his feet. But she was on hers before he was and had come around the table. One of her arms came about his waist, the other around his shoulders, and she moved against him and tipped back her head to look into his face.

"You are my friend," she said fiercely. "I love you."

He rested his forehead in the hollow between her shoulder and neck and closed his eyes as his arms came about her. She was not talking about romantic love, of course, despite the kisses they had shared out by the hills and at the lake. But there was a love that was a little more than just friendship. She loved him. And of course he loved her. Always had, always would. He had avoided putting a name to the type of love it was—except when he was eighteen years old and lived his whole life on raw emotion. Love was love. It did not always need to be defined or subdivided.

"I beg your pardon," he said after a minute or two, lifting his head and looking into her face. "I have learned to live my life without any extremes of emotion. I have liked it that way. It has given me balance and tranquility."

It had not struck him in all that time that perhaps he had repressed a great deal that mattered in life in favor of what was not, after all, real peace.

She raised the hand that was around his shoulders and cupped it about the back of his head. She smiled at him and kissed him. And he tightened his hold on her and kissed her back.

Someone coughed inside the workroom and then fumbled noisily with the door handle before opening it. Matthew had almost forgotten Ben was still in there. He released Clarissa at the same moment as she released him.

"Have you ever considered having an exhibition of your work?" Ben asked. "At a summer fete, for example? Or are they not intended for people to gawk at? You are a true artist, you know. You are not a mere dabbler."

"I had not thought of it," Matthew said. "Perhaps I ought."

"That owl," Ben said. "It is a masterpiece. Is it for sale? I would love to give it to my aunt for Christmas, although that is looking ahead quite a way."

"I would be delighted," Matthew said, with just a slight pang at the thought of parting with what was his favorite piece apart from the one that he kept in his bedchamber. "Is she the aunt who turned up so unexpectedly at Ravenswood during the fete a couple of years ago?"

"My mother's sister," Ben said. "Of whose very existence I knew nothing until that day. She lives with us at Penallen. It has turned into a happy arrangement for all of us."

"Then she will have her owl for Christmas," Matthew said.

"Thank you." Ben looked from one to the other of them. "I may come for it tomorrow?"

They left soon after that. Matthew stood at the top of the stairs watching them descend to the street. There was no sign of a carriage. They must have walked here.

Life had certainly changed for Ben Ellis two years ago with the arrival of Lady Jennifer Arden, sister of Lady Philippa's husband, as a guest for the summer. And then with the unexpected appearance of an aunt and a half brother to fill in some of his blank history on his mother's side. Apparently all he had known of her until then was that she had been the mistress of the late earl, his father, until her death when Ben was three.

Ben's life had changed for the better since then.

But his own? And Clarissa's? It was impossible to know yet. All they could do was live from day to day and face whatever changes came—either separately or together.

Together was not a word he had ever really associated with Clarissa and himself. Not, at least, since he was eighteen.

He sighed and went back inside his rooms and shut the front door.

A bright red door, he thought, the only specific feature yet planned for Clarissa's dream cottage. He smiled and then chuckled aloud as he went to fetch and then wrap the wooden owl, which was still poised for flight while holding his gaze with a stubborn determination not to be the first to look away.

Three mornings later the carriage from Ravenswood stopped outside the smithy. Matthew was already trotting down the stairs. Within a minute he was inside the carriage and it was in motion again.

"I could have walked up to the house," he said.

"And good morning to you too, Matthew," Clarissa said. "Our friendship is no longer a secret. Why should I not stop for you here, with perhaps half the village looking on? It does not matter."

"Your sons left yesterday?" he asked.

"They did," she said. "I felt guilty about not encouraging them to stay longer. But I know Ben was anxious to return to Jennifer, whom he should not have left in the first place. I know too that Owen brightened considerably at the prospect of spending a few weeks by the sea. Joy was over the moon that he was going with them. She has major plans for him."

"And you are happy to be alone again," he said.

"I really was sad to see them go so soon and to know they had come here only to make sure I had company and was not lonely," she said.

"And were not being devoured by a big, bad wolf," he said.

"There is that too." She smiled. "But I am happy to be alone again."

He was looking slightly pale, she thought. His manner was a bit strained. He seemed more like the old Matthew than the one who had lived and worked here for the past twenty years and more. It was hardly surprising. He was on his way to see and talk with the brother with whom he had had no dealings in more than thirty years.

They sat in silence for a while. Clarissa knew that nothing she could say was going to take his mind off the ordeal ahead. If he needed to talk, if he needed her to talk, then he would take the initiative. It was strange how she had forgotten, though he had not, the long silences that had characterized their friendship almost as much as all the intense talking and more relaxed chatting and laughing they had done. And it was what she had craved in the past few years, was it not? She understood silence more consciously now. It was through silence that she was becoming more comfortable with herself and the irrevocable turn her life had taken with Caleb's death six years ago. The members of her family had been precious gems of love and concern, making sure she was almost never alone, except in her bed at night, involving her in their own activities and conversations. Their great kindness had been part of her problem, though. She could wallow in it quite happily for the rest of her life if she chose. But at the end of it all, would she feel that she had somehow wasted the second half of her life?

Matthew spoke at last.

"There was a time," he said, "when he was my favorite person in the whole world. My hero, the person I aspired to grow up to be like."

"Reginald?" she said.

"Reggie, yes," he said. "The ten-year age difference seemed enormous when I was a child. He always seemed grown-up to me, and kind and indulgent and . . . fun."

She set her hand in his, and his fingers closed about it.

"He used to take me fishing," he said. "And birding. He never shot at birds. He taught me their names and their distinguishing features and their song. He would talk to me about the marvel of flight. How wonderful beyond belief it must be, he used to say, to be able to spread one's wings and soar into the sky. And to fly hundreds, maybe thousands of miles to a warmer climate for the winter and return for the summer. If one could understand the mystery of a single bird, he told me, one would be very much closer to understanding the mystery of everything. Of the whole universe."

Reginald Taylor had said that? He had always seemed very prosaic to Clarissa, like a man without any imagination at all.

"He would take me to work with him in the stables and the barns," he said. "He would take me up on a horse with him when he rode about the farm, checking on the crops or on the sheep and cows. He was very young at the time but very conscientious. When our father told him to do something, he did it. He understood things and would explain them to me. More than anything in the world I wanted to be like him. I wanted to be with him. I dreamed of the day when we could work together, side by side, shoulder to shoulder, and I would be as strong and as knowledgeable as he. We would live together and work together and be happy together for the rest of our lives, never needing anyone else."

And this had been Matthew as a very young child? Surely it must have been before the time he and she had struck up a friendship.

"It is strange how some long-forgotten memories can pop into one's head as if from nowhere," he said. "I cannot recall how old I was. Five? Six? No more than that. I was sitting at the table with Reggie and our parents. I did not always eat with them. I suppose I was still considered too young. It must have been some sort of special occasion. I can remember feeling that I might burst with happiness. Perhaps I had been helping Reggie and he had praised me and called me quite the little man. It is something I remember him saying more than once. I poured out all my dreams to my family at that table."

He fell silent for a few moments.

"Many parents could have humored me and laughed and praised me for being so eager to help with the farm work," he said, continuing. "My parents always prided themselves upon telling the truth, however. My father did not seem to recall or understand what it was to be a young child. He told me quite firmly at that table that there was no question of my remaining at home past the age of eighteen or of ever working alongside my brother on the farm. As the eldest, Reggie would inherit and I would have none of it. I felt the bottom fall out of my world. All my security was snatched from me. As soon as I grew up, I was going to have to leave my home. I was going to be all alone. Abandoned. Without home or family. Without my beloved brother."

"Oh," Clarissa said. "But did no one reassure you that it would not be quite like that at all?" Surely Reginald had. The Reginald Matthew remembered from that time anyway.

"How can one possibly know if what one remembers from that time in one's life is accurate or not?" he said. "It seems to me, though, that everything changed from that moment on. Reggie did try to reassure me, but our father told him to hold his tongue, and he did."

"Your mother?" Clarissa asked.

"They always worked as a team, my parents," he said. "My father had a talk with me in his study the following day—or week or month. I am not sure exactly when, but it was soon after. And he told me the bare truth—the primary virtue by which he lived. He told me it was time to stop following Reggie around like a shadow, getting in his way and slowing him down. He told me it was time to begin my schooling in earnest and learn the things I was going to need to know when I grew up so that after I left home I could have a gentleman's profession and a respectable income upon which to live. I can remember the terror I felt as he talked, and the panic I felt afterward when I ran to talk to Reggie and he looked at me almost as sternly as our father always looked and told me I must listen to our parents and do as I was told so I could be a proper man when I grew up. I did not realize it at the time, but it is almost certain that our father had had a talk with him too before he spoke to me."

Clarissa squeezed his hand. She had never quite understood why Matthew had been so very rebellious and badly behaved as a boy. She had understood his frustrations, yes, and the shortcomings of his parents, who had tried to force him into being the person they wanted him to be instead of nurturing him and coaxing him by small degrees toward an adulthood that would suit both him and them.

But she had not known of the blind terror of a little boy who had been told the bald truth of his future when he was far too young to understand it. His home would not remain his home after he grew up, he had been told. The work his brother did would never be his work. What might have been an exciting prospect if he had been allowed to grow up to the gradual realization that his life was going to be his own to plan had been a nightmare to him instead.

"I behaved badly," Matthew said. "Even when I was old enough to know better. He meant well, my father."

Meaning well was sometimes no excuse. Nor was telling the truth.

"And my mother always supported him," he said. "She was a good wife in that way."

And the world's worst mother, Clarissa thought viciously.

"Reggie tried to reason with me when I started misbehaving," he said. "Then he started withdrawing favors. He refused to take me fishing one day when he had promised he would and the weather was perfect and I was out of my bed early and eager to be on our way. I had got all my sums wrong for my tutor the day before, and when my father reprimanded me and sent me to my room without tea to do them again, I drew cheeky-looking squirrels in all the places where the answers were to go."

Clarissa smiled despite herself.

"You probably remember how poor I was at making creatures look like the ones I intended," he said. "My father thought I had drawn a caricature of his face, and when I looked, I had to admit he had a point. I even said so."

Clarissa winced and then laughed outright.

"Then a bit later Reggie cut all treats," he said. "He told me he would have nothing more to do with me until I had learned to be obedient to our father and take life seriously. I never called him Reggie after that day. Not until very recently, at least."

They sat in silence for a while as fields and hedgerows passed outside the carriage windows and clouds scudded by overhead to reveal the occasional glimpse of blue.

"How did this start?" he asked. "How did any of my self-pitying monologues ever start? Why should any of these memories matter after all these years? I have been contented with my life. I have done what I wanted to do. I have earned my living and been a burden to no one. The past is long gone. It is of no significance. I survived it. Reginald survived it. It is best not reopened."

Except that he was on his way to do just that.

"Do you think we should just turn around and go home?" he said.

"Did you write to tell your brother you were coming?" she asked.

"Yes." He winced. "Perhaps he has gone away on a full-day excursion."

"And perhaps not," she said.

"And perhaps not," he agreed with a sigh. "I wonder if this is how a man feels when he is on the way to his own execution. I would rather be doing anything else on earth than this. Lord, everything is starting to look familiar. I can walk over from your parents' house if you wish, Clarissa. I did it often enough when I was a boy. I will probably not get lost."

"The carriage will drop you off outside your brother's door," she told him. "You can walk over to us when you have finished."

He turned to take her other hand in his and squeezed them both tightly, almost to the point of pain. "I love you so much, Clarissa." She saw the dismay in his face as he realized what he had said. "I did not mean that quite as it sounded. I . . . I thank you so much. You are very good to me."

She smiled and leaned toward him and kissed him.

They were driving by his own property, she realized. The house, a sizable manor, was prettier than she remembered it. She usually drove to and from her parents' house by a slightly different route. Hollyhocks, hyacinths, and numerous other flowers were blooming against the walls of the house, and colorful window boxes hung from the upstairs windows. The garden surrounding the house was bright with smooth lawns and well-kept flower beds. White curtains fluttered at one open window downstairs.

And then the carriage was drawing to a halt outside the Taylor home, and even before the steps were set down, the front door opened and Reginald and Adelaide Taylor stepped outside, their son Philip with his wife behind them. The young people were smiling, Clarissa saw, while the older couple were not. This must be every bit as difficult for them as it was for Matthew, of course. But they had not fled on a day's excursion. Nor had they barred the door against him.

They all raised a hand in greeting to Clarissa when she waved from the carriage window, and then they turned their attention to Matthew, who was walking up the long path to meet them, his tall hat in his hand. The coachman put up the steps and shut the door, and Clarissa leaned back in her seat while the carriage rocked into motion again. She did not look out her window.

CHAPTER EIGHTEEN

The first half hour of Matthew's visit felt unreal. Downright bizarre, in fact. He sat with Reginald and his wife and Philip and his wife in the drawing room, which looked familiar but different—somehow lighter, brighter, larger than he remembered it. They sipped on tea, though Adelaide informed him that luncheon would be ready within the hour and they all hoped he would stay.

They made polite conversation. Yes, the farm was doing well, far better than it had used to do, now that more modern methods were being applied. And yes, Anthony, their younger son, was doing well in London, and Mabel, their daughter, was a happy wife and mother.

And yes, Matthew's business was going well, offering him a steady flow of work without overwhelming him. Yes, he was happy in Boscombe. He had some good friends there. It was a friendly place, in fact, a good place to live. And yes, he was proud of the sheep carving Emily had brought home with her last week, as he was of all his work. Yes, he carved during his spare time.

He ought to have brought another of his carvings as a gift for Adelaide, he thought too late. He had come empty-handed. That had been gauche of him.

Reginald and Adelaide had aged since he last saw them, a rather obvious thought to be having. They had been in their late twenties the last time. Reginald was sixty now. He had aged well, however. He was still lean. He still had most of his hair, though it was steel gray now. Adelaide had grown plumper and ruddier of complexion than she had been, yet she was still a pleasant-looking woman.

This was to be it, then? This uncomfortable meeting, filled with meaningless chatter? He was finding it impossible to shift the conversation to what was clearly in the forefront of all their minds. Half an hour was the expected limit of a social visit. Ought he now, then, to get to his feet, thank them for their kind hospitality, and walk over to the Greenfields' house to tell Clarissa that he was ready to leave when she was?

But he had been invited to stay for luncheon. Had it been a mere polite offer, which they expected him to refuse? Were they willing him to take his leave and end the embarrassment they were all feeling? They could hardly just ask him to leave, could they?

"If you will excuse us," Emily said, getting to her feet and smiling at Matthew. "We have promised to take the children outside for a walk before luncheon."

Philip got up too. So did Adelaide.

"I believe I will come with you if I may, Emily," she said. "The sun is shining nicely. But we will see you again at luncheon, Matthew?"

"Thank you," he said without actually saying yes or no. "You are kind."

And suddenly they were alone together, he and Reginald, and the silence in the room was loud.

Matthew drew a slow breath.

"Why did you do it?" he asked. No explanation. No context. Just the bare question about something that had happened more than thirty years ago. "I did not know. Not until Philip mentioned it when he came to see me last week. He assumed I knew. I did not. Why did you do it?"

"I assume you are talking about Grandmama's will," Reginald said.

"I could never understand it," Matthew said. "The only way I could ever explain it to myself was that she changed the will for Poppy's sake and the baby's and forgot to change it back after they died. When I heard about it, I imagined that you and our father—you especially—were hideously disappointed and probably furious too. You had always longed for the day when you would have a home and farm of your own and the prospect of the amalgamation of the two properties in time. Though I suppose you never longed for the deaths of our grandmother and father. But why did you give up your dream?"

"It was always Papa's dream more than mine," Reginald said. "I was never an ambitious man. I was like you in that. I still am. We are happy here, Addie and I. We have everything we could possibly need. And we have our family, all happily settled. We have good neighbors and friends."

Was it true, Matthew wondered—that Reginald had never been an ambitious man? He had always done his duty as the elder son of the family. He had worked hard. He had been an indulgent, affectionate brother—until he had not been. But ambitious?

"Grandmama never made a secret of the fact that she intended to leave her property and everything else to me when she died," Reginald said. "It was her right, of course. She could leave it to whomever she wished. But I was never comfortable with the way she talked openly about it rather than keep the contents of her will confidential. I talked to Papa about it a couple of times. Since she had only the two grandchildren, I explained, and I was set to inherit everything of his, would it not be better, kinder, for Grandmama to leave everything of hers to the one who would not inherit from her son-in-law? Unfortunately, Papa did not see things that way. He visualized a time when the owner of the combined properties would rival the Greenfields in prosperity and social prominence."

Why had Matthew assumed that his brother was just like their father? Perhaps because he had acted like their father?

"I wanted you to have that property," Reginald said. "I wanted you to live there and farm there. I thought that having it might at last restore you to . . . yourself. You adored being on the farm with me when you were a young child. You would work to the point of exhaustion in an attempt to keep up with me. You would prattle constantly, peppering me with surprisingly intelligent questions. You were adorable. I adored you. I think the great change in you came after you understood that you would not live here forever and work here as my partner, that you would have to find your own way in life when you grew up, with some profession suitable for a gentleman. But not as a farmer, since you would not be a property owner."

The great change in you . . .

"I *never* understood, Reginald," Matthew said, emphasizing the one word. "I heard only that when I reached the age of eighteen I was going to be tossed out into the wide world to fend for myself. Rejected and unloved."

"Papa could be blunt and tactless," Reginald said. "He did not mean—"

"And then you stopped loving me," Matthew said. He felt a bit like a petulant boy again.

Reginald closed his eyes and visibly winced. "Never that," he said. "Oh, never that. But you became impossible. Totally out of control. I tried everything I could think of. But Papa convinced me that I was part of the problem, that I was indulging your bad behavior and must stop doing so—for your own good. He was an unimaginative man, Matt. I always realized that about him. And Mama was such a mouse of a woman that she would never speak up against him. But he was not a bad man. He was genuinely concerned about you and your future. He could only ever see one way to go—become stricter and stricter with you and force you into compliance."

Matthew said nothing.

"The only person who seemed to have any influence on you was Clarissa Greenfield," Reginald said. "I do not know how she did it or why she did it, but I blessed her in my prayers every night and morning. I did not have the courage—"

"To what?" Matthew asked when his brother stopped abruptly without completing his sentence.

Reginald shrugged. "Simply to love you," he said. "And then, when you were already eighteen and showing no sign of settling down, you went and . . . impregnated Poppy and married her with no discernible plan for your future. And Papa at last admitted that he had failed with you, though I do not suppose he explained it that way to himself. He kicked you out, and it took some begging on my part to persuade Grandmama to take you in."

Ah.

He had not known that. Good God!

"I suppose," Reginald said, "you did it because Clarissa married Stratton. That must have been a nasty blow to you."

"I never had any expectation of marrying her myself," Matthew said. "That was not what our friendship was about."

"No, I suppose not," Reginald said. "And I persuaded Grandmama to change her will. It was not easy. I believe she did it eventually because for some strange reason she grew fond of Poppy."

"Poppy was not a woman to be despised," Matthew said. "She was a person. She was my wife."

"Yes. I am sorry." Reginald sighed. "I thought Grandmama might change her will back to the original after your wife and daughter died and you disappeared without a trace. We never talked about it. But she did not change a thing. And you did not come home, even after you returned to England. You never came home."

"No," Matthew said. "I did not know. About what you had done, I mean. I was not going to come back here and expect a prodigal's welcome. I was not going to come back to the poisonous atmosphere that very nearly destroyed my spirit. Yes, I was bad. Yes, I was out of control. I was also a child when it all started. Children need to grow gradually into an understanding of life. They need to be loved while it happens. Not disciplined in some perversion of love."

Reginald winced again.

"I have long forgiven my father," Matthew said. "And my mother. They did what they thought was right, and I did not make it easy for them."

"And me?" Reginald said. "Have you forgiven me?"

"You gave me a precious gift," Matthew said. "One I knew

nothing about until last week. Despite what you have said about ambition, I know it was a great sacrifice you made."

"I wanted my brother close by and thriving," Reginald said. "We could have been almost partners, as you had dreamed of when you were a child. My happiness would have been complete."

"I do thank you," Matthew said.

"But it was no substitute for love, was it?" Reginald said. "The love I withheld at a time when you needed it most. I did not have to listen to Papa, even though the habit of obeying him and convincing myself that he knew best was deeply ingrained in me. I was a young adult when I told you—the most nightmarish day of my life—that I would have nothing more to do with you until you learned to behave as you ought. I should have taken my own advice. I should have learned to behave as I ought. You were my brother, and I adored you and grieved over you. Effectively giving you property and income instead of love was no gift at all. You were right to stay away, Matthew. I did not deserve a relationship with you. But tell me now, because I have always worried—have you been happy?"

"Contented," Matthew said.

"And you and Clarissa are still friends?" Reginald asked.

"Friends again," Matthew said.

"I am glad," his brother said.

"So am I." Matthew got to his feet. "Maybe you will make my excuses to Adelaide. With thanks. I will walk over to the Greenfield house. Clarissa is there with her parents."

Reginald jumped up in what looked like near panic. "Don't go, Matt. Please don't go," he said. "I have never forgiven myself, if that is any consolation to you. And I understood your not returning here in all these years. I understood that the only way I could show my . . . love for you was to stay right out of your life and keep my family out of it. Philip is, of course, in his thirties. I could not forbid his writing to you a few weeks ago. I would never try to exert that sort of control over my children in any case. But I was sorry that you were to be bothered, that old wounds were perhaps going to be ripped open for you after all this time. And here you are as though to prove me right, obviously troubled by it all. Will you at least stay for luncheon? Addy will be upset if you do not. So will Philip and Emily."

"And you?" Matthew asked.

"And me too," Reginald said. "You cannot imagine how . . . good it is to see you again. Painful but good."

Matthew regarded him with a frown. "You loved me that much," he said. "I did not know it. You must have thought me the most ungrateful wretch in the world."

"Yes, I loved you that much," his brother said. "But I did not show it in the only way that mattered. One can never buy love. I am glad you did not know. And you do not owe me anything, especially thanks."

They stood gazing at each other.

"Unfortunately," Matthew said, "we can never go back to do things differently, can we? To do things right. We can only live on and try each day to do better than we did the day before. Which sounds very glib and preachy. Reggie, there has always been a hole in my heart where you were."

His brother's eyes were swimming with tears, he saw.

"Oh, Matt," he said. "In mine too. Where you were."

"To hell with thanks and forgiveness," Matthew said. "And pious platitudes."

"You will stay for luncheon?" Reginald asked.

"I will stay," Matthew said.

And somehow, excruciatingly embarrassingly, they were in each other's arms, choking and hiccuping, laughing self-consciously, and slapping each other's back.

"I ought to have brought Adelaide one of my carvings," Matthew finally said when he could speak clearly again.

"She would have liked that," Reginald said after stepping back and blowing his nose. "She will like it. You can bring it next time you come."

"There is to be a next time, then?" Matthew asked.

"Good God, yes," Reginald said. "You do not know Addy and Emily, Matt. Tyrants both. I predict with all confidence that they are going to organize some sort of grand party in your honor and invite everyone they know."

"Good God," Matthew said.

"Yes," his brother said, slapping a hand on his shoulder and indicating the door of the room. "Ghastly, is it not? I hope you brought your appetite with you. I believe a bit of a banquet awaits, early in the day though it is. Not quite the fatted calf, but not far off. After you."

He opened the door and gestured toward the dining room, from which Matthew could hear the voices of his sister-in-law and his niece-in-law.

"Good God," he said again.

When the time crept up to midafternoon but did not bring Matthew, Clarissa chose to take his lengthy absence as a good sign. Surely if the meeting with his brother had gone badly, he would have been here almost on her heels. Nevertheless, she was restless. She stood at the window of her parents' drawing room, looking out along the driveway and drumming her fingernails on the windowsill.

Her father had fallen asleep in his wing chair by the fireplace, his hands crossed over his waistcoat. He was not quite snoring. Her mother had just described the sound he made as he inhaled as clicking.

"And a bit annoying it can be at times," she said, gazing at him fondly. "I used to try to close his mouth with one very gentle finger. But he would always jump awake just when I thought I had succeeded and complain that he would never now know how that delicious dream he had been having of me ended." She laughed softly as she came to stand beside her daughter. "Still no sign? But you know what is said of watched pots, Clarissa. They are good neighbors, the Taylors, and good people. The elder Taylors were more puritanical, may their souls rest in peace. They missed many of life's joys in favor of righteousness. They were not easy to like."

"Unfortunately," Clarissa said, "they destroyed the joy of those under their care too."

"We must not judge," her mother said, rubbing her hand in a light circle over Clarissa's back. "None of us are perfect. None of us behave wisely all the time, especially toward our own children, whom we love most in the world."

"Like the time I sent Devlin away and he cut himself off completely from us for six interminable years," Clarissa said.

"Or all the times your father and I ought to have confronted Caleb with our outrage over his infidelities but decided it was better for everyone concerned to let sleeping dogs lie," her mother said. "Ah, here he comes."

And Matthew was indeed walking toward the house—with his brother. They were laughing over something, and Reginald was slapping a hand against Matthew's back. Clarissa felt the tension she had not realized she was experiencing ease out of her shoulders and neck.

"Reginald and Matthew Taylor are on their way here, Richard," her mother said, raising her voice just a little, and her father awoke with a snort.

"Just resting my eyes for a few minutes," he said. "Together, are they? And about time too."

The next few minutes were taken up with jovial greetings. Both men refused tea and cakes.

"I do not believe I will be able to eat another crumb until at least tomorrow," Matthew said, patting his stomach. "I have just been devouring a feast."

"And I will take no more of your time, Mrs. Greenfield," Reginald said. "We kept Matt rather longer than we ought. I know you have a distance to go, Lady Stratton."

"Clarissa," she said.

"Clarissa." He nodded. "You will want to be on your way. Thank you for bringing my brother to me."

"I am always happy for an excuse to spend time with Mama and Papa," she said.

He wrung his brother's hand but turned to look at them all before setting out for home. "I hope you are all free on Friday evening of next week," he said. "My wife and daughter-in-law are planning some sort of neighborhood party in Matt's honor, though I know he will have nightmares about it from now until then. I hope you will come too, La— Clarissa."

"If only to provide the carriage to bring Matthew?" she said, her eyes twinkling at him.

"I will be happy to send my own carriage to fetch him," he said.

"You were always his best friend. And I do mean best. We would be honored to have you at our party."

"I would not miss it for worlds," she said. "Thank you."

He nodded to them all again and was gone.

"What a lovely idea," Clarissa said, smiling at Matthew. "Nightmares notwithstanding."

He frowned. "I already feel like an impostor," he said. "But Friday of next week is bound to be ten times worse than today."

"Make that a hundred times, my lad," her father said. "Stiffen your backbone and grit your teeth and march valiantly into battle."

"Richard!" Clarissa's mother said. "You are frightening the poor man."

But the poor man was laughing, albeit a bit ruefully.

"And it really is time you were on your way," Clarissa's mother said as she always did when late afternoon was upon them and she knew her daughter had ten miles to travel in order to arrive safely home at Ravenswood before dark. "If you are quite sure you will not have any refreshments before you leave, Matthew."

"I really could not, ma'am," he said, patting his stomach again. "If it was not Adelaide pressing more food upon me during luncheon, it was Emily. And it is very hard to say no when people are being so kind."

Ten minutes later they were on their way. Not to go straight home, however. Matthew asked if they could stop at the church, which was at the far end of the village. Clarissa took his hand in hers. He gripped hard.

"Guilt and innocence are elusive concepts," he said. "The need to forgive and the need to be forgiven. It turns out that they are rarely entirely one-sided—one guilty party, one innocent. Everything is all jumbled up. Both guilty, both innocent. Both apologizing, both forgiving. No one more to blame than the other. Am I making any sense? Am I merely stating the obvious?"

"You are making sense," she said. "Perhaps in time you will understand how I felt—how I feel—about Caleb."

"I am not so sure of that," he said. "I cannot see how that was not clearly a case of guilt on one side and innocence on the other."

"I sent my beloved son into exile rather than confront the real cancer at the heart of my marriage," she said. "I put appearances before love. But I do not wish to discuss that now. I only mean to assure you that I understand exactly what you are saying. So Reginald is no longer the black-hearted villain?"

"Nor am I," he said. "Forgiveness always has to be given to oneself as well as to the other. I learned that years and years ago and applied it—except to the one crucial area of my life."

She set her cheek against his shoulder, but the carriage was already slowing outside the lych-gate that led to the church and the churchyard. She felt him draw a deep breath and hold it for a while before releasing it.

"I will wait here," she said.

He nodded. "I will not keep you long."

"Take as long as you need," she told him as he jumped from the carriage without waiting for the steps to be lowered and disappeared under the roof of the gate.

She watched as he came into sight on the other side, stepping off the path to the church in order to walk slowly among the headstones, many of them old and mossy. She realized after a while that he could not remember exactly where the grave for which he searched was. Her heart ached for him, and she could not watch any longer. She closed her eyes and rested her head against the cushioned seat behind her.

———

He found his grandmother's grave and his parents' first and stopped to acknowledge a pang of grief for them, though he had not allowed himself to grieve deeply when he heard of his parents' deaths—a long time ago. He thought of what he had learned today and knew that all humanity was flawed. No one was totally innocent. No one was entirely guilty. We are all varying shades of gray. *No man is an island* . . . His grandmother had rarely spoken kindly to him, yet she had given him a home when he was homeless. She had been kind to his wife. She had left him everything she possessed when she died.

It was a large, sprawling graveyard. He searched for an unkempt mound. At least he hoped there was some sort of mound. One would have thought the exact spot would be seared upon his memory. But he had been too distraught at the time. Not outwardly. Outwardly he had seemed dead to all feeling, even grief. He knew that because people had told him so—with disapproving frowns.

He missed the double grave for a while because he was looking for the wrong thing. When he saw the neat headstone and the well-kept grave with its cluster of pink pansies growing from the ground, he looked almost idly at what was written there. He had been feeling near to despair at the very real possibility that he would never know quite where they were buried.

Poppy Taylor, he read, *beloved wife of Matthew.* And beneath that, *Helena Taylor, cherished daughter.* And the dates, the first showing that Poppy had died at the age of twenty-four—she had been five years older than Matthew. The second date was singular.

Helena had been born and died on the same day in the same year. She had never drawn breath, never been given the chance to live.

But cherished nonetheless.

Someone had put the headstone here. Someone had composed the simple inscription. Someone had looked after the grave ever since, for more than thirty years. Someone had planted the flowers.

Someone had cared. Someone did care. Not past tense but present.

Matthew knelt beside the grave and pressed his hand to the stone so that the base of his palm touched Helena's name and the tips of his fingers touched Poppy's.

Ah, dear God.

His two women, the two he had vowed to love and protect for the rest of his life. The two who were supposed to be his salvation after a troubled boyhood and a misplaced romantic attachment. How different life might have been . . . Poppy, dead at twenty-four from some mysterious fever and convulsions coming seemingly from nowhere an hour or two after the midwife and doctor had left. And Helena, with no chance at life at all. The cord that had attached her to her mother for sustenance had been wrapped about her neck.

He had been helpless in the face of his responsibility to love and cherish them and keep them safe. And so he had failed in every imaginable way. And had fled. Briefly, as he crossed the channel from England, he had thought of dropping over the rail of the ship to the black waters below. But it was too easy a solution. He needed to suffer, to face himself and his many demons. And so he had forced himself to live on.

"Poppy," he murmured now. "I would have loved you for a

lifetime. Sometimes love is a deliberate choice. I would have made it. I did make it. I did love you. I am sorry it was not enough."

He moved his hand to trace the letters of his daughter's name.

"Helena," he said. "I could not save you. I could not die in your place. Life does not work that way. But I have always loved you with every breath I have drawn since you died. Forgive me for failing you."

And he pressed his hand to his mouth and clenched his eyes closed, swallowing the tears that had been more than thirty years in the making.

Eventually he got to his feet, patted the top of the gravestone, and made his way back to the carriage, where Clarissa awaited him.

Along with what remained of his life.

CHAPTER NINETEEN

T hey traveled home largely in silence, alone with their own
thoughts, though they held hands most of the way and occasionally laced their fingers. Their arms and shoulders touched. For
a while Clarissa tipped her head sideways to rest on Matthew's
shoulder. But she knew it was too soon for him to talk of all the
teeming emotions the day had brought him. And she had much to
think about herself. A great deal had happened since her return
from London.

"I need to concentrate upon work for the next few days," he said
as the carriage made its turn into Boscombe.

She needed to be alone again too.

"You will not neglect your archery?" she asked him as the carriage drew to a stop before the smithy.

He hesitated for a moment. "I will go three days from now after
I finish work," he said. "Weather permitting."

She knew he would need to practice. Not because his skills
would have grown rusty but because he would need to find that

source of peace and balance within himself that had been severely disturbed lately.

"I will not come to watch," she said. "But I will have tea taken out to the summerhouse. You may join me there when you have finished if you wish. But only if you wish."

He smiled at her and they left it at that. They both needed to be alone. They needed to sort themselves out. She did not know quite why she felt very close to tears as the carriage resumed its journey back to the house.

What if they did indeed sort themselves out and the way forward did not include each other?

It rained the following day. Even so she trudged up the hill to the temple folly, wearing rain boots and holding a large old black umbrella, which had belonged to Caleb, over her head. She sat under the roof of the temple all morning, breathing in the lovely country smells of wet earth and greenery and distant sheep. She had not brought a book with her. She had not read in over a month. She wondered if she ever would again. Perhaps when she was alone and cozy in her cottage by the river . . .

She thought of the letters that had been delivered this morning. They had come together in one package, one from Pippa, the other from Stephanie. They must have been talking to each other about her, for both had basically the same message. They loved her. They missed her. She might come to Greystone whenever she wished and for as long as she wished—that was Pippa. Stephanie would return to Ravenswood if her mother needed her and stay all summer and all winter too. Yet each understood—both had emphasized the point—her need to be free of family and obligation and even the distraction of entertainments for a while. They understood that she had reached a turning point in her life and needed time and solitude in which to make some decisions. They sent all their love.

It was a great relief to feel their understanding and to be assured that they were no longer puzzled by what she was doing, or offended by it. Perhaps it was because they were her daughters, without the strong protective instinct that characterized her sons.

How she loved them all!

And how delightful that Pippa and Stephanie were able to have time with each other without her constant presence with them too. There was a six-year gap in their ages. Pippa was twenty-five, Steph nineteen. It was an age difference that had distanced them from each other when they were younger, though there had never been any real hostility. Now, it seemed, the gap in their ages mattered less. They were becoming firm friends.

Ben and Owen and Joy had arrived safely at Penallen. Jennifer had written a brief note to tell her so. It had arrived yesterday while she was away. Jennifer was very happy to have her husband and daughter back home—she never called Joy her stepdaughter—and delighted that Owen had come with them. If her mother-in-law had come too, her happiness would have been complete. But she understood entirely her mother-in-law's need to be alone for a while. She would press no further invitations upon her, only the assurance that she would always be more than welcome.

Clarissa smiled through tears that never seemed to be very far off these days. How could she be distancing herself from a family that cared so much for her? How could she be dreaming of—and plotting for—a home of her own with a bright red front door she could shut against the whole world whenever she chose?

But they understood.

At last they seemed to understand.

She sat up in the turret room after luncheon. The rain had eased but not stopped entirely. She did not mind. It was the rain that kept the grass almost emerald colored and thick and springy to the touch. It was the rain that gave color to all the wildflowers blooming in the meadow and the cultivated flowers in their carefully weeded beds. And she was actually glad of the excuse to be lazy today, to remain at home, sitting and dreaming.

Devlin came with Gwyneth and the children the following afternoon after Clarissa had spent the morning, in her rain boots, strolling from one flowery nook to another in the dips of land between the house and the lake. She had stopped for what must have been a whole hour in the one with the small lily pond after checking that the seat was not still wet from yesterday's rain. She breathed in the scent of the sweet peas growing there.

They had called in for a day or two on their way to Wales, Devlin explained. Ravenswood was far off the much shorter route from London they would normally have taken. But when she pointed out that fact, Gwyneth explained that they had wanted to give her one more chance to go with them. She looked at her mother-in-law with a twinkling smile as she said it.

"We will not press the issue, Mother," she said. "We know you quite deliberately chose to come home to be alone and have probably been enjoying your freedom to come and go as you wish and do whatever you please. We guessed that you have been somewhat frustrated by the interruptions to your peace."

Clarissa merely smiled back at her. Making a detour here was Devlin's idea, not Gwyneth's, she understood.

"Gareth and Bethan will interrupt it even more when they wake up from their naps," Gwyneth said.

Clarissa laughed. "What are grandmothers for?" she said. "I have missed them. Has Bethan walked more than just that once yet?"

"She has not," Devlin said. "You asked the wrong question, Mama. You ought to have asked if she has run."

"Ah." Clarissa laughed again. "Let the fun begin, then."

"Is it any wonder," Gwyneth said, "that we want you to come with us?"

They stayed only until the following morning, during which time Clarissa played with the children and read them their bedtime stories. But while Gwyneth stayed in the nursery to tuck them into their beds and remain with them until they fell asleep, Devlin spoke with his mother in the drawing room.

"We came because I needed to talk with you in person, Mama," he said. He held up a staying hand when she drew breath to speak. "It is probably not quite what you expect. I have not come to object to whatever is between you and Matthew Taylor. You do not even need to explain to me or justify the relationship. We all reacted with rather ridiculous alarm to the hints various people dropped in the letters they wrote to us. As though you were a child. Or an imbecile. And I did not come to object to your remaining here alone through the summer. I have been assured, even apart from what you yourself told us before you came here, that it is what you want. You know there are several alternatives if you should change your mind, though I do not expect you will. I have come because both Ben and Owen have informed me that you have some sort of proposition to make to me and I had better listen to it carefully without dismissing it out of hand. Neither gave any hint as to what that proposition is."

And so she told him of her wish to build a cottage for herself down by the river, a home that could become a dower house after her time since it would be on Ravenswood land. She told him she had no wish whatsoever to move away from her family or cut herself off from them. She wished only to have a place all her own. She told him she intended to pay for it herself. It would not cost him a penny—only his permission to proceed.

His expression was black by the time she had finished speaking. Or so it seemed to her.

"It is still light outside," he said curtly after glancing at the window. "Show me."

They walked down the driveway and along the river path in silence until she stopped.

"Here," she said. "The cottage will go over there, just this side of the meadow, and there will be room left for a flower garden. Matthew says the chance of flooding is slim to none. And it will be very close to the house but separate from it. Devlin—"

He was still looking a bit thunderous. He held up a hand again.

"Just one thing," he said. "It will be on my land. It will be my property. I will pay for it."

He was not saying an outright no?

"It was my idea," she said. "It would be an expense you were not—"

His hand was up yet again.

"It is not negotiable, Mama," he said. "I will compromise on only one thing."

"What?" she asked warily.

"You may pay for what goes inside the house," he said. "And for what surrounds it. The furnishings and decorations. The lawns and flowers and hedges. It will be a considerable expense for you."

"You are saying yes, then?" She clasped her hands and held them beneath her chin.

"I am trying to understand all this, Mama," he said. "The need to be alone. The new friendship, which some of your neighbors, I might add, believe is probably more than just friendship. The need for a house of your own when Ravenswood is vast enough to swallow a village. The . . . independence from your own children. Gwyneth has tried to explain it to me as though she understands better than I do. Perhaps she does. Mama . . . she insists that you still love us."

She stared at him mutely for a few moments in the gathering dusk. "I let you down very badly once, Devlin," she said. "I sent you away because you had tried to defend my honor publicly. I suffered for that decision for six long years. I suffered because I love you, as I love all my children, perhaps more than I love my own life. But . . . I do love my own life too. I want to live whatever remains of it in my own way. But that does not include any separation from any of you. I love you."

He stared at her in apparent bafflement for a few moments before striding toward her and catching her up in a brief, fierce hug.

"We had better go back to the house before we have to feel our way in the darkness," he said. "And before Gwyneth organizes a search party. I will contact a good architect and send him here, Mama. You may explain your vision to him and he will draw up plans for your approval. I will explain to him that work on the house is to begin within the month and be finished before winter sets in. He can make all the arrangements."

"Oh," she said, taking his offered arm. She could not think what else to say. "Oh goodness."

Could some dreams really come true?

———

Matthew had discovered over the years that working could sometimes put him into a near-meditative state, especially if the project was one that required some creativity. It helped still his mind, focusing upon the task, letting both skill and artistry flow through his hands and into the wood.

He worked almost constantly through the two days following his visit to his brother and to the churchyard where his wife and daughter lay at rest, and the long carriage ride both ways with Clarissa. His whole being teemed with jumbled thoughts and raw emotions he had not experienced since he was a very young man. He did not try to control them. He worked instead, forgetting to stop for luncheon both days and stopping only long enough the first evening to make himself a thick sandwich, which he carried into his workroom and noticed an hour or so later, the bread hardening and dry on top. He ate the sandwich anyway rather than going to get something else. He forgot to go to bed that night until his eyes were watering so badly he could no longer clearly see what he was doing.

He stopped work the second evening only because he had said he would go to a birthday party Mrs. Holland had organized for Sally, her daughter, who was married to Alan Roberts, the school-teacher. Cam came to fetch him. It was a boisterous gathering, at which people all seemed to want to talk at once, raising their voices to be heard over everyone else's, while those who were not talking did a great deal of laughing instead. George Isherwood, the doctor, was there as well as Mrs. Proctor, the dressmaker, the Misses Miller from the shop, and John Roberts, the cobbler. Matthew was fond of them all and did as much laughing as any of them, despite the news the Misses Miller had brought to the party.

The Earl and Countess of Stratton and their children had arrived home from London earlier in the day. The sisters had seen their carriage from the shop window with their very own eyes as it drove past on the far side of the village green. The Strattons must have changed their minds about going to Wales.

"But I wonder why," Sally said.

Unusually, no one seemed able—or willing—to speculate upon the reason, and there were several uncomfortably silent moments while a few of the guests glanced self-consciously at Matthew.

He enjoyed the evening anyway and slept deeply that night. He worked the following morning until he was aware of a banging on his door and opened it to discover Mrs. Holland standing outside, a covered plate of leftovers from the night before in her hand.

"But you insisted I bring some home with me last night," Matthew said in protest. "I had cake for breakfast."

"Oh, did I?" she said with an almost comic look of surprise. "I forgot. Take it anyway. There is so much left Oscar and Cam will be eating it for a week."

"Well, thank you," he said, taking the plate from her. "You spoil me, Mrs. Holland."

"Someone has to," she said, patting the back of his hand after he had transferred the food to one of his own plates and given hers back to her. "His lordship's carriage drove away from Ravenswood a few hours ago. It looks as if they are going to visit her ladyship's relatives in Wales after all. They just stopped here for the night, I daresay. There is nothing better than sleeping in your own bed, is there? I don't believe the dowager countess went with them. And who could blame her? I would not enjoy traveling a few hundred or a few thousand miles, whatever it is, with two young children, no matter how good they are. So she is home alone again."

She squeezed one eye shut, rubbed it with a finger of her free hand as though a dust mote had attacked her, and clattered back down the stairs to the street.

Matthew took his bow and arrow to the poplar alley after cleaning up his workroom and casting a critical eye and hand over the almost-finished crib. Once he arrived at the wooded alley, he set up his equipment, noted with something that felt suspiciously like disappointment that he was alone, and began his practice.

It did not go well for a while. He almost gave up in frustration and despair. But what was there in his life that was so disturbing to him? He had work for some time to come, all of it both interesting and challenging. His friends were still his friends. Apart from the uneasy looks that had been cast his way last evening when the Misses Miller had talked of Devlin Ware and his family's arrival at Ravenswood, he was being treated as he always had been. He had not become any sort of pariah. His family had been restored to him, and he was as determined as they seemed to be to pursue the relationship, to normalize it if that was possible after more than thirty years of estrangement. Poppy and Helena were at peace in their neat, well-kept grave. He would visit them regularly, assure them that they would never be forgotten. He loved Clarissa. Yes, it was as simple as that. He was not sure of the exact nature of the love she felt for him, but even friendship would be enough, as it always had been. And they would remain friends. He was confident of that.

There was no reason, then, to feel out of sorts.

When he lifted his bow again after taking a short break and followed his breath for a while—in, hold, out, hold—he was finally there, one with his bow and his quiver and arrows, with the target and the space between, with the air and the grass beneath his feet and the sky above.

It had been a long practice, he realized when he finally came back inside his body and discovered that his bow arm was stiff and aching, that his fingers were sore and tingling from drawing arrows from his quiver, that his legs seemed almost locked at the knees. He went to pluck the last round of arrows from the target—all had found the bull's-eye—and looked ahead along the alley to the summerhouse. Even if she had come, he thought, she would surely have left by now.

But soon enough he saw she had come and she had not left. He could see her sitting inside the summerhouse in a light-colored dress, gazing back in his direction. He dropped the bow and quiver at his feet, decided against going back for his coat, and strode off toward her.

She was standing in the open doorway when he reached her and caught her up with both arms about her waist and swung her in a full circle. She wrapped her own arms about his neck and laughed.

"I am sorry," he said. "I lost track of time."

"And forgot your coat," she said. "But I like you in your shirt-sleeves. And I could watch you forever at your archery and not grow tired of it."

They stood gazing into each other's eyes, their arms still about each other. She was wearing a muslin summer dress with no shawl and no bonnet. She was rosy complexioned and bright eyed.

"Devlin came yesterday with Gwyneth and the children," she said. "They left again this morning. Matthew, I am to have my cottage. Devlin is going to send an architect here so I can tell him exactly what I want, and the building is to start within the next few weeks and be finished by winter. Can you believe it?"

It was difficult. He would have expected her son to put up all sorts of objections to her dream.

"He insists upon paying for the house," she said, "since, as he explained, it will be on Ravenswood land and therefore legally his. But I am to pay for all the furnishings and the landscaping and planting of the garden."

"Am I going to be allowed to visit you there?" he asked, smiling back at her. "Or will that red door be locked against me?"

"Oh," she said, her smile softening. "You must have a key of your own, Matthew."

He laughed, though he felt a stabbing of emotion at her words and the look on her face.

"Have you had your invitation?" he asked her.

"How delightful it was," she said. "Did they send one to you too, even though you are to be the guest of honor? The pleasure of your company is requested for refreshments, conversation, cards, and dancing if the young people and the young at heart insist upon it. And then, more prosaically, the date and time and Adelaide Taylor's signature. No mention of your name as the special guest."

"For which omission I am very grateful," he said. "Perhaps Adelaide is a bit afraid I will turn coward and not go and she will end up looking foolish."

"And feeling massively disappointed," she said. "You will go, Matthew?"

"I will," he said. "Will you?"

"Of course," she said. "Mama and Papa will be there too."

"Reggie insists upon sending his carriage for me," he said. "I daresay he will be happy for you to use it too."

She took her arms from about his neck and pressed her hands against his shoulders. "Come inside," she said. "Tea was brought out an hour ago, but I waited for you."

"Thank you," he said, sitting beside her on one of the sofas.

"Tell me. Are you closer to discovering what you came home to find, Clarissa? Despite all the interruptions?"

"I am," she said, taking his hand in hers and lacing their fingers. "I believe I am going to be able to have my own life and my family life too. It might be said that I have always had both anyway, but—"

"I understand," he said.

"I even read for an hour this morning after Devlin and Gwyneth and the children left," she said. "That must sound very trivial. But I have been unable to concentrate upon any book since I came home."

"And I was able to shoot today," he said.

"Yes," she said. "I saw. Is the turmoil starting to feel less . . . tumultuous, then?"

"It is," he said. "I have a brother and sister-in-law, and a whole family surrounding them. It is not going to be easy or comfortable sorting everything out, and I know I will dread the coming of next Friday almost as much as I dreaded my visit a few days ago. But . . ." He shrugged. "It will be done."

She tipped her head to rest on his shoulder, and he turned his head and kissed her—warmly and with deepening intensity as her free arm came about his neck again and her hand cupped the back of his head, her fingers pushing through his hair.

She was so beautiful, he thought, moving his head back a fraction from hers to gaze at her, heavy lidded and smiling dreamily back at him.

"What are you thinking?" she asked, her voice low.

He was thinking that he wanted to make love to her and that perhaps she wanted it too. But . . . in a glass-walled summerhouse in broad daylight, with gardeners forever busy in the park?

"I am thinking," he said, "that I could drink that whole jug of lemonade myself if you do not first claim a glassful."

She laughed and pushed away from him. "And all this food will grow stale if we do not eat it soon," she said. "That would be a shame."

"It would," he said, and told her, as she moved forward on the sofa to pour their drinks, about the party the evening before and the bundle of food he had taken home and the duplicate plate of leftovers Mrs. Holland had brought him earlier.

"The offering this morning was an excuse for her to let me know that your son's carriage had left Ravenswood, presumably bound for Wales," he said. "The Misses Miller brought the news of its arrival to the gathering last evening."

"Ah, the joys of belonging to a small rural community," she said, handing him his glass and an empty plate for him to fill himself.

Matthew took a mouthful of his lemonade and contemplated the feast set out before him.

CHAPTER TWENTY

Clarissa enjoyed the following week more than she had enjoyed any other for a long while, it seemed to her. She spent hours at a time alone, both indoors and out, and was thoroughly at ease in her own company. She was embroidering and reading again, though she spent a great deal of time too just sitting or walking and gazing about her, appreciating the fact that she was alive and healthy and in possession of an abundance of blessings upon which to build a future that would be personally fulfilling without also being self-ish. She wrote letters. She called upon friends and neighbors and received them when they called upon her.

An architect presented himself at Ravenswood a mere two days after Devlin left to look at and survey the piece of land she had chosen by the river and to make notes of what her ladyship wanted. He returned two days after that with detailed drawings of a two-story cottage, cozy enough just for her but large enough to allow her to entertain groups and accommodate overnight guests. There was to be a whole section at the back for the kitchen and servants' quarters. She expected that Millicent would move there with her, and she would need a housekeeper and cook, preferably all in one person, and a gardener and general handyman. Perhaps she would be able to find a married couple to fill the roles. There was to be space for a garden, which she planned to fill with shrubs and flowers as well, and a lawn. She pictured a vegetable and herb garden to the east of the cottage.

Her ladyship could expect work to begin within the next couple of weeks, the architect informed her with a bow as he took his leave. Clarissa felt a bit breathless. Could all this really be happening? And so quickly? Her dream of having a cottage of her own had only recently been conceived, as well as her search for the perfect setting.

She saw Matthew a number of times during that week. Their friendship was no longer to be hidden away. Mostly they met and strolled in the park in the late afternoon or evening, but once Clarissa walked into the village and, by prearrangement, met him outside the inn and shared a pot of tea with him in the dining room, enjoying the view over the village green from their table by the window. They even allowed themselves to be persuaded into eating some of the landlady Mrs. Berry's freshly baked rhubarb tart with their tea. Afterward they went together to the shop, since Matthew needed a few groceries and Clarissa wanted to look at a newly arrived batch of embroidery silks. The Misses Miller, wide-eyed and simpering, were almost visibly storing up the sensational news to spread among their customers for the rest of the day.

As they left the shop, Matthew reminded her his brother was insisting upon sending his own carriage to convey him the day before the party in his honor. Matthew was trying to persuade Clarissa to share the conveyance with him since she had been invited and fully intended on going.

"It seems a bit pointless to take two carriages, one behind the other," he said.

But Clarissa felt uneasy about accepting. Reginald had not specifically suggested that she travel with his brother. Perhaps he did not think it necessary to do so but simply assumed she would. She was not sure she wanted to give him and his wife the impression that she and Matthew were a couple, however. And were they? They had acknowledged only a friendship so far, though they frequently shared hugs and kisses and once or twice an altogether more heated embrace.

She did not know if she wanted them to be a couple.

She suspected he did not know if he wanted it either.

They were middle-aged and set in their ways. He had enjoyed independence for many years. She was just discovering her own. Perhaps the whole of their relationship would be ruined if they tried to take it further, and that would be incredibly sad.

As it turned out, she was saved from the dilemma of deciding whether to go with Matthew in his brother's carriage or take her own when yet another member of her family—and surely the last—arrived unexpectedly at Ravenswood two days before the Taylors' party.

Clarissa was in the turret room, a place in which she had spent far more time during the past month than she had in years past. She was dreaming of her cottage and of the grandchildren who would be born soon after Christmas. She was dreaming of Nicholas coming back to England soon, to stay, she hoped. She was dreaming of Owen finding his way in life and of Stephanie finding happiness. One thing she was not doing was reading the book she had brought with her. It was always virtually impossible to read in the turret room.

But she sat forward on the couch when she heard horses' hooves and carriage wheels. Looking out the windows, she saw that a traveling carriage was coming up the driveway, but not one that any of her local friends would be using so close to their own homes. It stopped before the front doors below and to the left of her, and out stepped her brother, George, and then Kitty. Their visit was unplanned and unhinted at in their most recent letters. Clarissa laughed softly to herself as she got to her feet and made her way downstairs.

"We decided we simply must spend a few days with Mama and Papa before going home," George said a few minutes later, after Clarissa had gone downstairs to greet and hug them. "I have been feeling guilty over missing Mama's birthday. A special one too, her seventieth."

"I insisted that we come anyway, late as we are for the birthday," Kitty said, beaming at Clarissa. "And I insisted too that we call upon you on our way there. I have missed you dreadfully."

They would have had to make a detour of many miles to come here. Ravenswood was not on their direct route from London to her parents' house. They intended to resume their journey after taking tea with Clarissa and relaxing for an hour or so.

"Mama and Papa will be delighted to see you," she said as she led the way to the drawing room, where tea was served almost immediately.

"Are you not lonely here all on your own, Clarissa?" her brother asked. "Though I daresay you have been making some new friends."

"One specifically?" she said while Kitty winked at her, unseen by her husband. "The one that has brought you here, though I am sure your desire to see Mama and Papa is genuine? Matthew Taylor is not a new friend, however, as you are well aware, George. We were close friends through most of our growing years, and we are friends again."

"Some of your neighbors have been a bit . . . concerned about it," George said.

"So I have heard. But I have also decided to let them be," she said. "It is really none of their business, is it?"

"I suppose you think it is none of mine either," he said, frowning. "Clarissa—"

But Kitty was patting his arm. "Mr. Taylor transformed Jenny's life when he made her that wheeled chair the year before last," she said. "It also happens to be a work of art. And he made the cane that has helped enable her to dispense with those useless crutches she used to have. I would like to be his friend too if only because of what he has done for my niece. Clarissa is a grown woman, George, as I have been explaining to you since we waved her on her way back to Ravenswood."

"I know," he said. "And she is five years older than me. You have been reminding me of that too, Kit."

She beamed at him and then at Clarissa. "We must be on our way soon," she said. "We still have another ten miles to go. I suppose you do not want to come with us, Clarissa? Nothing would make us happier."

"Well, as it happens, I do," Clarissa said, and watched as both their faces lit up. "I was going there tomorrow anyway. I have been invited to a grand party Reginald and Adelaide Taylor are organizing for Friday. It is in honor of Matthew. I am quite certain you will be invited too."

"I have a feeling," George said, getting to his feet, "that there is a story to be told here. You must tell it to us down to the last detail when we resume our journey, Clarissa. In the meantime, you have fifteen minutes to get ready to come with us."

"Have you always been such a tyrant?" she asked with a smile.

"Have you not noticed that I am a shadow of my former self?" Kitty asked her.

Clarissa hurried from the room, laughing. Fifteen minutes. But Millicent would rise to the challenge of packing what she would need for a few days. She, meanwhile, had only to change into a carriage dress and write a quick note to be delivered to Matthew.

M atthew was disappointed when he received Clarissa's note. The journey was a long and tedious one, and he would miss her company and conversation. However, perhaps it was just as well that they would not arrive together in Reggie's carriage. He did not want to give his family the impression that they were anything more to each other than neighbors and friends. No more, in fact, than they had been when they were growing up.

He was actually glad she had gone with her brother and sister-in-law when the following day brought not only his brother's carriage but Reggie too.

"What?" Matthew said after they had exchanged a firm handshake and Reggie stood inside his rooms, looking about with undisguised interest. "You decided to make a twenty-mile journey of it, here and back? Were you afraid I would change my mind and return your carriage empty?"

"This room ought to look like a hovel, Matt," Reginald said, ignoring his questions. "Instead it looks like a home. I want to see your work, though I suspect I am seeing some of it in this furniture and those candlesticks. May I see more?"

They spent more than half an hour in the workroom. Reggie ran a hand over the crib Matthew had almost finished making for Ben Ellis's child.

"I did not trust in your dream when you were a boy, Matt," he said. "I am so glad you dreamed it anyway. I feel humbled. Forgive me?"

"Perhaps we ought not to play the blame and forgiveness game any longer," Matthew said. "I did not know but guess now it is you who has looked after my wife and daughter's grave with such meticulous care. I did not know you cared at all."

"Addy and Emily are the ones who dispense with the weeds and coax the flowers to bloom," Reggie said. "I hope the inscription on the headstone is adequate. Just a few brief words, but I agonized over them for what must have been weeks."

"They are perfect," Matthew said. "Thank you."

They ate a luncheon at the inn and were on their way before the middle of the afternoon. His brother's arrival prevented Matthew from feeling the apprehension that had hovered over him for the past week. A generous gesture on his brother's part given the distance. But Matthew was now thinking he could accept that this party was something his family wanted to do for him. It was a sort of atonement, one that worked both ways. They would give the party, and he would attend it and do all in his power to enjoy it.

He felt love seeping into him. He had not realized quite how absent it had been. For most of his adult years he had loved in the abstract—and yes, it was a form of real love and essential to his being. But it had not been personal. He had friends and valued and loved them. But that deep sort of love that bound together certain individuals—family and the love of one's heart—had been denied.

Now he needed to complete—or at least continue—what he

had started to learn at the monastery. He needed to open his mind and his heart and his very being to all the risks of loving fully and unconditionally and of being loved.

It was not an entirely comforting prospect. It felt a bit . . . uncontrolled.

It was a necessary step, however, if he wanted to be whole.

He had not realized until now that he had never allowed himself to be whole, that he had suppressed a large part of himself lest he be hurt.

The family—his family—was very obviously excited by his arrival and by the preparations they were making for tomorrow evening's grand celebration, to which it appeared they had invited almost everyone they knew in the vicinity.

Philip and Emily bore him off soon after his arrival to meet their children, two boys and a girl, who proceeded to show him the treasures of the nursery. Mabel, his niece, arrived soon after with her husband, Albert, and their young son and daughter, and there was a flurry of introductions and hugs, loud conversation, and laughter. Adelaide shed tears over the wood carving Matthew had brought her of a woman sitting relaxed and dreaming in a rocking chair, a cat curled on her lap.

"I will treasure it always," she told him. "Look, Reggie. The chair actually rocks. And if that cat is not purring, there is something wrong with my inner ear."

Matthew allowed himself to feel happy.

Clarissa spent the day before the party talking endlessly with her parents, with George, with whom she had always had a close relationship, and especially with Kitty. They went for a walk in the park together during the afternoon, and Kitty, slipping a hand through Clarissa's arm, demanded to know everything there was to know about Matthew Taylor.

"I know," she said, "that he is a superb carpenter and wood-carver. I know the two of you were friends growing up. I know you are friends again now. I will not allow you to bounce our conversation off those few facts, Clarissa. We have been the closest of friends since we met in London as young brides, though most of our friendship has been conducted via letter, alas. Now we are face to face. Well, side to side anyway. And I want to talk about Matthew Taylor."

"There are friends and friends," Clarissa said after giving her answer some consideration. "There are those for whom we feel a warm affection, with whom we enjoy spending time. Those with whom we are comfortable. And then there are the friends with whom the affection and the communication run far deeper, those with whom we feel some sort of soul connection, if that is not too exaggerated a claim. Friends with whom we can and do talk about anything under the sun, including our deepest emotions. Friends with whom we can be silent for long stretches without feeling any discomfort or any disconnection at all. You have always been the second kind of friend to me, Kitty, though we are not often silent together, are we? There is always so much to say when we see each other so rarely. Matthew is also that kind of friend. He was when we were growing up, and he is now."

"But a little more than a friend?" Kitty asked. "Perhaps a great deal more?"

Clarissa was about to deny it. But this was Kitty.

"We were a bit in love when I was seventeen and Matthew was eighteen," she said. "When I decided to marry Caleb, though that was not entirely a calculated decision, I genuinely fell in love with him. And I never really regretted marrying him. Though perhaps . . . Well, it is complicated. He gave me my children, whom I adore. He gave me Ravenswood and my neighbors and friends there, and they make me happy. And he was genuinely charming and affectionate. Any deeper connection between Matthew and me would not have worked out well as we were at the time anyway. Not for either of us. We would have destroyed ourselves and each other. Perhaps. Probably. Who really knows?"

"You needed to wait until you were fifty," Kitty said. "You are there now."

"Yes," Clarissa said. "Almost."

"Was he the reason you went home to Ravenswood?" Kitty asked.

Clarissa looked at her in surprise. "No," she said. "I did not go there to find anyone but myself. Sometimes a woman can lose herself in her family. It can be a happy experience. For most of my life it has been for me. But sometimes a woman needs to pause to ask who she is in herself. Sometimes she needs to discover if her life is personally fulfilling. I went home early and alone because I was starting to feel a certain emptiness at the core of myself, if that makes any sense. I launched Stephanie upon society and then realized that all my active obligations to my children were fulfilled. What was left? It was rather a bleak feeling. Almost frightening."

"And does Mr. Taylor fill that emptiness at the core of yourself?" Kitty asked.

Clarissa frowned. "I am not sure I want him to," she said. "The core of myself should be filled with me, though I have no idea what I am talking about. What I am trying to say is that I should be able to stand alone as myself."

"I understand," Kitty said. "But does he make you happy, Clarissa? Does he make you feel that your life would be immeasurably enriched if he could be your friend—and perhaps more than your friend—for the rest of your life?"

Clarissa sighed. "Oh yes," she said, and Kitty squeezed her arm.

"I look forward to seeing you together tomorrow evening," she said.

"And what of you and George?" Clarissa asked. "Is your marriage everything you dreamed it would be, Kitty? Not that your personal life is any of my business. And how can you say anything but yes when he is my brother?"

Kitty laughed. "Do you really need to ask?" she said. "I am over the moon in love with him, Clarissa. I sometimes feel it is unseemly in a middle-aged woman like me. But why should it be? Why should anyone deny herself—or himself—the wonder of romantic love just because she is fifty or seventy? Or ninety? The miracle of it all, Clarissa, is that he is as deeply in love with me. Am I not the most fortunate woman on earth?"

"No," Clarissa said. "Only one of the most fortunate."

They both laughed.

By the following day, the day of the party, Clarissa was craving some solitude again. George was in the library with their father, and Kitty was in her mother's dressing room, helping her select a gown for the evening. Clarissa wrapped a shawl about her shoulders and stepped outside alone. The air was fresh and cool, and the sounds of nature were the only ones to assail her ears.

How she needed her cottage, she thought. Much as she loved company, especially that of her family and close friends, she had come to understand during the past weeks that she needed solitude too. And silence. Most of all silence.

She set out on a walk through the park. It was not entirely aimless. She had noticed something yesterday when she was strolling with Kitty. Something she would not have expected to recognize but did. She had not realized how deeply embedded in her memory it was. Perhaps it was that wood carving of Matthew's that had jogged the memory.

Yesterday she had recognized the tree against which she had leaned all those years ago after telling Matthew that she was expecting a marriage offer from Caleb the following day. She had been feeling excited at the prospect and deeply upset at the knowledge that she had hurt Matthew, and herself too, with her decision. She had stood against that tree bewildered by the extreme emotions only a seventeen-year-old could feel. Looking ahead, looking back, feeling the exultation and pain of the present. Aware of him standing silently not far off, not moving, not saying anything, the distance that would be between them for more than thirty years already an almost tangible thing.

She found the tree now and verified by looking around that yes, indeed, this was the one. She leaned back against it again after dropping her shawl to the grass. She felt with both hands for the trunk behind her and drew sustenance from the life force she could sense moving up to the branches from the roots belowground. She rested the back of her head against the tree and closed her eyes.

Just here. Where so much had ended. The day before so much had begun. Two men, one of whom had been her friend, her soul mate, the other of whom had become her husband and father of her children.

Two men she had loved on that day.

Did life offer second chances?

Though she could not chastise herself about choosing Caleb over Matthew at the time.

Was now the right time?

Would it be foolish to try to recapture a romance that had been about to blossom more than thirty years ago? Though perhaps that was not what was happening. Perhaps they were not trying to recapture anything. Perhaps what was happening between them was all new.

Ah. And perhaps she was the only one who was experiencing this turmoil of emotion and indecision. Perhaps for Matthew what was between them was nothing more than friendship with a few pleasant kisses included.

She opened her eyes and looked at the trees and greenery surrounding her. She tried to draw peace from her surroundings, a calming of the mind. There was so much for which to be happy.

Yesterday had been a day full of chatter and laughter and stories intended to fill in some of the long gap of the missing years. Matthew had felt so thoroughly welcome in his brother's home that he had quickly forgotten his self-consciousness and apprehension about the upcoming party. He had slept well in a bedchamber that had not been his when he was a boy—a touch of thoughtfulness on Reggie's part, he guessed.

Today was somewhat different. All was anxiety and busy activity as preparations were made for the evening's festivities, and Matthew spent most of the morning trying to stay out of everyone's way, mainly with Albert, Mabel's husband, as an accomplice.

"There is nothing more to be dreaded than a busy woman," that young man said. "She will invariably either accuse the men in her orbit of getting in her way or find all sorts of uncongenial tasks to keep them busy. It is far better to stay out of her way."

It was a vain hope, however. Mabel found her husband and Matthew talking at their ease behind a large potted plant in the conservatory and sent the former off to carry some chairs from one room to another since all the menservants were rushed off their feet. She looked in horror at Matthew when he offered to help.

"You are the guest of honor, Uncle Matthew," she said. "Mama would die of mortification if she saw you carrying chairs."

So Matthew did what he had been wanting to do since yesterday. He walked over to the Greenfields' house to call upon Clarissa and instead drank coffee with her parents and with George and his wife.

"I understand, Mr. Taylor, that the gathering to which we have been invited this evening is in your honor," George's wife said.

"It would seem so," he said, grimacing slightly. "The prodigal has returned. Until very recently I had not seen any member of my family for more than thirty years. It is a long story."

"I love long stories," she said, smiling. "But . . . another time. You will have come to see Clarissa."

"She went outside for a stroll a while ago," her mother said.

"She walked past the window of the library, where I was sitting with George," Mr. Greenfield said. "I daresay you will find her out there somewhere unless you would rather wait here. I suppose the Taylor women have driven you from the house."

"Only by refusing my help even in the conveying of chairs from one room to another," Matthew said. "They insist upon treating me as though I were someone special. I will go and search for Clarissa, if you will excuse me."

"You are excused," Mrs. Greenfield said.

He looked around after he had stepped outside but could see no sign of her. She might be anywhere. The park was not nearly as large as the one at Ravenswood, but there were more trees to obscure one's view. He set out in the direction they had taken most often when they were young. Then he thought of the last time they had walked here. It was a heavy memory of abandonment and grief, and for a moment he felt all the desolation of the boy he had been then. Yet there had been years before that when he had found consolation here and acceptance and the lightheartedness he had experienced rarely if ever at home.

He had found friendship here and a measure of love.

Did the same description apply to them now? Friendship, yes. And . . . a measure of love?

Was it enough?

And then he had an idea and changed direction. His footsteps slowed after a while as he sought out the exact tree and hoped he would recognize it—and that it still existed. He had carved the scene, but he had never come back here. Would she remember? Would it be important enough that she would try to find the exact tree? She had loved the carving, but would she—

And then he stopped walking abruptly and felt his breath catch in his throat.

She was standing with her back against the tree—and there was no doubt it was the tree—her arms slightly behind her on either side, her palms pressed to the bark. Her dark hair was dressed neatly on her head, not flowing as it had been that other time. Her dress was less full, more Grecian in line than the one she had worn on the earlier occasion. She was no longer that svelte, pretty young girl but a shapely, elegant, and beautiful woman of middle years.

But she was the same person. And she gazed ahead of her, as she had done then, though her expression was surely more readable. There was dreamy longing in her face, though he could see it only in profile.

He was not standing in exactly the same spot as before. He was close but out of her line of vision. He stood very still and drank in the sight of her. He yearned for her.

She could not see him. And she had given no sign of having heard him come. But she must have felt his presence after a couple of minutes had passed. She turned her head slowly, and they gazed at each other. She smiled very slightly.

He moved toward her and stood in front of her, as he had stood then. They continued to gaze silently at each other until he spoke.

"I wanted very badly to kiss you," he said.

"I know," she said. "You told me a while ago, but I knew it at the time. And I wanted you to kiss me, to force my hand, to make me change my mind. That was wrong of me. What I ought to have wanted was for us to kiss each other. A mutual embrace of equals. Alas, it is not how girls are brought up to think—or do. We are not taught to insist upon equality of decision and responsibility. Let us kiss now, Matthew."

She moved her arms away from the tree and twined them about his neck while her body leaned against his. He wrapped his arms about her and kissed her with all the ardor of his love and the sexual desire that thrummed through his body. She kissed him back the same way, until at last they drew apart, their arms still loosely about each other.

He drew a slow breath and released it while she smiled at him.

"Reggie is hoping I will move back here next year, after Captain and Mrs. Jakes's lease runs out on my house," he said.

"And will you?" she asked him.

"I am thinking about it," he said. "I could live the life of a gentleman. I would have a suitable home to offer."

"To whom?" she asked him.

"To you," he said. "I could ask you to marry me."

"You could indeed," she said after a short silence. "A gentleman and a man of property. And you might be happy here, back with your family."

"Yes," he said.

She released herself from his arms and leaned back against the tree again while her eyes searched his face.

"Or," she said, "you could continue to live in your rooms above the smithy and visit me at my cottage. You could continue to be Boscombe's carpenter and a wood-carver. You could even ask me to marry you and come to live with me at the cottage. And keep your rooms as your working space."

He swallowed. "Yes," he said.

They gazed at each other in silence for long moments.

"What do you really want to do, Matthew?" she asked at last.

"I want to be able to offer you a life at least somewhat similar to what you are accustomed to," he said.

She shook her head. "It is not what I asked," she said. "What do you want? The life of a gentleman here or the life you have lived for the past twenty years and more?"

He hesitated, though there was only one true answer.

"I want you," he said.

He might be way out of line. He might be destroying their friendship once and for all as well as any hope of a different sort of relationship with her.

"If I did not exist," she said, "what would your decision be?"

He continued to gaze mutely at her. For she did exist. It was impossible to imagine his life without that fact.

"I must confess," he said at last, "that the prospect of living in a house with a red front door has a certain appeal."

Her eyes smiled and then her lips too and she laughed softly.

"You can have it," she said. "We can have it."

He took both her hands in his and squeezed them tightly as he bowed his head over them and rested his forehead against them.

For more than thirty years the impossible dream. Was it really possible now?

He went down on one knee before her without releasing her hands and looked up at her. Her smile had faded, but her eyes were still bright.

"Clarissa," he said. "Will you take the utterly foolhardy step of marrying me? When all I have to offer is a steadfast and lifelong love?"

He watched the smile return, slowly and softly.

"It sounds good enough to me," she said. "Especially since I love you too—steadfastly and forever. Yes, Matthew, I will."

He kissed the backs of her hands and got to his feet.

"On the understanding that you will have a mere carpenter for a husband," he said.

"And a superbly talented wood-carver," she said. "And that we will have a cottage by the river in which to live," she said. "Yes, I will."

She came back into his arms and raised her face to his.

"With a red door," he said. "That is not negotiable." He kissed her.

They smiled at each other afterward, and she laughed and flung her arms about his neck.

"I had better go and have a talk with your father since Stratton is in Wales," he said. "Does a father in such cases take precedence over a son, I wonder? Then I must get back to Reggie's. My sister-in-law and nieces may panic if they think the guest of honor has gone missing."

"Are you nervous?" she asked him.

"About the party?" he said. "When between now and then I have to face your father?"

"He is such an ogre." She linked an arm through his.

He wondered if any moment now he was going to wake up from this strange dream he was having.

CHAPTER TWENTY-ONE

Not long after Matthew returned to his brother's house, having been persuaded to take some luncheon with the Greenfields, all became a frantic bustle as the ladies began to dress in their chosen finery and panicked over missing items and wanted the curling iron all at the same moment and worried that the first guests would arrive before they were ready to receive them and fussed over the two young children who had escaped from the nursery and called for their nurse to come and get them—and then called for the men to come and get ready too.

"At least an hour earlier than we need to do it," Reggie said, giving a mock sigh for his brother and his son. "But we had better go up anyway before the ladies have a collective apoplexy."

Matthew dressed in the evening clothes he wore on all such occasions and came downstairs at the appointed hour. He was feeling far calmer than he had expected, considering the whole event was in his honor. Perhaps it was because life here now was less about formality and rules and doing things right and more about warmth and love and family interactions. Reggie's household was nothing like Matthew had expected it to be. It was nothing like it had used to be under his parents' rule even though the house was the same, with very few real modifications.

The drawing room was the largest room in the house. Beyond it was another room of a decent size, variously called the salon, when he was a boy, or the library, or the music room, though there had been precious few books there and the only instrument in it was an aged pianoforte, always out of tune and rarely played. There were wide double doors connecting the two rooms. Matthew could not remember the doors ever being opened. They were open to-night, however, surprising him with the discovery that the combined space was impressively large. The pianoforte in the smaller room was new, or at least newer than the one it had replaced. The lid over the keyboard had been raised. There was music on the stand above the keyboard and a small pile on top of the instrument. There was a bookcase too, filled with books, along the back wall.

In the drawing room itself, the furniture had been pushed back against the walls and the rugs removed. The wooden floor of both rooms gleamed with a fresh coat of varnish. Candles burned in the candelabra overhead in both rooms, a rarity during Matthew's childhood, when creating too much light during the evenings was considered a sinful waste of money and candles.

In the dining room, which he had passed on his way down from his bedchamber, the table with all its leaves added was packed as full as it could be with plates and bowls of food. Two side tables offered what looked like a wide variety of beverages and a punch bowl.

But there was little time for a leisurely look around. The family was downstairs too in all their evening finery, smartly dressed

servants stood about, ready for action, and the first carriage was
drawing up outside the house.

"You must stand between Reggie and me, Matthew," Adelaide
said to him. "Philip and Emily, stand on the other side of Papa."

There was to be a receiving line, Matthew realized in some dismay. No effort was to be spared to show him off to the neighbors
as a valued member of the family—though he was only a carpenter.
No effort was to be spared to make him feel the joy his family felt
at having him back among them. It was a realization that brought
an ache of unshed tears to the back of his throat—and an intense
embarrassment as he wondered how the neighbors, some of whom
he had known as a boy, would feel about this grand gesture.

And then, of course, there was the whole matter of his engagement to Clarissa, which he had confided to Reggie and Adelaide,
but not to anyone else in the house.

But this was not the time to dwell upon that or the delight—and
surprising lack of shock—with which they had greeted the news.

D
espite the short distance between the two houses, Clarissa
rode to Reginald Taylor's house with her parents and George
and Kitty. It was a bit of a squash in the carriage, but there was
something of a wind blowing outside, and Clarissa's original plan
to walk over to the Taylors' house with her brother and sister-in-law
was abandoned in order to avoid arriving with shiny cheeks and
nose and hair that had been blown into an unruly bush.

They arrived early, something her parents had always done
when they were invited out and Clarissa still tended to do. Even so,
they were not the first to arrive. The house was buzzing with the
merry sounds of conversation and laughter when they were admitted.

It also seemed filled with light, very different from the gloom she remembered from the few girlhood visits she had made here. It hardly seemed like the same place.

She was amused to see a receiving line at the drawing room doors. Poor Matthew must be cringing with embarrassment. Yet he did not look particularly uncomfortable. He looked his usual placid, cheerful self as he stood between Reginald and Adelaide, who beamed at him while introducing him to friends and neighbors he had never met before. He was shaking hands and smiling and talking.

It was strange to see him tonight, a mere few hours after their encounter out at what she now thought of as their tree, knowing that everything had changed between them. That they were to marry. That they were betrothed.

She wondered if he had told anyone yet.

Kitty slid an arm through hers. "This is lovely to see, is it not?" she said. "George has told me some stories about what this home used to be like. He has told me what a rebel your fiancé was as a boy. Does that not sound wonderful—your fiancé? He is ruggedly good-looking in his carpenter persona. I have always thought so. But he looks downright handsome in evening clothes. Oh, Clarissa, I am so glad you have found romance in your life at long last. It is what you came home from London to discover, though you may not have known it at the time. George always calls me a hopeless romantic. But then he is one too, so it is a case of the pot and the kettle. Ah, it is our turn. I am so looking forward to the evening."

She released Clarissa's arm in order to pass along the receiving line with George.

"I am very happy you came, Lady Stratton," Adelaide said a few moments later. She leaned forward a little and lowered her voice.

"But soon I must beg leave to call you Clarissa. You are to be my sister-in-law and I could not be happier. Reggie could not be happier."

Ah. They knew, then.

"Please call me by my given name now," Clarissa said, and moved on to stand before Matthew and set her hand in his. They exchanged a lingering smile.

"No regrets?" he murmured.

"Not yet," she said.

But it was time to move on to Reginald, who took one of her hands in his and kissed her cheek.

"I am a happy man tonight," he said.

The people who were already in the drawing room stood in groups talking. George led their parents to a couple of unoccupied chairs against one wall and proceeded to introduce Kitty to other guests. Clarissa moved from group to group, as was her custom at social gatherings. But she enjoyed those in the country far more than she did the more glittering parties in London during the Season.

After a while it seemed the invited guests had all arrived. There was no more receiving line, and both the drawing room and the smaller room beyond it were full of people, chattering merrily and rather loudly. Reginald took his brother about, clearly bursting with pride and affection.

How touching and unexpected it was. Clarissa hardly recognized Reginald as the young man who had always seemed so dour and disapproving when she was still a child—so very much like his father, in fact. Even at her mother's birthday party he had seemed a bit stiff with her. She had not liked him. Now it was hard not to.

The guests soon disposed themselves into three familiar groupings. Those who wished to play cards moved to a salon close to the drawing room, where tables had been set up for them with new packs of cards awaiting their use. Those who wished to talk sat or stood in groups close to the walls or wandered to the dining room to fill a plate with dainties or a glass with a favorite beverage. A young lady Clarissa did not know seated herself at the pianoforte in the other room, and those young people who wanted to dance clustered about the instrument suggesting music and dance sets. Reginald, after huddling with them for a minute or two, announced a Sir Roger de Coverley. Lines formed, and the dancing began on a floor that was just large enough to accommodate those couples who chose to use it.

Clarissa watched the dancing for a while before going through to the dining room with her mother, who fancied a cup of tea. They stayed to converse with the vicar's wife and Mrs. Jakes and to sample a few of the savory dainties. Matthew was deep in conversation with Captain Jakes, she saw when they returned to the drawing room, though they were soon joined by other guests. Everyone wanted to have a word with him, it seemed.

After a while there was a break in the proceedings while servants moved around the perimeter of the room with trays of champagne they offered to everyone. The card players came in to swell the crowd, and Reginald moved to the empty center, a full glass in one hand. He held up the other hand to attract everyone's attention.

"I hope you are all enjoying the evening," he said. There was a murmur of assurances that indeed everyone was. "But before you resume whatever you were doing before I interrupted you, I invite you all to join me in a toast to Matthew, my brother, who has come home and been restored to us after more than thirty years."

There was another murmur, louder than the first, as everyone raised their glasses and drank the toast. Clarissa blinked her eyes in an effort not to weep openly. The servants moved about the room again, refilling glasses. Matthew nodded his acknowledgment of the toast and looked a bit sheepish. His eyes met Clarissa's across the room and he grinned.

"Thank you," he said when an expectant hush fell upon the room. "This has been a happy day for me. I will, however, be happier still when I am no longer the focus of everyone's attention."

Laughter greeted his words as Reginald held up a hand for silence again.

"And I have the honor of making another announcement," he said. "With the permission of those concerned."

Ah. It was going to happen, then, was it? All of Matthew's family was here except for one nephew. And Clarissa's own family was here, even though none of her children were.

"My brother is newly betrothed," Reginald said, "to the lady many of you will remember as Clarissa Greenfield, now Clarissa Ware, Dowager Countess of Stratton. You will join me, if you please, in a new toast to the couple."

His last words, though, were half lost in a swell of astonished and pleased exclamations. Soon everyone's glass was raised again in the new toast, and Matthew wove his way among guests to stand before Clarissa, take her hand in his, and bow over it.

"I believe we are fully committed now," he murmured to her.

"But I was committed this afternoon," she said.

And then they were surrounded by well-wishers, who came to shake Matthew's hand and squeeze his shoulder and slap him on the back and to kiss Clarissa's cheek and wish them both happiness and long life together and to ask what their plans were for the wedding.

Clarissa felt a bit guilty that all this was happening tonight, when none of her children even knew of her engagement yet. But they soon would. She had only to think of how fast they had learned of her friendship with Matthew. Besides, she would write to each of them as soon as she returned home, perhaps even before then. And besides again, her parents knew and were present tonight, beaming upon all who went to congratulate them. Her brother was here too, looking happy.

Oh, and she was happy. She was positively bursting with happiness.

Reginald, who was still standing in the middle of the drawing room floor, held up his hand once again after a while, and a sort of hush descended upon the room.

"The young people have been asking all evening for a waltz," he said, "though I understand very few of them actually know the steps. They have been relying upon someone to show them so they may try for themselves. George Greenfield and his wife have admitted to knowing the waltz. I understand it is quite popular at London balls these days. A few of our other guests have danced it too, including Lady Stratton, hardly surprisingly. And I have just learned from the younger Mrs. Greenfield that during an assembly at Ravenswood a year or two ago, the dowager countess waltzed with none other than my own brother. I do require proof, however. Now, without further delay."

There was a gust of laughter as Clarissa caught a look of dismay on Matthew's face.

"Good God," he murmured irreverently. Or perhaps it really was a plea to the divine to rescue him.

Clarissa laughed.

"We will see them waltz together now," Reginald said. "Everyone else who wishes to join them may do so after the first minute or two. Matt? Lead your betrothed onto the floor, if you please."

Everyone squeezed back closer to the walls to make the dancing space larger.

Someone began to clap slowly when Matthew did not immediately move, and others followed suit. Someone cheered. Someone else whistled.

Matthew shook his head, took Clarissa's hand in his, and led her onto the clear space of the dancing floor.

F or many country folk the waltz was still unknown, it seemed, or was merely a rumor of a dance that was not quite proper because it involved two partners dancing exclusively with each other and touching each other throughout. There were those, on the other hand, who had heard it was the most romantic dance ever conceived.

Matthew wished the dance to perdition. Yes, he had waltzed once, in a crowded ballroom a long time ago. But Reggie's guests, gathered to celebrate his homecoming and now his betrothal to the dowager Lady Stratton, were watching with avid interest, and Matthew was touched by their wholehearted welcome. He could feel their eyes upon him and Clarissa, a far from comforting feeling. But he owed them something. More important, he owed Reggie and Adelaide something. Not to mention Clarissa.

She was smiling at him.

"I hope I do not end up making a spectacle of you," he said. But he refused to do any such thing. He was about to dance with the most beautiful woman in the room, his lifelong friend, the girl with whom he had fallen painfully in love all those years ago, the woman with whom he was deeply in love now. And by some miracle she loved him in return. She had agreed to marry him—for who he was, without any attempt to change him into a more obvious and respectable gentleman, though he had made the offer.

Just as he was, he was her world, as she was his.

"You will not," she said, smiling softly into his eyes as he set a hand at the small of her back and took one of her hands with his other. She set her free hand on his shoulder, and there was a sort of sigh from the gathered guests. Even the card players had not yet returned to the salon and their games.

The young pianist struck a chord and began to play a relatively sedate waltz tune, one that enabled him to remember the steps and lead his partner with some confidence.

For a few moments, as they gazed into each other's eyes, he was aware of their audience and of his steps and hers. But the waltz—he remembered this about it from that set he had danced with her at Ravenswood—had a way of weaving its magic, and soon he forgot everything but the music and the gleaming floor beneath their feet and the candles glowing in the candelabra overhead and becoming one circle of light as he twirled her about a corner of the room. He was aware of evening gowns becoming a kaleidoscopic swirl of pastel shades and of jewels, whether real or merely paste, winking in the light. He was aware of other dancers joining them after a while. But his own world was bounded by their arms, his and his partner's, and centered in their bodies, close to each other but not touching. His focus was upon Clarissa herself and her smile. And his own overflowing happiness.

The waltz was indeed and by far the most romantic dance ever created. He did not want it to end. But, of course, it did—to enthusiastic applause.

No longer did he feel obliged to circulate alone among Reggie and Adelaide's guests. With Clarissa on his arm, he spoke with everyone, both old neighbors he remembered and new ones he had never met before tonight. And despite the fact that his new engagement was foremost in his mind, he also felt the warmth of homecoming.

He felt as though in the jigsaw puzzle of his life, the final piece, which he had not even realized was missing, had fallen into place so that now the picture was complete and he could be perfectly at peace. Not that life could ever be that simple and orderly, of course, but tonight he felt like a whole person, and he had his family to thank and Clarissa and her family—and even himself for opening his mind and heart to new possibilities after he had clung so long to his cozy cocoon.

"I want to thank you for all this," he said when they came upon Reggie and Adelaide a short time later in the hallway leading to the dining room. He hugged his sister-in-law and wrung his brother's hand. "I cannot tell you how happy your unconditional acceptance has made me."

"All streets have two sides to them, Matt," Reggie said. "We are grateful to you too for coming. And also to you, Clarissa. We were not at all sure our plans for tonight would not end in disarray."

"You have made us both very happy," Adelaide said, beaming at them. "Come and have something to eat. I do not particularly want to be serving the remains of this feast for the next week."

The party was still proceeding in lively fashion an hour or so later when George Greenfield came to tell them he and Kitty were taking his parents home.

"They are tired," he said. "You will squeeze into the carriage with us, Clarissa?"

Matthew opened his mouth to speak, but she answered first.

"No," she said. "You go on, George. Matthew is going to walk me home."

"Ah," George said. "We will see you back at the house, then."

"I am, am I?" Matthew asked after George had stridden away to assist his parents out to their carriage.

"Of course," she said. "It is one of the primary duties of a betrothed man to walk his beloved home when the carriage offered for her use is already filled with other couples."

"Rule 647, I believe?" he said.

"Rule 648," she said. "Number 647 is the one about him first fetching her bonnet and shawl and reticule while she takes her leave of her hosts."

"Right," he said. "I remember now. And 649 states quite categorically that he gets to kiss her good night after delivering her to her own door. I will see you out in the hall in two minutes."

Ten minutes passed before they left the house with a grand farewell from all his relatives, who had gathered in the hall to wave them on their way. By that time the card games in the salon close by seemed to be breaking up. In the drawing room the music had stopped and there were the distinctive end-of-evening sounds of neighbors taking their leave of one another. It was almost half past eleven, very late for a country party and a sure sign that everyone had been enjoying the evening and was reluctant to see it come to an end. Adelaide and Emily would be over the moon with gratification at the success of their party.

The sky was clear and the moon was almost at the full. The stars were at their brightest. Matthew did not take a lantern with him from his brother's house. It was not needed. They walked at first hand in hand and then with an arm about each other's waist, over the familiar route to the Greenfield house. They did not speak for a while. Instead they enjoyed the coolness of the air—there was still a steady breeze blowing—and absorbed the night sounds of insects whirring and an owl hooting in the distance.

She and Caleb had never walked like this. But she banished the thought from her mind before it could develop further. She did not want to compare and would not. She was happy now, and that was what mattered.

"You are not sorry you came, then?" she asked him after a while. "I know you were nervous about this party."

"It ought to have happened years ago," he said. "My reconciliation with Reggie, that is, not necessarily the party. But perhaps neither of us was quite ready until now, just as you and I were not. It is not always wise to try to hurry life along. No, I am not sorry, Clarissa. Not about anything that has happened this year."

"Not even Prudence Wexford's table?" she asked.

He laughed. "It made her happy," he said. "And I made it as tasteful as I could while still giving her what she dreamed of."

"I am not sorry either," she said. "Though when I came home to take a long and solitary look at my life to determine where it ought to go in the future, I had no idea my search would lead me to you or to a cottage by the river, or to the discovery that though my children are very protective of me, they also respect my wishes when they understand just what they are. I had no idea about any of this. I have always called regularly upon Mama and Papa, and I have occasionally met some of their neighbors. But I have always avoided your brother and his wife whenever I could. They seemed a dour couple to me, and I blamed Reginald for not loving you as he ought to when you were a boy. I did not expect that I would be proved wrong and come to like them exceedingly well."

"Do you want to go directly home, Clarissa?" he asked when her father's house came into sight.

"Do you have anything else in mind as an alternative?" she asked him.

"I have been wondering," he said, "what our tree looks like by moonlight."

"Well," she said, "we have the perfect night to find out."

They changed direction and walked in silence toward the rolling lawns and trees farther into the park. It was not as easy to find their exact destination as it had been in the daylight earlier today. The trees, though not thick, were plentiful enough to cut out some of the moonlight and starlight. But they found the tree eventually— the one he had carved with such exquisite skill and pulsing emotion a few years ago. Where she had told him she was going to marry Caleb, though she was half in love with him and knew him to be more than half in love with her. Where this afternoon he had created new memories by asking her to marry him. Or was it she who had asked him to marry her? Did it matter? They had asked and answered each other, and there was no more melancholy to be associated with this place.

He turned her so her back was to the tree, on the side against which she had spread her right hand on previous occasions, and pressed her to it with his own body. He searched for and found her mouth with his own and kissed her with unleashed passion and urgency. Her arms went about his shoulders and her fingers pressed through his hair while his hands explored her body with a bold disregard for subtlety.

He wanted her. And almost instantly she wanted him too.

"Are you going to make me wait until our wedding night?" he asked, his mouth still on hers. "Whenever that is likely to be."

"Whenever everyone has been summoned to celebrate with us," she said. "Perhaps after a cottage has been built by the river and furnished. Perhaps after a couple of babies have been born and their mothers are able to travel. Who knows? But whenever it is likely to be, it is far, far too long to wait."

It had been so very long. She had been celibate for more than half a decade and had not experienced the joy of unbounded passion for some time before that. She wondered briefly if Matthew . . . But she did not want to know. It did not matter.

The past did not matter. Nor did the future. Tonight mattered. Now mattered.

"Make love to me," she said.

It was not, she supposed later, the most comfortable encounter in the world. The ground was hard and uneven. They had only his coat to lie upon and her shawl with which to cover themselves afterward. The wind was a bit chilly. A number of insects had to satisfy their curiosity by buzzing about them and even crawling upon them. Dealing with their clothes without actually removing them all was tricky.

But it was only afterward she thought thus. While it was happening, nothing could have been more perfect.

She shook her head when he would have taken her on top of him to shield her from the hardness of the ground. She wanted to feel his weight on her. She wanted him to take her from above. And it was glorious and wonderful and any other superlative the mind cared to offer her. The foreplay had happened while they stood against the tree. On the ground he entered her almost immediately, his hands spread beneath her to cushion her, her legs twined about his, her pelvis tilted so he could come deep and deeper. And he took his time. They took their time as she matched him thrust for thrust, almost lazily for a while as they savored all the unfamiliarity and all the pleasure of their joining. After a while their lovemaking became more urgent, more frenzied, deeper and faster, until she was hot and slick inside and they were both panting and searching out each other's mouths again.

And then it was over with a final burst of energy and passion, a moment of excruciating pleasure—or was it pain?—as they reached the climax together, and a descent into the utter relaxation of a sated desire.

"My love," he murmured against her mouth.

"Matthew."

They did not sleep. They did not even linger very long. Someone would surely be waiting up for her at her father's house. And they were going to have to make a probably futile attempt to put themselves back to rights before going there so no one would suspect the truth. But they relaxed against each other for a minute or two, murmuring love words Clarissa could not even remember afterward. It did not matter. Some things were beyond words.

They walked back to the house with fingers twined and shoulders touching.

"We could just elope," he said before they arrived.

She laughed, though the suggestion was surprisingly enticing. "To Gretna Green?" she said. "Your family would be severely disappointed. So would mine."

"I suppose," he said, "weddings are for families, are they not? I am unaccustomed to thinking of families in connection with my own life. Throughout my adulthood I have done just as I please, when I have pleased."

"I thought," she said, "that was going to be the outcome of this year for me too. And to a certain degree it is. But my family is at the heart of my life. I cannot live totally independent of them or in disregard of their feelings. I believe you will learn the same thing of your brother and sister-in-law and your nieces and nephews, Matthew, now that you have found them again. It can be irksome at times, but the rewards are beyond measure."

"So no elopement," he said. "And no hasty wedding."

"Irksome, is it not?" she said, and they both laughed.

They stopped outside the door and wrapped their arms about each other again.

"I love you," he murmured against her lips.

"I love you more," she said.

"Most."

"Very most."

"A superlative cannot be added to. I win," he said, and deepened the kiss.

George opened the door, clearing his throat as he did so. He must have been standing behind it, waiting for them, Clarissa thought. Kitty stood beside him, twinkling at them both.

"I was beginning to think you were walking all the way back to Ravenswood," George said.

CHAPTER TWENTY-TWO

The new building being erected on Ravenswood land, across the river and somewhat to the east of the village of Boscombe, attracted a great deal of attention during the following months.

Word quickly spread that it was to be a dower house, though it soon became clear that it was no small mansion, as many such houses on large estates were. Even the word *manor* would be a bit of an exaggeration. This was merely a sizable cottage with an upstairs and a down and a thatched roof to make it impossibly picturesque. It had clearly not been designed to accommodate many overnight guests. But then, who would need to stay there when the vast mansion that was Ravenswood was just a short walk away?

The cottage went up with astonishing speed, the Earl of Stratton having apparently instructed the architect that there was to be no dillydallying, that it was to be completed before winter descended upon them. It made the perfect picture against the backdrop of the meadow, in which sheep continued to graze, undismayed by all the noise and bustle of the workmen who sawed and hammered and shouted out instructions and questions all day long. One could only imagine how much more perfect the cottage would look when it was finished and a garden had been mapped out and planted with grass and flowers and shrubs and perhaps a few trees, and when hollyhocks and hyacinths and other tall flowers grew against the walls of the house. And would there be a rustic fence?

It was going to be a cottage worthy of a storybook cover.

It was to be the new home of the Dowager Countess of Stratton, the earl's mother. When that rumor was confirmed as actual fact, some of the inhabitants of the village were disturbed, even outraged. Was there some rift within the family, as there had been ten years ago after the calamitous ending to the ball at the summer fete? Was her ladyship being banished from Ravenswood itself by her vengeful son, whom she in turn had banished after that ball? Was she to be hidden away on the riverbank, out of sight of the main house itself?

Common sense soon prevailed when it was pointed out that the earl was not a vengeful man. And they were reminded of the dowager countess's preference for solitude this past summer and of her friendship with Matthew Taylor. Rumor had it then—and it was soon confirmed by those in the know—that the couple was betrothed, that there was to be a wedding in the foreseeable future. That the cottage was to be their love nest, so to speak.

Most of the villagers were enchanted by the romance of it all. A number of them acquired the habit of strolling along the riverbank on the Boscombe side even when they had no reason to do so except to gaze across at the small army of workers erecting the lovely new building, future home of two unlikely lovers.

The wedding was to take place before Christmas in the village church. That news too became general knowledge long before it was officially announced. And everyone was to be included in the celebrations, just as they had been when the present earl married Gwyneth Rhys a few years ago. There was to be a grand feast for all in the ballroom at Ravenswood the night before the wedding. And though the church would be reserved for invited guests for the wedding itself, there was plenty of space to stand outside and get a good view of the bride and groom and all the fancy guests in their wedding finery. Sir Ifor Rhys, the church organist and choirmaster, was to give an organ recital the following day before the wedding decorations inside the church were taken down.

It was a marvel to many that Matthew Taylor did not change at all during the months of his betrothal, while the cottage was being built and plans were being made for his wedding to the dowager countess and the village buzzed with the excitement of it all. He did not suddenly become the gentleman he was by birth. He did not grow idle or conceited. He continued to live and work in his modest rooms above the smithy. He continued to buy his food at the Miller sisters' shop and take the occasional tankard of ale at the village inn. He still mingled with everyone, whether of high or low estate, never refusing an invitation.

As for the dowager countess, she remained as charming and gracious as ever. And perhaps more beautiful than ever, some said, even though her fiftieth birthday was celebrated during the autumn.

Clarissa forced herself to stay away from the cottage during the daytime while it was being built. She did not want to get under the feet of the workmen, who were toiling so diligently over its construction. Most evenings, though, she walked down to see what progress had been made, even when darkness started to fall earlier. Sometimes Gwyneth or Devlin or Owen went with her once they had returned to Ravenswood in the autumn. Often Matthew met her there and she would lean back against his chest while his arms came about her waist, gazing in wonder at her growing dream and planning with him exactly what the garden would look like when work on it could finally begin next spring.

"I must have daffodils," she said.

"And snowdrops," he said.

She had a gardener. He was also a general handyman. Millicent had cleared her throat and actually spoken while brushing Clarissa's hair one evening at bedtime. It was a week or so after she had been told about the cottage and asked if she would continue as Clarissa's personal maid. She had a brother, she explained now, who was an avid gardener but was leaving his position at another grand house because of conflicts with the new head gardener there. The brother's wife worked as an undercook at the same house but had long dreamed of being fully in charge of her own kitchen and even of having the running of a smaller establishment. Millicent had spoken with them, and they were eager to be considered for the position at Lady Stratton's cottage.

"We have always been very close, my brother and I, Your Ladyship," she had said. "And my sister-in-law and I get along very well too."

Clarissa had interviewed the couple, liked them, and agreed to employ them as soon as the cottage was finished. That would be soon, before the wedding, which she and Matthew had set for the first week in December. She wanted to spend her wedding night in their new home. And it was theirs, not just hers. Although Devlin was paying for the house itself, which would belong to the estate, it was Clarissa and Matthew who furnished it. And he insisted upon sharing all the costs.

"Otherwise," he explained when she protested, "it will never seem like my home, Clarissa."

He made the dining room table himself and other items of furniture. She embroidered new cloths. They purchased what neither could make.

Devlin and Gwyneth had come home from Wales late in the summer and Owen had come back from Penallen soon after. Nicholas, finally home in England to stay, had a week's leave to spend at Ravenswood in the early autumn. He lifted Clarissa off her feet and twirled her about by way of greeting and in spite of the old war wound to his leg that had left him with a slight limp. He headed off to the village soon after his arrival to interrogate Matthew—his word—and then shake him by the hand with a grip that had come close to crushing every bone in it. Or so Matthew had reported later to Clarissa.

Nicholas looked almost achingly like his father. He had the same rugged, fair-haired good looks and the same openhearted charm. But he was not Caleb. There was a firmness about his jaw, a military uprightness to his bearing, an occasional hardness to his eyes that proclaimed him a man of firmer character.

The Taylors meanwhile did not neglect Matthew. They came several times to call upon him, sometimes Reginald and Adelaide, sometimes Philip and Emily, once Mabel and Albert. On one occasion his brother and sister-in-law brought Anthony, their younger son, the one who lived in London. He was making a brief visit to his parents, he explained, while his wife and sons went to spend time with her sister following the latter's confinement. He seemed pleased to meet his uncle, though he looked about the rooms above the smithy with unconcealed astonishment.

And finally the cottage was finished. The new furniture was moved in and arranged, rugs were laid on the floor, pictures were hung on the walls, books were properly organized in the bookcase, favorite carvings were displayed, most notably the one of the girl against the tree in the place of honor on the mantel above the fireplace in the sitting room—it would have been too pretentious, they agreed, to call it the drawing room. And all was ready.

The cottage was far more wonderful even than it had been in Clarissa's dreams. For it was not just a dream house. It was a home in which to live. And love. And make memories. There was no garden yet, only the wide riverbank beyond the red door, somewhat churned up by the workmen and their supplies. But that did not matter. It left more dreams to be dreamed and goals to be worked toward.

But before Clarissa and Matthew took up residence, there was to be a wedding.

Everyone was coming, all Matthew's family and all Clarissa's. Nicholas had been granted a two-week leave from his new posting at the Horse Guards. Even Jennifer was coming from Penallen with Ben and Joy and Ben's aunt. And Philippa was coming too, all the way from Greystone with Lucas and the twins, even though both she and Jennifer were expecting their babies not long into the New Year. They were coming because . . . how could they not? That was how Jennifer explained it, anyway, after Ben had lifted her out of the carriage and set her down in her wheeled chair upon their arrival. Stephanie came with her sister and family.

Jennifer was the sister of Lucas, Philippa's husband. Her child and Pippa's would be cousins and very close in age. That would be lovely for them at family gatherings in the future, Clarissa thought. She had a mental image of them playing together before a crackling fire in the sitting room at the cottage.

Soon all became the familiar madness of preparation for a grand event at Ravenswood, except that now it was Gwyneth who assumed charge of all the planning, insisting that her mother-in-law was not to be allowed to do a thing except what related to her role as bride—the choosing of her wedding dress, for example, and of Joy and Matthew's great-nieces as her bridesmaids. And the music, which she and Matthew jointly discussed with Sir Ifor.

Clarissa was quite content to leave all the planning and arranging to everyone else. She did think wistfully a few times about Matthew's joking suggestion that they elope. But she remembered too that weddings were for families more than they were for the bride and groom. Let them enjoy themselves, then.

She enjoyed herself meanwhile dreaming of the future and walking hand in hand with Matthew about the park in the late afternoons after he had finished work.

CHAPTER TWENTY-THREE

M atthew was feeling smart and slightly uncomfortable in the new coat and breeches—the new everything, in fact—he had decided he needed for his wedding. He had actually gone to London to be measured and fitted for them, accompanied by Lord Hardington and Reggie.

The evening clothes he had worn to every evening event for the past number of years just would not do for the occasion, he had admitted to himself somewhat ruefully—though he had worn them to the wedding eve community banquet in the ballroom at Ravenswood last evening. It had been hosted by the Earl and Countess of Stratton and had been a large and merry affair. The whole family had been there, his own as well as Clarissa's, though they had been far outnumbered by all the neighbors for miles around. Indeed, Matthew could not think of anyone who had not been there.

He had surprised himself by enjoying himself enormously. Clarissa, flushed and resplendent in a figure-hugging scarlet gown, had enjoyed herself too. They certainly had not behaved like a couple who were longing to retreat from the world. But how wonderful it was, he realized, that they could do both after today—enjoy socializing with others and being alone together as well.

"You are looking very smart indeed," Reggie said, coming through the door from Matthew's living room into his bedchamber. He stood in the doorway, admiring his brother's appearance.

His tailed coat was black, his breeches buff colored, his boots black and shining. His shirt and neckcloth were white, his silk waistcoat ivory. A red rosebud was pinned to his lapel.

"And all done without the services of a valet," Reggie said.

"I would have felt like an idiot," Matthew said. Stratton had offered the services of his own valet. So had Colonel Wexford and Lord Hardington.

"Shall we walk over to the church?" Reggie said.

He was Matthew's best man. He had already walked from Ravenswood, where he was staying with his whole family. All of Clarissa's family was there too—her parents and her brother and his wife, and all the Wares, even the Duchess of Wilby and Lady Jennifer Ellis, both of whom had been looking rather large with child but blooming with good health last evening.

"It is a little early," he said. "But perhaps if we go now we can creep inside without anyone seeing us."

His brother laughed as he shook his head and slapped him on the shoulder. "You are dealing with aristocracy here, Matt," he said.

They were not going to escape anything, of course, as Matthew saw even while they were descending the stairs outside his rooms. He did not have to reach the bottom and see the church farther along the street. The village green was already half crowded with people. So was the street itself. It was a chilly December morning, though the sun was shining and the wind was down. But the cold had not deterred those who wished to watch the guests arrive at the church—and the bride and groom leave it after the wedding service.

Someone set up a bit of a cheer, and those standing in the street opened up a sort of pathway for Matthew and Reggie to pass through. Matthew grinned and waved to the crowd before turning into the churchyard and ducking inside the church. It was decorated with white lilies and red roses and winter greenery, and the full reality of the moment hit Matthew like a physical thing.

"It is my wedding day," he said aloud.

"I am very relieved you have remembered," Reggie said, laughing.

Sir Ifor Rhys, seated at the organ, was practicing some piece with a whole lot of intricate trills.

C larissa had decided upon simplicity. She wore an ivory-colored velvet dress, the sleeves long, the neckline and waistline high, the skirt narrow at the front and sides but flowing at the back to allow ease of movement. She would don the matching cloak and bonnet before she left the house. She was going to carry a rather lavish bouquet of red roses and fern. Joy and Matthew's two great-nieces were to wear red velvet.

She was dressed early. Millicent had finished with her hair. She stood in her private sitting room now, looking out at the wintry landscape, the branches of the trees bare against a pale blue sky. She loved the changing of the seasons. She loved winter. She was glad there were a few months of it still to come.

It would be the last time she would stand here like this, belonging in this room, in this house. She had stood here all those months ago after returning from London alone, wondering what the future held in store for her, wondering if she was going to be able to shape it into something meaningful, something that would make her happy and give her a renewed zeal for living.

And here she was on her wedding day. These were the last few moments of her solitude—until after the wedding anyway. And then it would not be solitude she would be seeking.

She smiled and turned from the window when a tap on the door heralded the arrival of Stephanie and Pippa and Jennifer wheeling herself in her chair.

"Oh, Mama," Stephanie said, hurrying across the room to hug her. "You look beautiful."

"Even unadorned as I am?" Clarissa asked.

"You do not need adornment, Mother," Jennifer said.

They were all dressed smartly for the wedding. They were soon followed into the room by Ben and Nicholas, who was looking resplendent and a bit formidable in his scarlet dress uniform, and by Owen and Gwyneth.

"I have been holding the little girls back," Gwyneth said. "I did not want them to get in your way, Mother. They are very excited. May I bring them? And by the way, you look gorgeous." She smiled warmly.

Her bridesmaids looked like rosebuds, Clarissa thought, though they lacked the serenity she associated with those flowers. Joy had apparently taught the other two girls to bounce—or perhaps it was in the nature of young girls to do so when they were excited. Had Pippa been the same? And Stephanie? Had she?

"We had better be on our way to church," Gwyneth said. "Mother cannot go until we do, and she will not want to be late."

There was a great deal of noise as everyone hugged her before leaving the room. Ben took Joy by the hand and led her out while Gwyneth took Matthew's nieces.

"We will meet at the back of the church later," Clarissa said.

And then she was alone again, though only for a few moments while she went into her dressing room and Millicent helped her on with her cloak and handed her the bouquet. By the time she returned, Devlin was standing in the doorway.

"I don't know about you, Mama," he said after looking her over slowly from head to foot. "But I am feeling a bit emotional. Are you really as happy as you have been seeming for the past few months?"

"I am," she said. "Not least because you have all accepted the life I am choosing. It has not been easy for you, I know."

"Well, it was a bit of a shock at first, I must confess," he said. "But I ought to have trusted you from the start, Mama. You have chosen a life that is perfect for you. He is a good man. I think he will prove himself to be the husband you always deserved." He paused and frowned for a moment as though remembering his father, but he shook his head firmly and smiled. "I am happy. We all are."

She smiled back at him.

"I can only hope," he said, "I do not start bawling at church when I have to give you away."

They both laughed.

"Mama," he said, "I love you."

"And I will love you too if you get me to church in time," she said.

As he drew her hand through his arm and led her downstairs and out to the waiting carriage, the reality of it all struck her anew.

This was her wedding day.

M ore than ever, as he sat in a front pew with the church filled behind him and he imagined the crowd outside swelling as the time of the marriage service drew near, Matthew realized that weddings were indeed for the families of the bride and groom and for their friends and neighbors. And he was glad they had not eloped, Clarissa and he, though his suggestion that they do so had not been a serious one.

He had been surrounded by happiness yesterday, first with the arrival of Reggie and his whole family and then with the banquet last evening. And he had not held himself apart from it. He had been happy too. So had Clarissa.

It felt very good indeed to be an integral part of something larger than himself. He had ignored his family for far too long. He had held himself at an emotional distance from everyone all his adult life, though he had not quite realized it. He had been contented and at peace and had not looked for happiness. Now he had found it—in himself, in his relationship with Clarissa, and in his dealings with their families and neighbors and friends.

He was feeling nervous. He was also feeling . . . happy.

Sounds of a flurry of activity from the back of the church rose above the soft hum of conversation within, and he knew Clarissa had arrived. The Reverend Danver, in his church vestments, was signaling him to rise. Reggie was feeling around in a pocket, no doubt checking to make sure the ring was where it was supposed to be. A loud musical chord silenced every other sound, and the organ began to play.

Matthew turned to watch his bride approach along the nave, her hand drawn through the arm of her son, the Earl of Stratton.

And yes, he was a part of something that involved two whole families and this whole neighborhood where they lived. But it was something else too. It was something just for the two of them. It was for Clarissa and him. They were about to marry.

And then all he saw was her.

The music ended and the congregation was seated again. The

young bridesmaids arranged themselves about Clarissa, and Joy took her bouquet. Devlin gave her hand to Matthew and took his place in the front pew beside Gwyneth.

"Dearly beloved . . ." the Reverend Danver began.

The day was a whirlwind of activity and celebration after that—the wedding itself; the stepping outside to a cheer from the gathered crowd and waving handkerchiefs and showers of petals from some of the younger guests, who had come outside and lain in wait on either side of the church doors during the signing of the register; the ride back to Ravenswood in a carriage beautifully decorated but also deafeningly noisy, with all the pots and pans tied beneath it; the hugs and kisses as all the guests returned too; the wedding breakfast for both families; the speeches and toasts.

It was all a bit overwhelming for a man who had spent most of his adult years living quietly in two small rooms above a village smithy, never seeking attention, never looking for excitement, never expecting more than he already had.

But what he had now, after a summer and autumn of change, was everything he could ever have dreamed of—if he had allowed himself to dream. He was no longer a man living somewhat on the periphery of life, a bit afraid perhaps to plunge into it lest he be hurt more than he could bear—as he had been during his childhood. Now, today, he was at the very heart of two families, the Taylors and the Wares. He was one of them. He belonged. He mattered to them as they mattered to him.

It was an immeasurable gift these past months had brought him.

Yet now, today, there was so much more—for what anchored

him to the day and prevented him from being completely over-whelmed was Clarissa. The love of his life. The joy of his heart.

His wife.

Beautiful and vibrant and charming and happy.

And his.

It was hard to believe. Once or twice he wanted to pinch himself. Yet whenever she looked at him, which she did frequently, just as he looked at her, he saw the truth there in her sparkling eyes and in her flushed cheeks.

He was the love of *her* life. He was the joy of *her* heart.

Her husband.

He touched her hand when all the speeches were finally over and everyone stood to move to the drawing room, all talking at once, it seemed.

"Shall we go home?" he asked her.

Her eyes softened and her lips parted. But even now old habits reasserted themselves.

"And abandon all the guests?" she said.

"But they are not your guests, are they?" he said. "They are Gwyneth and Devlin's."

Her lips curved into a slow smile. "It is true," she said. "I am free. How absolutely marvelous. Oh yes, Matthew, let us go home."

They could not simply slip away, of course. That would have been ill-mannered. And she could not simply step out of the house. It was December. She had to send a servant to fetch her cloak from her old room while Matthew had a quiet word with Devlin.

No, they could not simply slip away, for by the time the cloak had been brought and she had hugged Gwyneth and thanked her for the breakfast and everything else she had done to make this a perfect day, and Matthew had gone to shake Reginald by the hand and hug Adelaide, everyone had discovered that the bride and groom were about to leave, and all had gathered in the hallway to shake hands, slap backs, kiss cheeks, hug tightly enough to deprive one of breath, and talk and laugh and wish them well. Even the children had spilled out of the nursery, the bridesmaids looking like slightly bedraggled rosebuds. They darted among adult legs, giggling and shrieking and generally getting in the way.

But finally they were walking away from Ravenswood, hand in hand like young lovers, and taking the familiar route along the terrace, down the driveway almost to the bridge, and then along the river path, which had been widened a little since the summer and paved.

Their cottage awaited them. It was finished and fully furnished but had not yet been lived in, except by Mr. and Mrs. Hoover, Millicent's brother and sister-in-law, who had taken up residence in the servants' wing of the house a few days ago and dusted and scrubbed and polished every square inch of the interior since then, according to Millicent, as well as the front door, the knocker, the front steps, and the windows outside.

The windows winked at them now in the light of the late afternoon sun. The red door seemed to glow in contrast with the muted winter colors all around. And smoke curled out of the chimney, a welcome sight on what was a crisp winter day.

"Home," she said.

"Home," he agreed.

And they stopped by mutual consent to gaze at it, the cottage she had not even dreamed of when she came home alone back in the late spring. The cottage that seemed like a palace to him after his rooms in the village, he had told her, laughing, a few days ago.

"Mr. Hoover must have lit a fire in the sitting room," she said. "Shall we go in, Matthew? It is chilly standing here."

Strangely, she felt a bit nervous.

"I hope he has also lit one in our bedchamber," he said.

And a bit breathless too.

They had made love awkwardly, somewhat painfully, altogether wonderfully beside their tree on the night of their betrothal. They had not made love since. It was amazing how little opportunity everyday life offered a well-bred lady and an honorable man who respected her reputation.

She wondered if their butler/gardener/handyman would have thought of warming the bedchamber in the middle of the afternoon. Or if Mrs. Hoover had. Or Millicent.

The front door opened even as they reached the two steps leading up to it. Mr. Hoover, very stiff and formal in a black and white uniform worthy of any butler, held it for them and bowed. Mrs. Hoover stood beaming behind him, and Millicent, almost smiling, beside her.

"Welcome home, ma'am, sir," the butler said, indicating the small porch in which he stood as though it were the vast hall of a mansion.

Clarissa smiled at him and at the two women.

"Thank you, Mr. Hoover," Matthew said. "But stand back, please. I need a little more room."

And quite unexpectedly, he turned to sweep Clarissa up in his arms. She shrieked as he climbed the steps with her and carried her over the threshold of the cottage before setting her feet on the floor.

Their new home. The new chapter in their lives, which had begun so gloriously today.

Millicent, she noticed, was fully smiling now.

"There is a fire in the sitting room and in the main bedchamber, sir," Mrs. Hoover said. "There is extra coal beside the hearth in both rooms if you should need it. Will you be requiring a tray of tea and freshly baked scones immediately, ma'am?"

"No," Clarissa and Matthew said together.

"Perhaps later," Clarissa said. "I can smell them now, and they smell delicious. I will have no need of you for a while, Millicent. Why do you not have tea with your brother and sister-in-law?"

The three servants needed no further persuasion. They disappeared back in the direction of the kitchen, and Clarissa turned to Matthew, who took her in his arms.

"I am going to like them," he said. "They understand a thing or two. Perhaps we had better go up and see if that fire needs tending to."

"I am quite sure it does," she said.

He smiled at her before kissing her nose. "Red," he said. "Like our front door."

"Why does no one else's nose turn red at the mere suggestion of cold weather?" she asked.

"Perhaps because you are unique," he said. "And uniquely beautiful. And uniquely my wife."

"At last," she said with a sigh. "At long, long last, Matthew."

"At last," he agreed, turning her toward the staircase and their room beneath the thatched roof.